MENDELEVSKI'S BOX

ROGER SWINDELLS

ISBN: 9789493056114 (ebook)

ISBN: 9789493056107 (paperback)

ISBN: 9789493056602 (hardcover)

Publisher: Amsterdam Publishers, The Netherlands

info@amsterdampublishers.com

CONTENTS

This book was born out of my love for The Netherlands, its people in general and the wonderful city of Amsterdam in particular.
I am extremely grateful to the volunteers at the National Holocaust Museum and the National Holocaust Memorial in Plantage Middenlaan, to the patient staff of the Stadsarchief in Vijzelstraat and to all those in Amsterdam, too numerous to mention, whose brains I picked and whose memories I explored.
Finally, thanks must go to my sister-in-law Sandra Arthur (née Mendell), who encouraged me to write. I await her verdict with interest and some trepidation.

FOREWORD

Much is known and, quite rightly, much has been written, about the fate of Europe's Jews in the extermination camps of the Holocaust. Much less is known, and even less documented, about the life of survivors on their return to their homes.

Jews living in The Netherlands suffered the lowest survival rate, just 27 percent, of any Western European Jewish community in WWII. Only eighteen of the 34,000 Dutch Jews transported to Sobibor survived the war. Questions have been raised about the attitude of the general Dutch population to the deportations and to property left behind by their Jewish neighbours.

This is a work of fiction, based (albeit loosely) around immediate post-war events. It seeks to encompass the day to day life of an Auschwitz survivor returning to his native Netherlands in September 1945, and the experiences of Amsterdam residents following the 'hunger winter' and liberation.

The book was also inspired by the discovery in 2009 of a suitcase of family items hidden by a Jewish family in a cupboard in a house in Beethovenstraat in Amsterdam.[1]

1. https://www.dutchnews.nl/features/2016/05/a-suitcase-full-of-secrets-found-in-amsterdams-jewish-quarter-after-70-yearssterdam-flat-stirs-memories-of-long-gone-lives

THURSDAY 20TH SEPTEMBER 1945

'Ten guilders? Ten lousy guilders?'

'It's just an average painting, it won't be going into the Rijksmuseum, the girl's features are, well, amateur at best. So that's my best offer, take it or leave it.' His hand, white, thin and immaculately manicured, reached out to retrieve the crumpled notes.

'But the frame alone is worth fifty,' she pleaded, covering her wedding ring, 'it's all I have. Look at the gilding.'

The man smiled, revealing gold teeth below a neatly trimmed moustache. 'For twenty guilders I could buy a dozen before lunchtime, dear lady. Everyone in Amsterdam is poor, the Nazis have left our country on its knees. Like I said, take it or leave it.'

She shrugged, reluctantly picking up the notes and watching the painting disappear beneath the counter. *Not everyone is poor*, she thought, looking at the white cuffs of the man's freshly laundered shirt, waistcoat with a gold watch chain, and neatly pressed trousers. Her worn shoes and threadbare dress showed clearly that some had done better from the war than others.

'Collaborator,' she mumbled under her breath as she left. Out from the darkness of the shop and into the early autumn sunshine, she started to make her way back along the Keizersgracht towards the Leidsegracht and the Jordaan.

Suddenly she heard a voice from across the canal.

'Mevrouw Blok! Grietje! Over here!'

She turned to see a tall young man, his clothes hanging loosely about his thin frame, running towards the bridge while frantically waving.

'Grietje, it is you, how wonderful to find someone! It's me, Simon, Simon Mendelevski, you used to work for my father before the war, cleaning at his workshop in Peperstraat, don't you remember me? We lived on the Dijkstraat. I think you came there once.'

'Simon, yes of course I remember you, I just...' She tailed off, unsure what to say.

The man's face was familiar and looking carefully she could just see in him the handsome teenage boy she had known before the war, but the four years since she last saw him had clearly taken their toll. Gone was the ruddy faced youth to be replaced by a man older than his years with a straggly beard, sunken cheeks and fear in his eyes. The cheeky muscular lad she had chased with her broom was now a thin, haunted man in worn clothes. The jacket, several sizes too large, hung from his shoulders, exacerbating his skeletal appearance.

'I'm sorry, I just didn't recognise you at first. You've changed, well, we've all changed I'm afraid. The war was hard on all of us. I don't suppose I look the same as I did in 1941.'

He smiled, showing missing and bad teeth, 'I'd recognise you anywhere Grietje, beautiful as ever. Can I say that now I'm no longer a boy?' He laughed. 'I'm so glad you came through it all.'

'Don't embarrass me, Simon. And you and your family? How did you survive? I heard nothing for two years after you went into hiding, then I was told you had all been arrested and put on a transport.'

He fell silent for a moment, looking at the ground. 'We didn't survive, I'm afraid I'm the only survivor. I've been looking and asking since I got back to the city two months ago, but no one can tell me anything. There is no trace of my family; in fact I can hardly find any friends or neighbours to even ask about them. The whole area is virtually deserted, looted and stripped bare of anything wooden. Most of the houses on Jodenbreestraat and Weesperstraat are derelict, some have even collapsed. Were they bombed?'

She shook her head and was about to tell him about the hunt for fuel during the recent winter when he continued, the words flooding out as he recounted his return to his old district.

'The better places on Nieuwe Keizersgracht are still there of course, who is in them I don't know. The one belonging to our friends, the Kok family, was boarded up. The houses that are still intact seem to have been occupied by non-Jews, I don't think they expected any of us to return. I went to our old house. There is a Dutch family in there now. I told them it was our family home, but the man said that wasn't possible as all the 'dirty Jews' were dead, and he slammed the door in my face. The workshop building looks alright but it's boarded up and I couldn't even find a door, but then I have no key anyway. Father never registered the business and he closed the workshop after the first arrests in 1941, so I assume he cleared it out then.

She nodded, remembering his father packing his most precious possessions from the workshop when it closed. 'The Germans had made it a law that non-Jews couldn't do domestic work for Jews anymore, so I had had to leave you anyway. Please go on, what did you all do?"

'We didn't hide until the middle of 1942 when they started taking everyone and fencing off the area to make a ghetto. In June they'd started calling all Jewish boys aged sixteen and over 'to work in Germany', so they said. They found us after six months and we were taken to the theatre on Plantage Middenlaan with hundreds of others. There were some families like us who had been in hiding, but almost all the other people had just been rounded up from the street. Then we were taken to Centraal Station and put on trains. After that we were at a camp called Westerbork before we were transported to Auschwitz. I didn't see my mother and sister again after we arrived. As for my father, I know he died there. The Red

Cross are saying that less than a thousand of us Jews, out of the sixty thousand who were sent there, have survived.' His voice began to break and he sobbed, 'I'm sorry, I can't go on.'

'Come Simon, come home with me.' She put her arm around his shoulders and tried to lead him away. 'It's only a short walk from here.'

He forced a smile. 'Walk? But where is your bicycle?'

'Jaap managed to keep a bicycle when the official confiscation was on, but the tyres gave out and he said riding on wooden tyres or on the rims was noisy and uncomfortable, so he gave up. I'm certainly not going to use it until there are tyres available again. At least the Germans left it behind—they took most of the rideable bikes with them.'

'Ah yes, of course, Jaap. I had forgotten his name. Enough about me, how is Jaap and how are your children?'

It was her turn to fall silent. 'Not now, please. Come on, we can talk more at home, I must hurry, my neighbour can only look after my daughter until four.'

They linked arms and walked towards the Jordaan. The better canal-side houses on Keizersgracht and Prinsengracht were still grand and sparkled in the sun, and they came across several well-dressed groups at the corner cafes and bars still celebrating liberation. Once they crossed into Elandsgracht and walked deeper into the Jordaan, amidst the remaining signs of Nazi occupation with 'V' for victory signs, some altered to 'W' for Wilhelmina, daubed on the walls, they merged seamlessly with other war-worn citizens struggling to go about their business.

'Come in, I'm on the first floor. It's not much, I'm afraid. Jaap said that after the war we would be able to move out to the Spaarndammerbuurt as there would be much more work on the docks, but it never happened.'

Squeezing past two tyre-less bicycles in the hallway they climbed the near vertical stairs to the first landing and a heavy dark brown door. She unlocked it. 'Please go on in, I need to collect Irene from Maaike downstairs, she minds her while I work but she has to work herself from six.'

He looked around what was a dark living room overlooking one of the narrower Jordaan streets, whose houses prevented the entry of sunshine through even the largest windows. The furniture was old and equally dark wood, and the carpet was worn with a hole showing just inside the door. It reminded him so much of the place where his family had hidden for six long months, which had also been somewhere in the Jordaan.

His thoughts were interrupted as the door opened and Grietje led a beautiful little blond girl into the room. 'Simon, this is Irene, my daughter, she's three. Irene, this is Simon, a friend of mine, he's come to visit.'

The girl hid behind her mother's skirts, eyeing him suspiciously.

'I'm sorry, I think it's the beard,' she said apologetically. 'She never saw her father with a beard.'

He laughed. 'Don't worry, I think I probably look pretty frightening generally, not just with the beard, I've been sleeping rough in derelict houses for two weeks. A quick wash at Centraal Station every few days obviously isn't enough.'

His smile clearly placated the girl as she came out from behind her mother and stood between them.

'Goedemiddag meneer, I'm Irene, I'm named after the Queen's grand-daughter and I'm three and a half.'

He extended his hand. 'I'm Simon and I'm pleased to meet you.'

Grietje interrupted the introductions with a question. 'Are you hungry? I can make some food but I don't know if I have much that you can eat. We have nothing that is kosher.'

He grinned. 'Don't worry, I may be a Jew but if I had a strict diet I gave it up a long time ago. I was happy to eat anything just to survive and yes, I'm starving, but please, I don't want to take your food.'

'Nonsense, you are a guest here and anyway there are just the two of us to feed so there will be plenty.'

'What about Jaap and the boys?'

A sad look passed over her face and she turned to the girl. 'Go to the bedroom and play with your doll, I must talk with Simon.'

5

When the girl had left, she continued speaking. 'Jaap and the boys won't be coming home, they are all dead.'

'Oy gevalt! What happened?'

Her chin and lip trembled and the tears came and he wanted to hold her but was unsure if it would be the right thing to do.

'Please, please, I'm so sorry I asked you, I would not upset you for the world.'

She sniffed and wiped her nose. 'No, no, I was going to tell you when you asked about them out on the street but I wanted to wait until we got home. That's partly why I suggested we came here.'

'You don't have to tell me at all.'

'I must, I want to, there have been so few people I could talk to and I'm sure you will understand, after all the damn war treated you cruelly too. All three of them were killed within five months. Hendrik, my eldest, was twelve. You met him, I had to bring him to work with me one day in the holidays before the war—he was only six or seven then. Last winter was cruel, many died of starvation and the cold.'

He nodded. 'I heard that from people while I was asking about my family.'

'He wanted to help us, to provide, to be a man like his father. He was out in January collecting wood to burn on the fire. He was with some other boys stripping a door frame over in the Jodenbuurt, probably one of the houses you saw. The stone lintel collapsed, and his skull was crushed. He died two days later. Jaap was devastated to lose his first-born son and so angry. The Germans eventually allowed the British airforce to drop food and supplies but for many, including our eldest son, it was too little too late.'

By now she was sobbing and he reached out and took her hand. Feeling the hard skin and callouses from many years of cleaning for people like himself he was ashamed.

'Please Grietje, no more, you don't have to.'

'Jaap was killed by the Germans in April, just three weeks before we were liberated. He was shot with two others as they were leaving a safe house. I knew he had been working with the resistance while he was on the docks. He used to go out at night

6

and not tell me what he was doing. I asked a number of times but he said it was better for me that I didn't know. The Germans must have been aware of him since the dock strike in 1941, so when he became more actively involved in the resistance he was quickly identified. Within weeks our little boy Johan was killed, also by the Nazis. He was just eight years old. He was shot standing right next to me and Irene in Dam Square on the 7th of May just as we were celebrating our liberation. Many people died that day when some German sailors in a drinking club overlooking the square started shooting down into the crowds. Bastards! The war was over. They'd already surrendered. He died in my arms. I had to bury them all. The men in my life are all dead because of the Nazis. Thank God Irene was spared.'

She clung to him and he put his arms around her, smoothing her hair as her whole body rocked with grief.

'Mama!' Irene appeared at the door to the bedroom and ran towards her mother. 'Mama!' By now she too, seeing her mother's tears, was crying.

'It's alright my darling, your Mama was just being silly, don't be upset.'

'I'll go, you and Irene need to be alone, she doesn't want a strange bearded tramp sharing her table.'

'No, you will stay! Please, I need someone here and besides I didn't realise you had nowhere to sleep, wash or eat. It will be a tight fit but you can sleep in the box beds in the small back room the boys used, Irene sleeps with me these days anyway. There is no bath and the toilet is shared, it's out the back downstairs but you can wash up in the kitchen, I will boil a kettle for you. Oh, and it's chicken soup for dinner, more soup than chicken I'm afraid, and there's some fruit, bruised and given away when the market closed, but you are welcome to it.'

She was smiling again, the big smile he remembered from before the war.

'And get that beard off! You'll find Jaap's razor under the sink.'

FRIDAY 21ST SEPTEMBER 1945

He woke with a start, bathed in sweat and gripped with fear. The boards of the top bunk were just inches from his face and for an instant he was back in Auschwitz, lying in his narrow space on the boards stacked three high. But there was no one above or below him, no cries of pain, no smell of stale sweat, faeces or death. In their place just the fine dawn light filtering through the curtains, the smell of a fresh pillowcase under his head and the sound of the Westertoren bells.

Suddenly a fresh terror overwhelmed him, the sound of heavy boots on the stairs coming down from the rooms above. He froze, recalling the day three Dutch policemen and a solitary German soldier had arrived at the family's hiding place to arrest them, expecting the door to crash in at any moment. The boots passed by and continued down to the ground floor, along the hallway and out of the front door into the street.

He lay quietly, waiting for his sweating and heart thumping to subside. He could hear Grietje moving in the next room. Irene wanted the toilet, woken no doubt by the noise on the uncarpeted stairs.

He swung his legs out of the box bed, stretching his limbs and massaging his stiff neck. Grietje's description of it being a tight fit had been an understatement. His face was raw, Jaap's razor was blunt and Grietje hadn't been able to find the strop. He had cut the beard as closely as possible with a pair of kitchen scissors before resorting to the razor. He had no experience of shaving anyway; this had been the first time. Perhaps he should have left the beard and just tidied it up, he was Ashkenazi after all and his father had never shaved.

He must have fallen asleep almost immediately, safe, warm and fed for the first time in over two years, and had slept so soundly that he had not heard Grietje come into the room and remove his filthy clothes. In their place on the chair lay clean underwear, a shirt, trousers and a thick blue jacket. He dressed quickly, grateful there was no mirror to capture his emaciated nakedness, prominent pelvis, fleshless ribs and pitiful limbs and pleased to have clean clothing.

Grietje was in the kitchen, making porridge on the gas stove and Irene was eating bread and cheese at the table. She gave him a hard stare, decided it was the same man but without the hairy face he had had the night before, and turned her attention back to her breakfast.

Turning from the stove, saucepan in hand, Grietje smiled, taking in his new appearance. 'Good morning, I hope you slept well.'

'The best night since we left Dijkstraat. But who was that on the stairs earlier? It gave me a scare.'

She laughed. 'It was old van Beek, Aart, he lives in the top-floor room. If you can manage the stairs it's the best room in the house for daylight anyway, but it was far too small for us—we were a family then. He's a tram driver and he is on early shift this week. Did he disturb you in his working boots?'

'I was already awake, but he frightened me for a moment, bad memories of the day they came for us.'

'I'm sorry, I didn't realise.'

'Don't be silly, it's not your fault, after all he can't be expected to creep down the stairs in his socks, can he?'

She put a bowl and spoon down on the table across from the girl.

'Sit down, Irene has finished off the cheese and bread so it's only porridge and it's watery, more like gruel as I was short of milk.'

'I can't let you feed me like this, you need everything you have for yourself and Irene.'

'It's not a problem anymore, starvation is over, thank God, and some food is reasonably plentiful, take a look at the markets. I just need to go shopping after work today, that's all.' *Not that I can do much with just ten guilders*, she thought.

'But you are feeding me and clothing me too. Where are my clothes by the way?'

'Most of them are in the rubbish. Your shirt, vest and pants I'll take to the laundry woman with our things this afternoon. That jacket and the trousers look well on you.'

Suddenly she looked worried. 'They're Jaap's of course, I hope you don't mind a dead man's clothes.'

'I wore dead men's clothes for over two years. We fought over them, often before the owner was cold.'

She looked down, avoiding his eyes, not knowing what to say.

'I'll move on today, I have some more places to check out in the old streets and I want to find the place where we hid. I know it was in the Jordaan somewhere but it's just a rabbit warren for someone like me, I don't know this part of the city at all. I'll keep in touch and hopefully repay you somehow. You have been too generous already.'

She fixed her gaze on him and suddenly he was, to her, a boy again 'You'll stay here until you get sorted out and at least have somewhere to sleep. No arguments, and anyway, you have to wait here for your washing.'

'I can't allow you to do all this for me, I'm a young fit man, or soon will be, I hope. You're a widow, alone and with a child. You work hard I'm sure, but money must be short. If I stay I must contribute something. I need to—for my pride if nothing else. Would it save you some money if I look after Irene for you?'

Her voice hardened. 'No. That's impossible, Maaike relies on me for the few guilders I give her. She's alone too and just does a little bar work in the evenings. She needs the money even more than I do. If your pride won't let you stay unless you contribute something, then go and get a job somewhere.'

'But what can I do? I've never worked, you know that. I was just sixteen and still studying before the war, father was supporting me and anyway I have no papers just the one they gave me saying I am a Jew who was in Auschwitz, and this of course.' He pulled back his shirt sleeve to reveal his tattooed forearm.

'Speak to Maaike, there are always jobs in the bars and cafes that don't ask for papers. She's originally from Friesland, she arrived here with her father but he was taken for forced labour in Germany so she found herself a job paying enough to keep the room downstairs and for food.'

'I'm sorry, I'm feeling sorry for myself, pathetic really.'

He felt her hand on the back of his neck.

'You've been through hell. No one can possibly comprehend what it was like. Even when the camps were liberated and reports started to come through we didn't believe it possible. Now we are all ashamed. We stood and watched as you went past in trams or were marched down the Damrak on the way to the station. We saw, but few of us actually did anything. Most of us just carried on as normal. I want to help you. You have your pride while I have guilt for all my countrymen. We need each other, you and I, we can support each other and hope we can both be repaired.'

She fell silent for a moment remembering, then noticed the time.

'I'm in a hurry, I need to get ready for work, it's past Vondelpark and I have to walk so can you please take Irene downstairs for me and introduce yourself to Maaike while you're there.'

Suddenly her mood changed and, giving him a mischievous glance, she giggled. 'Oh, and please don't forget to make it clear you're only the lodger.'

They stood in the bare unlit hallway, the girl banging on the door.

'Maaike! Maaike! It's me, Irene.'

'I'm coming little one.'

The key turned and the door opened. A pretty, fair haired, young woman with sad blue eyes, virtually still a girl, for she could be no more than eighteen years old, stood between a pair of crutches with just a single leg showing below her skirt.

'Come in, come in. Where is mama today?'

'She's getting ready for work so I brought her down for you, I'm Simon by the way.'

She smiled. 'And I'm Maaike, Grietje told me all about you. Well, not everything of course.' She appeared flustered. 'I mean she said she had a guest, a good looking Jewish boy, she said.'

'Why thank you, but not a boy anymore, I'm afraid.'

'Come in please, don't stand out there in the dark.'

She moved expertly backwards on the crutches to allow him to pass into the room. Identical to Grietje's but at street level it suffered even more from a lack of natural light and was lit by a single bare bulb. Irene was already over in the corner near the fireplace with a box of old soft toys and dog-eared books.

'Read me a story, Maaike, read to me please, Maaike.'

'In a minute, darling. Please sit down for a moment, Simon.'

She dropped down into a large worn armchair by the window. Her skirt lay flat on the chair and showed her left leg had been amputated at the middle of the thigh. What light there was from the window highlighted her shoulder-length hair and innocent face.

'How long have you been back in Amsterdam?'

'Since July. The first repatriation trains left in June for the displaced persons camps but they were for women, children and families. As a single man I had to wait, but there was much work to do as so many were sick and needed care. Also I thought I might find my mother and sister in the hospital, but there was no trace. Then I thought they might have been put on one of the first transports out, so I came here hoping to find them. I've been looking for them, other relatives and friends, but I can't find anyone at all. Anyway, what about you? I was born here but from your accent I think you were not.'

She smiled. 'No, you're right, I'm not an Amsterdammer. I'm from Friesland and the accent is strong, I know. My father worked on the Afsluitdijk and when it was finished he had no work so he moved us to Rotterdam. I was five years old. He worked on many projects in Zeeland, so my mother and I were often alone. We were alone when the Nazis bombed Rotterdam and our house received a direct hit. Mother was killed and I was left with this.' She touched the end of her stump and her pretty face registered sadness.

'But how come you are in Amsterdam?'

'We had nobody in Rotterdam, we had no house and there was no work, in fact there was virtually no Rotterdam, so my father brought us here when I left hospital in 1941. We took this place as it was cheap and easy for me on the ground floor. Amsterdam staircases are not for people like this.' She smiled wistfully and once more indicated her one-leggedness. 'We had been here for a year or so when my father was taken by the Germans to do work somewhere near Dresden, so I am alone.'

'Have you no relatives in Friesland?'

'There are relatives in Leeuwarden but travel to other areas was difficult during the war and anyway I must stay here in case my father ever comes home. I haven't heard from him since the city was bombed in February, but I pray he is alive somewhere, maybe in hospital.'

'I'm hoping to find family too but I fear the worst. Hopefully your news will be better.'

'I hope so. How rude of me, would you like coffee?' She went to stand, reaching for her crutches.

'No, thank you. You have Irene to look after and I want to look around the area. Grietje says you are working and that you might be able to give me some ideas.'

'I just work in a bar, its evenings only but it just about pays the bills. It's the Café van Loon on the corner of Nieuwe Leliestraat and Tweede Leliedwarsstraat.'

'It sounds complicated, why can't the streets have short names? Singel and Spui I can handle. I'll call in tonight if I may, that's if I can find it of course!' he laughed.

'It's not far, even I can walk there,' she smiled. 'Between Bloemgracht and Egelantiersgracht if you get lost. I don't know if Jos can help you but he knows all the other bar owners.'

'Will it matter that I'm a Jew?' The label still hung heavy around his neck.

'Don't be silly, I'm sure it won't and anyway I won't tell him if you don't.'

'I warn you I've never worked in a bar.'

She smiled. 'Don't worry, neither had I.'

He moved to the door. 'Don't get up, I'll see myself out and thank you.'

As he left he turned to see Irene, clasping a book, climbing onto Maaike's single knee and the story had already begun as he emerged into the narrow street.

He got back, footsore, hungry and deflated, in the late afternoon.

'Simon, is that you?'

'Yes, it's me.'

'How are you? What did you do today? I'm in the kitchen, come and tell me. Did you talk to Maaike?'

He walked through the living room.

Irene was sitting at the kitchen table eating while Grietje was once more at the stove. 'It's *stamppot*, have you ever had it before and are you allowed to eat it? It has sausages, but I don't have a clue what they are made with,' she laughed.

'If we had it, which I doubt, I'm sure we didn't call it that but I'll eat anything, I'm tired and starving.'

'Sit down and eat then tell me everything.'

'This is tasty, if this is what pork is like what have I been missing?'

'And you a good Jewish boy.' She laughed again. 'What has the war done to you? Well, did you talk to Maaike and isn't she nice? Irene adores her.'

'She's lovely and yes, we spoke. She's much younger than I expected, younger than me I guess. You didn't tell me she had only one leg.'

14

'Why would I? Does it matter? She's simply a neighbour who has suffered from the war. What difference does a missing leg make?'

'Nothing, I was just shocked, that's all, she's so young and pretty, it seems unfair.'

'Life's unfair, you above everyone should know that. She's been alone for over two years since her father was sent to Germany. She was only fifteen or sixteen, a disabled teenage girl in an occupied city. Anyway, what did she say?'

'Well, she said she would ask her boss about a job. I'm meeting her at work later. She told me her father was made to work in Germany, that he's missing and she doesn't know if he is still alive.'

'You have a lot in common then.'

'I wouldn't say that exactly, but she's a nice girl.'

'So what did you do all day?'

'First of all I found out the name of this street, which was just as well as I got lost at least three times. It's a very complicated neighbourhood, some of the street names go on forever. I thought I ought to know where I am living even if I can't find it again.'

She laughed once more. She seemed a totally different woman to the one he had met the day before. 'If you can't find your way home just look for the billiard hall on the corner and the big advertisement painted on the wall.'

'You seem happy tonight, Grietje. It's lovely to see you like this.'

'I had a good day at work, my boss wants me to work more hours. I'll have to speak to Maaike about that. You might end up helping out with Irene after all. There were lots of bargains at the market this afternoon and you're staying. Do go on, what else did you do?'

'I didn't fancy going to my old area, so I explored round here. First I found the bar where Maaike works. Then I set out to walk the area, stupidly I thought I might find the house where we hid but I only saw it from the outside twice, once when we arrived and once when we were taken away. All I remember is that we were upstairs, I think it was above a garage or a warehouse, I'm not sure. I seem to remember large green wooden doors. We weren't allowed near the windows overlooking the street for obvious reasons. Anyway, all the houses look the same apart from those on the canals and I didn't find anything remotely resembling it.'

'Don't worry, you'll soon find your way around. I'll send you shopping to the Noordermarkt tomorrow, it's fairly close. You might find a strop for the razor while you're there.'

'It seems a very poor area, very rundown, lots of the streets have derelict houses with awful wooden steps leading up to them and the people are, well, lower class.'

She spoke suddenly and fiercely. 'You should fit in well then, rich Jewish boy, except you're not anymore, are you? You're as poor as we are. It's poor, yes, and the houses are old and in need of much work but Jodenbreestraat was hardly the Royal Palace. What with the war and everything it's hardly surprising. The people are hard working, unlike some.'

'I'm sorry, I didn't mean, I ...'

'You forget I cleaned for your father for years and visited your home. Just one of the clocks or watches in his workshop was worth more than Jaap and I earned in a year. You should remember that the Jordaan has given you sanctuary on two occasions now, this street may be one of the worst, but it's home and the people are honest folk.'

'What can I say? I just found it so different, so strange, I'd just never seen housing like this. I wouldn't insult you or the people of your neighbourhood for anything. I'll leave, how can I stay after hurting you like that?'

'I'm sorry too, but there's no need for that, I overreacted, I forgot that you were used to better things and what you have been through in the last three years. I was wrong too. Please can we both forget any harsh words and start again?'

They sat in silence, both too embarrassed to say more.

She broke the stillness first. 'What time are you going to see Maaike? Do you want to wash first? There is a clean shirt for you in your room, another one of Jaap's. I'll put Irene to bed and see you later.'

'Thank you Grietje, I don't deserve you.'

He left the house just before seven, knowing Maaike would have started work at six.

It was a beautiful early autumn evening in Amsterdam. The narrow streets of the Jordaan were still fairly busy, especially with cyclists despite the alleged shortage of both bicycles and tyres. More must have been hidden away awaiting liberation than he realised. Small shops, their windows still decorated with faded homemade red, white, blue and primarily orange flags for the celebration five months before, were still open along with bars and cafes and he started to get a feeling of community, something he had missed so much. He was not yet part of it of course, but the possibility that he might belong somewhere again raised his spirits.

Café van Loon was right on the corner as Maaike had said, housed on the ground floor of an imposing four-storey building, the first, second and top floors of which had huge windows. The double doors, above which was a rusty Heineken sign, went across the corner of the building and a rough bench sat under the window outside. To the side a set of wooden steps led up to what he presumed was the entrance to the private accommodation above.

Inside the space was larger than he expected. The bar was to the right with a line of stools at which sat two older, obviously local, men drinking beer. Straight ahead, up five wooden steps, was a raised seating area with a number of bare wooden tables and chairs lit by two more large windows on the side street. To the left was a large cast iron stove, the chimney of which disappeared at an angle out through the wall.

Three men were engaged in a noisy card game at the table in the furthest corner. Below the raised area a small set of steps led down, he assumed, to the cellar. The ceiling, from which hung an old wooden three bladed fan, and to a lesser extent the walls, were stained dark brown from hundreds of years of smoke.

Maaike, in a white lace edged blouse, was sitting on a high stool behind the bar, an old two-tap polished brass beer pump in front of her and her crutches propped up close to hand. She greeted him with a smile. 'You made it, I told you it was close and easy to find.' She jumped down from the stool and gave a little hop to steady herself before putting the crutches under her arms. 'I told Jos about you, he's in the back, I'll just get him.'

She crutched gracefully across to the steps, climbing them expertly, her single foot first then the crutches. She went over to one of three doors, opened it and called his name.

A voice boomed out an acknowledgement from somewhere inside.

She gave him a huge smile. 'He'll be down in a moment, I think they are eating.'

He looked around, noting a collection of old enamel signs advertising Amstel, Brand and a dozen other beers and numerous old faded photographs of jolly pre-war evenings in the Café van Loon. Above his head was the underside of a curving stairway presumably leading from the steps he had seen outside up to the accommodation above. Perhaps Jos and his family did not occupy the whole house.

The door crashed open and an enormous man in both height and width appeared, sporting a huge grizzly grey beard, moustache and a stained brown apron. He extended a huge hand, while asking, 'Simon? I'm Jos van Loon, goedenavond.'

'Goedenavond Meneer van Loon.'

'Please call me Jos, everyone else does, except my wife of course, her names for me are often very unflattering.' He laughed loud and long at his own joke. 'Do you want a beer?'

He intended to decline as he had never drunk alcohol in his life and had no money but Jos was already calling out to Maaike, '*Fluitje* for Simon please and jenever for me, I'll collect them.'

'Now Maaike tells me you are looking for work but that you have neither experience nor papers.'

He nodded, cautiously sipping at the beer. Why people liked it he didn't understand.

'You're a Jew, yes?'

Simon glanced at Maaike behind the bar.

'No, she didn't tell me, I guessed. I could tell just looking at you. Half starved, someone else's clothes and you look haunted. It doesn't matter to me, you poor sods deserve a chance after what the

Nazis put you through. I took part in the strike in 1941 when they started shipping you all to the camps, it nearly brought them down here in Amsterdam but the NSB and police bailed them out. I'll never forget how the police co-operated. A lot of the NSB went into the SS and fought in Russia. That got rid of plenty of the bastards. The only good thing the Germans did was abolish the bicycle tax but then they stole them when they left. Anyway, you're looking for your family right?'

'Yes, right on both counts, Meneer, sorry, Jos. We are, sorry were, originally from Lithuania, we are Ashkenazi. My father came here with his new wife, my mother, in 1919, just after the Great War. I think everyone is dead, even my young sister. I need to support myself, everyone and everything we owned have gone.'

'There are lots of bars and cafes round the Jordaan looking for staff, things are hopefully picking up now those Nazi bastards have left. The gas and electricity are back on, the trams are running, there's some petrol available - if you know where to look that is - there is more food, beer supplies are back to normal, thank goodness no one bombed the brewery, and we are starting to live again. They need staff on the Prinsengracht too but the bars and cafes there are a bit more upmarket than this place. They serve food and fancy drinks so it's waiters and professional bar staff they need plus they'll want people who are all legal and registered so you pay tax.'

'I've got no experience, in fact I've never had a job, I was a student when we went into hiding.'

'No use to the posh bars then eh? Plus you're hardly dressed for it, are you?'

'I'm sorry, but these clothes are all I have until I get a job.'

'It's somewhere round here for you then. I could recommend you to a dozen bar owner friends of mine in the Jordaan but why would I pass up a good honest Jewish boy who actually wants to work? What about coming here? I took a chance on the lovely Maalke over there, her father was a regular in here for over a year until the German bastards sent him away and she was like you and needed a job. She's been great but for obvious reasons she can't do the cellar work or serve drinks to the tables. Do you think you two could work together?'

'I'm sure we could if someone teaches me.'

'I'll soon show you the cellar and Maaike will show you the bar, we only do two types of beer on tap, four or five in bottles, jenever and whisky, brandy and vodka if I can get it, although now a lot of the Canadians have gone home and Amsterdam is not their city for leave anymore that will be harder. My wife and I do eleven in the morning to six when Maaike arrives plus I have to do the cellar in the evenings as and when, and frankly I want more time off. I would need you here from four in the afternoon till closing Tuesday to Friday and from eleven on Saturdays. Oh, and Wednesday mornings too, the brewery delivers then. The drayman and I will do most of it until you know what to do. Perhaps you can hold the horse for now.' He laughed loudly. 'By the way you're not one of those who can't work Friday evenings and in the daylight on Saturdays are you? It's a busy day with the markets.'

'No no, it's a long time since I followed any strict stuff like that, you ate anything you could get and there were jobs to do in the camps every day of the week. It felt like the Sabbath when there were no bodies to move.'

'That's awful, I hope the full story about what those bastards did comes out one day.' He paused for a moment, deep in thought. 'Then it's agreed?' He extended his huge hand again. 'I need a rest, in the war I worked on the docks and I ran this place. That's where I knew Jaap Blok, you're staying with his wife in Slootstraat, at the same house as Maaike, I'm told. Jaap was a good friend and a brave man.'

'Thank you Jos, I won't let you down.'

'I know you won't, same rate per hour as Maaike once you know the job, yes? Now are you drinking that beer or just warming it? Get it down you and I'll show you the cellar.'

Simon followed him down the steps, smiling and mouthing 'thank you' to Maaike as they passed.

Jos let Maaike leave early and Simon walked her home. It was dusk and the street lights were coming on. Maaike swung smoothly along on her crutches and he found himself having to walk a little quicker to keep up.

As they got to the bridge over Egelantiersgracht she stopped and looked along the canal. The lights shimmered on the water and the trees were starting to take on autumnal shades. 'I love this city, so different to Rotterdam and this neighbourhood with all its problems and deprivation is so welcoming and warm.'

'I'm starting to agree, until yesterday I knew only the Jodenbuurt but the Jordaan is growing on me. I upset Grietje this afternoon by criticising it, but I think I was wrong. I need to find a new home to start my life again and I think this might be it.'

SATURDAY 22ND SEPTEMBER 1945

Unlike the night before he didn't sleep well and was awake long before dawn. Whether it was the excitement of getting a job or the uncomfortable child's bed he didn't know. He listened to the silence, another rare commodity in the camp, broken only by the chimes of the Westerkerk. Suddenly he was back in the hiding place, keeping quiet in case anyone below heard them.

Eventually Aart's boots on the stairs broke his chain of thought. He had not yet heard Grietje so he decided to get up and made coffee for her. She had been in bed when he got back the previous night. He was slightly disappointed she hadn't waited up to hear his news but it had been late, Maaike having decided to take the long route back.

He and Maaike had talked at length on the way home. He was right, she was just 18, three years younger than him, but far more streetwise and he was amazed that she walked home alone every night, even though the bar had closed much earlier during the war. She had been unable to work for short periods in the winter if the pavements had been covered in snow or ice but other than that she had doggedly refused to miss a day, despite often being hassled by German patrols checking she wasn't a Jew breaking the curfew and, more recently, by on-leave Canadians. He'd thanked her over and over for getting him the job and apologised for the fact that he appeared to be getting more hours than her. She'd told him not to worry, the hours she had suited her, and she was paid a little by Grietje for looking after Irene.

He couldn't wait to tell Grietje his news, so he took coffee to her room, knocked and heard a sleepy: 'Who is it?'

'It's me, Simon, can I come in? I have lots to tell you.'

'Just a moment, OK, come in. Quietly please, Irene is still asleep.'

The room was in darkness, but he could make out it was much larger than his and that a large brass bed dominated the centre. Grietje was silhouetted against the window drawing the curtains. As she turned she let her robe fall open revealing her large bare breasts. Below the waist she wore black knickers and thick wool stockings held up with a suspender belt. He looked away, frightened and shocked. He had only ever seen his mother in her underwear and that by accident when he was a young boy.

She gathered the robe around her. 'Oh God! I'm sorry! What must you think of me? Please put the coffee there by the bed and go to the kitchen. We'll be there in a moment.'

Irene began to stir as he hurried from the room.

They came into the kitchen a few minutes later. Irene was still in her nightdress, Maaike had told him she did not have to look after her as Grietje did not work on Saturdays. Grietje was in her dressing gown, thankfully now tied tightly at the waist.

'I'm sorry about that, how awfully embarrassing. Now tell me how things went last night.'

Ten minutes ago he had been bubbling over with excitement and pride to tell her all about the job but now he was confused and embarrassed and found it hard to even remember, let alone tell her about it.

She encouraged him. 'Come on, do tell.'

'I met Jos van Loon, he knew Jaap and Maaike's father by the way, and he gave me a job there, at his bar, working with Maaike.'

For an instant he thought he saw a frown cross her face. 'So you'll be working with Maaike, that's nice.'

'Mainly I'll be helping her with the things she can't do because of her leg. I'll be working with Meneer van Loon as well in the cellar and with his wife in the bar. It will be a lot of hours though, more than I expected, more than Maaike in fact, so I don't know if I will be able to help you much with Irene after all.'

She smiled and patted his hand. 'That's fantastic, I am so proud of you, the first steps to getting back on your feet and getting your confidence back. Don't worry about Irene, I can do the extra cleaning around your work and Maaike's.'

'I'll be able to pay you for my rent and keep now too until I can find a place, so that will help.'

'You can stay here as long as you want, you know that, and keep your money until you get some decent clothes and buy yourself a few possessions.'

'Thank you, you're so kind to me,' he smiled, 'but if I am to stay, can we please do something about those bunk beds, I just don't fit.'

'Of course, I know a friend of Jaap's who might be able to make a proper bed out of them. But now I need you to go to the market.'

'I have to work today at eleven, Jos says Saturdays are busy because of the markets.'

'It won't take you that long, it's not a long list, vegetables, fruit depending on what you can get, some meat or sausage too if possible and eggs, bread and cheese. It all depends on what is available. We may not need the distribution cards anymore apart from for coffee and clothes but some things are still not plentiful. You might have to shop around to get the best price, it's a farmers' market so there should be a good choice.'

'I understand.'

'They were charging twenty-five guilders for a loaf on the black market in January and February,' she said, shaking her head in disbelief, 'that's why it was difficult to feed people in hiding through the war, they had no distribution cards and the black market prices went completely crazy at the end.'

He looked shocked. 'I had no idea.'

'I got paid yesterday so I bought milk, I think it's still alright.' She sniffed the jug. 'I'll buy more when he comes around today, but your budget is ten guilders and try not to get change in those awful Nazi zinc coins. The new ones should be available now but the market dealers will be trying to pass off all the zinc stuff. Next week will be interesting, they're calling in all the old notes and those who got rich on the black market will have to explain where all their money came from.' She laughed and said, 'Not that it will affect me, or you, for that matter.'

'You do know I have never been shopping in my life?'

'Good day to learn then and if there are any of the second-hand stalls look for a razor strop. If they see your face you might get it free! Out of here, follow Anjeliersstraat right down to Prinsengracht and turn left at the end. While you're out I'll iron your shirt, vest and pants. The woman on Marnixstraat who does the washing did me a favour and did it all, and Maaike's, in a hurry in exchange for an hour's cleaning.'

'Jos didn't actually say so but I think he wants me a bit smarter.'

'You'll be in a clean shirt and underwear at least today and I'll press your trousers when you get back.'

'I badly need shoes and more clothes, I can't wear Jaap's forever.'

'I can't help with shoes, Jaap had huge feet. You'll need to go over to your old stamping ground on Waterlooplein when you get your first pay packet. It's starting to get going again, they'll have some good second-hand stuff there from the north but you have to be early and fight for it, half of Amsterdam is in rags at the moment.'

'It has to be better than my stuff. When I first got back they were giving out coupons to get clothes at a place on the Nieuwendijk, but they were no better than the rags I was already in and the shoes were even worse. Some of the others went to a shop on Koningsplein but when I got there everything was gone. Jaap's clothes are the best I have had since we arrived at the camp.'

'Don't worry, you'll soon be able to clothe yourself. Now if you want breakfast, go!'

'Shall I take Maaike's washing down to her on my way out?'

'No need for that,' she snapped, 'I'll take them later, besides I think she is probably staying in bed this morning as she doesn't have to look after Irene.'

He found the market and managed to get many of the items before running out of money. He suspected he had been either short-changed, he had not handled money for nearly three years, or the stallholders had put up the price realising his inexperience. One gave him some of the wartime zinc coins he had been told to avoid saying the new American coinage still wasn't available, but when he tried to spend them again the next stallholder refused to take them.

He remembered something Grietje had said about getting fruit cheaply, or even free, if it was bruised, when the market was closing so he left the fruit and vegetables hoping perhaps that he could get out from work for a few minutes late in the afternoon.

He had no luck with the razor strop, but he could have purchased amongst other things dozens of pairs of ice skates, a wide range of allegedly antique crockery, numerous branded beer glasses and a German helmet. That part of markets and second-hand and antique shops had always fascinated him, but he had never even been allowed to visit Waterlooplein alone. His mother had always accompanied him and his sister and taking time to explore and examine things was not permitted.

Back in Slootstraat Grietje seemed pleased with his purchases but was disappointed he had no vegetables and angry about the handful of zinc he brought back. She was in the kitchen with a flat iron heating on a gas ring on the stove. His clean shirt and underwear lay over the back of a chair, already ironed.

'I'll go myself this afternoon, after all it's your first day at work so you can't really ask for time off to go back to the market and anyway I can either get the price down or flutter my eyelashes and get things for free. Now get those trousers off so I can press them and go and change your underwear and shirt. I've put out some socks for you, they will be too big but better than too small and yours are more holes than socks.'

He changed and waited for his trousers, but when they did not appear he went, rather self-consciously in his shirt and underpants, back to the kitchen.

He was greeted by Grietje, shouting, 'Simon! Simon! It's just been announced on the radio that Eduard Wirths is dead. He killed himself two days ago. He was an SS doctor at Auschwitz they said, is that right? Great news, yes? A monster has gone from the earth, you must be pleased.' She threw her arms around him excitedly.

'Of course. But he's escaped justice and thousands are still dead. If anything, it brings it all back.'

'I'm sorry, I thought you would be pleased a beast like him was dead.'

'I am, and I expect more of them will kill themselves before too long. The big trials start in November. Now can I have my trousers, please?'

'So long as those bastards Seyss-Inquart and Mussert get their just desserts, I want them to hang.'

Jaap's trousers were still worn, thin and too big around his waist but now they had immaculate creases. With them, his clean shirt and an apron from Jos he might actually look the part.

Grietje made him a late breakfast, bread with a slice of old cheese and a fried egg. She called it *uitsmijter*, another dish never seen in the Mendelevski household. She and Irene also had a slice of the ham he had bought at the market, but he declined. After all it was the Sabbath and he thought he ought not to break two rules on the same day.

After they'd eaten she took some towels and set off with Irene, via Westerpark, to visit friends in the Spaarndammerbuurt who had a bathroom. He was tempted to go down to see Maaike but he resisted, knowing he would see her at six. Instead he set off early for the bar, anxious to appear keen on his first day.

The streets were by now very busy indeed, more so than the previous evening and much busier than when he had made his way to the market earlier. Crowds of women, laden with shopping, relieved no doubt to be able to obtain food again, made their way home. Bicycles were again in evidence, but not as many as in pre-war

Amsterdam; most were still on wooden tyres or their metal rims. A few cars, their drivers fortunate to have found petrol, drove slowly along Egelantiersgracht. The whole area was bustling and the chairs outside those cafes and bars which were still in business were occupied by Jordaan residents enjoying the late summer sun and, more importantly, their freedom and a return to comparative normality.

He arrived at Café van Loon just after ten. Jos had been right, the place was crowded, and a number of men sat on the bench outside smoking, drinking beer and exchanging stories. He approached the bar, all the stools were taken so he stood hopefully behind the row of drinkers trying to catch the eye of a tiny middle-aged woman with dyed red hair, narrow lips and an angry expression who he assumed to be Jos's wife.

Finally she noticed him. 'What can I get you?'

'I'm Simon, I'm here to start work, Jos is expecting me. I'm rather early.'

'Ah, so you're the Jewboy.' She looked him up and down. 'You'll have to do I suppose, he didn't ask me about employing you. I'm Mevrouw van Loon by the way. He's in the cellar, drinking I suspect and staying out of the way so he doesn't have to work, the lazy bastard. Go down, he'll be hidden away somewhere, tell him to give you an apron. It might cover up that awful shirt and trousers a little bit.'

He wanted the ground to swallow him up as the drinkers turned to look at him. How different she was to her husband.

'Thank you mevrouw,' he smiled weakly and turned away.

She shouted after him, 'And bring up three crates of Amstel, two Brand and two bottles of jenever, one of them bessen.'

Jos van Loon was in the far corner of the cellar, behind a pile of old broken bar furniture and surrounded by a haze of smoke. He had a jenever bottle by his side, a glass in his hand, and was smoking a large foul-smelling cigar. Behind him in his hideaway were six cases of Canadian Club whisky and a stack of American cigarettes.

'Simon! My God, you're early boy.'

'Your wife sent me down, you have to give me an apron and I have to take beer and jenever upstairs.'

'Ignore the miserable bitch, you're early, sit down and have a drink.'

'No, please, I want to get off on the right foot, I'm here to work.' He was afraid the obviously drunken landlord was going to insist and put him in a difficult position, but he needn't have worried.

'You're right, get on the wrong side of her and your life will be hell, believe me, I know. There's a fairly clean apron over there, you know where the beer is and the jenever is in that cupboard.'

He struggled up the steps from the cellar to the bar with the two crates of Brand beer, still not as strong as a man of his age should be. He realised he had tried to carry too many of the heavy wooden crates at once. He put them down rather heavily behind the bar.

'One crate under there as it is and then refill that shelf with the others and if you can't manage, just carry one crate at a time. We can't afford breakages, you'll end up paying out of your wages. Take the empty one back down with you and get those jenevers up here quickly, Jewboy.'

'Empty crates over there, Simon,' van Loon indicated a corner near the trapdoor and poured himself another drink, 'I'll be pleased when Maaike gets here, then the old cow will go upstairs, out of the way.'

I'll be pleased when she gets here too, he thought, returning to the bar with the two bottles of gin.

'I said one *bessen* idiot, don't you know what *bessen* looks like? It's the coloured one, its blackcurrant-flavoured. Whatever made him employ you I don't know. Bloody Jew!'

Everyone in the bar was staring, or at least he felt as though they were. There were certainly a number of drinkers looking but most were casting sympathetic glances at him, they obviously knew Mevrouw van Loon of old.

He brought up and refilled the shelves with the Amstel without any problem and managed to get through to five thirty without further incident. Van Loon's wife had asked him to serve some customers but just as he was about to point out that he didn't know how, her husband emerged from the cellar red-faced with the butt of his cigar clamped between his teeth. 'I'll do that, Maaike is going to teach him the bar work when she gets here. Can you collect the empties, please Simon?'

Jos, despite his obvious excessive jenever consumption, started to serve customers, often three at a time, noting what they had on the already open tabs clipped on a board behind the bar, while holding a conversation with someone sitting upstairs and refreshing drinks without apparently even being asked. 'Take this up to Wim, he's the ugly one at the back near the gents, then see if anyone outside needs a drink. We don't do pavement service so normally, if they are too idle to come in, they get bugger all, but as you're here and an extra pair of hands you can go and see. If anyone wants to leave tell them they'll have to come in to pay.'

He was standing outside taking a breath of fresh air when he spotted Maaike coming towards him. He waved, and she paused for a moment to let go of a crutch to wave back.

'Hello Simon, you're here and working hard already.'

'You're early too.'

'I wanted to see you, I mean to see how you were getting on. I saw you going out this morning, you were very early.'

'And I wanted to see you too, I'm glad you're here. Jos is drunk but managing very well and his wife has disappeared upstairs, thank goodness.'

'Oh, you've met our very own Führer have you?' she joked. 'She's a nasty piece of work, I'd like to say her bark is worse than her bite, but it probably isn't.'

'You likening her to Hitler isn't far off, I get the distinct impression that she doesn't like Jews.'

'Don't worry, she doesn't like anybody, how she hasn't driven all the customers away I don't know. I don't think she likes me that much. Jos is like a father and I was hoping to get close to her too, but I know she makes remarks about my leg and calls me a cripple.'

They went inside. Maaike was greeted by a number of the customers and Jos, who announced, 'And here is the little lady all you lot come in to see, isn't she beautiful?'

With that he took her jacket, stumbled up the steps, hung the jacket on a peg and disappeared through the door marked 'Private'.

'It's just the two of us then. Are we going to be able to manage? It's very busy.'

'Easily, it will die down after about seven or eight and I will be able to show you how to serve the beer, teach you the prices and introduce you to the more determined regular drinkers. Until then can you do empties and take trays up the steps for me.'

'I've already stocked the bar and I saw Jos changing the barrels, which is a good thing as I've already forgotten his short lesson last night.'

'If you collect the dirty glasses I'll show you how to wash them. It's not just a simple sink, the water is always running and there are brushes in the water to wash the glasses and a tap to rinse the suds out, then you put them upside down on the brass drainer there. Watch me, it's easy.' She slid down from the high stool and hopped towards him. Holding on to the bar with one hand, she expertly washed a full tray of glasses in an instant with the other. She hopped back to the stool and smiled at him. 'OK, so now you try.'

The evening passed quickly. He enjoyed her company and he thought they worked well together. As promised she showed him how to pour draught and bottled beers, the different glasses and how to measure spirits, and talked him through the price list.

She introduced him to, and he actually served, a couple of the hardened regulars but when it came to adding up how much customers owed he was useless compared to her mental arithmetic.

Jos came down after a noisy argument with his wife, audible to everyone, bringing them a supper of *bitterballen* and cheese. 'Here, have these you two, see how I spoil you kids. I have to look after the staff, don't I?'

He settled himself at the end of the bar, drinking small glasses of beer and chatting to a couple of the regulars. They were still there at ten, but all the other customers had paid and left, all the glasses were washed, and between them they had wiped the tables and tidied the bar area.

'Off you go Maaike, I'm not staying open much longer, and take this lad with you, he looks absolutely tired out.' Jos turned to Simon. 'Well done, a good start.'

He fetched her coat and held it for her.

She balanced on her one leg with tiny hopping movements while she put her arms in the jacket. She took her crutches and moved confidently to the door. She called back over her shoulder, 'Good night Jos, thank you, see you Tuesday.'

They walked back together via Egelantiersgracht and Lijnbaansgracht. She said how much she loved to walk the canals at night. As they approached the door she tripped and stumbled, almost falling. He caught her and held her for a few moments until she steadied herself.

'Oh Simon, thank you. I feel so stupid doing that in front of you. What must you think? Honestly, I haven't done that for ages. I've been like this for a long time now, I used to fall a lot in the beginning but I'm usually pretty safe on my crutches now. It's not surprising nobody wants a girl with one leg if she keeps falling over.'

'Don't be silly, it's very dark, the lamp is out and the streets are full of potholes, the whole city seems to be falling apart since the war.'

She smiled. 'Thank you, you are a kind man. Good night.'

MONDAY 24TH SEPTEMBER 1945

'Simon! Breakfast, come on, some of us have to work even if you don't.' She had laid out his food: bread, jam, a little butter and coffee. Now she was struggling to get an uncooperative Irene ready and down to Maaike. She started work earlier on Mondays and finished later as it was Maaike's day off.

The two women had spent part of Sunday together. Grietje had invited Maaike up for lunch then they had taken Irene to Westerpark. Simon had been out all day over in the Jodenbuurt, still looking, still hoping. She wasn't sure for what anymore, but she feared he was doomed to fail again.

He wasn't back when she went to bed, which was early, as she had a particularly busy day ahead.

'Simon, come on, please, stir yourself, I have to go soon.'

'I'm coming, I'm coming.' He appeared at the kitchen door, even more dishevelled than usual.

'What the hell happened to you? You look terrible. What time did you get in last night?'

'About two.'

She looked shocked. 'What on earth were you doing until then?'

He looked ashamed. 'Drinking, you see I met someone.'

'Drinking?' She looked angry now. 'You don't drink and what do you mean you 'met someone', not a woman I hope?'

'No, no, I met someone I knew and who remembered me. Not a relative or even a friend really. It was old Bart van Dieten, you remember him, he had the workshop above father's, making jewellery.'

'Oh yes, I remember him, he used to try to touch my backside when I was cleaning the landing.'

'Yes, well,' he ignored her and carried on excitedly with his story, 'it was fantastic just to find someone. He's not a Jew, of course, so he only comes into our old neighbourhood to work, he lives somewhere out in the west, but he knew me straight away.'

'How did you end up drinking half the night?'

'I went to the Red Cross, they're accessing the registration cards from the City Registry to help in tracing people so I hoped they might know more about my mother and sister, but they were closed. There are fewer trains coming back now so there are less and less of us registering and looking for help. They are still putting up new lists all the time of those who have survived and returned and those who will not. I checked them as I haven't been over there for a few days but there's still no news. I went to the free kitchen, it's still there and I thought I might be able to get a meal but it was closed as it was Sunday so...'

'Simon, I have to work, get on with it, please.'

'I went for a walk around the old area, hoping against hope to see someone, anyone, and I went up to father's old business again and that's when I saw Bart. He was on his way to his place, recognised me, and let me in. I told you it was all boarded up, but I forgot the little side door down the alley.'

'And?'

'Father's workshop is still there, it's not been stripped or damaged in any way, I presume because Bart and the other man were still working there. It was locked but I looked through the glass panel and could see his bench, the desk, cupboards and one of the lamps. There was nothing else. Father obviously cleared out all the stock and tools and stuff when he closed down.'

'I remember that, he had to pay me off.' She sounded hurt and angry. 'I helped him to pack and move things to Dijkstraat, it was the last time I worked for your family. As a matter of fact, it was the last time I saw you.'

'I spent the rest of the day with Bart, he bought me a late lunch. He's trying to build his business back up so he's working seven days a week at the moment, and we went to a bar on the Spuistraat, then on a tram out to his home and then out again to a bar in his neighbourhood. We stayed there talking about my father, what had happened to us, what it was like for him here while I was away, how the area was destroyed last winter, everything in fact. Before I realised it was midnight and I had to find my way back here. I'm not used to drinking, in fact I don't like it, I feel terrible today. I didn't know the way, so it took me a long time.'

'That will teach you. You are lucky you didn't fall into a canal.'

'It was worth it though, just finding someone. We're going to keep in touch whenever I am there checking the lists. He's going to ask around for me if he sees anyone he thinks might know me. He said he'd heard a rumour that the City Council is thinking of charging returning Jews the rent and taxes which have been unpaid on their properties while we have been away. Surely not, that can't be right, can it?'

'I wouldn't worry about it, you said some locals were living in your family's house so unless you try to take it back or want to re-occupy the workshop, I'd just keep a low profile. No one knows where you are or even that you're here. Look, I'm late, now I have to go, we'll talk tonight, but I'm pleased for you.'

She took Irene down to Maaike on her way out while he ate his breakfast and washed. He really needed more sleep, but the bed was so uncomfortable he opted to go for a walk instead in the hope of clearing his pounding head. He passed Maaike's door, wanting to see her and tell her his news, but decided against it.

It was a hot day and he wandered aimlessly for what seemed like hours, half hoping to find the hiding place, but it was useless, it could just as easily have been down past Elandsgracht as up near

Westerstraat and he was afraid he would not recognise it even if he saw it.

It was about three when he got back to Slootstraat. He knew Grietje was working a little later than usual and that Maaike would be in looking after Irene so he decided to call on her.

'Simon! I was hoping you would drop in on me, the day seems so long when I am inside all the time. I was going to come up to see you but you know, the staircase is steep and I have little Irene.'

'And I wanted to see you too, but I felt quite ill this morning.'

He recounted the story of his Sunday while she made coffee in the kitchen. Irene sat on his knee with a stuffed dog, which she insisted he stroked every few minutes.

'Bring your coffee through here, we can sit more comfortably.'

He followed her into the sitting room. She was wearing a sleeveless summer dress and as she came into the room she was silhouetted against the window and he could see her stump clearly through the thin skirt.

'Here, sit next to me.' She patted the settee. 'Irene seems to have claimed the chair. Great news that you found a friend yesterday, but still no news on your family?'

'Sadly no, and nothing on your father either I assume.'

'No, nothing.' For the first time since he had known her he thought he saw a tear.

He wanted to put his arm around her and comfort her but he was afraid. 'I'm sure you'll get a letter soon or, better still, he'll walk through that door.'

'I hope so, I don't think I can stand not knowing for much longer. Anyway,' she sniffed and dried her eyes, 'what are you doing this evening? I often do what I call my canal walk along Brouwersgracht, it's my favourite. We could stop somewhere for a drink or a coffee. I often have to rest.'

'I'm sorry, I need to spend the evening with Grietje, I was out all yesterday until very late and I haven't seen her today as she has been working.'

'Oh, I understand,' she said but she sounded upset.

'I haven't got any money for coffee anyway.'

'Don't worry, I would have paid, I think we are all going to be short of money for a week. They are withdrawing all the old notes on Wednesday so I don't know how Jos is going to pay us, we don't want old notes which are no good on Thursday. He might struggle to explain all his money to the bank, it's part of identifying black market profits or something.'

'Jos, black market, surely not.' He laughed.

'I don't really understand, it's a bit like the new coins. They are supposed to be limiting everyone to ten guilders in the new money, a five guilder note and two two and a half guilder coins to tide them over for the first week, but it won't go far and how do you pay for cheap things, how do you get change, will the German zinc coins still be used? I don't really understand it at all. They cancelled all the hundred guilder notes two months ago, but that didn't affect me of course.'

'Everyone? I haven't been paid at all yet, how will I get the ten guilders?'

'I don't see how you can, you have to show your ration distribution card at the bank when you get the new ten guilders and you don't have one as you were in hiding and in the camp when the new ones came out last year, so you don't exist officially. I don't know how I'll get my new money yet either and it's getting very close.'

'What if you have more than ten guilders to exchange?'

'That's something else I don't have to worry about, especially if Jos doesn't pay me more than ten guilders this week. I think if you have more than ten guilders they will want you to open a bank account, where your funds are going to be immediately frozen until they are satisfied it's not black money. It won't affect people like us but it's going to be difficult for a week at least. They say people are spending all their money now on just about anything to get rid of it before Wednesday.'

'Shame we haven't got any to spend, we could go out tonight and live it up.'

'Grietje will be pleased if you stay in with her, she's attracted to you, you do know that, don't you?'

'What! Don't be silly, she's twenty years older than me.'

'Twelve, she told me, she's only thirty-three.'

'I thought she was just being kind to me as she knew me when I was young and she worked for my father. She seems guilty about something, possibly because of the way we were treated by the Nazis and wants to look after me, or so I thought. I should feel guilty if anything, I don't think we paid her at all well.'

'Well, just be aware that's all, she's a widow and vulnerable, make sure she doesn't jump on you,' she giggled. 'After all underneath that hair and stubble you're a handsome man.'

They spent the rest of the afternoon chatting and entertaining Irene. Just before six there was a knock on the door. It opened and Grietje walked into the room. Irene ran to her.

'Simon! What are you doing here?' She looked surprised and a little angry. 'Don't you see enough of Maaike at work, you shouldn't be bothering her today.'

Maaike stood up and hopped on the spot ignoring her crutches. 'It's alright, he just came down for a chat. He's lonely, poor boy,' she joked.

'I'll look after him tonight, I'm cooking, and I've got a chicken. See you tomorrow, Maaike. Can I pay you then? Otherwise you'll have to wait a week. Come on you two.'

'Yes, goodbye Maaike.' He gave her a big smile which, to his delight, she returned. He left, together with Irene, feeling like a small boy again.

Grietje cooked a wonderful meal of roast chicken and potatoes. It was quite late by the time they had eaten so she put Irene to bed while he washed the plates. Afterwards they sat and listened to the radio and talked.

He was still a bit unnerved by Maaike's revelation and he realised that allowing her robe to come open in front of him might not, after all, have been accidental.

She tried to explain to him about the withdrawal of the old guilder notes. She had slightly more than the permitted ten guilders as she had been paid again by one of her employers, anxious to get rid of his old notes no doubt, so she had spent

38

money that night on the chicken, was going to pay Maaike tomorrow and hoped to spend the rest before the deadline.

'I don't have any black money but I don't want to have any more than ten when I go to the bank, I don't want all the hassle and I don't really want to open an account but I can't afford not to use it. It all seems crazy to me but the Finance Minister, Lieftinck, I think his name is, has come up with the idea. It's to catch all the black money and to sort out how much is in circulation. Apparently we have just been printing too much money under the Germans.'

He still wasn't sure he understood it correctly that everyone in the country had to manage on ten guilders for a week and make a declaration where their money came from, or that she and Maaike understood it either, but as he had no money it didn't affect him apart from his wages from Jos.

'I've arranged for someone to come round tomorrow morning to look at the box beds and see if he can build you a proper single bed. He's the husband of a friend but he won't want old money either, so he probably won't do it until next week when I can pay him in the new notes. The mattress will be a problem, we'll have to look around for a clean second-hand one nearby, we'd never get it back here if we went to Waterlooplein for it.'

He told her in more detail about his visit to his father's workshop. She seemed interested in where all his tools, stock and other things had gone.

'There was so much stuff, I was helping him fill big old tea crates with it.'

He nodded, remembering the crates arriving at Dijkstraat. 'I'm fairly sure he sold it all while we were at Dijkstraat, while people could still deal with Jews. I remember he took a few things with him when we went into hiding. I recall him trying to work on watches in the dark but I suppose the Germans or the police got them when we were arrested. He certainly took nothing other than clothes when they put us on the train.'

She changed the subject, not wanting to discuss his father and tired of hearing of his day with Bart. 'How are you getting on at work?'

'I've only actually done one shift. Jos seems to like me but his wife doesn't, although I'm told by Maaike that she doesn't really like anybody.'

'And how are you getting on with Maaike?' It appeared to him to be a very pointed question.

'Very well I think, she's nice and she's good at her job so she's teaching me well.'

'She's sweet on you, I know that, I can tell.'

He saw a chance to finish both rumours. 'There's no point in anybody being 'sweet' on me, I've got no money, no prospects and no confidence or self-esteem, I wouldn't be any good for any woman.'

'I wouldn't say that Simon, you are honest, upright, young and you will get back on your feet soon I'm sure, someone will snap you up. Well, I'm so tired, it's been a long day, I'm off to bed, goodnight.' She leaned over and kissed his cheek and went through to her bedroom.

He toyed with the idea of going down to see Maaike. He was going to suggest a walk the following morning but he realised she would have Irene in her care again. The evening was out as well as they were both at work so, still tired from the previous night's drinking session with Bart, he too went to his room.

WEDNESDAY 26TH SEPTEMBER 1945

He'd slept much better as the husband of Grietje's friend's had been round, looked at the box bed and taken off the end board of the lower one and removed the top as an interim measure. It meant he could at least stretch out, although his feet hung over the end and the mattress finished at the middle of his calf.

He still woke early, early enough to actually see Aart van Beek as he passed carrying his chamber pot. He said good morning, Aart grunted. He was at the bar early to help with the delivery. Jos had said the previous evening that nine would be fine, but it was only eight thirty as he banged on the door of the Café van Loon.

Jos appeared wearing his cellar apron but otherwise immaculately dressed in what were obviously his best suit trousers and a white shirt and dark blue tie. He'd combed his hair and even trimmed his beard. The suit jacket was hanging on a peg nearby.

'Morning Jos, very smart for taking a delivery, aren't you?'

'Cheeky young sod, I've got to go to the bank today with her upstairs and our distribution cards to get our twenty new guilders and to pay in last night's takings. I'm also taking my account books for the bar, so they can see I run a legitimate business and that my account isn't full of black market money. It's bloody ridiculous, we might not be back by eleven so I'll lose money not being open. You haven't got any old notes, have you? I'll pay them in for you if you do so you don't lose the money.'

'I haven't got any notes, in fact I haven't got any money at all. I was hoping you would pay me today but with only ten guilders I don't see how you can.'

'See me tonight,' he winked, 'I'll see you alright then. There are ways and means you know. Those clever buggers in government think they've got it all tied up but they don't know how a Jordaan lad works.'

The brewery wagon pulled by two large horses arrived, as Jos had guessed, at nine exactly. He held the horses while Jos and the dray driver dropped barrels of beer down onto a thick padded cushion before rolling them down through the trapdoor into the cellar. Crates of beer were slid down the slope but the crates of empties were much harder work so he went down to help Jos get them up to street level so the drayman could load them. Jos signed a receipt, took his copy and the horse and dray moved off towards Bloemgracht. The whole thing took only about twenty minutes and he wondered for a moment why Jos had asked him to be there.

'There, that wasn't too painful was it? He's a good one, that driver, but a couple of them are lazy and don't do any more to help than they have to. You'll need to make sure they don't deliver one case short, thieving devils. You'll soon get the hang of it, you'll be doing it on your own in no time. You can bugger off now until four.'

I don't know about that, he thought, but he was grateful to be finished so early. He'd left before breakfast so he headed back home. He knew that Grietje would be at work by the time he got back and after he'd eaten he was going to see Maaike.

She was sitting on the outside step as he arrived, watching as Irene played in the street with two other small children from across the road.

'You were quick, I heard you go out but didn't expect you back yet.'

'It was all very easy really, Jos was waiting, he has to go to the bank and he and the drayman soon did the job. I think he expects me to supervise it soon, no doubt he'll want to stay in bed sleeping it off on Wednesdays.'

'I'll have to go and change my money today too somehow, I've got it down to just ten guilders and a few zinc coins, about fifteen cents which don't matter. Grietje is finishing early so she should be here by two to take Irene back. I'll go to the bank on Haarlemmerdijk and then straight to work. Trouble is if she pays me it will be in old money and then I'll have more than ten guilders. I don't know what to do.'

'I expect it's a problem lots of ordinary people will have today but don't worry, Jos will sort it out I'm sure, knowing him he'll have a way around it. Can I come with you? We could do that canal walk you mentioned and still be at the bar by four.'

She smiled. 'That would be very nice. If you watch Irene I'll make coffee, I think I have just enough for two cups.'

'I'll have to go upstairs, I haven't eaten yet.'

'Let me get you something to eat, bread and jam or cheese, OK? I have eggs if you want.'

'No, really, just coffee and bread will be fine, I don't want to bother you.'

Secretly he was delighted to be spending this unexpected time with her. Last night at the bar had been very busy, everyone was trying to get rid of all their folding money before it became worthless and what better way than to exchange it for drink? They had had little time to talk and she had wanted to take the quickest way home as she was tired.

Grietje arrived just after two and, as expected, paid Maaike in old notes. She had already been to the bank for her new ten guilders, which she showed to Maaike.

'The banks are busy, Maaike.'

'Simon and I are going now that you are home, we thought we'd try Haarlemmerdijk and then go on to work.'

Grietje frowned. 'You're going to the bank too, Simon?'

'Just to keep Maaike company and I have to be at work at four anyway.'

'Don't you need to eat?'

'Jos often gives us a mid-evening snack, so I'm alright thank you.'

'I'll see you later then, depending on what time you get back.' She sounded disappointed but took Irene by the hand and disappeared up the stairs.

They were nearing the end of Lijnbaansgracht, the pavement was very narrow and he had to walk behind her as she swung between her crutches, her single foot appearing to hardly touch the ground.

'We need to cut across here. This will take us to the bridge over Brouwersgracht so we can get to Haarlemmerdijk.'

They turned into Palmgracht; the canal, long since filled in, left a wide road and pavements so he was able to walk alongside her.

She suddenly stopped and turned to him. 'You're not embarrassed or ashamed to be seen with me, are you?'

'Whatever do you mean?'

'Being seen out with a one-legged girl, people do stare you know.'

'They shouldn't, but let them, I don't care, I like being in your company. You're very pretty, why should I be ashamed? You're the one who should be embarrassed being out with a scruffy chap like me.'

She smiled weakly and moved on.

Suddenly it was his turn to stop. 'Maaike! Stop!'

'What's the matter?'

'That smell, what is it?'

'What smell? I can't smell anything.'

'But you must be able to, it's quite strong.'

She breathed in deeply. 'Oh, that smell. It's the gin distillery, they make jenever just down there somewhere.' She indicated a side street across the road. 'Why, what's wrong?'

'It's here, it's here somewhere that I was hiding with my family, I just know it, that smell, it all comes back to me. I'll never forget that smell. Come on, we must look down there.'

'But the bank, I have to get my new money?'

'Change it tomorrow, lots of people won't cash their old notes in today. You won't need money before then, you won't need to spend anything tonight and Jos will probably sort it out for you. Come on, please, we must look, it's here somewhere, I just know it.'

'I'm coming, I'm coming as fast as I can.'

'Where does that road go to?'

'Out onto the Brouwersgracht and Lijnbaansgracht corner I think, I don't really know all the little streets around here.'

He almost ran into the side street she had indicated. The sign told him it was Driehoekstraat. 'Come on Maaike, I'm sure we're close.'

She was still crossing the wide Palmgracht. 'Wait for me, Simon, please.'

He ran ahead, past a bar on the corner, looking from side to side as he went. The jenever distillery premises were on the left and also straight ahead where the street forked. He vainly looked at the houses on his right, hoping to see the doors he remembered or on the left the view he had glimpsed of the house opposite when he had sneaked a look out of the window.

She finally caught up with him.

'I can't see it, I can't see the green doors, I was so sure this was the place.'

'Perhaps they've been painted.'

'No, no, it doesn't look like anything has been painted here for years and anyway the view's wrong as well, the street is too wide.'

'Well keep going, a bit further and maybe you'll see it.'

'But it splits in two, look.'

'Check both ways then, I'll stay here at the junction, I need a rest.' She sat on a window ledge of the distillery office, which looked closed.

It was only mid afternoon but all was quiet at street level. The doors of what he guessed were distillery storerooms or garages were shut. *Perhaps they aren't delivering today because of the money thing,* he thought. The distillation process was obviously continuing, he could hear someone moving about inside and a tell-tale aroma was coming from the building.

He hurried down the right-hand fork to Brouwersgracht and

then along the left-hand fork to Lijnbaansgracht before returning to her.

His face told her everything. 'Nothing, in fact not many houses, a few sets of doors but most of them under warehouses, nothing that matches what I remember.'

'Never mind, it must be around here somewhere but there are so many identical little streets in the Jordaan, it might even have been on the other side of Brouwersgracht somewhere. Come on, let's go.'

'Just one more place, Maaike, please.' He almost begged her. 'I think we are so close. What was that little alley we passed back there?'

They retraced their steps a few yards to the corner of Kromme Palmstraat.

'I'll just check down here, please be patient with me.'

'You go ahead, it looks very uneven. I'll wait here.'

He hurried down the alley. Halfway down there was a dogleg to the left, he turned the corner and suddenly there it was. Two large green doors and next to them a single small door leading to the rooms above. He looked up, seeing three grimy windows at both the first and second floor levels, all hung with dirty lace curtains and a smaller window up in the gable. Opposite, a mere five or six metres away, were a number of typical Jordaan houses.

He ran back to her screaming, 'Maaike, Maaike, I've found it, it's here! The doors, the windows, the house opposite, even the little room at the top where father tried to work on watches, it's all there. It's definitely the place. Quickly come and see.'

They walked back down the alley and stood outside the double doors. Above was a faded sign with yellow lettering still just legible as 'A.F. de Jong & Zonen'.

He tried the small door, the paint was peeling but it was securely locked. Looking at the filthy tattered curtains, the upper floors were obviously unoccupied so knocking was useless.

'What do we do now?'

'I need to find someone to ask about who owns this place, maybe they hid us, maybe they betrayed us. I need to get inside.'

46

'What are you hoping to find?'

'I don't know, I just need to do it.'

'But there's no one around, let's go, I have to get to the bank. You can do it any time now you know where it is.'

There was at least a two hour wait at the bank so they went straight on to work arriving at Café van Loon just before four.

Jos was behind the bar himself. There was no sign of his wife or any customers for that matter, with just a solitary regular on the first stool inside the door. 'Hello you two, you're early, Maaike, it's going to be a quiet evening in here I think. They all spent their old money last night, I took twice as much as usual but tonight no one wants to part with their precious new ten guilders, if they've even got any new money yet that is.'

'They do have to make it last a week. It seems crazy to me, how is it going to work?' She looked worried. 'I haven't got my new money yet, the bank was too busy.'

He winked at her. 'Don't you worry, I'll see you alright.'

'But I've got more than ten old guilders. I've got twenty-five because Grietje Blok paid me in old money.'

'I told you, don't worry, there are ways and means you know, and you, young fellow, you've got no money to change have you?'

'No, and I don't expect you can pay me yet, people are saying everything will be delayed by a week.'

'I told you, I'll see you alright, both of you.'

He reached under the bar and took out a thick leather wallet. 'Right, here we are, twenty guilders for you, Maaike, and twenty for you, Simon.'

To their surprise he handed each of them two new five-guilder notes and four new two-and-a half guilder coins.

'But this is too much, more than my usual wages, how did you...?'

'I told you, ways and means. I sold all my excess old guilders, the ones the tax man doesn't need to know about, at a two for one rate. There are those who are buying them and who have their own ways of getting around the controls. The black marketeers are making even more money out of the government's plan to stop black money. It's crazy. There's been a delay in producing other denominations of the new notes and coins apparently. The British are doing the notes, and they and the Yanks the coins, so it may go on a while. Call it a bonus. Now give me your old notes.' With that he produced yet more new notes and coins from the wallet. 'I'll change yours on a straight one for one basis Maaike, here you are, twenty-five guilders in our sparkling brand new currency. They said they would release my bank account in a week as it's all in order.' He laughed. 'Jos van Loon is officially totally honest, and his money is completely clean so there will be no problem with next week's wages.'

'Thank you, I told Maaike you'd look after us somehow.'

'Just make sure you keep it to yourselves. Now come on you, we have work to do in the cellar, this morning's delivery still needs stacking away. Maaike, you can manage up here, somehow I don't expect a rush. I'll still accept old notes but the beer price if they pay with old ones is double, alright?'

Down in the cellar they shifted all the crates, stacking them neatly against the back wall, making sure to cover a square metal plate set in the floor.

'I've got a few valuables down there, I went in for a little gold, jewellery and things when the Nazi's withdrew the one hundred guilder notes a month or so ago. Everyone was doing it. Not a word to my wife though, our secret eh? I'm trusting you now.'

'Of course. Now can I tell you something? You might be able to help.' He told him about finding the place in Kromme Palmstraat and explained he was trying to find out who owned it or who might have arranged for his family to use it.

'I'll ask around for you, I know a man who runs a bar on Palmgracht. Oh, and while you're here, take these.' He handed him a razor and strop. 'As you can see I haven't used them in a while.'

He was right, there were no more than three customers all night. One, a regular with a drink problem, tried to spend his precious ten guilders in new currency but Jos, in yet another act of generosity, refused to take his money and extended him credit, telling him he could pay in a week.

The bar was empty by eight and Jos sent them home. Maaike was relieved to have new currency in her bag and he was just relieved to have money of any sort. They discussed going to the Waterlooplein market together to get him a change of clothes and shoes but as she looked after Irene every day it was decided he would have to go alone.

'You'd better discuss it with Grietje first though,' she smiled, 'I have the distinct feeling she might want to go with you and supervise her little boy.'

He left her at the door and ran up the stairs, anxious to tell Grietje about finding the hiding place and to finally pay her some rent.

FRIDAY 28TH SEPTEMBER 1945

Maaike had been quite right, Grietje insisted on coming with him to Waterlooplein to look for clothes. In fairness she argued that she would be much better at bargaining than him, pointing out that he had never tangled with the Waterlooplein dealers before. He'd told her all about finding the hiding place in Kromme Palmstraat. She seemed pleased but she clearly wasn't as excited or as enthusiastic as him, merely asking what he intended to do next and saying she hoped it would put an end to his obsession. She had refused his offer of rent or housekeeping saying she would wait until the following week when he got his second week's wages.

As soon as she had dropped Irene off with Maaike they set off for Waterlooplein.

'I don't have to be at work until noon today, so we have plenty of time to look around the market, there might not be the choice there used to be and there will be a lot of rubbish. We can't have you looking worse than you already do.'

'At least I've had a proper shave thanks to Jos.'

'And taken half your face off too by the look of it!'

'Maaike and Jos both laughed at me last night, but at least it looks better than it did yesterday morning.'

'It's finally stopped bleeding you mean. Come on, let's go, we'll walk rather than spend money on the tram.'

They made their way across to Kloveniersburgwal via Oudemanhuispoort. Only two or three of the booksellers were open. The passageway with its numerous lockable alcoves stacked with second-hand books was somewhere that fascinated him and he had spent many hours there as a student before the war, searching for medical books as he dreamed of becoming a doctor.

Crossing the bridge at the end of Staalstraat they arrived at the market. It didn't look to him as large as it had before the war. There were certainly fewer traders but the shortages and hardships brought out those in search of cheap goods, particularly clothes it seemed, in large numbers despite the monetary limit the change of currency had imposed.

'I bet these poor devils will be paying with the old zinc rubbish, half of them don't look like they have ten guilders to change into the new money.'

They approached a pile of clothes on the ground.

'This is no good, half of it is just army boots and greatcoats, let's move on.'

They found another pile and, elbowing her way through a crowd of women to the front, she pulled out five shirts and three pairs of trousers. 'These don't look too bad, nothing a good hot wash and iron won't put right. Here, hold them up against you.'

He did as he was told. One of the pairs of trousers was far too short so she dived back into the pile again, emerging with another pair and a leather belt.

'Right, these will do, now let me go and sort out a price. Give me some money, the new coins not the notes, he can't have change, there's nothing smaller than two and a half and I don't want the old zinc stuff. Then we'll look for shoes.'

As promised she got the shirts and trousers for a good price and in lieu of change the seller threw in some underwear, socks and a scarf. 'That's how you do it, come on, shoes next.'

He grimaced. 'I'm not sure about the underwear.'

'It'll be fine, I'll boil them, don't worry, beggars can't be choosers.'

The pile of old, worn and odd shoes looked a real challenge, many were worse than the ones he was wearing. Eventually, after much hunting for the left shoe, she found a pair of the right size in black leather, newly re-heeled but lacking laces. He tried them on, surprised at the good condition and quality. He guessed they had been looted from a Jewish house nearby.

She secured the purchase with a handful of old coins and his old shoes in exchange and then deftly removed and quickly pocketed the laces from another pair of shoes in the pile. 'Right, that'll do for today, I'll get these washed and ironed for you. You'll have to get a coat, maybe an ex-army one, when winter comes. That jacket of Jaap's will have to do for now.'

He checked the latest Red Cross lists while they were in the area but there was still no mention of his mother or sister. The list of those confirmed dead had grown, which should have given him hope, but the list of known survivors was still less than half a page.

'Shall we go and see Bart?'

'No, we won't, he'll probably want to grab my arse again, you can see him the next time you're over here. Come on, I have to get to work.'

They set off for the Jordaan.

'Put the underwear in the bucket in the kitchen, boil the kettle and leave them to soak, I'll take the shirts and trousers round to the woman for washing when I get home. Tell Maaike it will be about five and ask her to feed Irene for me.'

She gave him the clothes to take back to Slootstraat and left him on Prinsengracht.

He hurried through the small side streets, very conscious of the bundle of dirty second-hand clothes over his arm. He was embarrassed about the clothing and took it straight upstairs before calling on Maaike.

She opened the door almost before he knocked, 'Simon, hello, I saw you coming down the street but then I heard you going upstairs, I hoped you would drop in. Please come inside quietly, Irene is sleeping. Have you eaten yet?'

'No, I was going to buy something on the way back but I only have the two and a half guilder coins so I didn't know how I would get change. How is anyone managing with the new money?'

'I don't think they are, it will probably be quiet at work again this evening unless Jos gives everyone credit. How did you get on at the market this morning? I noticed you were carrying clothes and you have smart new shoes.'

'The clothes are rather dirty but Grietje is going to get them laundered and ironed for me, better than the clothes in the camp I suppose.'

'Cheer up, they'll look nice when they're washed. Everyone is badly dressed at the moment, some clothes are still on ration so it's difficult and if you don't even have a ration book, like you, then it's even worse. I've just got hold of a pair of overalls from a girl who worked at the tram depot. I'm altering them to fit, women are wearing trousers these days you know. I'm not sure how I'll look but I'll give them a try.'

'You'll look lovely, I'm sure. I quite like the shoes, they're comfortable and not full of holes but Grietje had trouble finding a pair.'

'It's much easier if you only need one like me,' she laughed and looked down at her single foot. 'I'm sorry I don't have coffee, I need to go shopping. I hope Grietje isn't late home.'

'She said five and please can you feed Irene. Don't worry about coffee, I'm going up to Palmgracht to have another look around.'

She looked disappointed. 'I'll see you at work at six then.'

He made his way to Kromme Palmstraat. The premises were still deserted with the large double doors closed. He noticed the windows had heavy dark drapes behind the dirty grey lace curtains, something else he remembered. They had lived mainly on the first floor and at the back of the house to not show any light, but he and his sister had often crept to the front to steal a look at the street through the curtains. He hadn't noticed it before, but he could just make out the name 'Smit' in faded fancy script on the front door and the number 3b on a blue and white enamel plate next to it. He hammered on the door without any response.

'There's nobody there, it's been empty for years.'

He turned to see a woman standing at the door of the house opposite.

'There were some Jews hiding there in the war, but the Germans arrested them one night. Someone used to visit while they were there and for a day or so after they were taken, but I haven't seen him for ages. The stable has been rented out for three or four years, I think it's used as a store. A man in a car comes occasionally.'

'Thank you, I was looking for a friend, that's all,' he excused himself.

The woman went inside and he looked through the crack between the two big doors. As she had said, it was an old stable. The cobbled floor was worn with two distinct grooves from the movements of cart wheels over the years. The walls and low roof were originally whitewashed and there were four stalls on each side, half of which were filled with furniture and packing cases.

He moved away, conscious of the eyes watching him from behind the curtains opposite, and made his way slowly to work.

Jos greeted him from behind the bar. Once again there was no sign of his wife or of any customers. 'Hello Simon, very prompt as usual.'

'It's quiet again here.'

'Normal for a weekday afternoon, it'll pick up when they leave work and drop in for a beer on the way home, I hope so anyway. Same as yesterday if they want to pay with old notes, then it's double the price. I'll take them, but it will cost me to get rid. No zinc stuff either and if old Hendrik or Daft Willem look like throwing their new money about try to keep them to three or four beers, make a note and give the silly buggers credit. You can manage until Maaike gets here, can't you?'

'As long as I can add the tabs up, no problem.'

'Good lad, I'll be down the cellar keeping out of her way.' He looked up at the ceiling. 'Oh, and while I remember, I might just have found someone who can help you about the time you were in hiding, but no promises.'

'That would be wonderful, thank you.' He started washing glasses and putting out clean beer mats with a long overdue smile on his face.

Maaike arrived at exactly six. There were a few more customers, some at the bar and two upstairs, but he had managed on his own although he wasn't sure they realised Jos had put the prices up yet.

'On your own?'

'He's down the cellar having a drink and counting his money I guess. It's been quiet, and I managed alright, you are a good teacher.'

He took her coat while she settled herself on the stool, then he told her about his visit to the house and stable, the neighbour and Jos thinking he had found someone to help.

'That's good, but where do you think it will take you?'

'I'm not sure, but I just have to know how we were betrayed and who by, it's eating away at me and I owe it to my family.' He suddenly looked sad. 'Esther was only eleven.'

'Esther, what a nice name. You've never told me her name, in fact you've hardly mentioned her before.'

'I'm sorry, it's just too painful. She was my little sister, I should have looked after her and mother. They were separated from my father and me when we arrived there on the train. I never saw them again. If they are dead, and I fear they must be, I hope they didn't suffer for weeks or months or worse.'

She stood down from the stool and hopped to him, putting her arms around him. 'I don't know what I can say, but I will be here for you.'

The doors opened and 'Daft Willem' came in, took his normal stool and ordered a beer and a jenever, bending to sip the gin from the glass as it stood brimful on the bar.

'Goedenavond Maaike, goedenavond Simon.'

'Hello Willem, what have you been doing today?'

'Waiting at the palace as usual to speak to Wilhelmina about beer prices.'

She desperately tried to stifle her laughter and he made an excuse and headed for the cellar.

They walked home together along the canal as usual.

'It's Saturday tomorrow, I start work earlier and work all day. I really must spend more time with Grietje somehow, she's been so good to me. She's not working on Sunday—perhaps I can spend the day with her and Irene.'

'She'd like that, I know she wants to spend more time with you too. We often have lunch together on Sundays and she likes to go to the park in the afternoon.'

'I just wish she had taken some money from me for my keep. Jos gave me twenty guilders after all, and the clothes were not as expensive as I was afraid they would be.'

'You could pay for some of the shopping at the market tomorrow, if she sends you again.'

'Yes, that's a really good idea, and I could buy her flowers too perhaps.'

SATURDAY 29TH SEPTEMBER 1945

He rose early, anxious to go to the market before work. Grietje was up and about making coffee and breakfast for Irene when he came through to the kitchen.

'You're early today, it's your day off, isn't it?'

'Good morning, yes, but I have lots to do. I am taking Irene to see her grandmother and grandfather, Jaap's parents, in Utrecht this afternoon. It's a last-minute decision really, I got a letter from them a couple of days ago. I'm leaving about lunchtime and I need to go shopping first. I want to take some food and things with me as I will be staying the night.'

'I was hoping we could spend the day together tomorrow.'

'I'm sorry, that would have been nice, but they haven't seen Irene since Johan's funeral in May. Another weekend, perhaps. I'm not sure what time I'll be back on Sunday as the train service is still not very good and the trains themselves are awful.'

'I can go to the market again if it helps.'

'Thank you, but I need to go myself. Come along if you like, I'll ask Maaike to have Irene just for an hour, it'll be quicker if she stays here. I need to get some food in for you today and tomorrow.'

'I'm at work for most of the day today but I'll be here all day tomorrow.'

She fried him two eggs and served them on the last of the bread. He had hoped to buy the food for her, but as she was going with him to the market he knew she wouldn't let him and as she was going away the flowers idea was out too. Perhaps he could buy some later for her return on Sunday.

Maaike answered the door still in her dressing gown. She agreed to look after Irene until they got back.

On the way to the market he told her about Jos possibly finding someone who might know about his time in hiding. Like Maaike she questioned what he hoped to achieve, but said she understood that he needed to know exactly what had happened.

'If you find out who betrayed you I hope they arrest the bastards and lock them up, there are still lots of NSB and collaborators detained in camps, you know. It's ironic actually, there are hundreds of NSB in hiding now so they don't get arrested and taken to the camps just like you were. Whoever told the Germans about you deserves to be there too, unless you kill them first.'

'I have had thoughts like that but it's not really me. It's like all the Nazis who are committing suicide before they can be tried and hanged, it achieves nothing and it won't bring my family back, will it?'

They were back from the market by nine thirty. He had watched with amazement at her shopping and hard bargaining powers, so different to his amateur efforts of a week before.

She wasn't going to be around for the free fruit and vegetables at the end of the day, but she still managed to get them plus the bread, butter, cheese, eggs and ham at a very good price, and at least two stallholders looked relieved to agree her price simply to get rid of her. She also bought a chicken and some under-the-counter coffee to take to Utrecht.

She collected Irene from Maaike and made coffee for them both.

'My friend's husband is coming around on Sunday morning to finish building your bed, just let him in. Now, you are going to be alright while I'm away, aren't you Simon?'

'Stop worrying, I'm a big boy now, the young lad you remember had to grow up fast.'

'I'm sorry but I still worry about you, you're alone and still look a bit, well, lost.' She reached out and squeezed his arm. 'Oh, by the way, your new underclothes are clean, dry and ironed in the kitchen. I can't get the washing back until Monday so you can't have the shirts and trousers yet. There's still one clean shirt.' She laughed and said, 'I'm afraid you'll have to manage in Jaap's trousers a bit longer. Now off you go, get to work!'

The bar was as busy as the previous Saturday, there were obviously a lot of men like Jos who knew how to lay their hands on more than the statutory ten guilders. Either that or a lot of his customers were prepared to pay extra for their beer in old money.

Jos's wife was behind the bar. She greeted him quite civilly and he immediately set to work in the cellar, changing a barrel without incident, stacking crates of empties and re-stocking the bar with bottled beers, jenever and some black market whisky and vodka. He also managed to keep up with clearing and washing empty glasses.

Of Jos there was no sign, which meant his wife had to work most of the afternoon. It was obvious from her demeanour that she was getting increasingly angry at his absence.

'Where the hell is he? Out drinking with some of his cronies, I bet. If he's not getting pissed in our cellar he's out spending money in other people's bars.'

She decided at about four that she had had enough and, obviously believing he could manage on his own, disappeared upstairs with a large glass of vodka in her hand.

Thankfully the afternoon rush was over and to his surprise he managed alone, even totting up customers' bills quickly and hopefully correctly. He noticed that Jos's wife had been adding her own supplement to the bills, presumably expecting many to pay with old notes. He attempted to make the necessary adjustments if new currency was offered.

He quite enjoyed himself, sitting behind the bar talking to the line of customers on the stools and taking the odd tray of drinks upstairs. There was a feeling of camaraderie among those sitting at the bar and he began to feel part of it. They all smoked, most rolling their own cigarettes with strong Dutch tobacco and consuming small glasses of beer.

Jos arrived at about four thirty, appearing to be relatively sober. 'On your own? The old bitch left you, did she? Bet I'm in the shit, have you managed alright?'

Before he could answer Jos poured himself a large jenever and a beer and continued, 'I've got some news for you, lad. I've traced someone who might know who was looking after you and your family while you were in hiding.'

'That's marvellous, what does he know? Who is he? I can't wait, when can I see him?'

'Steady, steady. Slow down. There's a problem. His name's Theo but I don't know when he will be able to see you, he's a crew member on a Rotterdam Lloyd ship and my friend didn't know when he'll be back in Amsterdam. I'll go to the shipping office tomorrow, I know someone who works there, and find out what ship he's on and where it is.'

'How long do you think it might be?'

'I've no idea, it depends what he's on and where he is now with all the shit that's going on in the Indies at the moment. They've let the Japs carry on running the place in the absence of a proper police force or any Dutch or British troops although the war's over and they've actually surrendered. Plus, there are thousands of Dutch folks there waiting to be repatriated and now Sukarno has declared independence. We'll have to send troops, there'll be another bloody war, I reckon. If his ship gets sent there he could be gone for months.'

'I see, but what do you think he knows, and how sure are you he knows anything?'

'You'll have to ask him yourself. He'll want to be sure about who you are and that you were part of the family in Kromme Palmstraat before he tells you anything I suspect. I'm told a relative of his was involved. How I'm not sure. He himself might have been one of a group placing people in safe houses.'

'I wonder if he is the one my father was paying, or worse, if he had anything to do with us getting caught.'

'Absolutely not, I can tell you that for sure. No chance of that. He is one hundred percent as far as I am concerned plus he knew Jaap Blok, so that tells you something about what he did in the war. He was no collaborator, that's for sure.'

Jos joined him behind the bar, checking the till and the remaining unpaid tabs.

'Can you manage here until Maaike arrives? I'm going to sit outside and have a smoke and another drink before I go up and see the dragon.'

Just before five a man came in dressed in a long filthy overcoat and an old peaked cap. His face, pale and drawn, much like Simon's own when he met Grietje, bore a huge scar totally covering the left side and affecting both his eye and his mouth.

'Is Maaike de Vries here?'

Jos had followed him in, no doubt wary of him because of his appearance. 'Who wants to know and why?'

'I have a message from her father.'

'Really? And who might you be?'

'I'm Henk Claassen, I've come from Rotterdam with a message for Maaike de Vries.'

'From her father?'

'Yes.'

'Is he on his way home?'

'No. He won't be coming home I'm afraid, he's dead. I promised him when we were in hospital together that I would tell his daughter if he didn't make it. He promised me the same about my wife.'

'Shit! Who's going to tell her Simon, you or me?'

'You've known her longer, Jos.'

'No, no, it has to be me, I promised her father and she needs to know what happened,' Claassen interrupted.

Jos sat him down with a beer and the story came out. Like Maaike's father, he had been sent to Germany as forced labour and they had met in a factory in Dresden. They suffered three nights of Allied bombing in the middle of February, much of it with incendiaries, and their factory was hit. 'There were no shelters for us, all the foreign workers had to take cover where they could, between their machines. Our workshop caught fire, it raced through the building, and many of us were trapped. Maaike's father and I were badly burned but came out alive.' He took off his cap revealing that virtually his whole scalp was horribly scarred and without hair. He removed his right hand from his pocket and held it up, showing it to be no more than a bright red, scarred, fingerless pad. 'We got to one of the hospitals that wasn't hit, but there were hundreds if not thousands already there. They say there were over sixty thousand refugees in the city fleeing west from the Russians in addition to the normal population. We were seen after four days; my burns were superficial compared to Kees's. They eventually found places for us in some sort of overflow building, like a soldier's hut. I was there for a week before they discharged me as they needed the bed. Then I slept rough on the streets with hundreds of others, they were clearing the rubble and removing the dead. I visited him every day. He died in agony after a month—his burns got infected. Before he died he made me promise to find his daughter.'

Jos grimaced. 'You can't tell her all the details, she mustn't hear all that.' He got Claassen another drink. 'So how did you get back here?'

'I walked. I stayed in Dresden until the end of March. I had no papers, no belongings, nothing, just these old boots and this greatcoat that I got from a dead German soldier. The barracks we had been staying in were hit too so the few bits I owned were gone. We heard the Russians were very close, so I left with thousands of others, mainly German I think. I've heard they took the city in early April. I was in a DP camp in the British area until last month. They thought I was German at first. I haven't been home yet, I came straight here.'

'I'll take Henk here up to that back table, it's clear up there at the moment. Send Maaike up to us when she arrives. You look after the bar and get rid of anyone who's left. Tell them we're closing early.'

The doors opened a few minutes later and Maaike came in. 'Hello Simon, still very quiet in here.' She called up to Jos, 'Hello boss, how are you?'

'He wants to talk to you, you'd better go up.'

'What's the matter, am I in trouble?' She crutched smoothly up the steps and sat down next to Jos, laying her crutches on the floor beside her.

Simon had turned away to usher the three remaining drinkers out of the door, ignoring their protests, when she screamed. He spun around to see her in Jos's arms shouting hysterically. 'No, no, no, Papa, no! Please, please, no!'

Jos looked down at him. 'Give Henk twenty guilders out of the till so he can get food and get home to his family, in the new coins mind, then get brandy for Maaike and a whisky for me.'

Claassen took the coins in his good hand and gave him a lopsided smile. He looked back at Maaike and said, 'I'm so sorry. Tell her I did what I could for her father and I kept my promise,' and with that he left the bar.

Simon locked the door and took the drinks up to Jos and Maaike. Just then the door to the private accommodation opened and Jos's wife appeared. 'What the hell is going on? What's all the wailing about, why are we closed and where the hell were you all afternoon?'

'Just go back upstairs, woman, Maaike has had bad news about her father. We'll fight later, just go. Now!'

His wife obviously sensed the venom in Jos's voice and for once she did as she was told without protest, withdrawing her head and softly closing, rather than banging, the door.

Maaike was still sobbing uncontrollably. At first she refused even a sip but Jos persuaded her to at least taste the brandy. She coughed, spluttered and nearly choked as the spirit hit her throat. 'What am I going to do? I always believed he would come back, I suppose I was fooling myself. But he's gone, I have no one. Thank God he was killed instantly and didn't suffer.'

Jos had obviously persuaded Claassen not to tell her the full awful truth. For that he was grateful, and he made a vow she must never know. He looked at Jos who winked and gave him a reassuring smile. 'Take her home, Grietje Blok will look after her. Unless you want to stay here for the night of course, Maaike, you would be very welcome.'

'Grietje is not there, she's gone to Utrecht, but I'll look after her, if you want to go home, that is, Maaike.'

'Yes, please, take me home.' She started to cry again. 'I need to be there, that's where I lived with my father and the last place I saw him before he went off to Germany.'

The normally foul-mouthed ex-docker and bar owner looked at her benevolently with love and care in his eyes. 'I don't want to see you back here until you are ready, take as long as you need and if there is anything at all you want, or anything I can do, just tell Simon and he will let me know.'

They walked home without speaking. Maaike cried quietly all the way. He wanted to put his arm around her and console her, but her crutches made that impossible.

'Are you sure you're going to be alright? I'm just upstairs, if you need me in the night, call me.'

'Please come in and sit with me, it's still very early. It's going to be a long night and I don't want to be alone yet.'

'Of course, anything that helps you, I don't know what I can say to you but I'm a good listener.'

He warmed some milk as she still had no coffee while she changed into her nightgown with a dressing gown on top. He settled himself on the settee leaving the large chair for her but she came over and sat beside him.

They drank their milk and sat in silence for what seemed like an age.

'What am I going to do? I'm on my own, I have nobody. I know you are in the same position, but you are a fit young man and I'm still really just a girl, a girl with only one leg.'

'Can't you go back to Friesland to your family there? You said you had relatives.'

'I do, cousins and an aunt too, I think. My father had a sister, oh dear, I'll have to write to her to tell her he's dead, won't I? I haven't seen them since before the war. I suppose my father told them mother had been killed but I don't know whether he told them I had lost my leg.'

'But that doesn't matter surely, you're family, they'll help you.'

'I'm not so sure, I hardly know them, I don't know what they'd think if I turned up on their doorstep.'

'You must tell them when you write.'

'I don't know how to put it. 'Your brother's dead, I had my leg off when I was thirteen and I want to come to live with you'—I don't think that would sound right somehow.'

'Then you must stay here. I'll always look after you and I know Grietje will too. Jos loves you like a daughter and you will always have a job with him, you know that.'

'Yes, but it's all changed, I always believed father would come back one day.' She started to cry again. 'Now I feel totally alone, without hope almost, after all I'll probably never find anyone.'

He put his arm around her and she moved close to him, resting her head on his shoulder.

'You're a very beautiful girl, someone somewhere will fall for you and love you.'

'Like this? Who would want a cripple?'

He stroked her hair. 'You must look to the future now. It's hard, I know that, and at times you'll think it's impossible. I learned that in the camp. You'll come through it, really you will, believe me.'

'You're a kind man Simon but I can't imagine life without my father. I know I've been without him for over two years, but I always felt he was out there somewhere thinking about me and watching over me somehow. Now I know he was lying dead in the ruins in Dresden—at least he wasn't horribly burned like his friend.'

Please God, don't let her ever find out the truth, he thought to himself.

'All I have of him are the few possessions he rescued from our house in Rotterdam, a photograph in a frame, a silver box, that's about it.'

They sat close together without speaking. It was by now very dark.

'Come on, it must be very late, you need to rest, sleep if you can. I'll be around all day tomorrow and Grietje will be back in the afternoon.' He passed her the crutches and she went through the kitchen to the bedroom. He followed as she sat on the bed. She took off her robe and standing on her single leg she hopped towards him. He could see her breasts and her narrow waist through the thin material of her nightdress. He could also see her short, rounded stump swinging backwards and forwards as she tried to keep her balance.

'Thank you, with your help I'll get through this somehow.'

She reached out and grabbed his shoulders, steadying herself against him, and gently kissed him on the lips.

He was taken aback and pulled away, never having kissed a woman before. 'I must go, please get into bed.'

'Stay with me, don't go, I need you with me tonight.'

'I'll sit with you until you fall asleep then I'll go.'

'No, I mean I need you to stay with me, I want you to hold me.' She looked away, embarrassed or confused he didn't know. 'I mean in the bed.' She threw back the covers. 'Please, sleep here with me tonight.' She finally fell asleep in the early hours and, taking care not to wake her, he disentangled himself and crept upstairs.

SUNDAY 30TH SEPTEMBER 1945

He lay awake until dawn wondering how he and Maaike could face each other after the night before, desperately hoping she would not mention it and that their friendship would not be spoiled. He was strongly attracted to her but had been shocked and frightened as he had no experience with women and had certainly never shared a bed with one. He reflected that the same almost certainly applied to her with men, and he convinced himself that the previous night had been purely a cry for company and compassion and nothing more. He wanted to help her as he knew that within seconds of waking she would remember about her father's death, so she would need him until Grietje arrived.

He need not have worried, she met him at the door with a sad smile. 'Please, come in. Thank you for looking after me last night, you are a good friend. Have you eaten?'

'Yes, thank you. Grietje left me enough food for a week.'

'She does like to look after you. What are you doing today?'

'I thought I'd spend the morning with you if that's alright. The husband of Grietje's friend's is coming around sometime to finish building a new bed for me so I need to let him in but otherwise I'm all yours until Grietje gets home. I will be with you when you speak to her about your father.'

'That's nice, but I'm afraid I won't be very good company. Every time I think about my father I cry, part of me still can't believe it but I know it's true.'

'I'll get Grietje's coffee, she won't mind in the circumstances.'

They sat and talked. She showed him a photograph of her parents. Her mother looked very young and beautiful while her father looked older and very stern.

'He didn't like the camera,' she explained. 'He was a very old-fashioned Frisian man. Moving to Rotterdam, then here, was like emigrating to him. I wonder what he thought of Dresden?' She started to cry. 'The rotten war and those hateful Nazis sending him away from me and taking my mama too. I know he hated Germany, I still have his letters, he was so sad. I'm pleased he found a friend in Meneer Claassen.'

'He's a good man, he obviously thought a lot of your father.'

Her hands trembling, she took a bundle of letters from a drawer in the bureau. Hitler's image stared at them from the stamps on the envelopes. 'This is all I have of him now.'

It hurt him so much to see her breaking her heart. 'You have memories, they will always be there for you.'

The man arrived to work on his bed at ten. He left him upstairs alone as Grietje said he could and persuaded Maaike to go for a walk.

It felt decidedly autumnal as they made their way slowly along Bloemgracht towards Prinsengracht. The last of the morning mist still hung over the canal as the sun came through and the leaves on the trees had started to turn.

She stopped outside number eighty-two. 'It was here that Jaap was shot by the Germans. I came here with Grietje, who wanted to see where it happened.'

They stood in silence for a moment. She was obviously still thinking about her father, but he was thinking about the tragedies Grietje had suffered. Between the three of them the war had taken a terrible toll. They sat for a while outside the Noorderkerk, people were leaving after the eleven o'clock service had ended. He remembered the large numbers leaving the shul on Friday evenings and twice on Saturdays. Even if the shul was open he wondered if there were enough men left to form a minyan. He feared the Jewish population of Amsterdam would never engage in their enjoyable pre-war Shabbos activities ever again. There were still some Jews in Amsterdam; many had been hidden and actually survived the war without being found. He had met some of them while looking for his family but none of them were relatives, friends or people he knew from the shul.

He felt her looking at him. 'What are you thinking about?'

'Just how things were in my community and how it can never be the same, no matter how many survived and eventually return.'

She took his hand and looked up into his face. 'You're not alone you know, just like you told me last night, I'm here for you, we could sort of belong together now somehow, in a way, couldn't we?'

He squeezed her hand. 'We should get back, I'm not sure what time Grietje will be home.'

'I'll make us some lunch,' she said, looking a little disappointed.

They walked back along Westerstraat, he was still deep in thought but she clearly wanted to talk.

'It's time you got registered so that you actually exist again. I don't know how to do it, but you can't just live like a displaced person. You belong here, you were born here, it's your home city even if your house and family have gone.'

'I'll have to ask at the Red Cross, they have my details from the camp list but I don't know how to prove I am who I say I am, I just have a piece of paper they gave me when I left the camp which I suppose could belong to someone else. I have no identity card, nothing at all. I don't know what things father took with us to the hiding place or what happened to them—taken by the Germans or the police when they searched the house probably. Maybe whoever betrayed us took them. We were told just to take clothing when we were arrested.'

'I'm sure the Red Cross have dealt with lots of people in your situation.'

'I'll find out, it's something I didn't think about when I was on my way home, I just wanted to get here to look for my family. Lots of others who survived went into displaced persons camps under the Americans and British, some even went with the Russians to Odessa I think, but I refused and came straight back here. They tell me the Americans were working to improve conditions and give help to get people out of the DP camps; they're probably better off than I am here.'

'Don't say that, you're home here.' She smiled. 'You're as Dutch as I am, just a different religion, that's all.'

'Maybe, but I don't have an identity. Our cards were all stamped 'Jood' and I suppose the Germans took them when we were arrested. I doubt they went to the camp with us, but I just don't know. There's something called a Jewish Central Registration Office in Eindhoven, I've given them my details and those of my parents and sister, maybe they can advise me. Will the authorities just take my word?'

'You could try the Town Hall as well, I suppose. Ask Jos, he'll know or find out. I read somewhere they were talking about making payments to Jewish camp survivors, reparations I think was the word they used. I don't know who is going to do it or when, but you need to be on a list or something.'

'No amount of money is going to bring my family back.'

'But it might help you rebuild your life.'

'I'll talk to some of those who hid and weren't arrested, they will know what to do, they've been sorting things out since they came out of hiding in May.'

'They might also know how you can get your family's house back.'

'Maybe, but it won't be a family home anymore, will it? I know my father cleared his workshop, Grietje helped him pack, and I think he disposed of almost everything apart from the fixtures. He was supposed to put our money in a bank on Sarphatistraat. He said it was a Nazi bank, the Germans made it compulsory, but I don't know if he did deposit it. He left instructions about everything in the house too. It's almost as if he knew we wouldn't be coming back and anyway anything that was left was probably looted by

Dutch people who hate us Jews, a bit like the ones in our house now.'

'Please don't judge us all like that. Many Dutch people did all they could for their Jewish friends and neighbours and many of those who just watched did not realise what they were witnessing until it was too late.'

'I know there were a lot of Jews hidden by Dutch people in the cities and out in the countryside on farms. One of the families I met spent the whole war up in your part of the country in Friesland with a local family. I know a lot of people also tried to help with fake ID cards and deleting names from the lists of Jews but many just stood by. The police rounded up the Jews on the Germans' behalf and a lot of those in hiding were betrayed, like us, by Dutch people who the Jewish families had actually been paying to hide them. If only there had been more like Jaap. Now to make it worse, they have taken our homes.'

She fell silent and he was afraid he had upset her. He touched her shoulder as they walked. 'I'm sorry, you have suffered awfully too because of the Nazis. You lost both your parents and your leg.'

She smiled weakly. 'I was coping until I got the news about my father last night. I suppose if I am honest I was expecting it, but I just hoped against hope, just as you are still doing about your mother and sister.' She stopped. 'Hold me a moment, please.'

He held her shoulders and as she looked up at him, his lips met hers in a soft kiss. She gripped his elbows and, raising herself up on the toes of her single foot, she pushed her lips firmly against his, hardening and prolonging the kiss. 'Stay with me again tonight, I need you, I want you.'

He felt her raise her stump and push it between his thighs. He pulled away from her both embarrassed and feeling strangely aroused.

'You know that's not possible.' He tried to cover his confusion, 'Come on, we must go, Grietje will be home soon and you have to tell her about your father and you have to write to your aunt.'

She looked away. 'I'm sorry, I didn't mean... I just want you...'

They walked the rest of the way in silence. Grietje still wasn't home. Maaike started to make lunch while he went upstairs to check on the progress on his bed. Not only was it finished but somehow the husband of Grietje's friend had found a full-size mattress to go on it.

Grietje and Irene arrived back at two thirty.

He was still in Maaike's room, but they heard her come in and met her in the hall.

'Hello you two, nice cosy weekend together?' she joked.

If only you knew, he thought. 'I'm afraid Maaike has had some bad news, can you come in?'

Maaike threw herself into Grietje's arms, her crutches falling to the ground. She sobbed, 'Oh Grietje, he's dead, my papa is dead, a man came and told me.'

Irene, seeing Maaike so distressed, also began to cry.

'Simon, please take her upstairs for me while I talk to Maaike,' said Grietje.

Grietje came up after about an hour. 'She's calmer now, I said I would send coffee down and some tablets I had after Jaap died. Will you take them, please?'

'Of course. Did she tell you everything?'

'She said her father was killed when the British bombed Dresden and a friend he had made out there came to the bar to tell her.'

'Yes, but she thinks he was killed outright. That's not true, he was burned and died in agony weeks later. She must never know.'

'The poor sod, he must have suffered.'

'What's she going to do?'

'She's managed on her own since she was fifteen, with our help she'll carry on like before, the same as all of us. We'll just have to support her a little more, that's all.'

While they waited for the coffee he showed her the new bed and mattress. 'It's marvellous. It's going to be wonderful to be able to stretch out, but where he got the mattress from I don't know. It was such a surprise, I was expecting to have to sleep on bare boards like in the camp.'

She smiled. 'I managed to arrange it before I left, he said he would deliver it for me. I want you to be comfortable here, it's your home now, here with me, for as long as you need it. You'll have all your new clothes clean and ironed tomorrow.'

More confused than ever he took the coffee to Maaike and together they drafted a letter to her family in Friesland.

WEDNESDAY 3RD OCTOBER 1945

He had intended to spend his day off on Monday at the Red Cross and around the Jodenbuurt asking about his family and making enquiries about how to obtain documentation. He had also been hoping to talk to others from his neighbourhood but Grietje had been working and she had asked him to keep Maaike company and to help her look after Irene.

He had collected the washing for Grietje from the woman on Marnixstraat, then they had taken Irene to the park, posted the letter to Maaike's family and had lunch together. Neither of them had mentioned the Sunday walk home but there had been a tension between them, and he had not felt as comfortable as before in her company.

They had also spent Tuesday morning together. Maaike had been very tearful and upset about her father and he had wanted to hold her and comfort her, but had felt uncomfortable about doing so. He had actually been relieved to go to work in the afternoon while Maaike had stayed at home, not yet ready to return.

Tuesday evening at work had been very quiet. Jos's wife had been in the bar when he arrived, but she had disappeared upstairs almost immediately leaving him alone with just a handful of customers all evening. Jos had appeared briefly at nine and had sent him home early, giving him no chance to ask if there was any news about the seaman who had the information so important to him.

Wednesday morning arrived, and a chance to talk to Jos couldn't come quickly enough so Simon found himself at the bar nearly an hour early for the brewery delivery. The bar was still closed and there was no sign of Jos or his wife.

He knocked on the doors and eventually Jos appeared red faced from the cellar. 'You're a bit early, couldn't you sleep?'

'Not really no, I want to ask you about the man you said might have something to tell me. Have you found out anything yet about when he will be back in Amsterdam? I'm desperate to know.'

'Hang on there, young man. First things first. How is Maaike?'

'Not good, she's still very emotional, especially in quiet moments. It doesn't seem too bad when she's busy looking after Grietje's daughter and doesn't have time to think about it. I helped her write to her father's family in Leeuwarden. I don't think she will be back at work yet though.'

'I don't want her back here until she is ready, please tell her that. By the way, can you open up and manage here on your own for a while today, there's virtually no cleaning up to do, it was very quiet last night as you know. My wife will hopefully stay out of your way. I'm going to the bank again. My account should be released, it's been seven days, so hopefully I can draw out money as normal to pay bills, and you two of course. The takings have been so poor I just don't have much cash in the till. It will probably be quiet again today, no one has any money left but tomorrow will hopefully be busy,' he laughed. 'That stupid 'ten guilders for a week' restriction will be over, people will be getting paid and able to settle debts, including mine, and pour alcohol down their throats again.'

'Jos, will you please tell me about the sailor, when is he coming home?'

'In a minute, let's have coffee first. It's not a big delivery today, things have been so quiet I don't need much, so I expect we'll be low on his list. There's plenty of time. You look very smart today by the way.'

'They're my new clothes, well not new but you know what I mean. At least these trousers fit me.'

'Not for long the way you are going, you've put on weight already, living with Grietje Blok obviously suits you. She seems to be looking after you rather well.'

They sat in the raised area and Jos brought a coffee pot and two cups. 'I went to see my friend in the office, it cost me a bottle of Canadian Club by the way, but I found out the ship is on its way back from the Indies via the African coast. It's due here in ten days and then it will probably be requisitioned by the government to take troops and equipment out to the Indies. They've only just got the damn ship back from the Yanks who chartered it during the war. Anyway, it will be leaving again virtually straight away, the troops and equipment will be here in Amsterdam waiting, and it will be returning with released internees. It's likely to be one of many trips that vessel will make. It's all getting very nasty out there as I feared, the locals are causing all sorts of shit with this independence business, there's virtually a revolution going on. The cities are still under control apparently, the company has ships in harbour at Medan and Batavia, which Sukarno's lot is calling Jakarta now. But out in the country it's very sticky already.'

'Are you saying he'll go off again to the Indies for however long it takes?'

'They'll try and keep the same crew on board if they can, it's not a situation where there's any danger to shipping but they're all signed on as merchant sailors, not navy or anything like that, so if they want they'll be able to sign off when the ship gets back to Amsterdam.'

'And Theo, will he stay on board or sign off?'

'My guess is he'll sign off. He's got a wife and a sister, a widow who he's responsible for, so he won't want to be committed to a long-term contract if it's going to drag on out there. My friend in the office is going to tip him the wink and arrange something closer to home on a coaster or something running to the UK.'

'So he'll come in here as soon as he gets home?'

76

Jos laughed. 'Well, I think he might go and see his wife before he fancies one of my beers, don't you?'

'Don't make fun of me, Jos, you know how important this is to me.'

'I'm sorry, of course I do, now drink up, the drayman's here.'

Unloading was quite an easy job. Jos hadn't ordered many crates of bottled beer and there were fewer than usual to return so it was just a matter of three barrels to roll down the cellar and only one empty to manhandle back up. He opened up the bar and gave the drayman a beer and the horse some water while Jos went off to the bank. It was, as Jos had expected, his last delivery so the drayman hung around for a second free beer. By twelve there were just three customers sitting on stools at the bar. They all wanted to know how Maaike was and when she was coming back. Of Jos's wife there was, thankfully, no sign, but it meant he couldn't take orders for *bitterballen* or cheese.

The customers were all talking about the situation in the Indies. Although news was sparse it looked bad, and two of them were concerned about relatives who had already been interned under the Japanese for over three years. He understood little about the Indies independence problem, but he listened more intently when the upcoming trials of leading Nazis were mentioned.

Most of the conversation, and hatred, centred around Seyss-Inquart, not so much because of his involvement with the deportation of Jews but because of his order to execute strikers, resisters and political prisoners. Simon hadn't realised how involved he had been in the forced labour order, which had resulted in the death of Maaike's father.

'He did allow the Brits to drop supplies last winter though.'

'Eventually, too little too late though, I hope the bastard burns in hell.'

'He'll get the rope, that's for sure.'

'The Queen's going to Rotterdam this Friday. She's unveiling a memorial to the poor devils they shot in March. There were twenty of them I think.'

'What about Mussert then?'

'He's even worse if anything, he was one of our own, look at all those boys who joined the NSB because of him and fought for the Nazis. Hope he gets what's coming to him as well. I think he's going on trial here.

'They're talking about releasing the NSB lot from the prison camps, they'd better not show their faces in here.'

'Who's that? I need all the customers I can get.' Jos crashed in through the door, obviously the worse for drink.

'NSB, Jos.'

'Oh, those bastards, they're banned, they won't get a drink in here. Anyway half of them are still in hiding shitting themselves.'

He joined Simon behind the bar and poured himself a beer. 'Hope you're keeping these three in order, Simon.'

'He's doing a great job, and he won't give us credit either.'

'Good, too many of you lot owe me money. Have you seen her from upstairs at all?'

'No, not at all.'

'Good, I'm down the cellar if you need me.'

By six, much to his surprise, the bar was extremely busy. Jos emerged from the cellar clearly as surprised as him.

'Looks like I'm not the only one who got to his money today. Move up, I'll give you a hand.'

He looked on amazed as Jos worked the bar, serving three people at once, keeping a tally of everyone's account and engaging in small talk. He was washing glasses as Jos prepared an order on a tray for four men up in the balcony area. He'd seen the men in the bar before although they weren't among the regulars.

'Send them up with the Jew kid, Jos, get the little fucker working.'

'It's alright, I'll take this myself.' Jos lifted the tray and bounded up the steps.

'What did you say?' Jos spoke softly to the leader of the group.

'I was talking to the Jew, dirty slimy fuckers, I thought they were all dead but they're still everywhere. What are you doing giving him a job?'

Jos leaned across the table, his eyes blazing, and, picking him up by his collar, threw the man over the railing and down onto the floor of the bar below.

'Throw the little shit out for me, boys, while I remove these three.'

The remaining men hurried out of the door while the regulars at the bar helped their friend unceremoniously on his way.

Jos went to the door and shouted out into the street, 'And don't come back if you know what's good for you.'

He turned back into the bar. 'I'm so sorry, Simon, I'm ashamed to say they are my fellow citizens. You won't see them in here again, I promise you. It's not often we have trouble in here. Thank God Maaike isn't at work.'

'Why, what have I missed?'

They all turned to see Maaike standing in the doorway. 'What's been happening?'

'Maaike, what are you doing here?' Jos went over to her and put his arm around her shoulders. 'You shouldn't be back yet.'

'I got bored and had too much time to think just sitting at home, besides I was missing you lot. Now what's been happening?'

'Some men were insulting Simon, so we persuaded them to leave.'

'I saw them in the street, one of them was holding his back, did he fall?'

Jos laughed. 'You could say that.'

'Serves him right. Now move over and let me get behind the bar.' She leaned her crutches against the bar flap and hopped over to and up onto the stool. Straightening her skirt over her stump she smiled at the row of drinkers. 'Now gentlemen, is anyone ready for another beer?'

'It's great to have you back, Maaike.'

'It's great to be back, Jos.'

'Well, I'm sure you and Simon can cope with this crowd, so I'd better go upstairs and face her.'

The rest of the evening passed quickly. The bar was busy all night and he had to bring up crates of bottled beers as well as change the Amstel barrel. They were a good team, Maaike like Jos seemed able to serve more than one person at once and keep track of their bills, all from the stool from which everything was within reach. He was kept busy taking orders to those not sitting at the bar and washing glasses.

Before he knew it, Jos appeared. 'Come on you lot, it's past eleven. All ashore that's going ashore, the liberty boat's leaving.'

Eventually all the drinkers dragged themselves away, the hardened regulars from the bar stools bringing up the rear.

Jos closed and bolted the door. 'Now then you two, wages time and a drink I think, you've done well tonight, your busiest evening since you started, Simon. Beer for you, and no protests, and a small *bessenjenever* for you, Maaike?'

He took a bundle of the new notes and a handful of new coins from his pocket and made both of them a generous payment over and above their wages. They sipped their drinks cautiously, neither being used to alcohol.

'I expect you've both struggled with this new currency restriction thing and anyway, you both deserve a bonus. For different reasons, of course.' He looked at Maaike and smiled sadly. 'You buy yourself something nice and Simon, get Grietje Blok a present or a bunch of flowers or something.'

'Thank you, I'll be able to pay her for my keep now.'

'And I'll be able to buy coffee even if it is at black market prices,' she said and laughed.

'How lovely to see you laugh again. Now get off home you two, it's a late one tonight and I expect it will be even busier tomorrow when they all start spending again and settle all those outstanding bills.'

They took the most direct route home, walking much of the way in silence. He sensed there was still tension between them. 'About the other day...' he started.

'No, please don't say anything, I'm sorry I embarrassed you, I just like you a lot and I wanted you to hold me, not like my father but like, well, something more, more physical.'

'I like you too, I just don't know how to react. I find you very attractive, but I've never been with a girl, it felt strange but somehow nice to feel you pressed against me.'

'And I've never been with a man before, I'm only eighteen and I'm well, hardly pretty, a cripple.'

'But you are pretty, the prettiest girl I've ever seen, and I want to be with you as much as I can.' He took her in his arms and kissed her.

FRIDAY 12TH OCTOBER 1945

'You're up early, I was going to let you sleep.' Grietje was getting breakfast for herself and Irene. 'You and Maaike were so late back last night, you seem to be getting later every night. Has it been very busy in the bar?'

'It's been busier since the money thing was sorted out, in fact Jos says things are getting back to how it was before the war.'

It wasn't a total lie, the bar was staying open until eleven most evenings, but the real reason for him and Maaike getting back late was their slow walks home and the long talks they had sitting on 'their' bench on Egelantiersgracht. Maaike was looking after Irene five or sometimes six days a week, so they rarely had time to actually go out anywhere together and they never seemed to be alone.

'Why are you up so early? You're not at work until four.'

'I know, but I want to check the lists at the Red Cross again then I want to go to the market to see if I can find a thicker coat and I'm going in to work early, today's the day Theo's ship docks. He might come to the bar so I want to make sure I'm there.'

'If you wait until tomorrow I'll come and help you find a coat.'

'I'm a big boy now, Grietje, I think I can manage to choose a coat on my own.'

She looked hurt. 'I was only trying to help, to make sure you don't get swindled. You're paying me now, so you can't afford to waste your money.'

'I'm sorry, I just want to do it on my own. It's part of rebuilding my life, getting more confident, I suppose. I've got a job, thanks to you I've got a home, I pay my way and I'm trying to get registered so I actually exist again. Anyway, you're working this Saturday, so I'll be going to the food market for you.'

'And for Maaike too, I suppose?' She gave him a hard stare and banged the kettle down onto the gas ring.

'Yes, if she needs anything. After all she's looking after Irene and you know she has problems carrying shopping.'

'I'll do you a shopping list this evening.' With that she went into the bedroom to dress Irene while he ate his breakfast.

She emerged again, saying, 'Oh, and get a haircut while you're at it.'

'I will, I didn't realise how long it has been, don't forget my head was shaved for years. Haircuts are not something I have had to think about.'

It was another beautiful morning but there was a distinct chill on the breeze as he made his way over to Waterlooplein. More and more leaves littered the surface of the canals. He wanted to go to the Oudemanhuispoort to browse and perhaps buy some books now he had money. He loved books and missed his own. They had taken just a small selection into hiding with them.

He cut through the Begijnhof enjoying its peace. Exiting through the side gate he saw a barber's shop and following Grietje's instructions he went in for a haircut.

Seated in the chair he was taken aback and didn't know what to say when the barber asked how he would like his hair cut. It brought back memories of having his head shaved by a fellow prisoner given the task of camp barber, who tended not to enquire of his customers what they would like.

In the end he settled for a simple trim, asking the barber to 'just tidy it up'. The barber asked if he also wanted a shave, clearly having noticed his own less than expert efforts. Never having experienced a professional shave before, he agreed, sat back and relaxed while the barber went to work.

Feeling clean and relatively smart for the first time in almost three years he strode across Rokin towards Oudemanhuispoort.

Six of the damp alcoves were open and he once again immersed himself in his great love, browsing through the piles of old and musty smelling volumes, totally losing track of the time. Half an hour turned into two hours before he realised, and he set off hurriedly to the market.

It was clear he was too late as he searched in vain for a good winter coat among the pile of Dutch army greatcoats and ragged overcoats, all clearly examined at length and rejected by many discerning Dutch women before he even arrived.

'Simon Mendelevski, over here!'

He turned to see a wiry little woman he estimated to be in her late thirties frantically waving from the next row of stalls and trying to make her way over to him through piles of shoes, clothing and old tyre-less bicycles.

She came up to him, red faced and out of breath. 'It is you, Simon. Shalom Aleikhem. I knew it was although you've grown, and aged. Don't you remember me? I'm Sarah Lewandowski, your mother's friend from Jodenbreestraat.'

'Of course. Aleikhem Shalom Mevrouw Lewandowski. A gutn tog. Vas makhstu?'

'Existing, that's about all. And you?'

'The same I suppose, how long have you been back?'

'Since June, but my house is gone, it's just a pile of bricks, my family all died so I am alone, I am staying with a Jewish family out west.'

'My house has a Dutch family in it now.'

She nodded. 'It's a problem for many, and when you went into hiding the Germans would have taken everything you left behind anyway.'

'My father died, I know that, but I am still checking the lists for my mother and sister.'

She looked up at him and placed a hand on his arm. Her face,

84

so excited just a few moments before, creased with pain. 'They're both dead, Simon, I'm sorry.'

His body shook, and he thought he was going to collapse. He held onto her and they walked slowly to sit on a wall nearby.

Through tears he looked at her and said, 'Thank you for telling me. Deep down I knew they could not be alive. Every day the list of newly identified survivors gets shorter, I think all those who are coming back are already here and any others who are alive are listed as being in a DP camp. Please tell me they didn't suffer too long.'

'I was with you all when we left the train. You and your father and my husband went one way with the men. Your mother and little sister were with me. I was chosen for work, I was younger, and fitter I suppose, than your mother and she had your little sister with her. They were killed that day. Please don't ask me how I know it but believe me, they went to their deaths together and very quickly after we arrived.'

'Sarah, I have to know, is there more? Please tell me.'

She paused for a moment. 'I saw their bodies carried out of the gas chamber. Your little sister was still in your mother's arms.'

He broke down again and she squeezed his hands. 'That's why I didn't want to say anymore. But they were together, and your mother held your sister to the last.'

He calmed himself, thanked her and they said their farewells. He took her address although like his own, she was hoping it was temporary. She wanted somehow to rebuild her life with the circle of any friends who might have survived. She urged him to keep in touch and tried to encourage him to return to the shul, which was open once more and hoping to welcome the remains of the old congregation, but he no longer felt part of his old community. In fact he had been putting off a return to the shul. There was no one left, either of his family or, it seemed, his age group. His life now was in the Jordaan with Maaike, Grietje and Jos.

He walked back to Slootstraat in a daze, his thoughts racing, all his hopes dashed. He was the only survivor; even little Esther was dead. Why had he survived? Why couldn't he have died instead of her?

Maaike met him in the hallway. 'Where on earth have you been? I made lunch for us, you have to be at work in an hour.'

'I'm sorry, I forgot the time then I had some terrible news. The worst news, something I have feared but hoped would not be true.' He began to weep.

'Whatever is it?'

'My mother and little Esther, I met a woman today who was my mother's friend, she confirmed they are both dead. They were killed just after we arrived at the camp.'

'Oh Simon, I'm so sorry, please come inside quickly.'

She put down her crutches and hopped up to him, opening her arms. He buried his face in her shoulder and wept. Irene looked at them quizzically, then she too began to cry.

'It should have been me, I should have died instead of them. Why did I survive, who decided I should be spared?'

'Please don't punish yourself, there was nothing you could do, it was the Nazis, they decided who lived and who died. Stay here with me until Grietje comes home. I will go to work early in your place and explain to Jos, he will understand I'm sure. You can stay at home with Grietje.'

'No, I must go, Theo, the man who may know about what happened when we were hiding, may come to the bar today. I was going to get to work by two in case he came in early.'

'If you can look after Irene until Grietje gets back I will go in at four and you can come in at six, we'll just swap our shifts around. It will give you a little time and I'm sure if the man is around he'll wait for you.'

Grietje was back early so he only had to look after Irene for a short time. She was very good, almost as if she sensed he was unhappy. After her initial surprise to find him looking after her daughter, Grietje heard his news with great sadness, having known his mother and sister.

'I am so sorry, you were always so optimistic. It breaks my heart, let me hold you.' She took him in her arms and stroked his hair as if he was a child. 'It's just you, me and Irene now.'

She wanted him to stay at home so she could 'look after' him but he insisted on going to work. Like Maaike he wanted to be busy so as not to think too much about his devastating news, and he was now even more anxious to see Theo.

The bar was busy when he arrived, and Jos was behind the counter with Maaike. 'Sorry I'm late.'

'That's alright. Maaike told me your bad news, I'm so sorry, I don't know what to say. Those damn Nazis, I just hope they get what's coming to them at Nuremberg.'

'I just didn't want to let you down as it's so busy.'

'Perfectly alright, I've rather enjoyed working with the lovely Maaike here, she's much prettier than you.' As usual he laughed at his own joke. 'Now I know what you're going to ask me, and the answer is yes, the ship's in, but no he hasn't been here yet. He's obviously not very thirsty.' He laughed again. 'Nice haircut by the way.'

'Thank you, you know how badly I need to find out what happened and after today somehow it's even more important.'

By nine the bar was absolutely full and both he and Jos were helping Maaike by taking orders to the tables. He kept watching the door as people came in, taking particular notice of any faces he didn't recognise. Just before ten a stocky red-faced man in his fifties with grey thinning hair entered, stood behind the drinkers on the bar stools and, leaning between them, spoke to Maaike. She pointed over to him and Jos and the man approached them.

'Jos van Loon? I'm Theo Visser, lately a deckhand on the motor vessel Brastagi. The office said I might be able to help you.' He extended a large workworn hand to Jos.

'Thank you for coming, this is the young man you have come to see; this is Simon Mendelevski.'

'Goedenavond Meneer Visser.'

'Goedenavond Simon and please, call me Theo.'

'As you can see it's very busy tonight, I can spare you Simon but you'll have to talk in the cellar, it's the only place that's quiet and private.'

'Thank you.' He indicated the steps down to the cellar. 'Go ahead please, Theo.'

'And get Theo a beer or two while you're down there.'

They sat in the cellar, Simon on two crates and Theo in the old chair in Jos's 'hideaway corner'.

'Now first of all I need to be sure I am talking to the right man for reasons which will become clear later. Who are your family members?'

'Were, past tense, I'm afraid. They are all dead, but they were my father Aviel, they called him Avi, my mother Ruth, my little sister Esther and me of course.'

'So just the four of you?'

'Yes, but I discovered today that I'm the only one who survived.'

'And where were you in hiding?'

'As far as I can recognise it we were in the house next to, and above, a stable with two big green doors in Kromme Palmstraat, the house door is numbered 3b and has the name Smit. The sign above the stable is A.F. de Jong & Zonen.'

'And when were you there?'

'From the middle of 1942 for six months, then we were discovered.'

'Betrayed.'

'Were we? That's what I needed to know. Who was it, Theo? Tell me, please.'

'I don't know, but I think so. It cost your family their lives and a member of mine his life too.'

'What do you mean? Who? How?'

'Hold on there. First of all, who came to the house to help you while you were there?'

'I don't know who found us the place or who took us there, it was at night and all very secret, of course. There was a man who used to come regularly. A tall, thin man with fair hair. Dutch, not a Jew, he brought food I think. My sister and I weren't supposed to see him but we often peeked. Maybe he was the one who betrayed us.'

'No, no. Absolutely not. He was my sister's husband Gerrit. It's complicated, it was his job to look after you while you were in hiding. He was working for de Jong as the caretaker of the house and stable so he had the keys. De Jong was a fruit wholesaler who kept their horses and carts in the stables but they closed the business down when the Germans invaded in 1940. The house above was rented out to the Smit family for years but they left in the 1930s. De Jong then furnished it for three employees to live in but they left when the Nazis arrived and the company closed down. That just left my brother-in-law looking after both empty premises. A general dealer hired the stable in 1942, I think to store furniture and things. The house, which was still furnished, was vacant, so the resistance put your family in there with Gerrit in a different sort of caretaker role, looking after you all. They were going to put another family in with you, but you were discovered. Gerrit also acted as caretaker looking after people in hiding at other addresses. He was arrested three days after you were discovered, taken to the prison in Scheveningen and tortured about other safe houses before he was executed somewhere in the sand dunes on the coast.'

Simon was horrified. 'Because of us?'

'No, not just because of you, it was because he was in the resistance, but whoever gave your family away told the Germans he was looking after you. There were many, many brave people working against the Nazis. For example, all the ration cards which got food for your family were either stolen, gifted by resistance people working in the ministries, or forged. The number of people in hiding was huge, not just Jewish families but Dutch people too who the Nazis wanted to arrest.'

'It was his job to look after us?'

'You and others at other addresses.'

'But who betrayed us and your sister's husband then?'

'That I don't know, but I have my suspicions about the man who was using the stables for storage. Some families were paying the landlords of the houses where they were hiding and when they couldn't get any more money out of them the landlords betrayed them for a reward. People who betrayed Jews to the Nazis got seven guilders and fifty cents for each person—did you know that? Your family was worth just thirty guilders.'

'Paying the landlords?'

'Of course, the resistance placed Jewish families but often the landlord charged them for it, they thought all Jews were rich. In your case the place was empty anyway and de Jong knew nothing about you being there. Tell me, did anyone else ever come to the house?'

'I think my father had a visitor he said was important on one or two occasions, but it may just have been your brother-in-law, I don't know, I didn't see who it was. My father worked in the attic room, it was forbidden for us to go up there.'

'That explains the box.'

'Box? What box?'

'Your father hid it in a false wall in the attic. He put it there every night in case they came for you all. He asked my brother-in-law to look after it if he was arrested and to keep it for him until he returned. It's now yours by right.'

'What's in it? Where is it now?'

'The police and Germans took everything you left behind but they didn't find the box. Gerrit removed it the next day and took it home and hid it again. It stayed with my sister until the war was over. When no one came for it she asked me what to do as she did not want it in the house—it reminded her of her husband. She passed it to me.'

'What's in it?'

'I don't know, I haven't opened it, all I know is that it's very heavy, how your father got it in and out of its hiding place every day I don't know. It's not mine to open. It's in my house, still padlocked just as your father left it. You can collect it tomorrow afternoon, I have to go to the shipping office to sign off the ship, settle up and look for another berth in the morning. I live at 81 Knollendamstraat in the Spaarn dammerbuurt, it's on the ground floor. Jos will know where it is.'

'How can I ever thank you, Theo?'

'Don't thank me, thank Gerrit or rather his widow. Tot ziens.'

Theo drank his beer and left, anxious to get home to his wife while Simon raced into the bar bursting to tell Maaike and Jos.

He gave them both the full story after closing time as they had simply been too busy to sit together and take it all in earlier. He was so excited everything came out in the wrong order.

'Simon, slow down, slow down, please.' Jos held up his hands to halt his excited gabble. 'Your father left a box behind and Theo has kept it safe for you?'

'Yes, yes, and he doesn't know what's in it as he has never opened it and he says I can have it tomorrow afternoon.'

'But he doesn't know who betrayed you?'

'He has an idea but that's all, he didn't give any names. Maybe the box will help. I can get it tomorrow, did I say?'

'About five times,' she smiled. 'And you've got to tell Grietje all this as well when we get home.'

'Tomorrow afternoon, what a shame, you're working from eleven.' Jos tried to keep a straight face but collapsed with laughter. 'Of course you can go. Do you know the way? I'd better come to show you and how big is this box anyway?'

'Thank you, Jos, I've no idea, but Theo said it was heavy.'

For once they rushed home, with no slow romantic stroll with a stop to talk halfway. He wanted to get back before Grietje went to bed to tell her his news for the second time that day. The awful revelation of the morning had turned into excitement about what was to be his father's legacy to him and a route perhaps to uncovering the truth about their betrayal.

They kissed goodnight out of sight before reaching the house. Maaike was tired and went straight to her room, unable to manage the stairs up to the first floor.

Simon ran into the room calling Grietje's name. She emerged from the bedroom in her nightwear, her fingers to her lips, 'Sssh, you'll wake Irene, what's all the excitement about?'

She sat beside him and he started to tell her all about his meeting with Theo and the box when he became aware of her pulling at her gown to show her thighs. She half turned towards him, slightly parting her knees as she did so and he could see she was naked underneath.

Suddenly tongue-tied and in a total panic, he stopped midway through the story as she put her hand on his thigh and began slowly moving it up between his legs.

'I'm so pleased for you, Simon, it's good that you might find out about your time in hiding but you got some heartbreaking news this morning and I thought you might want me to comfort you.'

She started to unbutton his trousers, pulling the gown open at the top with her other hand, revealing her breasts.

'No, Grietje, please. I can't. I don't want... please, no.'

'I want you, Simon. I need you, please.' She almost pleaded with him as he stood up and hurried from the room.

In just one day he had experienced anguish, elation and now total shock and confusion. He wished he could talk to Maaike.

SATURDAY 13TH OCTOBER 1945

He slept badly, in fact he barely slept at all, his mind in a total turmoil, excited about getting his father's box but shocked and unsure about how he could possibly face Grietje after the night before. Hanging over both thoughts was the empty feeling of despair knowing that, despite all his wildest hopes, his mother and sister's deaths were now confirmed.

He could hear her in the kitchen. Then he remembered it was one of the Saturdays that she had to work, and that he had to go to the market for her before going to work himself. He dressed and went through to the kitchen with no idea what to expect.

'Good morning, I've boiled a kettle so you can wash, you have a clean shirt and the shopping list is on the table.'

To his relief she smiled at him as if nothing had happened. 'I've left some money with the list, can you put in the same and call it your rent for this week? I'll drop Irene with Maaike on my way out and tell her to give you a list of the things she wants.'

'Yes, thank you, that'll be fine.' He couldn't leave things unsaid and therefore he began, 'About last night Grietje, I don't know if I can stay here anymore after...'

'It didn't happen, alright? I'm a silly, lonely old woman who thought she just might still be attractive. It won't happen again, and

I don't want to spoil our friendship, just promise me you won't tell Maaike, I couldn't bear it, and please, please, don't leave.'

'You're not silly, you are attractive and you're certainly not old. I value your caring and love but not in that way.'

She forced a smile, turned, and, taking Irene's hand, started down the stairs.

He washed and put on a clean shirt before going down to Maaike's door. She opened it, wearing the overalls she had told him she was altering. He stared at her.

'Close your mouth before you swallow something and come in,' she joked. 'Well, do you like it?'

'I'm sorry, it's just so, well, different.'

'Haven't you ever seen a girl in trousers before?'

'No, actually I haven't, and it's a bit unusual especially, well, like that.' He indicated where she had cut off the empty left leg and sewn it up to fit her stump.

'Are you shocked? Do you hate it? I just didn't want to have the empty part hanging loose or folded up so while I was altering them I cut off the leg. Clothes are hard to come by and these overalls were virtually new, my friend got three pairs when she started work at the tram depot and she only stayed a few weeks.'

'I don't hate it at all, in fact you look sensational. It's going to get a lot of attention at work.'

'I couldn't possibly wear this at work, or could I?' She giggled. 'Anyway, how are you feeling today after yesterday's news?'

'Still a little shocked but I am very excited about father's mysterious box. But first I'm on my way to the market for Grietje and I wondered if you wanted anything.'

'Oh yes please, Grietje said you would be going, I've just got a short list. She'll be home by two by the way, so tell Jos I'll come in as soon as she's collected Irene. I thought it would help him out for me to start early so you two can go off to get the box, if you can wait that long, that is.'

He was back at the house with all the shopping, including some coffee he had managed to find for her, before ten.

They spent half an hour together before he had to leave for

work. She was in the kitchen putting away her groceries while he entertained Irene.

'You're getting quite good at the shopping, holding your own with all the ladies. It's all here and the fruit and vegetables are good quality.'

'Yes, I'm getting used to it now.' He remembered his first visit to the market. 'It's still a bit unnerving though, some of the women are frightening.'

She laughed. 'Frightening? In what way? You are funny.'

'I'm just an innocent young lad when it comes to bargaining and getting the best price. Seriously, I'd never had to buy food or provisions before, my mother did it all for us.'

He fell silent remembering his innocent schoolboy days, cosseted and protected by his parents. It all seemed so long ago.

'I'm able to make you coffee at last, can you come through and get it and take mine too, please?'

They sat and talked while Irene played happily in the corner. He felt totally at ease in Maaike's company and somehow being with her eased his pain. He hoped she felt the same.

'I've had a reply from my Aunt Nel in Leeuwarden. They want me to go up there.'

'To live or just a visit? Only a visit I hope, sorry, I am being selfish. If they want you to live with them, it might be better for you.'

'Only for a visit to start with. They haven't seen me for years and father didn't tell them about my leg, so I suppose they think I need help now I'm on my own. I'd like to see them, but I don't want to live back in Friesland. We left when I was five, there's nothing for me there. I belong here now, and you're here of course.' She looked at him with laughter in her eyes and a smile on her lips and said, 'Don't get big-headed about it.'

'How will you get there?'

'If I go it will have to be by train I suppose, but I think I would have to change trains in Amersfoort or Zwolle or both, which will be difficult and of course I can't manage a suitcase and these damn crutches. That's if the lines are even open and running again, they suffered a lot of damage in the war plus the Germans ripped up the track from the north in retaliation for the railway strike last year. That's one of the reasons we all nearly starved. They say it will take years to get everything repaired and running again.'

'We'll have to work something out. Grietje might know, she used the trains recently when she went to Utrecht.'

'My aunt will be surprised to see me if I do get there.'

'She certainly will if you arrive in that outfit. A woman in trousers in Friesland, there'd probably be a riot!'

He was a few minutes early for work, but the bar was already busy with the usual crowd of Saturday morning men seeking sanctuary from work and their wives, and women, many loaded down with goods from the market, seeking their husbands or a drink or both.

Jos's wife was behind the bar and Jos was taking drinks to the bench outside.

'The Heineken needs changing and we're short of Brand, bring a couple of crates up. Come on, jump to it, we're losing money here.'

At that moment Jos came in and hearing the exchange murmured, 'Jawohl mein Führer,' under his breath as he followed Simon into the cellar.

'You take the crates and I'll change the barrel, I don't know when we're going to get away to collect your box, it's very busy up there and the wife is not very happy at having to work.'

'Maaike has already thought of that. Grietje gets back about two and as soon as she has collected her daughter, Maaike is coming in to work so she should be here by half past two instead of six. I'll go up and help your wife until she gets here, then maybe we can go?'

'Up you go then, you're a braver man than I am. I'm staying down here, out of her way.'

He and Mevrouw van Loon worked together over the lunchtime period. He washed glasses while she complained, he took out trays of drinks while she moaned, and he tried to help her with pouring drinks while she criticised. Anyone asking for *bitterballen* or other snacks got short shrift.

At about one she disappeared upstairs with the words, 'You can manage, can't you? Get my lazy drunken husband up out of his hiding place if you need help.'

Jos must have heard her as he appeared almost the instant his wife disappeared.

'Has she gone? Thank God for that. Right, so it's just me and you, young Simon, let's get these thirsty buggers served.'

Maaike arrived just before two thirty and took her place behind the bar. It was still very busy. Jos was unsure about leaving her on her own as it was clear his wife was not going to reappear.

'Just go you two, I can manage easily, they'll just have to come to the bar and collect their drinks, that's all.'

'If you're sure. Simon has stocked up on bottled beers and I've put a new barrel on.'

Jos turned to him. 'I've just had a thought, how big is the box going to be? Theo said it was heavy and he didn't know how your father put it in the hiding place every night.'

'I've no idea.'

'Right we'll take the barrow from the cellar, the one I use for crates. Can you get it for me while I tell this lot they'll have to go to the bar and get their own drinks and can we go through Kromme Palmstraat? I'd like to see the place.'

They walked down Palmstraat, the barrow rattling on the cobbles. 'It's just down here, it turns to the left halfway down and it's in the second part of the street.'

'Let's have a look then.'

'Look, there's someone! There's a car and a man just closing the doors. He must be the one who rents the stable. Quickly, let's speak to him before he leaves.'

'Hang on there, lad, we don't know who he is or why he's here, let's just watch.'

The man, in his mid forties, smartly dressed, slim with dark hair and a moustache, snapped the padlock closed on the doors and, carrying a small bag, got into the car and drove away, turning right onto Lijnbaansgracht.

'But we could have challenged him, we've missed our chance.'

'What exactly were you going to say to him? No, not yet, lad, not yet. Did you see the number of his car? No? Well, I did. Old Jos knows a lot of people and has a lot of contacts, leave it with me.' He smiled, tapping the side of his nose with his index finger.

They walked across the bridge on Brouwersgracht, across Haarlemmerplein under the railway line and into the Spaarndammerbuurt. It was his first time in that neighbourhood and he was impressed by the clean open streets, the smart blocks of red brick apartments and the modern architecture. It wasn't like the city he knew at all. He remembered Grietje's ambition to move there from her run-down Jordaan address, a dream shattered by Jaap's death.

A large woman in her late forties with bleached hair, bright red lipstick, a plunging neckline and smoking a cigarette answered the door at 81 Knollendamstraat.

'Mevrouw Visser? Goedemiddag, I'm Jos van Loon and this is Simon Mendelevski. Is Theo at home? He's expecting us.'

'He's still not back from the office, probably out drinking somewhere with his mates from the crew the bastard, but he said you were coming for the box. Come in.'

They went into a small dimly lit hallway. The place smelled of tobacco smoke, fried food and cheap perfume.

'I'm pleased he's found you, young man. I'll be glad to see the back of the bloody thing. It's been in the cupboard under the stairs since Liberation Day when his sister palmed it off onto him. I told him he had to get rid of it, but he wouldn't. I asked him to open the thing, it might be a body or something for all we know, but he wouldn't do that either. I said it had to go when he got back from this last trip to the East or else.'

'Thank you for keeping it for me.'

'I'm just glad you and your family have come back to claim it.'

'We haven't I'm afraid, it's just me, my parents and sister are dead.'

'Whatever, just get it out of here. I ought to charge you rent.'

'I'll see your husband gets a drink or two and I'm sure we'll do something for your sister-in-law, won't we, Simon?'

She sounded disappointed. 'He gets enough to drink already, and all his sister did was to ditch the thing here. Just get it loaded and out of my house. It's in here, you'll have to get it out, I can't move it.' She threw open the cupboard door and stood back, indicating a brown wooden chest.

'Bloody hell, I thought Theo said it was a box.'

'It's my father's travel trunk, he always called it 'his box'. Look, his initials A.M. are on the side. He brought it from Lithuania with him after the Great War. It was in his workshop and then at Dijkstraat, but I don't know how it got to the hiding place. I don't remember us taking it with us.'

Together they manhandled the crate out of the front door and onto the barrow as the woman, without another word, slammed the door shut behind them. It was heavy as Theo had said, and it was secured with two large padlocks.

Jos laughed loudly. 'No wonder poor old Theo goes to sea, she makes my wife look almost friendly. Come on, let's get this back to the bar.'

The bar was still crowded when they got back and Maaike was on her own with no sign of Jos's wife.

'You help Maaike, it looks like there are a lot of glasses to wash and tables to clear. I'll put this in a safe place down the cellar for now.'

'But I want to open it Jos, I must see what's inside. Please, it's all that's left of my family.' He was almost pleading.

'We can't do it now, it's too busy. First things first, there's work to be done and money to be made. We'll do it tomorrow when the bar is closed.'

'Can't we just break it open now?'

'You don't want to break it open, you'll damage it if you prise the hasps off. I'll get a hacksaw tomorrow and we'll cut the padlocks. There are two locks on the trunk itself, if they are locked we'll have to get help if we don't want to force it.'

He reluctantly agreed, but he didn't know how he was going to contain himself until the next day.

Jos kept the bar open until midnight and he and Maaike stayed on for the extra hour on the promise of overtime. It was later than usual therefore when they started to walk home.

They sat on their bench talking. He had so much to tell her, especially about seeing the well-dressed man with the car leaving the stable. It was nearly two when Grietje, woken by a noise, looked out of the window and saw them kissing in the street below.

SUNDAY 14TH OCTOBER 1945

It had been another disturbed night but for totally different reasons than the one before. He was so excited about opening his father's box that he was awake before dawn. His mind was racing about the events of the last few days. Who was the man they saw leaving the stable, and was he the one who was renting the place while he was hiding upstairs with his family?

He dressed and went down to the kitchen to wash. Grietje and Irene were still asleep, and he tried not to wake them. Once again he was bursting to update her but it was still very early. He made his own breakfast, anxious to get to the bar, but Jos hadn't suggested a time and as it was his day off, and that of his fearsome wife, he was afraid to arrive too early.

He slipped out into the street. Dawn was breaking and the Jordaan was still asleep, the normally bustling narrow streets were deserted. It was the first time he had seen the area at such an early hour and he found it captivating. The smell of autumn was on the air and the surfaces of the canals were increasingly carpeted with fallen leaves. Resisting the temptation to go to Kromme Palmstraat again and the even stronger temptation to go to the Café van Loon, he wandered slowly and aimlessly around the maze of streets. He reflected with sadness that so many canals had been filled in only to emerge as featureless wide roads. Those that remained, especially the smaller ones in the Jordaan, were especially beautiful at this early hour and he wished Maaike was with him. How she did her 'canal walk' on crutches he didn't know, by the time he got home he felt exhausted and he realised that, although he had put on weight, he had still not fully recovered his health and strength.

Grietje was eating breakfast with Irene as he came inside.

'Good morning Grietje, good morning Irene, what a beautiful day, it's wonderful out there.'

'What are you so cheerful about?'

'I wouldn't say cheerful, every morning when I wake up I remember my parents and sister, it's always there, it never goes away, but there is some better news. Jos and I found my father's box yesterday. It's at the bar, we're going to open it today.'

'Where have you been anyway, why were you out so early? You were very late last night.'

'Jos didn't close until midnight. I couldn't sleep so I went for a walk and for a think.'

'About your beloved Maaike I suppose?'

'What do you mean?'

'I saw you. I saw you kissing her last night.'

'I like her very much. We're good friends, similar people I suppose.'

'It looked like you are more than good friends. How can you be attracted to her, a one legged girl, what is it she's got that I...'

'Please, it's not like that, she's just lovely, that's all, we get on.'

'You and I get on, at least I thought we did.'

'We do, Grietje, we do. You are very, very special to me, I'll never forget what you have done for me and your love for me, just not... not like that.'

'I suppose you're taking her to the grand box opening ceremony?' Her sarcasm was evident. 'I was hoping you and I would spend the day together, it's my only day off and I was going to cook. I have a Texel lamb joint, at least he said it was from Texel, with vegetables and potatoes.'

'I have asked her, yes. Can't you cook this evening instead of lunchtime? You know how important my father's box is to me, whatever is in it is all I have left of my family, all I have left of my life.'

'I suppose so.' She looked at him, then grudgingly said, 'Ask Maaike to join us, if she can manage the stairs that is. Now, breakfast?'

'I've already eaten, thank you.'

'You'd better go and call for her then.'

He collected Maaike and they set off for the bar. 'I was out walking at dawn this morning, the canals looked beautiful.'

'Why didn't you call for me? I would have loved to have come.'

'It was so early. I couldn't sleep but I thought you would be tired after last night. Grietje saw us kissing by the way.'

'Oh no, is that going to cause a problem?'

'Im not sure, she was a little strange about it, but she's asked you to come for a meal this evening after we get back.'

'But won't it be difficult?'

'I hope not, after all we all have to live together. You could ask her about the train service. Tell her the food's good, it's Texel lamb apparently. Whatever that is.'

'I love Texel lamb, it's the best. It's from the island of Texel which is just off the coast of Friesland, we used to have it a lot when I was a child.'

They arrived at the bar just after ten. Jos was up and about, cleaning up after the late session the previous evening. 'Hello you two, beautiful morning. Thank you for working late last night. If you go in and sit down, I'll make coffee and bring up the box.'

They went up the steps to the raised area where the tables were larger. He took Maaike's coat and crutches. Jos brought coffee and disappeared down the cellar, reappearing with the box on his shoulder.

IIc put it down on the floor next to the table and turned to Simon. 'What are you expecting to be in here?'

'I haven't a clue, I thought my father would have disposed of the box with everything else from his workshop when it closed down.

Grietje remembers putting some of his workshop things in it with him. When we left the house to go into hiding we just took clothes and a little money as far as I am aware. I didn't even know father had taken the box.'

Jos produced a hacksaw. 'We'd better get started then, over to you, young man, it's your box, get sawing.'

He'd never used a saw before in his life and after a few minutes of making no impression on the first lock and cutting his hand when the saw slipped, Jos took over.

'Give it to me, you're hopeless. I can see I'll have to teach you a lot more than changing a barrel of beer. Look, you make the saw do the work.'

He sawed smoothly and quickly, and the lock fell away to be followed soon after by its partner.

'Well, here we go, if its closed with those other two built-in locks we're in trouble, I'll have to get a contact of mine.' He winked. 'If he's not in jail, that is. Go on then Simon, open it.'

He prised the hasps free of the staples and tried to lift the lid. His face fell as it refused to move but with one extra effort the stiff hinges creaked and the lid opened.

Covering the contents was what appeared to be a beautiful piece of gold and brown silk cloth wrapped in tissue paper and a piece of black and white striped cotton cloth.

He lifted them out reverently, his voice trembling. 'Mother's best dress, she only wore it on special occasions. I remember her in it at my Bar Mitzvah. They were obviously keeping it for after the war. She'll never wear it again. And this is father's tallit, his prayer shawl, it was so precious to him.'

He began to sob and Maaike put her arm around him. 'Look, if this is too much for you we don't have to do it today, do we, Jos?'

Jos shook his head. 'We can take as long as you need.'

'No, it's alright, I want to carry on. I should have realised it might be upsetting, I just didn't know what to expect and seeing Mother's dress...' He broke down again. 'I'm sorry, I'm being stupid.'

Jos put a hand on his shoulder. 'Not at all, lad, you've been through hell.'

He reached into the box, removing a layer of old newspapers to reveal a large flat metal box about twenty centimetres deep and virtually the same dimensions as the outer trunk.

His eyes lit up. 'I know what this is, it's father's work box, it sat on his bench or his desk, it used to have all his delicate tools in it. He must have been using it up in the attic when we were hiding. I thought he'd sold it all when he closed the workshop. He must have tried to keep the business going so he kept these tools.'

He tried to lift the box out, but it was a tight fit all around and heavier than he expected. His fingers kept slipping in his excitement.

'You help him Maaike, I'm no good, my fingers are too big to get down the side.'

Between them he and Maaike lifted it far enough for Jos to get hold of one end and together they lifted it out and put it on the table.

Simon opened it to find all his father's tools; hundreds of small implements, minute screwdrivers, drills, a stand for holding watches and hundreds of parts, wheels, springs and other pieces of metal he didn't even recognise. At the end of the box was a thick pile of paperwork, letters and invoices and another flat, wooden, highly polished box. It was locked but the key lay beside it and with his fumbling fingers he unlocked it and lifted the lid.

'Bloody hell!' Jos stared with an open mouth. 'I'm so sorry about the language Maaike, but just look at those.'

'That's alright, I've heard worse, mostly from you.' She laughed and joined them, staring at four gold pocket watch cases and three complete gold pocket watches.

'Were these your father's or was he repairing them for people?'

'I don't know, I presume the cases were for watches he was making but as for the complete ones I've no idea. I always thought the watches he made went into silver or base metal cases. Perhaps they're repairs.'

'They're yours now, lad, don't worry about it, they belong to you.'

'They must be worth a lot of money,' said Maaike.

'You're right there, thank God your father didn't sell them and put the money in that Nazi bank like he was supposed to, Simon.'

'I was sure he sold some things for cash, this isn't all of his stuff. It must have been the first time in his life my father broke the law when he kept this lot back.'

'He obviously wasn't going to let the Nazis have everything he'd worked for.' Jos pointed down into the trunk, indicating at least two more inner boxes. 'And there are those yet.'

'I recognise that one, it's more of father's tools.' He indicated a polished wooden box with an arched hinged lid. 'That's the one with a slot for each item and a watch holder in the centre.'

Jos opened the lid. It was just as he had said, forty or fifty specialist tools, each in its own place. 'No gold watches in this one.'

He reached in and lifted out a cardboard box. Much lighter than the others, it appeared to be full of papers.

'Our identification cards.' He held up four cards, each headed 'persoonsbewijs' and stamped prominently with a letter 'J'. 'This is little Esther's, and this is mother's.'

Maaike reached out her hand. 'Can I see them, please? She looks a lovely, kind lady and what a beautiful little girl...'

'Look, here's a copy of my birth certificate, and Esther's. Mother's and father's from Lithuania are here too. At least now I can prove who I am and where I was born.'

He unearthed two albums of family photographs and a huge bundle of letters in an elastic band. He clutched the photographs tightly and began to cry again.

'These are so precious, more than the tools and the watches, they're a record of my family and our life, and I think these are love letters from mother and father to each other.'

'You won't be needing these bloody things anymore.' Jos reached into the box and brought out a sheet of yellow cloth stars inscribed 'Jood'. 'You know your father actually had to pay for these. It was compulsory to have them on all the clothes you wore outside. You were allowed four per person, they cost four cents each and you had to use your clothing coupons as well.'

He recoiled, not wanting to touch them, 'Mother had one on

each of her coats, so did father. I had one on my jacket, that must be what was left. Mother wasn't like you Maaike, she was no seamstress, she must have only cut out and sewed on as many as she absolutely had to. They only became compulsory a couple of months before we went into hiding, so we wouldn't have needed many. I think it was the main thing that finally decided my father that we had to hide, that and our identification cards being stamped with a letter J. We were too easy to identify and anyone with a star was being arrested.'

Jos lifted out some more official looking papers. 'Look here.' He opened them out. 'An insurance policy on your father and documents about a house in Dijkstraat.'

Maaike smiled and squeezed his arm. 'It might help you to get your home back, Simon.'

'You need to go through all these papers and the ones from that first box very carefully. Your father was obviously a very methodical man, not just trying to hide all this but keeping lots of documents he thought important, you just don't know what might be here.'

'Thanks Jos, I will. Can I leave the main box and all the tools here for now?'

'Of course, but even the watches? You trust me with them?'

'I trust you with my life, you're a good friend. I think I may need your advice on lots of things before all this is finished.'

'It'll all be quite safe in the cellar, I'll put the watches with my valuable things in the special place.' He looked sideways at Maaike and put his finger to his lips. 'Right, push the big box over here and I'll put those tools in. Make sure you have all the paperwork.'

Simon pushed the box along the floor to Jos, who took hold of the edge to pull it nearer to him.

'There's something wrong here, it's still heavy, too heavy in fact.'

'It's empty. I can see the bottom.'

Jos looked at the box. 'You think you can, you can see a bottom, yes, but it's not the real bottom. Look.'

'I can't see anything.'

'Maaike, lend me one of your crutches. Now look.' Using the crutch as a measure he placed it inside and then outside the box.

There was a difference of at least ten centimetres. 'Now do you see? It's a false bottom. I've seen them fitted in all sorts of crates down the docks to smuggle things past the customs men. Let's try and work out how to get into it.' He scratched around in the box for a few moments, then disappeared down the cellar and returned with a screwdriver. 'Right, watch and learn.' Scraping with the screwdriver in each of the four corners he uncovered a screw-head hidden with a layer of putty. The screws turned easily and the whole floor of the box lifted in one piece.

Three heads craned to look inside. The false compartment was subdivided into six, two large and four smaller sections, to stop the contents sliding around. There were items wrapped in hessian cloth in the two largest compartments. Three of the smaller compartments held cloth bags and the other a package wrapped in brown paper.

'Oh Simon, it's so exciting.' Maaike gripped his hand, her nails digging in. 'Come on, open them.'

He picked up the brown paper package and tore it open. 'It's money! Jos, Maaike, look, it's money!' He removed the rest of the paper wrapping. 'But they're all old guilder notes, what can I do with them?'

'My God, they're five hundred and two hundred guilder notes, I haven't seen them for years and I certainly haven't owned many. There must be thousands of guilders there.'

'Yes, but what can I do with them? They're no good now. I can't think where he got them from, these must be either my father's savings or the proceeds from what he sold off when the business closed. There were a lot more things than the two boxes of tools; drills, other things attached to the work bench for cutting little wheels and things, and a big stock of parts. He said he wasn't going to tell the Germans or put the proceeds into that 'Liro' bank they were running to collect all the Jews' money but I had no idea it was this much. He obviously couldn't know that they'd change the currency after the war.'

'Don't worry, leave it to old Jos, there are ways and means. You can't just change them at the bank, that's for sure, amounts like this are just what they are after, it looks like money from the black market. I know it's not, but you can't prove it. Being in such large notes doesn't help either, in fact the five hundreds might have been withdrawn during the war. I can do it through contacts of mine, but it will be two for one or maybe even a worse rate.'

'Do you have a contact for absolutely everything, Jos?'

Jos laughed. 'Pretty much Maaike, pretty much.'

He reached in and took out the first large parcel wrapped in hessian. Releasing the string he revealed an oil painting of a boy in a gilt frame.

'I remember this, father had a pair of them above his workbench at Peperstraat, there was a boy and a girl. He obviously valued them very much.'

'Open the other one.'

He hurriedly unwrapped the second package, expecting the second painting. 'This is father's stamp collection. I wonder where the picture of the girl can be? He loved his stamps, he used to go to the stamp market on Nieuwezijds Voorburgwal. I know he spent a lot of money on stamps and never told mother just how much. There were a lot of Jews there dealing in stamps, even though it was on the Sabbath, but so many were arrested that he eventually didn't go anymore.'

'Go on, open one of the bags.' Maaike was getting more and more excited.

He took the first cloth bag, loosened the draw string, emptied the contents onto the table, and sat back in shock and surprise.

'It's all my mother's jewellery. She hardly ever wore it. I think some was her mother's, or maybe some was from my father's family. Father would have done anything to stop the Germans getting this.'

Jos cast a knowing eye over it. 'There's a lot of silver but some gold, look at the rings, it's going to be worth good money.'

'It's worth more than money to me. This is going nowhere, I'll never sell it.'

'Of course not, I'm sorry, I didn't think.'

'Will you keep it here with the money and the watches, you know in your special safe place?'

'Of course, lad, but come on, you've still got two bags to open.'

'You open one, Maaike.'

'I can't, they're yours, your father wanted you to have them.'

'Please, you do one and I'll do the other.'

She took the first of the two remaining bags, untied it and emptied a pile of gold coins onto the table. He did the same, doubling the number of coins.

Jos gasped. 'I'm sorry Maaike, close your ears again. Bloody hell, do you know what you've got here?'

Jos looked closely at the coins. 'They're gold five and ten gulden pieces, they stopped making them in the early thirties I think. Look, there's our Queen Wilhelmina. There are some with her as a young girl with long hair and there's some of King Willem, from when?' He picked up a coin. 'This one's dated 1875. There are some silver guilders. The Nazis stopped us using them and issued those horrible paper one silver guilder vouchers. There's even some old German gold twenty mark coins from before the Great War. Where could he have got this lot from?'

'I've no idea, but they're old currency just like the notes surely.'

'Wake up, lad. No one has been spending the gold ones since about 1933. It's not the guilder value here that matters, they're gold, think about it, gold. That's where the value is. They're not bits of paper, they're like gold bars but circular and flat.'

'How much are we talking about?'

'I don't know, it all depends on the price of gold. The ones of King Willem are earlier, they might be purer gold. I think the price must have gone up in the war. I paid through the nose to buy that gold jewellery of mine, but that was because I was getting rid of a little bit of, shall we say, surplus money.' He winked conspiratorially.

Maaike had been counting. 'There are eighty-two of the gold twenty gulden ones, a hundred and thirty of the gold five gulden, a lot of silver guilders, I remember those, we used them until quite recently, and fifty-two of those gold German twenty marks ones. There are six of these too, I think they're Russian fifteen somethings from 1897.'

'Whatever they are, they look like gold too. Like I said, the value depends on the weight and the price per gram. I'll find out.'

'I'll take all the paperwork and leave everything else here if that's alright?'

'It's fine with me if it's alright with you.'

'Let's go home, Maaike. I want to go through this lot, it'll take us all day tomorrow if we do it together, and I want to show Grietje. She helped father pack up the workshop, perhaps she knows something about the contents of the box. We'll have to hurry, I forgot about Grietje's lamb. Goodbye Jos and thanks for everything.'

They hurried back to Slootstraat. He was quiet and she realised that, far from being excited at his newfound wealth, he was more distressed than ever at the loss of his family, brought home to him by the personal items carefully stored in the box by his father in the desperate hope that at least some of the family might survive and one day return.

MONDAY 15TH OCTOBER 1945

The day dawned wet and miserable. He lay in bed as long as he could, listening for Grietje dropping off Irene and going out to work before he got up. The lamb had been wonderful but overall the atmosphere during the meal had been strained to say the least, and he wished he hadn't subjected Maaike to it, with Grietje making veiled references to the two of them being a couple all evening.

He'd arrived back very excited, as always, to tell Grietje his news. She, however, seemed unmoved and possibly even jealous when he mentioned the watches. He remembered how she had cleaned for his family for years, almost certainly for a pittance, so he had not told her any more details, deciding not to mention the cash or the coins in the false bottom, asking instead if she knew about the correspondence and other contents of the box.

She told him his father had actually packed the box, that she had just passed items over to him and that the contents they had found yesterday were different to those on the day she and his father had cleared the workshop. This made sense, as clearly his father would have added the more valuable items at Dijkstraat. She remembered the pictures, insisting his father had packed the pair, not just the one they had found.

Grietje had been unable, or unwilling, to help with any advice on train travel and suggested Maaike would need to check at Amsterdam Centraal whether her journey was possible.

He got up and made coffee. The news on the radio from the East Indies was bad—the Indonesian People's Army had declared war on the Netherlands and the British troops together with the Japanese peacekeepers were under attack. Dutch troops had yet to arrive. Jos had said the East Indies' demand for independence would turn into a war, and that he was surprised that, after years of Japanese occupation, there was a willingness for more fighting and bloodshed in the colony.

He and Maaike, Irene permitting, were going to sort through all the paperwork, both personal and business, found in the box together. He was excited about finding his personal papers, which would confirm his identity if not actually his existence, but saddened at the thought of seeing all the photographs of his family in happier times.

He put the cardboard box and loose paperwork down on Maaike's kitchen table.

'Where shall we start?'

'Let's do this stuff first, it looks like it's all invoices and papers relating to father's business.'

They sat next to each other. She took out each document and passed it to him. Irene sat opposite and wanted to join in, becoming agitated when he wouldn't give the papers to her.

'Here, look, this is a blank invoice pad, can she have this? I'll give her a pencil so she can draw. It will keep her quiet, we'll never get through this or have a chance to study things carefully otherwise.'

She handed Irene a stub of pencil and he slid one of his father's invoice pads across to her after checking it was all empty. Peace reigned as Mendelevski Senior's precious invoices were covered with flowers and butterflies.

'Look, these are all copy invoices, and some are dated middle to late 1942. Weren't you at Kromme Palmstraat by then?'

He looked at the dates. 'August, September, October, yes we were. These must be for repair work he did or watches he sold while we were hiding. I knew he was trying to work upstairs but I didn't know he was actually trading. How did he get the invoices out to the customers? By post through Gerrit I suppose, but how did people pay him and how did they get their watches? Surely he didn't give them the address.'

'The invoices have got the Peperstraat address on them, so any payment would have gone or been taken there.'

'But what about the watches? How did they get to the customer after he'd paid? I'll ask Bart if he knows, he was still upstairs at the workshop address. How many invoices are there and who are they addressed to?'

'There are five after the middle of 1942, one to Matthijs van der Meer on Johannes Vermeerstraat, one to a Mevrouw de Groot on Wilhelminastraat, one to a Cornelis Dykstra on Tolstraat, one to a David Meijer on Rapenburg and one to an Edwin Berger on Lijnbaansgracht. Are you thinking one of them could be the one who betrayed you?'

'I suppose if they knew the address it's possible, but not David Meijer, he was a family friend, a Jew from our shul. He was like an uncle to me and Esther.'

'The others then? We'll have to find them.'

'And then what?'

'I don't know, ask how they knew my father I suppose, and if they got watches from him during the war.'

'I think three are probably for repairs, judging by the price, and the other two look like they're for four very expensive new watches. They're hard to read though.'

He smiled. 'That was father, he kept everything in duplicate but refused to get new carbon paper. Are any of the earlier invoices to any of those names? That will tell us if they were long-standing customers from before the war.'

'There are hundreds here, it will take a long time.'

'Sorry, my father never threw away anything to do with the business.'

'Leave them with me and I'll go through them tonight after Irene's gone.'

'What else have we got?'

'All these seem to be invoices for things he purchased for the business. I can't see anything being bought after 1941 at first glance.'

'That would be right, but can you check those for those names too? It might help to know who he knew well and who knew him. Can you look for the purchases of the gold watch cases as well, I've no idea of their value.'

She laughed. 'I'll be up all night at this rate. Right, the next lot seems to be letters, you'd better check those in case they're personal family stuff.'

'Alright, but I doubt it. Knowing my father, he wouldn't have mixed the business with personal things, they'll be business letters for sure, he even used to keep copies of letters he'd sent. I'll do them later.'

'Let's see what's in the cardboard box, then.'

'Well, there are these.' He held up the ID cards. 'They're the ones the Germans insisted were issued to everyone. It says April 1941 and soon after that we had to take ours in to be stamped with the 'J' for 'Jood'. Father said once that the resistance was getting false ID cards for Jews but he thought it was too dangerous, so we just kept our cards and as we didn't go outside at all while we were hiding we didn't need them really, they were never used. I suppose I can still use mine now as proof until I can get a new one issued.'

'I don't know how long they're valid for, until you can get a new one probably. You'll have to check, but it's more than you did have. Mine is from when I was fourteen and it was issued under the Germans too. Everyone's will need renewing, I suppose, if we continue with them, that is.'

'I hope I can get a new one soon, I hate this one because it was issued on the orders of the Germans and even more because it showed we were different and easier to identify. At first father said he would not register himself as a Jew and wouldn't get a card with 'Jood' on it, but in the end he had to. Just look at little Esther's face and my mother, she was lovely.'

'Please don't upset yourself, Simon.'

'I can't help it. Why did they die when I lived? How can that be right?'

They both fell silent. He looked at the four cards laid out on the table, reluctant almost to put them away yet reticent to touch them.

She gathered them up and put them in the pile for him to take. 'These are all the birth certificates.' She passed across an envelope. 'Two are your parents'. I can't read them. Is that Lithuanian—some of the letters look strange?'

'It's a slightly different script I think, but I don't really know. We always spoke Dutch at home, Esther and I were Dutch and didn't really know anything else, well just a little bit of Yiddish maybe. Father wanted to integrate and become a Dutchman, not a Lithuanian. He and mother spoke Lithuanian Polish, Lithuanian Russian, Yiddish or all three together sometimes as mother's Dutch was poor.'

'If I read it correctly your father was born in 1894 and your mother in 1898 in Vilnius, and I think this must be their marriage certificate. They were married on 4th of March 1919.'

'That's about right, they came to Amsterdam soon after they were married. My father wanted to come earlier, as soon as the war was over, but he didn't want to leave without my mother and her parents insisted they were married before they left but wouldn't let her marry until she was twenty-one. There was a local war going on after the Germans left at the end of the Great War. Father said the Russians took over just before he married mother, and then the Poles took over in April and fighting went on until 1920. Father and mother left in the summer of 1919.'

'And here's your birth certificate: 'Simon Nojus Mendelevski born Amsterdam 17th of July 1924'. Nojus?'

'It means Noah. Father wanted a Dutch name, I was nearly a Johannes or something, but mother insisted on keeping it traditional.'

She giggled. 'I'll be alright if there's a flood then.'

'I love it when you laugh, you are so beautiful.' He leaned over to kiss her.

'Stop it, we'll never get this done.'

'Sorry, I couldn't resist.'

'Right, so you've got the ID cards, birth certificates and your parents' wedding certificate. What's next?'

He reached into the box. 'Old newspapers by the look of it. I wonder why he kept these?'

She opened them out. '*Joodsche Weekblad*, I've never heard of this one, or this, *Cetem*, it seems to be sport.'

'Now I know exactly why he kept them. This one, the *Joodsche Weekblad*, was a newspaper issued by the Jewish Council, the Judenrat. The Germans started them all over Europe under the leadership of local prominent Jews. Father said the idea was for the Jewish Council to pass on instructions to the Jewish community and help things to go smoothly. It was organised by a sort of council of elders, they asked him to be part of it as he was an important man at our shul, but he refused, he didn't trust them or Cohen, the leader. He thought the Council would be manipulated by the Germans to get the Jews to do as they were told. He told me they were putting together a record of all Jews, but it was actually only helping the Germans to identify Jews, so they could be sent to the camps. They also told Jews not to hide and to cooperate with the invaders. There was other Jewish news in it too, births, marriages, Bar Mitzvahs and things—this one must have had something of interest to him.'

'That's awful, you mean a Council of Jews worked with the Germans?'

'He said they were meant to look after Jewish people, but the Germans started to put pressure on them and they started to cooperate with them instead of resisting.'

'What about this, the *Cetem*?'

'Oh, that's easy, let me look.' He took it from her. 'I thought so, this is very precious, it has memories for me and clearly had for my father as well. It's the local paper, it was printed in the Jodenbuurt on Sundays after the football matches. This is the last match he ever took me to, the big match, Ajax versus Feyenoord, before he resigned as a member at Ajax.'

'What do you mean resigned? Was he a player or something?'

'No, silly, he was a member of the club. He resigned and so did a lot of other Jews when the Germans started to make rules about where we could go in the ground and things. It was only a matter of time before we were banned from going to matches. Jews weren't allowed to play for them anymore and father resigned before the club followed the Germans' wishes and cancelled his membership.'

'Did he like football?'

'Like it? He virtually lived for it and for his precious Ajax. He was passionate, it broke his heart not going anymore. The last game we went to was the most important one of the season, Feyenoord was our biggest rival. Sunday afternoons when Ajax was playing was the best part of the week, I couldn't wait for it. The Jodenbuurt was always busy on Sundays with all the Jewish market stalls, lots of Jews worked but father's business meant he didn't have to. We used to catch a tram from Weesperplein, it was always crowded and the atmosphere was very exciting to me. I was a young boy, only about eleven, when father first took me. Ajax had just moved to a new stadium: de Meer. We went to every home game for five or six years, we even went after the Germans came. The *Cetem* paper was sold in our neighbourhood every Sunday, it had all the football results from the whole country and people used to wait in crowds for it to arrive.'

'So he kept this edition to remind him of his last match?'

'I think he was hoping to see his beloved Ajax again one day, but deep down he probably knew that would never happen.'

They sat in silence for a few moments.

'I'll make coffee, you play with Irene for a while, we've been neglecting her.'

He drew birds, horses and dogs for Irene among her rows of flowers and her sky full of butterflies.

She looked up at him. 'Simon, why did you kiss Maaike?'

He paused. 'I thought she was upset so I kissed her, just like your Mama kisses you when you fall over.'

'Oh, I see.' Apparently satisfied she returned to her drawing, her tongue out of the side of her mouth as she concentrated.

Maaike finished making coffee and called through from the

kitchen, 'Very well put and very quickly thought out. Can you come and get the coffees? There's a drink of milk for Irene and a biscuit. Grietje said she needed building up, all the little children suffered terribly in the winter. She's nowhere near as big or strong as she should be for her age. Now, where were we?'

'There's the stamp album and the album of photographs, I thought we could look through them together if you're interested.'

'Not the stamps maybe, but photos of you in your school uniform and short trousers, I'd love to see those.' She giggled again. It was infectious, and he giggled too.

'These letters between my parents, I can't understand a word, but I must keep them. Maybe if I find anyone from the shul who was close to us and speaks Lithuanian I can get them translated one day. There are some letters from people in Amsterdam which might be of interest, I'll read them tonight.'

'That just leaves these.' She handed him the insurance policy envelope and the papers about Dijkstraat.

'There are four policies here, one each on mother and father, one on me and one on Esther. What can I do with them?'

'What are they exactly?'

'Mother's and father's are for life insurance. Mine and Esther's are twenty-five-year policies which look like father took them out when we were born.'

'Can you cash them?'

'Presumably yes, I'll have to get in touch with the insurance company, it's in The Hague. It doesn't feel right getting money because they're dead.'

'Don't be silly, that's exactly why your parents took the policies out, for you and Esther when they died.'

'To pay for their funerals maybe, but they never had funerals, did they? Their bodies were burned, they have no grave, and I had nothing to pay for.'

'But you're entitled to the money, plus of course yours still has four years to go then it pays out to you, which is what your father set it up for.'

'But will they pay out anyway? The premiums won't have been kept up, nothing has been paid since we went into hiding.'

'You'll have to find out, get in touch with the company, you won't be the only one in that position. Also there are those,' she pointed to the paperwork about Dijkstraat. 'They might prove the house belongs to your family, not those Dutch people.'

'How do I go about that?'

'You'll have to ask...'

He interrupted her. 'I know, don't tell me, I'll have to ask Jos.'

They both collapsed with laughter.

'This is a new start for you, you have money, maybe property. Think what you can do, you're a rich man. You can get new clothes, go to the dentist, you're always saying you hate your teeth, get your own place to live.'

'I'd rather have my family and anyway, I can't enjoy any of this until I find out how and why we were betrayed, I owe that to my father, mother and Esther. When I do start to enjoy this good fortune, I want you to share it with me, I want you to share my life with me.'

She smiled, not knowing what to say. 'Don't be silly, that sounded like a proposal. I'll make lunch and then we can start reading the rest of those papers.'

The afternoon passed quickly, and they didn't have an opportunity to discuss what they'd found or look at the photographs before Grietje arrived to collect Irene. 'Well, this is cosy, have you two been together all day?' She sounded irritated.

'There's just so much stuff to go through, Maaike and Irene have been helping me. Irene has done some nice drawings for you.'

'Thank you darling, that's beautiful.' She took the drawings from Irene. 'Oh, by the way, did you hear, the French have executed Laval, the Vichy leader who helped the Nazis against the French resistance. They shot him for treason this morning. Let's hope Mussert gets his too.'

'I'll come up with you, Grietje. I'll see you tomorrow, Maaike. I'll finish my lot of papers tonight and then we can compare notes and see if there are any clues.'

Grietje looked dubious. 'Have you thought about that you might have betrayed yourselves? You might have shown a light, you might have been seen at the window or made a noise. It may not have been some evil individual known to you at all.'

'I know, and I have thought of that, but if I can identify anyone who had dealings with my father after we went into hiding then I can maybe eliminate them. I'm concerned that one of father's customers might somehow have got our address, perhaps father did something stupid, I don't know. Once I've explored every possibility then us making a mistake with lights or even Gerrit being seen going into the house with bags of food will be all that's left. I just think father buying from and selling to people while we were hiding is worth checking out.'

'Jaap once told me that they suspected there was a large group of men, collaborators, employed and paid by the Nazis to find and betray people who were in hiding. Their leader was a man called Henneicke or something like that, there were twenty or more Jaap said. He told me there was a 'special operation' against him in 1944 and he was killed by a resistance group. If it was any of his gang then they probably had nothing to do with your father at all.'

'I know, it's probably an impossible task, but for my family's sake, and mine I suppose, I just have to try.'

'It sounds like you and Maaike are going to have to work very closely together then.'

TUESDAY 16TH OCTOBER 1945

'So what are your plans for today?'

He and Grietje were having breakfast together. She was rushing to work as usual and he was anxious to speak to Maaike about the paperwork. He had sat up until the early hours looking through the letters and the photograph album. There were photographs of family occasions before the war that he had totally forgotten, everyone was happy and smiling, still ignorant of the horror that was to come.

As he expected, most of the letters were of a personal nature. He couldn't read them but they appeared, from the dates, to have been written during his parents' courtship in Lithuania. There was, however, a number of letters which appeared to relate to business matters. This puzzled him as he knew how strict his father had been about keeping business records, even if the business they related to was occasionally less than legitimate. He found it strange that they were mixed with what was obviously private mail. He tried to remember the names Maaike had read out from the 1942 invoices as he thought some of them might match the ones on the letters.

'Simon, answer me please. What are your plans for today? Are you going to speak to those people you told me about?'

'No, not yet. I want to try to work out which were reliable, regular, loyal customers of my father and which might have somehow betrayed him, then maybe I'll go to see them.'

'You're going to take Maaike, I suppose?'

'Not necessarily. Some of the addresses are too far for her to walk so we'd need to take trams and I haven't a clue about them, not in this area anyway, plus of course she only gets one full day off.'

Grietje sounded angry when she said, 'She gets good money from me for looking after Irene, she doesn't do it for love you know. I don't get much free time either, but I can come with you at the weekend if you want, I know the tram routes. I don't have work this Saturday. We could take Irene along when we talk to the people, as if we are a family.'

Her idea disturbed him and he frantically looked for an excuse. 'I have to work early on Saturdays and during the week I start work about the same time in the afternoons as you finish, so it might be difficult. I think I'll have to start off on my own.'

'Just as you like, the offer is there if you need me.' She was obviously disappointed that her idea had been turned down.

She went straight out and, after collecting the letters and photographs from his room, he took Irene down to Maaike's.

'Good morning! How are you this wonderful day?'

She yawned. 'Tired, I was going through your father's sales and purchase invoices half the night. Coffee?'

She disappeared into the kitchen.

He looked out of the window. 'It's a lovely day, we may not have many more mornings like this, autumn is here.'

'We should go out, take Irene to the park or something. Coffee's ready.'

'But we still have to cross check all the names and things in father's papers.'

'I've looked through every sales invoice from 1939 to when you all went into hiding and every purchase invoice for the same period, and there's only the one sale to Berger on Lijnbaansgracht, the one we found last night. The strange thing is there are only three purchase invoices for things your father bought after the middle of 1942. One from a regular supplier from before the war, one from David Meijer, whom you said he knew well, and one from Berger just days before the sales invoice. He didn't deal with your father in any way at all before then.'

'What's your point?'

'Don't you think that's a bit odd? Your father did no business, buying or selling, with Berger before you went into hiding when your father was trading at Peperstraat, but they did business together afterwards? How did he find your father? How did he get in touch? Why did he buy a watch from him? At least I think it was a watch purchase, I can't read it clearly and there's some other writing, but it was over two thousand guilders, so I don't think it was a repair.'

'What do you want to do?'

'The address is fairly close, let's have a walk down there.'

'And speak to him, you mean?'

'No, not yet, let's just see what sort of house it is and if it's one where the owner can afford two thousand guilders for a watch.'

It was further than Maaike thought and both she and Irene were tired before they got to the address. They crossed Elandsgracht and she stopped, easing her hands from the crutch handles.

'It's somewhere here, just one more block, you sit somewhere, and I'll go on.'

'I'm alright, we must be close now.'

He walked ahead calling out the numbers. '189, 190, 191, it's here, it's a shop.'

'And it's empty.' Her voice echoed her disappointment. 'Now what?'

He looked up. 'Well, that's his name alright, look above the door, 'Edwin Berger Antiek'.'

He tried to look through the shop window, but it had been covered with old newspapers from 1942. Through the letter box he could see uncollected mail lying on the floor. He turned to her, clearly frustrated, 'There's no notice saying where he's moved to.'

'Perhaps he's gone out of business, perhaps he's dead or was taken for work in Germany like my father, who knows.'

'I suppose that's one we can cross off the list then.'

'Not yet, there's a cafe on the next corner, let's have a drink and a rest, and maybe we can ask the owner if he knows anything.'

A little voice piped up, 'Can I have a glass of milk, please?'

The café on the corner of Looiersgracht was not unlike Café van Loon. He went to the row of stools in front of the bar while Maaike and Irene sat at a table. He ordered coffee, lemonade for Maaike and milk for Irene.

It was approaching lunchtime and he bought two slices of an apple pie from under a glass dome sitting on the counter. The man behind the bar reminded him of Jos, he was jolly and fussed around Maaike and Irene with forks and a second plate. Irene ate enthusiastically while he shared with Maaike.

'We were looking for Meneer Berger at 191, the antiques shop, but it's empty. Do you know what happened to him?'

The man eyed him suspiciously. 'Are you relatives?'

'No,' Maaike cut in, 'just friends.'

'Well, if you find him tell him he owes me ten guilders, he just disappeared one night in early 1942. I thought he'd been arrested by the Germans, but someone came in a van and took away his stock. It wasn't the Germans or the police stealing it like they usually did when they'd arrested someone, it was a local haulage firm. The driver came in for a beer. I got talking to him and he said Berger was moving to another shop somewhere in the city, but his stock was going into storage until it was ready or possibly until the war was over, he wasn't sure. No one has seen him or heard of him since. Perhaps he was arrested after he left here, perhaps he's dead. Who knows these days? Maybe he was in the NSB and he's in a camp somewhere awaiting trial. He's gone, that's all I know. I don't even know who owns the shop. I think it was rented, maybe he owes the landlord money too.'

'Did he live above the shop?'

'No, the door at the side goes to the apartment upstairs where an old lady was living but she died of cold or starvation or both last winter so it's empty too. I've no idea where he lives, I only ever saw him after he closed up each day. If I knew where he lived I'd be knocking on his door for my money. He obviously wasn't short of a few guilders, that's why I gave him credit. There was a huge amount of stock and it was good quality stuff too. It wouldn't surprise me at all if some of it was from Jews who'd been deported.'

They thanked him and left, making their way back to Slootstraat.

Simon was disappointed. 'That's the end of that one then, there's nowhere to go now, it's a dead end.'

'Maybe, but just think, how did he get the watch from your father? According to the invoice he bought it while you were in hiding, but the café man said he left the shop early in 1942.'

'Maaike, I don't follow at all.'

'Remember we thought your father must have either posted the invoices or that Gerrit delivered them? He would also have had to post the watch or get Gerrit to deliver it. How could it happen that way if Berger had already left the address?'

'Go on.'

'Look, as far as your father knew, according to the address he put on his invoice, and you said he was very particular about his records, Berger was still at the Lijnbaansgracht shop. The invoice Berger sent to your father a few days earlier was on his Lijnbaansgracht notepaper, although he had already left there. How did Berger's invoice get to your father, he couldn't have posted it as he didn't know where your family were and how did whatever he sold to your father get to him? There's nothing to say your father had any clue about where Berger was other than Lijnbaansgracht. Something's wrong somewhere.'

'Thank you, Miss Detective.' He smiled at her. 'I think I understand but what can we do? There's nowhere to go, like I said, it's a dead end.'

'I've no idea, it's your turn now, I've done my bit of deduction.' She smiled back at him.

Irene joined in the smile.

He got to work at four and told Jos about their investigation and what they had learned from the paperwork.

'There's still a lot to do, we've only looked at one of father's customers, it seems he had others even while we were in hiding. They're all possibles for betraying us.'

'I know the old bugger in the bar on the Looiersgracht corner, maybe I can get some more out of him or ask him to make enquiries for us, especially if he's owed ten guilders, he's a mean old devil.'

'Is there anyone you don't know, Jos?'

He thought for a moment. 'No, not really.' He laughed and lit another disgusting cigar.

'Do you think it's possible to contact Theo Visser again? I need to ask him if he knew whether his brother-in-law delivered anything from my father as well as taking food to him.'

'I think he'll be away at sea again by now. You can go and ask the dreadful Mevrouw Visser if you're brave enough. I'll ask at the office for you. If he's on a short sea vessel like they said he should be back in the country every few days, it all depends on where in the Netherlands the ship is running from.'

'Did you find out anything about the man in the car yet?'

'Give me a chance, I've got a contact in the police. I haven't seen him yet, it's only been two days and I have to cross his palm and loosen his tongue a bit to get him to check for me.'

'I'm sorry. Did you find out anything about the old banknotes or the gold yet?'

'Bloody hell lad, you don't want much, do you? I have spoken to someone about changing the notes, he's, how can I put it, keeping a low profile at the moment, but I knew where to find him, and I saw him this morning. He'll change them but I'm afraid it's three for one because they're such large denominations. He won't be able to just spend the money, it's not actually legal tender anymore after last week but if someone could get it paid into a bank account then they could draw it out as clean new money, If you know what I mean. If you don't want to do that, he's willing to change it for some nice gold trinkets but you'd have to keep them for a while for them to cool down.'

'Cool down? What do you mean?'

'Oh dear Simon, you have a lot to learn. It's still quiet, just these three drunken old sods. Pour a couple of beers and I'll get her upstairs to come down here for a while, and we'll have a chat in the cellar. We need to work out if it's best to take the new guilders or the slightly dubious jewellery.'

'I'm not sure I like the jewellery idea, it's not exactly legal, is it?'

'Not exactly, no.'

'I hope it didn't come from looting and robbing Jews.'

'I can't be too specific, but you have my word that is not the case. This stuff came from very rich gentiles who, shall we say, forgot to close all the windows.' He laughed at his own joke as usual and, opening the connecting door, shouted up to his wife.

'She's coming down, we'll get out of her way and try to decide what you should do. You haven't even counted the cash yet, and I didn't like to do it without you. How much there is will decide whether you go for cash or jewellery.'

'I really need money now, I couldn't afford to keep the jewellery until it was safe to sell it, and anyway, would I get its full value?'

'There, you see? You're learning fast, we'll make a villain out of you yet.' He laughed loudly, downed his beer and reached for the jenever.

'Shift those crates, you know where, so you can get to my little under-floor hidey hole. I've put your cash, the coins, the watches and your mother's jewellery in there for safety. Your father's box with the tools is over there, near the spirits cupboard.'

'Think about it, 10,200 guilders, change it for new notes and it's still nearly 3,500. You're a rich boy.'

They sat in silence just looking at the money. The peace was suddenly shattered by a screech from the bar upstairs.

'Jos van Loon, get your lazy fat arse up here.'

'She's obviously had enough already, it's still very quiet up there by the sound of it. She just wants to go back upstairs and put her feet up. Go and relieve her will you, before she drives away the few customers we have got. Maaike will be here soon and it won't get busy just yet. I'm staying here.'

He managed the bar quite easily on his own. It filled up in the hour before Maaike arrived, but he was becoming quite proficient at managing a number of customers' bills at once while chatting to the regulars. They were getting to know him too and he felt quite at home gossiping with them. In many cases, he even knew what they wanted as soon as they came in the door.

Maaike arrived exactly on time at six to the delight of those sitting at the bar, who clearly found her company far preferable to his. She settled on her stool while he collected glasses from the tables and washed them. He wanted to tell her how much money there had been in his father's box and how much Jos had said he could exchange it for but couldn't while there were six pairs of ears at the bar.

Jos emerged from the cellar in a cloud of cigar smoke, clearly the worse for wear and jenever. 'Maaike! Hello beautiful, you look wonderful tonight as usual, how are you?'

'Tired, Simon had me up half the night looking at his father's papers and we had a long walk this morning.'

'So I understand. You have some interesting theories I hear, quite the little detective, I understand.'

'Don't tease me Jos, I just thought it through that's all, it proves nothing and we are no nearer to finding out who betrayed Simon's family.'

'Give it time girl, you've only just started. Right, if everything down here is under control I'm off upstairs. I'll be down about nine and if it's still quiet we'll close up and talk then. I know Simon here has something to tell you.'

Everyone fell silent and all ears were tuned in, awaiting the verbal explosion that would signal Jos meeting his wife in their living room above the bar. They were not disappointed; a tirade of abuse and, by the sound of it, crockery, clearly headed his way. Everyone smiled and ordered more beer.

The bar got busier than expected, and he didn't have a moment all evening to speak to Maaike. Jos came down, saw there were still a number of customers, and instead of closing disappeared into the cellar. Eventually he emerged, ushered the last few hardened drinkers out of the door and locked it.

'Can you two help me to clear up a bit? It's the brewery delivery in the morning and I've put in a larger order than last week now all that money business is sorted and people have got funds to spend again, so we need to tidy up tonight.'

Simon helped Jos with the ashtrays, sweeping the floor and wiping the tables, while Maaike finished washing and putting the glasses away. He and Jos brought up six cases of bottled beers and re-stocked the shelves, then they moved the crates of empties and two empty barrels towards the cellar hatch, ready for the next morning.

'Right, that's sorted, thank you both. Let's have a drink unless you want to get away?'

He had a small beer and Maaike had lemonade while Jos had his usual beer and jenever. He told Maaike how much money there was and what Jos had found out about changing it.

'That sounds wonderful, but is it legal?' She looked at Jos. 'I don't like the sound of it.'

Jos grinned. 'Changing the money is not illegal as such, after all it's not black money or stolen money, but because Simon doesn't have a bank account and his identity is still unresolved then opening one with such a big amount, and in old, large denomination notes as well, is certain to prove difficult. My man has a way of doing it but it costs him and Simon doesn't want the money frozen by a bank, he needs it now. That's right, isn't it, Simon?'

'Yes, I need clothes, a dentist, somewhere to live maybe, just a few personal possessions. One thing's for sure, the jewellery route most definitely isn't legal, but I don't want to go for that option anyway. Three for one doesn't sound good, I agree, but I trust Jos to get me the best rate.' He looked at him and said, 'After all, he has experience in this area.'

Jos laughed and playfully punched him in the shoulder. 'Cheeky young sod, how do you put up with him, Maaike?'

She touched his arm. 'Actually he's quite nice. Whatever you do, it's still a huge amount of money, more than I have ever dreamed of, and you still have the gold, the watches, the insurance policies and the house. You'll be a rich man, but you certainly deserve it after what you've been through.'

He reached across and held her hand. 'It's a new start for both of us, we deserve it.'

Jos noticed the interaction between them and smiled inwardly. 'Well, I hope I'm not going to lose you two when you're a rich couple.'

Maaike blushed and Simon nearly choked on his beer. He asked Jos about his ID card, the insurance company and how to approach repossessing the house.

'That's three more jobs for old Jos on top of the gold, the car we saw at Kromme Palmgracht, Theo and the owner of the bar on Looiersgracht. The things I do for you, or should I say you two?'

She blushed again.

'So can I go ahead with changing the cash for you?'

'Yes, please, and can you keep the money for me with everything else in your special place? I'm worried it will still be too large an amount for me to open an account without lots of questions. I can take money out as I need it.'

'Another job for me then. I'll find out about a bank account for you as well while I'm at it. Get off home, you two.' He winked at Maaike. 'And no canoodling on the way.'

They walked slowly along the canal.

'It's all very exciting, I've never seen so much money. Did you mean it when you said it was a new start for both of us?'

'Of course, Maaike.'

THURSDAY 18TH OCTOBER 1945

'You two were late again last night.'

'We were so busy right up to eleven. I was there at ten in the morning for the brewery delivery but the driver was an hour late and Jos had to get into the centre of town, so he was delayed too. I had to work with his wife all afternoon. It was hectic from four until six then Jos, Maaike and I worked all evening.'

'Where was Jos all afternoon? Out drinking, I suppose?'

'No, no, it was business, the bank and things.'

He didn't tell her that Jos had been out meeting his contact to change the old notes before making enquiries at the bank about opening an account for him and asking at the shipping office about Theo Visser.

There was, as they feared, a problem about the bank, they had told Jos that to open an account the account holder had to go in personally with identification documents. His old ID card would apparently suffice, but they would need proof where the money, if it was over a thousand guilders, had come from. There was however good news; Jos had managed to get 3,700 new guilders in exchange.

The Ned Lloyd office had told Jos that Visser was currently on a small vessel trading up and down the English coast, but would be back in about a week.

Jos had of course been for a drink, but he claimed it was while making enquiries on Simon's behalf about Berger at the Looiersgracht bar and at another bar on the Spui, the Hoppe, where he had met his police contact about the mystery man's car. He said he had made no progress on either, but that his police contact was 'working on it'.'

'I didn't really get anything done at all yesterday. I wanted to find an overcoat, it was cold and wet late night, and I wanted to talk to Bart and the Red Cross people over in the Jodenbuurt.'

He didn't mention visiting any more of his father's customers from the 1942 invoices in case she wanted to come with him, and also because he hadn't had a chance to look at the papers again although he knew Maaike had found a few more things out.

'If you're seeing Bart, don't go drinking with him again, remember what happened last time. You've got work at four, don't forget, and if you're going to Waterlooplein for a coat make sure you don't end up with rubbish, the women over there will eat a young lad like you for breakfast.'

He called in to see Maaike on his way out. 'I'm trying to make up for lost time yesterday, so I'm going to see Bart to ask if any of the customers replied to father's invoices by post or even sent money to the Peperstraat address, or if Gerrit ever picked letters up there for him. Then I'm going to the Red Cross to tell them my search for mother and Esther is over and I'll take advice about my ID if they can help, I'm sure I won't be the first not to know what to do. I'm going to look for a coat too, I was wet and cold last night.'

She laughed. 'Lucky I cuddled up to you then. But why are you going to the market, you've got money now to buy a new one. There are places you can get them without coupons now. By the way, I've looked at your father's invoices again.'

'Can we look at them when I get back, unless there's anything about David Meijer? I thought I might go to see him, he's just around the corner from Peperstraat. And I haven't got any of my money yet, we were so busy last night I forgot to ask Jos so a new coat is out.'

'Never mind, it's pay day tomorrow for us normal hard-up

people. As far as Meijer is concerned there's the sales invoice we found the other evening, and one of the last purchase invoices I found was sent from him to your home on Dijkstraat in June 1942, so he knew your father had stopped trading at Peperstraat. I suppose it's possible your father never actually received the goods or paid it before you were all...'

'Arrested, you mean? It's alright, don't be upset. David will know, if I can find him.'

He went straight to Waterlooplein, resisting the urge to browse the book stalls knowing he would not find a decent coat if he was late yet again. He arrived in time to turn over a pile of overcoats with only minimal competition from the usual housewives, finding a reasonably smart dark blue top coat among the still unsold pile of ex-army items.

The Red Cross office was quiet. Most of the returning survivors had already arrived and all those still in displaced persons camps were, presumably, now accounted for. He explained he had met an eye witness to the deaths of his mother and sister and that their names would no doubt eventually appear on the list of victims and not, sadly, on that of survivors. Their advice about his ID card and other official matters was to contact either the registry at City Hall or the relevant government department. They also suggested the Jewish Registration Office, which he was already registered with, might be better placed to help with such problems.

Unable to make progress he set off to Peperstraat where Bart was hard at work over an intricate piece of jewellery.

'Simon, welcome, come in. I won't be a moment and we can go for lunch and a beer.'

'I can't stay, I'm sorry, I have so much to do today and I have to work at four. I have just called in to ask you something.'

'Just ask, I'll help if I can. Is there any news on your family yet?'

'Sorry, I forgot I haven't seen you since I heard. Mother and Esther are both dead, I met a woman who was with them in the camp she saw their bodies. I already knew father was dead as we were in the same hut. Now I know about mother and Esther. It's as I feared, there is no one left.'

'I'm so sorry, I don't know what to say to you. Your father was a wonderful man, we were neighbours in here for years. I often called down to see him and he came up to see me. We would have coffee and put the world to rights. I usually arrived as he was at a delicate point on a watch or clock and he always seemed to turn up as I was mounting a stone. I remember your mother calling here too, she was a lovely lady. So sad, damn war. Now what can I do for you?'

'Where to start. My father left a box behind with lots of tools, photos and other stuff. There were piles of purchase and sales invoices, you know what a hoarder he was when it came to business records.'

Bart nodded. 'Go on.'

'It appears he continued trading after he closed down here, in fact he continued even after we went into hiding and he bought and sold things and issued invoices. I'm checking all the people he had dealings with after we went into hiding in case one of them somehow betrayed us. I'm trying to work out how father paid them, how they paid father and how they got their watches without them knowing about our hiding place.'

'I don't see how they could, but you know some of your father's dealings were, how can I put it, dubious'

Simon nodded, 'Did anyone ever call here to pick up mail, for example?'

'Not as far as I know, and I assume your father handed in the keys so only the landlord would have access. I certainly didn't see anyone.'

'Did anyone ever try to deliver or collect items?'

'I remember a well-dressed, middle-aged, military looking man who came looking for your father, but he had already closed down here so I sent him to Dijkstraat, did I do wrong? I didn't know where you all were, so I didn't give you away.'

'No, no, not at all. If we were still at Dijkstraat it would have been alright and if we had already gone into hiding he would have found Dijkstraat empty, or full of those Dutch people who moved themselves in.'

'Yes, I heard about that, the bastards, it's been happening all over the Jodenbuurt, what's left of it, that is.'

'Does the landlord come to father's old workshop often?'

'He came a few times in the months after your father left, but then he boarded up the windows on your father's floor and I haven't seen him since, he hasn't even emptied the place.'

'Do you think there might be mail lying there?'

'I can't see how, since I became the only occupant that side door is locked so mail is just put through the outer box, and it's all for me anyway. I wasn't here every day in the war, even the Germans couldn't find a job for a sixty-seven-year-old jeweller thank God, but the postman wouldn't have been able to get in to go up to your father's door and I never found any mail for your father in my box.'

'That seems to be the end of that then, I was hoping there might be mail here as this address was on all the invoices father sent out. The landlord must have had it. Can you remember anything else about the man who was looking for my father?'

'Well built, dark hair, very well-dressed for around here, middle-aged, I think he'd been wounded in some way, so I guessed military. Sorry, that's all I can remember.'

'Thank you, it was worth a try. If the customers didn't send payments or goods here, how did my father get them, I wonder? I must go, I'm off to Rapenburg to see David Meijer, he was from our shul and dealt with father.'

'You know you'll be lucky to find him alive.'

'I must try tot ziens Bart, we must have a drink and take food together again soon. Grietje really gave me a lecture after our last evening out, you know.'

'Ah Grietje, lovely bottom.' He laughed, remembering old times. 'Give her my love.'

12 Rapenburg was a three-storey house in a narrow street not unlike the Jordaan. 12B appeared to be on the first floor, there was no separate bell so he knocked loudly on the outer door. After a few moments the top window was thrown open and a woman's head and shoulders appeared. 'Who are you looking for?'

'David Meijer. I'm sorry to bother you, I think he lives at 12B.'

'Little grey-haired Jewish man, about seventy?'

'Yes, that's him. Does he still live here?'

'Not anymore, the Germans took him and his wife in 1942 I think. I didn't really know them, they kept themselves to themselves and I only moved in here a couple of months before they were taken away, just after my old man was sent to Germany. I doubt they'll be back, must be dead I think. The place is empty, still vacant. The Germans took all the furniture and everything, totally stripped the place. They had trouble getting it downstairs, they wanted to use my hoisting beam and pulley, but I told them to fuck themselves.'

'I see, thank you anyway.'

'Did he owe you money or something?'

'No, he was just a family friend.'

'You a Jew then? I thought you were all dead, all of them round here must be, I haven't seen one since the war. How did you survive?'

He turned to walk away. 'Sometimes I really don't know.'

Maaike was sitting at the table with Irene on her knee, comparing invoices, when he got back to Slootstraat.

'How did you get on? That coat looks quite nice, let me see.'

'Apart from this, not very well.' He handed her the coat. 'In fact a complete dead end as far as Peperstraat and David Meijer are concerned. Bart hasn't seen any mail for my father since he left, if there was any the landlord must have got it. No one delivered or collected money or anything that could have been watches or parts. There was someone who asked for my father but that's it, and David Meijer and his wife were arrested in 1942 and must be dead like all the others. Their place is empty. I'm not sure this is going to get us anywhere. Grietje did try to talk me out of it.'

'Maybe, but we're not going to stop now, there are still people to see. Someone must have known where you were hiding.'

'What if we showed ourselves, someone detected a movement, a light? Grietje said there was a gang of men just looking for Jews to claim the reward.'

'We'll worry about that if checking your father's business

137

contacts gets us nowhere.' She looked up at him and handed the coat back. 'You did well with this, it's good barathea material. Forces, I think, probably Navy. Let's see it on you.'

He took off Jaap's old jacket and put on the overcoat.

'Oh yes, my handsome sailor!'

'Stop it! Let's look at the rest of these invoices, I have to be at work at four. But first, what exactly was on the two invoices to and from David Meijer?'

'I think I've solved two of the questions, the ones about payment. I'm not sure there actually was any.'

'What do you mean?'

'Meijer's invoice to your father was dated June and it was sent to Dijkstraat, so he obviously knew by then that your father had left Peperstraat.'

'We knew that already. They were friends and Peperstraat is just around the corner from his home in Rapenburg.'

'Give me a chance. Look at Meijer's invoice. 'One gold watch case March 1942'. It's March not June, he had supplied the watch case to your father three months earlier, three months before he invoiced it. He must have actually passed it to your father while he was still at the workshop, he probably walked around the corner and gave it to him.'

'But why didn't he invoice my father earlier? Was it because he delivered it by hand and then forgot to raise an invoice for three months? But why didn't my father pay him at that time in June or much earlier?'

'That's the whole point, your father never intended to pay him.'

'What?' He sounded incredulous. 'Father wouldn't do that.'

'Calm down. Look at your father's copy invoice to Meijer, I know it's hard to read as it's a poor carbon copy, but look closely. Your father invoiced Meijer for a complete watch, which he obviously made to order for him as it says 'inscribed DM', but look, down there, your father has then deducted the price of the case from the total cost, so no money changed hands for the case at all. The invoice is just for the cost of the mechanism and your father's labour. I can't really understand why Meijer bothered to raise an invoice to your father at all really.'

'I can, knowing my father, he was so strict about paperwork he probably insisted. That explains how father got the cash to Meijer, or rather why he didn't. Father could have sent out his invoice by post, it's dated September and we were hiding by then. How did Meijer pay father and how did father get the watch to him?'

'Unless Gerrit delivered the watch and collected payment I don't know, but I think it's possible Meijer never paid your father at all. You told me today he was arrested, perhaps that happened before he even got your father's invoice. He might have been arrested before you.'

'Perhaps he never got the watch either.'

She laughed at him. 'Exactly, the light has come on at last! I don't think he ever did, unless of course Gerrit took it to him and tried to collect payment, and we'll probably never know that. Maybe Gerrit did take it and found Meijer had already been taken away. We know the invoice wasn't sent, or delivered, until September, and Meijer was possibly in Westerbork, or worse, by then. The main reason I don't think he paid is that your father hasn't marked the invoice. It appears he always marked his copy invoices 'paid', but not this one.'

'You're right, he was very meticulous about things like that. So, if father didn't get the money, where's the watch?'

'If Meijer hadn't been arrested by then and Gerrit delivered it and took Meijer's money but didn't hand it over to your father, then I'm afraid the Germans have got it somewhere. But if I'm right, then I suggest you look at the three complete watches in your father's box for one with an inscription.'

He bent over to kiss her. 'Maaike, you're a genius.'

Irene looked alarmed. 'Is Maaike upset again?'

'Can we look at that remaining purchase invoice you mentioned?'

'It's from Prins Horloges BV in Arnhem, they look like a big legitimate company. Your father appears to have been buying parts from them for many years. This last invoice is dated June 1942, but they probably invoiced thirty days after sending the goods, so I think your father probably received these parts in April or May. Look, the invoice is addressed to Dijkstraat, so they must have known the Peperstraat address was no longer in use. I think these are the parts we found in your father's box, parts he was going to use for the watches he was hoping to make while you were hiding. He's marked it 'paid June 3rd'.'

'That must have been the last thing he did before we left Dijkstraat. I can't remember the exact date'

'Don't worry, I think this one's alright, there's nothing to suggest they knew your Kromme Palmstraat address and they appear legitimate to me.'

'In that case purchase-wise it just leaves Berger.'

'Yes, but there are still these three sales invoices to customers to check out.'

The bar was quiet when he arrived, and Jos's wife disappeared upstairs as soon as he walked in. Jos wasn't there, so he couldn't ask him for any of the money. He couldn't look at the watches either but he decided it would be nice to wait until Maaike arrived anyway to put her theory to the test.

He made small talk with and served beers to the usual faces at the bar and the downstairs tables. The talk was mainly about the upcoming Nazi war trials in Germany, the many NSB members and collaborators held in Dutch camps awaiting trial in the Netherlands, and the worsening situation in the East Indies where independence forces were fighting the British while Dutch troops were still to arrive.

Two younger patrons were concerned about the Dutch economy and lack of work considering the vast amount of rebuilding that was needed, but the others pointed out that the country had only been liberated a little over five months and a large programme would take time to organise. Most thought the Labour Prime Minister Schermerhorn should call a general election and that the Catholic party would win. An argument ensued as to whether either could turn the country's economy around very quickly. Much went totally over his head as he had no experience of political matters whatsoever. All he really knew, from Maaike, was that Rotterdam, the second city and trade port, would need totally rebuilding.

The topic of the housing situation in Amsterdam in general and in the Jordaan in particular came up. He was asked about the Jodenbuurt and some of the older drinkers, having spent their entire lives and the whole of the war in the Jordaan and northwest of the city, were surprised at the dereliction of the area although he realised many must have been aware of, if not actively involved in, the hunt for timber.

Maaike arrived early, clearly keen to find out about the watch and, he suspected, to get her wages from Jos. He knew she was struggling for money but didn't know how to help her financially without offending her.

Jos arrived about seven, fresh, it appeared, from a number of local bars run by fellow landlords.

'Maaike! Simon! My two young friends. How are you both?'

'We're fine, Jos, thank you.' Simon looked at Maaike and she nodded encouragement. 'Can we talk? Downstairs, preferably.'

'Of course, my boy, follow me.'

Jos settled himself in his corner. 'What can I do for you? You two aren't going to elope and leave me, I hope.'

Simon ignored the joke. 'No, nothing like that. First of all, I need some of my money if that's alright.'

Jos looked hurt and reached for the jenever. 'Of course you can, it's your money, you don't have to ask, I'm not keeping it from you.'

'I know that, I'm sorry if you misunderstood but I forgot to ask, sorry, tell you. I needed money last night and I didn't want to go into your special place when you weren't here.'

'I understand, you're a good boy, I should have realised. Maybe it's time you had your own special place down here until you can get the money into the bank.' He stood up and moved the crates to reveal the metal plate covering the hole. 'How much do you want?'

'I don't really know, don't laugh but I still don't really know what things cost. I want to buy the groceries for Grietje this week and for Maaike too, she's been feeding me at lunchtime. I'd like to get them both presents and treat myself to some clothes and a dentist visit.'

'You can certainly afford all of that and more. It's in that envelope, don't wait for me to hand it out, it's yours, just take what you want. Take about three hundred, I guess that will be enough, but keep it safe and don't forget I'm paying you tonight.'

'I need to look at the watches too.'

'Help yourself, they're yours not mine.'

He started to explain what he and Maaike thought had happened with David Meijer's invoices and watch, but it was clearly too complicated for Jos. One by one he took out the three complete watches and examined them. He selected one and, taking the money, he ran up into the bar.

Maaike was sitting on her stool. The place was virtually deserted, most of the drinkers wandering home for an evening meal cooked by their ever patient wives, no doubt.

He stood in front of her and opened his hand, revealing the back of the watch and the initials DM. 'You were right, you clever thing.' He kissed her on the cheek, making her blush, and she pretended to push him away.

Jos appeared behind them. 'That's quite enough of that, you two. Right, it's wages time, thank you for another week's hard work. More of the same please, it's going to get busy soon, I hope.'

He took the watch back down to the cellar, trying again to explain to Jos the story behind it. 'So you see, the mechanism is mine but the gold case isn't.'

'It's all yours, stop worrying, take it from me, your friend David would have wanted you to have it. All you have to do now is sell it to someone with the same initials.' He laughed at his own joke and reached for a bottle of beer.

SATURDAY 20TH OCTOBER 1945

Grietje called through to Simon's bedroom, 'Give me all your washing. I'll take it this morning and should be able to iron it tomorrow evening.'

'Thank you, there's no rush, I bought some shirts and two new pairs of trousers plus socks and underwear yesterday when I went into town.'

'New ones? Not from the market? Quite the well-dressed man-about-town, aren't we? A nice overcoat two days ago and now new shirts and trousers.'

'I just wanted to look a bit smarter, that's all, and you don't have to keep taking my washing and doing the ironing so often if I have more clothes.'

'Have you come into money then?'

'Well, a little, there was some money in my father's box.'

'Really? You didn't mention it. Not too smart to do the shopping at the market for me today, are you?'

'Not at all, it's your Saturday off, of course I'll do it.'

'You can drop the washing off too if you want, then I can really have a free day. Irene and I are going to my friend's to have a bath later. Can you ask if Maaike has any washing on your way past? No doubt you'll be calling to see her. She'll want shopping too, I expect.'

He came into the kitchen and she looked him up and down.

'Oh yes, very smart indeed, and a tie too. It's cold and damp out there so you'll need that overcoat. I've sponged a few stains off it and brushed it for you. Breakfast is ready, and the shopping list and money are on the table. I'm going to get dressed and get Irene ready.'

'I won't need the money, I'll be paying for the shopping in future. I don't pay much rent, and you cook and clean for me, get my washing done and do the ironing.'

'There's no need for that, I can't let you do it.'

'In that case I'll pay more rent, we'll sit down and work it out. Jos pays me the same as Maaike now I've learned the job. You can't keep subsidising me, no arguments.'

She smiled and looked at him. 'Yes, sir, anything you say, sir. My, my, how the young boy has grown into a man. I'm proud of you, your parents would be too. What happened to the person I took in a month ago?'

'It's thanks to you, you know that, you saved me, fed me and housed me, helped me to start rebuild my life, I suppose you'd call it. Thank you.'

'I think Maaike might have had a hand in it too, don't you?'

Maaike answered the door still in her dressing gown. 'Good morning, come in. I'm not dressed yet, you're an early bird.'

She crutched ahead and turned to look at him. 'You look very smart, is that outfit all new?'

'I went into town yesterday, they didn't ask for clothing coupons. I didn't want to wear them for work last night.'

'Come here handsome, I want a kiss, it's not often we're alone.' She moved towards him and as she swung between the crutches her dressing gown parted slightly and he saw the end of her amputated leg. 'Oh no, I'm so sorry and embarrassed.' She quickly covered herself and turned away from him, almost in tears.

'Don't be silly. It doesn't matter, you are a beautiful woman. I've only ever known you with one leg, I had to see your...'

'My stump.'

'Yes, your stump, I had to see it sometime if we're going to, well, you know, be a couple. It doesn't matter to me. Now, I thought I was going to get a kiss.'

She smiled weakly and went carefully up to him. Letting her crutches fall to the floor, she put her arms around his neck and they kissed. He could feel her soft breasts against him, and the stump of her leg pressing against his groin. He felt himself becoming aroused, so he ended the embrace.

'I have to go to the market for groceries, but I am taking the washing for Grietje first, have you got anything you want me to take for you?'

Her impish grin had returned. 'The things you'll do to get hold of my underwear.' She laughed, but he was embarrassed and didn't share in the joke.

'I'll do your shopping too if you have a list.'

'If I get ready quickly, can we go together? I'd like to do my own shopping if you can carry it back for me.'

'You'll have to hurry, I have to be at work at eleven. And I'm paying, you can't afford to keep feeding me.'

She looked angry and hurt. 'I'll pay for my own food, I'm not a charity case, don't insult me.'

'But I have all that money, I don't need it or know what to do with it. I want to share it with you. I didn't mean to offend you, I'm sorry. I just want to help.'

'Not by paying my bills, you won't. Please don't mention it again, I can look after myself. I'll get dressed and we'll go, we'll have plenty of time and we can have coffee back here before you leave. While you're at work I'll look at the invoices again and find out where the addresses are for tomorrow. We'll have to take trams, I think.'

'I've no idea where they go from or where they go to, so it's up to you.'

They delivered the washing and soon finished the shopping. He thought he had become quite proficient but Maaike held her own and bettered many of the crowd of hardened women he had competed against for three weeks. Bargain followed bargain as she charmed successive stallholders.

'You're excellent at this, who taught you to shop like that?'

'It's amazing what a sad smile and a pair of crutches can achieve, being disabled helps sometimes.'

'Nonsense, it's being beautiful that makes the difference.'

She squeezed his hand. 'Let's go home.'

'I just want to buy flowers.'

'The chrysanthemums are beautiful and so are the carnations, they're my favourites.'

He bought two bunches of each and she looked at him quizzically. 'Grietje is going to love all those.'

'They're not all for Grietje, the carnations are yours.'

She stretched up and kissed his cheek.

Back at Slootstraat he took Grietje's flowers and groceries upstairs while Maaike made coffee and put her flowers in a vase. 'I've put Grietje's in a bucket of water so she can arrange them herself when she gets back.'

'It'll be a nice surprise for her.'

'Right, where are we on our research for tomorrow?'

'Mevrouw de Groot on Wilhelminastraat, I suspect from the price that it was a repair but there's no sign of her paying and both the original and duplicate copies are here. It looks like the bill was never sent and maybe the watch is still in the box. Dykstra on Tolstraat: sounds like he's from Friesland, looks like another repair judging by the price but it's an awful copy and it's torn, I can't see whether it's marked paid or not. I suspect both de Groot and Dykstra were repairs that your father started at Peperstraat, or even Dijkstraat, but didn't finish before you all went into hiding.'

'I'll check the box for them tonight and we can take them with us if I find them. If they didn't know how or where to get in touch with father for their watches, it seems unlikely they could have betrayed us. What about the third invoice?'

'It looks like three brand new watches, certainly not repairs, and very good ones obviously, it's for 6,000 guilders. It's a very expensive address. Your father has marked it as paid so he must have got them to him somehow and he got paid. If you discount David Meijer's watch, there are only two left so these three can't still be in the box.'

'Who did they go to and whereabouts is he?'

'Matthijs van der Meer on Johannes Vermeerstraat, I think it's near the Rijksmuseum. It's not round here that's for certain, in fact none of the addresses are as far as I know. I really haven't a clue, I haven't been far from the Jordaan, walking long distances is not exactly my strong point.' She smiled weakly.

'So how are we going to find these places tomorrow?'

'We'll have to ask Jos tonight, maybe he has a map or perhaps he can give us directions. I don't think we'll be able to do them all in one day, all three of the streets are obviously very long judging by the high numbers of the addresses. We might have to go on Monday as well. We can take Irene with us.'

'I hope you will be able to walk to some of them with me at least.'

'We can take the tram, either on Marnixstraat, where we took the washing, or on the Singelgracht, or even on Rozengracht depending on where in the city we have to go. Beyond that I don't know my way anywhere and some of the trams haven't started running again yet.'

'Don't worry, neither do I.' He laughed. 'I'd hardly been out of the Jodenbuurt until I was arrested. I've only just started to realise what an innocent, spoiled eighteen-year-old I was, I knew nothing about nothing, except my studies of course. You're only eighteen now and you are much more experienced with life than me.'

'You've had to grow up quickly since then though, you've been through things many will never have to experience, and you have had to become a man very quickly.'

'Maybe, but I sometimes still feel like a little boy. Money is strange to me, shopping for myself, finding my way around the city, I'm still innocent in all of those things.'

She leaned over and kissed him. 'And with the ladies,' she laughed.

He managed an embarrassed smile. 'I must get to work, it's nearly eleven. Can you write those three addresses down for me?'

The bar was packed with Saturday shoppers. Jos and his wife were working and virtually every table and the benches outside were occupied. Jos disappeared down the cellar as soon as Simon arrived, but only to change a barrel and to bring up some bottles of spirits. Thankfully he reappeared quickly and his wife went upstairs almost immediately, much to the relief of both of them, he suspected.

By two the bulk of the morning trade had disappeared, the women back to their houses with the shopping and the men either to watch Ajax or back home to their wives for an afternoon sleep.

While things were quiet he showed Jos the list of addresses he and Maaike hoped to visit the next day.

'You'll do well to get to all these in a day if you're walking and Maaike definitely won't manage it. If I were you I'd try to do two, which ones I'll leave to you.' He brought a map from upstairs and pointed out all three streets. As Maaike had observed all three were long and the map didn't show at which end the addresses might be.

'It's only a guess, but I think the numbers start near the centre of the city and go up as the street goes outwards, so at least two of your three are going to be a long way out. You'll have to take a tram to Overtoom if you're going to Wilhelminastraat, or you could stay on to Museumplein if you're going to Johannes Vermeerstraat. Tolstraat is right down in the Pijp.' He pointed to the map. 'Stay on until you get to the Amstel.'

'It sounds complicated, can you tell Maaike all that when she gets here or, better still, write it out for her?'

'I spend more time working for you than I do for myself.' He laughed and slapped him on the back. 'Oh, that reminds me. Theo Visser will be arriving on the Triton in the Westerdok on Monday morning. It's near his home but I think he'll go for a beer first. Well, if you were married to her, wouldn't you?' He laughed again. 'We'll go down and meet him if you think it's going to help, but I don't see what else he can tell you.'

'I'm just hoping that he or his sister might know something

about any errands Gerrit might have carried out for my father. Someone must have found out where we were, unless we gave ourselves away, of course, and anyone who had contact as a customer or supplier might be the one.'

'But won't you have spoken to them all by the time we see Theo again?'

'Some of them, but I want to check their stories if possible. One is almost certainly dead, we're seeing two tomorrow hopefully and the other on Monday afternoon. Then there's Berger, the Lijnbaansgracht man who's disappeared. There's also the man we saw at Kromme Palmstraat, is he the 'general dealer' Theo knew about or is it a different man? Did Gerrit ever mention anything about him, did he see Gerrit going into the house with food? There are still so many possibilities.'

'This is getting like a detective story, I just hope you can solve it. I might know who the man in the car is quite soon, I'm seeing my man from the police records section next week.'

'That would be wonderful, I hope it answers some questions. I still think that whoever rented the storage in those old stables is the most likely person to have known we were up above.'

'I just hope for your sake that you can identify the bastard who gave you away. If you can't, it will gnaw away at you forever, I reckon.'

He reflected for a moment. 'Possibly, Jos, possibly. Can I look in the special place? I want to check the two other watches.'

'Go on then, don't wait for me. I trust you, and bring two crates of Amstel up with you.'

Both watches were, as Maaike suspected, older ones his father had clearly had in for repair, unlike the new one intended for David Meijer. One was unmarked except for small dents and scratches but the other, like Meijer's, was engraved. Worn, but still legible on the back were the initials 'WdG'.

He showed it to Maaike when she arrived. 'Meneer de Groot's watch, his wife never got it back and she never paid, it all fits in with your father still having both copies of the invoice.'

'All I need to know then is how it got to my father, if it was before we went into hiding Mevrouw de Groot is not our man, sorry, woman. I want to go to de Groot's and to Tolstraat tomorrow. I would like to return their watches, if at all possible. I couldn't get David Meijer's to him, but I hope I can finish the job my father started on these two, it's important to me.'

She smiled at him. 'What a lovely man you are, Simon.'

SUNDAY 21ST OCTOBER 1945

He was afraid Grietje would be upset that he would be out all day with Maaike. He knew that she liked them to spend Sunday together. He dressed and went into the kitchen with some trepidation, but he needn't have worried.

She was in a good mood, making him a cooked breakfast of eggs. 'Simon, good morning, how are you today? It's a nice, sunny morning.'

'I'm fine, thank you, you're up and about early.'

'I've got lots to do. Cleaning this morning, then I'm going to collect the washing, then I'll do the ironing, and then I'll cook. Thank you so much for the flowers, they're lovely and for the shopping too, I notice you slipped some extra items in. You really shouldn't have.'

'Don't be silly, I told you I don't really pay my way, so I thought some extra bits and pieces might be appreciated.'

'I'm going to cook the chicken with all the vegetables today, if that's alright.'

'Grietje, I'm sorry, but I'm going to be out all day looking for more of father's customers.'

Her face fell for a moment then she smiled and said, 'With Maaike I suppose. Never mind, I've got lots to do this morning, so

I'll cook this evening. Ask Maaike to join us again, she won't be able to cook anything if she's out with you all day.'

Irene looked up from her breakfast. 'Yes, please, ask Maaike to come, please, I like Maaike. Please, Simon.'

Maaike opened the door wearing her coat, clearly ready to go.

'Good morning, I'm ready, it's quite exciting, isn't it?'

'I'm not sure about that, it's all a bit sad, really. Jos says it's becoming a bit of a fixation for me.'

'Understandable. What are you going to do if you do find out who betrayed you?'

'That I don't know. Come on, let's go. Grietje wants you to come for a meal this evening by the way.'

'Oh no, really? Again? The last time I ate with you two was very difficult if you remember.'

'Don't worry about it, I'm sure the atmosphere will be a lot less frosty this time, she seems to have accepted that we are...how can I put it?'

She smiled and touched his arm. 'A couple?'

'Are we? Yes, I suppose we are. I hope so.'

They took the tram from Marnixplein as Jos had advised. Maaike struggled a little with the steps up onto the tram as they were quite steep but, as it was quite early on a Sunday morning and they were virtually the only passengers, the driver kindly waited until they were seated before moving off.

He couldn't remember any journeys by tram other than those with his father to see Ajax and an almost empty tram, as opposed to one with men hanging on outside, was very different. The rest of his travel had only been in the immediate vicinity of the Jodenbuurt and had always been undertaken on foot.

They changed trams at the junction with Overtoom and, on consulting Jos's map, they decided to get off halfway down Overtoom in the hope that 174 Wilhelminastraat would not be too far to walk either way.

174 was an unpretentious four storey house like all the others in the lengthy row. The porch had two bells with the name de Groot next to number 174A.

Maaike, already obviously tiring, sounded relieved. 'Thank goodness it's the ground floor.'

The door was opened by a tall slim elegant lady with silver hair piled on top of her head. He estimated she was in her late forties. She wore an expensive dark purple dress and sported equally expensive jewellery.

'Goedemorgen, Mevrouw de Groot?'

She looked him and Maaike up and down. 'No, thank you, I'm not buying today.' She started to close the door.

'Please, you don't understand, I'm Simon Mendelevski and my friend is Maaike de Vries, I'm here about your watch.'

'My watch? What watch?'

'I think you left it with my father for repair, a gold pocket watch.'

'The Jewish watchmaker, you mean? Yes, of course, I remember, I haven't seen him or the watch since. He's your father, you say?'

'He's dead, my whole family is dead. I'm the only one who survived. I'm sorting out my father's affairs and I found the invoice for repairs to your watch.'

'It wasn't my watch. It belonged to my husband, I sent it for repair just after the Germans came. It's a long story, you'd better come in.' She looked at Maaike, then down at her crutches. 'You look tired out dear, please come inside.'

She showed them into a sitting room tastefully decorated with expensive curtains, paintings and old photographs. A tall, well-built man of about fifty with a military bearing rose from an armchair to greet them.

'Willem, this young man is the son of the watchmaker who had your gold watch, and this is his friend.' She turned to Maaike. 'Please sit down, dear.'

Maaike sank down gratefully in a chair as de Groot offered Simon his hand.

'I'm Willem de Groot.'

'I'm Simon Mendelevski and my friend is Maaike de Vries.'

'I'm pleased to meet you both. Now, about my watch, you say.'

'I'm sorting out my father's affairs. He died in Auschwitz and we found paperwork to suggest he was repairing a watch for Mevrouw de Groot.'

'Yes, it was my watch, my wife took it to your father in early 1941, he'd been recommended as the best watchmaker in Amsterdam. She knew the watch was important to me. She wanted to do something special for me after I got home from the POW camp. I was a major in the regular Dutch Army and I was wounded and taken prisoner by the Germans in Zeeland during the fighting in Middelburg, two days before Rotterdam was bombed and we surrendered. Because I was a regular soldier and because I was captured before the capitulation I was sent to a POW camp in Germany. I was released in late 1940 on the understanding that I signed an undertaking not to raise arms against Germany again. When I recovered from my wounds I went to your father's business premises but he had gone, it was all empty and closed.'

'And you spoke to Bart, the man downstairs.'

'That's right, he was a jeweller or something, he sent me to your home. I can't remember where it was, but that place was empty too.'

'And this was in 1942.'

'Yes, late summer I would say, just before the Germans recalled all the regular officers and sent us to POW camps in Germany. I hid for a while but in the end I was taken as a POW. I only got home in May.'

'We hid too, that's why you couldn't find my father at either of the addresses in 1942, but we were betrayed. I'm the only survivor.'

'I'm sorry to hear that, young man.'

De Groot's wife came back in with a tray. 'There's tea or coffee and biscuits, which would you like, Maaike?'

'I have something for you.' He took the watch from his pocket and handed it to de Groot. 'All repaired and running and there is even a key.'

De Groot took the watch and turned it over in his palm. He ran his thumb gently over the engraved initials. 'I don't know what to say to you, I am touched that you've taken the trouble to find us and return the watch. It was my father's, he was a Willem too, hence the engraving. It's very precious to me, I didn't think I'd ever see it again. You could have sold it, we would never have known. Thank you so much.'

'My father hid some items so the Germans didn't get them before we were transported to the camp, and Maaike here worked it all out through father's unsent invoice.'

'Oh, of course, how rude of me, how much do I owe you?'

'Please, I don't want money, I am just finishing the job on behalf of my father as he couldn't do so himself. He was an honest man and I would not want his memory soiled by anyone thinking he had kept any of their property, especially a nice, much valued gold watch.'

He thought it best not to mention that he was also checking out his father's customers to see if one of them had betrayed his family.

Maaike and de Groot's wife chatted in the corner while de Groot proudly showed him some of his army photographs and one of his father, the original owner of the watch. 'I never surrendered to the Nazis, I was wounded and still fighting when I was taken prisoner. I signed the paper to get out of the POW camp to get home to my wife, but I never cooperated while I was free. I'm just so sorry we couldn't do more to save your people.'

They walked back to Overtoom and took the tram again. Maaike was apparently refreshed by the coffee and biscuits.

'Those two didn't betray you, that's for sure, what a lovely couple. He fought to the end, was a wounded prisoner, got home to his wife and was taken back as a prisoner for a second time.'

'I'm just pleased the watch is back where it belongs, it will run and run for years, my father's legacy I suppose. Now, when we change trams, do we go home or press on?'

'Let's press on to Tolstraat, it's on the tramline we pick up at the end of Overtoom, I hope! Anyway, I fancy speaking some Frisian with Meneer Dykstra.'

'What's the position with him invoice-wise? There was no engraving on it but it's the last watch, so it must be his, unless he got his back some way and didn't pay.'

'There was only the carbon copy invoice, which was torn, but it

155

doesn't appear to have paid written on it. Presumably your father sent the bill out, but that's all we know. The invoice was dated August 1942, were you in Kromme Palmstraat then?'

'I think so, but it looks like it was sent out somehow. Hopefully Gerrit posted it, surely father didn't go out and post it himself.'

She studied the map and notes Jos had written. 'Tolstraat is a long street like Wilhelminastraat and the address for Dykstra is number 97. Jos said we should stay on this tram until it reaches the Amstel. It's a long walk along the river to Tolstraat, but it looks like if we change trams at the junction of van Woustraat it will take us down to Tolstraat, about halfway down in fact, so 97 might be close.'

She was right once again, and they found it easily without too much walking. There were two front entrances, a door at street level for 97A and, through an archway, a flight of steep stairs up to the landings and presumably the front doors of 97B and C.

'Which one is it?'

She laughed. 'I don't know, all I remember is 97. I hope it's the ground floor, let's try that one first.'

A young boy answered the door. 'Miserable old man? About eighty, bit smelly? You want upstairs, first floor. I think he's in.'

He stared at the crutches. 'Did your leg get shot off in the war?' He turned and slammed the door.

'Can you make it?'

Maaike looked at the steep flight of stone stairs. 'I think so, I'm not too bad on stairs, I can get up to Grietje's, but can you go up behind me in case?'

He followed her as she crutched slowly and methodically up the stairs.

'I hope he's in after all this,' she joked. 'I'm not going down without a coffee and a sit down.'

He was in and the door opened a few inches. 'Who's there? What do you want?'

'Goedemiddag. Meneer Dykstra? Cornelis Dykstra?'

'Bugger off, you bastard Germans, you've taken it all already.'

'We're not Germans, please don't be afraid.'

Maaike put the tip of her crutch in the door before he could close it and spoke quietly to the frightened man. Simon hardly understood a word, he assumed it was that strange Frisian dialect she had mentioned but the old man clearly did. It worked wonders, the door opened wide and the man started smiling and chattering away.

'This is Cornelis, he's from Friesland like me.'

He held out his hand. 'I'm Simon Mendelevski, I'm sorry, I don't understand Frisian.'

'No, I'm sorry, I haven't spoken to anyone in Frisian in years apart from my lovely wife Sytske. I'll speak Dutch now, it was just nice to hear Frisian again and to speak with your wife. Come in.'

'We're just friends, Cornelis, I'm not his wife.'

The old man smiled. 'Well, you should be.' He turned to Simon. 'Why haven't you asked her?'

He stood back and they entered the main room. It was very dark and smelled of the old man's cigarettes, damp and boiled vegetables. The man's hair was lank and unwashed, and his woollen cardigan was stained with food and missing a button. The absence of a woman's touch was clear; there were mountains of old newspapers everywhere and layers of dust and cobwebs.

He felt himself blushing at the reference to Maaike as his wife. He looked at her. She was desperately trying not to laugh, so he quickly changed the subject. 'So you're from Friesland too? How long have you been in Amsterdam?'

'Probably since before you two were born. I'm seventy-five, Sytske and I arrived in 1922. She died last winter, starved and frozen to death thanks to the Nazis.'

Maaike settled in a chair and smiled up at him, sensing his sorrow. 'Why did you come here, Cornelis?'

'I worked on the railway building the line in Friesland. We finished it in 1913. The two railway companies were in financial trouble after the war, I don't know why they were affected, we were neutral, but for some reason they were so we moved here, and I worked on the track between Centraal and the big depot at Amersfoort.'

'It was the same for my father, he moved to Rotterdam looking for work after the Afsluitdijk was finished.'

'So how did you get here?'

'We were bombed when the war started, my mother was killed and my father is dead now too.'

'Will you go back to Friesland?'

'I don't know, Simon wants me to go on a visit to see my aunt but I don't really want to stay there, unless of course he comes with me.'

'He will if he has any sense at all. And what about you, young man, are you from Amsterdam?'

'I was born here but my parents came from Lithuania originally.'

'You're a Jew, I think, yes?'

'Yes, I am.'

'And you survived the war. There don't seem to be many Jews left, there used to be quite a lot living around here but now there is no one.'

Apparently satisfied that everybody's background had been fully explored, he sat down opposite her. 'Now then, young lady, what can a lonely old man do for you?'

'Well, it may be what we can do for you. Simon, why don't you explain?'

'We are here about your gold watch.'

'My watch! I don't have a watch anymore!' He suddenly grew very agitated. 'I took it for repair, I paid his invoice, but the thief never returned it to me. I think he probably sold it to the Nazis, the bastard.'

'No, you don't understand. The watchmaker was Aviel Mendelevski. I'm Simon Mendelevski, the watchmaker was my father.'

The old man looked confused. 'But why are you here? I paid your father's bill, but he kept my watch.'

'He kept it because I think he was arrested and sent to Auschwitz before he could send it to you. How did you pay him? Where did you take the money?'

'I didn't take it, I sent him a cheque. Wait a minute.'

He crossed the room and frantically looked through a pile of letters and papers stacked high on an old bureau.

'Wait, it's here somewhere, I know it is. Ah! I have it. Look. He sent me this by post in August 1942, I've written 'received 15th August 1942' on it and I sent him a cheque by return. It was cheque number 233, I noted the number.'

'You sent it by post? What address did you use?'

'I posted it to the address on the invoice, Peperstraat, the same place I took the watch. He had it for a long time, I know that.'

'That would be right, my father left there in 1941 and worked from our home until the middle of 1942. This is an old invoice, I suppose he just forgot about the address and sent it out. A lot of things were happening. We were in hiding by then and I think he probably finished working on your watch at that time. I don't think he could have got your cheque. Was it cashed?'

'I've no idea, it was so long ago. I assumed it was but maybe not, I don't know. My wife used to check the bank account. I just remember sitting here waiting for my watch to arrive and when I went to try to collect it the place was boarded up.'

He exchanged a smile with Maaike and reached into his pocket, 'Well, it's finally arrived, I'm sorry it's so late.'

She dried a tear as the old man reached out, his pale bony hands shaking almost uncontrollably, to take the watch from Simon. Like de Groot earlier, he turned the watch over and over in his hands, his nicotine stained fingers exploring and remembering the dents and scratches in the gold case.

'What can I say to you, Simon Mendelevski? You have returned my watch, the watch my wife bought for me so many years ago. It's all I have left of her. I thought I would never see it again. I am so sorry I doubted your father, please thank him for me.'

Before he could speak she interrupted, 'Simon's father is dead, his whole family is dead, but he wanted to finish his father's business.'

The old man sat in silence for a moment. 'I have no words,

young man, what a wonderful gesture that you should seek me out today. I can never thank you enough.'

They left Dykstra sitting in the chair in the dim room, holding the watch to his ear. Simon went slowly down the steps in front of Maaike in case she needed support and they walked in silence to the tram stop.

She was the first to speak as they waited for the tram. 'I don't think it was him either, but how was your father ever going to get the cheque?'

'We'll never know, maybe Gerrit was supposed to pick up the mail at Peperstraat, maybe father just got confused and forgot about the address on the invoice, but then he could hardly change it to Kromme Palmstraat, could he? Probably the Peperstraat landlord got it. Anyway, I'm not going to worry about it, we'll never answer every question. One thing I do know is Cornelis Dykstra didn't betray us, I'm sure of that.'

They got back to Slootstraat at five thirty. Grietje had a beautiful meal waiting and the atmosphere was very different to the last time they all ate together.

'Tell me, did you two make any progress today?'

'Yes and no. We saw two of father's customers and I think we established neither of them betrayed us to the Germans, but as far as who did we're no further forward.'

'I think we made them both very happy though,' Maaike said and looked at him. 'Simon gave them both their gold watches back. He finished his father's work in a way.'

Grietje looked surprised. 'So there were gold watches in the box? You didn't tell me that.'

'Yes, but the watches weren't mine, father didn't manage to get them back to their owners so I did it today.'

'That's wonderful, Simon.' She looked at him and then at Maaike. 'He's a wonderful boy, it's no less than I expected of him. You're a very lucky girl.'

MONDAY 22ND OCTOBER 1945

Jos hadn't specified a time to go down to see Theo Visser at the Westerdok, so he was outside the Cafe van Loon far too early and had to hammer on the door to attract attention.

Jos's wife threw open a side window and looked down. 'What do you want? It's Monday, we're closed. What are you doing here anyway?'

'I'm here to see Jos.'

'He's still in bed, lazy bastard, he was out with some of his drunken friends last night. You'll have to wait.'

He sat on the bench outside.

She had left the window open and he heard her cursing her hungover husband.

Jos cursed back and after a few minutes the door opened. 'Simon, for goodness' sake, it's still night time, come in, come in, I'll get dressed.'

'I'm sorry, but you didn't say what time.'

'Have a seat in the bar, I won't be a minute. I'll bring down some coffee. We don't have to be down at the dock until at least eleven.'

He told Jos about the visits he and Maaike had made the day before and how he thought neither of the two watch owners could have betrayed his family.

'So that's two of the watches your father left you gone.'

'Yes, but they weren't mine at all really, in fact they always belonged to de Groot and Dykstra, they just gave them to my father for repair. I had to return them to their rightful owners.'

'You're a good boy but it's cost you a few guilders.'

'Not when they weren't mine anyway, father may have put them in the box for safekeeping but I'm sure he wanted to return them after the war and I know he would have if he'd lived.'

'How many watches, complete ones not just cases, are left now?'

'Just the one that should have been David Meijer's. I've still got to see van der Meer, he had three according to father's invoice—somehow he must have got them. His invoice is marked 'paid' as well, we just don't know how.'

'It could it be him then, the man who betrayed you all?'

'We're going to see him this afternoon, he lives on Johannes Vermeerstraat. I'll tell you tomorrow.'

'Nice address, there's money there, probably a rich bastard who did well out of the war. Black marketeer or collaborator, you'd better be careful, it could be him.'

The Westerdok was very busy with small coasters, so different to the huge vessels from the Indies Jos had helped to unload out on Java-eiland and KNSM Island.

'I can't see her, *Triton*, registered in Groningen and owned by Becks. She should have a blue funnel with a 'B' on it. She could be anywhere along this quay, perhaps we're too early.'

'There it is.' He pointed to a small vessel, painted light grey with white accommodation topped with a dark wood stained bridge, in the process of tying up on the opposite side of the dock.

'Well spotted, your eyes are younger than mine and she's a 'she' not an 'it'. Come on, let's go before he goes ashore.'

They hurried down to the lock gates and crossed to the other side of the dock. A crewmember was struggling to put out a gangway and Jos took hold of the end and pulled it further onto the dockside. 'Lucky she's in ballast, if she was loaded he'd never have got that gangway up and onto the quay.' Jos clearly enjoyed being around docks, ships and shipping again.

He called across to the crewmember who was busy securing the end of the gangway to the hatch cover. 'Is Theo Visser aboard?'

The man grunted and shrugged his shoulders just as Theo emerged from the door leading out onto the deck.

'Theo! There you are. Thank goodness I asked where you were, but this miserable bugger doesn't seem to understand basic Dutch.' Jos started down the gangway onto the ship.

'Of course, he does. He's from the Indies, he's been on here for years, all through the war apparently, but he's started to be a problem ever since that independent Indonesia shit started. It's got worse this trip since he heard about the fighting around Surabaya —that's where his family is. He hasn't been home for years, but his family survived the Japanese and now they're in the middle of a civil war.'

'I would have thought he could have rigged a bloody gangway by now then.'

'He's really the cook and in fairness he's damn good. There are only five of us on board, the old man, the mate, the engineer, him as cook and me as the only AB. He helps me on deck, that's why he was doing the gangway. It's a bit different to the big Rotterdam Lloyd ships, that's for sure.'

'Can you go ashore, or do you have to stand by the ship?'

'The old man said I can go as I live so close, but I have to be back by six as we're moving across to the big silo to load grain for England.'

'Have you got time for a beer with me and a chat with Simon here before you go home?'

'I've got time for a beer and a chat instead of going home,' he joked. 'Seriously, I'll have to call in to see the old girl, but so long as she doesn't know exactly what time we got in all is good. I'll just get my washing and we'll go.'

They walked across to Prinseneiland passing two customs officers on their way to the ship and entered a small, very old, bar on a corner.

Jos knew the landlord, and so did Theo.

'What are you having? These are on Simon.'

Simon paid for the drinks, beer for him and beers and jenevers for the two men.

'So what else can I do for you? What was in the box? Thank you for collecting it, one less thing for my wife to complain about.'

'First of all, thank you and thank your sister for keeping it safe for me. My father had put lots of our family's valuable things in there for safekeeping and there was some of his paperwork which I'm hoping will be helpful in the search for whoever betrayed us and your brother-in-law. Next time I see you I'd like to give you something for your sister for her trouble and for Gerrit's sacrifice for my family.'

He waved his hand dismissively. 'That's not necessary. What can I do for you today?'

'I appreciate it's a long shot, but do you know if Gerrit did any favours or ran any errands for my father or did he simply deliver our food and check on us?'

'My sister might know more, she knew a little bit of what he was up to. I had an idea he was minding a Jewish family in hiding but I didn't know who or where until you and he had already been arrested, until my sister told me about the box in fact, but I do know he posted letters for your father.'

'Ah, yes! That would have been the invoices. I know now that some went out while we were hiding, my father was still working, you see, but I didn't know how.'

'My sister told me he also made deliveries on at least two occasions. One in particular he told her about, no details, you understand, just that there were three solid gold very expensive watches, worth more money than Gerrit had ever seen.'

'Van der Meer's watches. That solves one mystery at least. Did he ever mention Lijnbaansgracht?'

'I'm sorry, lad, I don't know. I'll ask my sister but Gerrit was very careful about what he did. He kept it secret for the Jewish families' sakes as well as for his own. I think he mentioned running errands almost in passing as part of his general duties looking after you. As for the watches, I know he wouldn't have given any details about you or your address, the less my sister knew the better for her. He probably mentioned it just because they were so valuable. How he knew, I don't know.'

'I think he collected the money for my father too, that's how he would have known their value and, honest man that he was, it got to my father safely.'

Jos broke in. 'Your sister's husband was a brave man, what a shame there were not more like him.'

'I'm sure you did your bit too, Jos.'

'Not like that, a bit of sabotage on Nazi equipment and stuff down the docks. I took part in the docks strike and did a bit of thieving to keep people warm and fed last winter, that's all.'

More beers and jenevers followed. Jos and Theo chatted about Theo's trips on the *Triton*, the dock strike in England, the state of the wharves on the River Thames and in Hull following the wartime bombing, the ongoing detention of NSB members, and the situation in the East Indies.

He listened intently to the two men, both worldly-wise, discussing subjects he knew absolutely nothing about, realising his life and knowledge were limited to his small corner of the Jordaan district. At that moment he somehow knew that to make a new life he would need to spread his wings, possibly even away from Amsterdam and the Netherlands.

They walked to Haarlemmerplein together. Theo, either drunk or still finding his land-legs, left unsteadily to see his wife while he and Jos made their way back to the Jordaan.

Maaike was waiting for him at Slootstraat with a sandwich. 'Tell me, how did it go? Did Theo know anything?'

'He did actually, no names or details but I think he has answered some if not quite all of the questions. Gerrit posted letters for father, which explains Dykstra's invoice and maybe Berger's too, but not how the one from Berger got to father. He didn't know anything about Lijnbaansgracht but what he did know was that Gerrit mentioned to his wife that he'd delivered three very expensive gold watches. They must be the ones to van der Moor.'

'So if van der Meer gave the money to Gerrit, it explains why your father was able to mark his copy of the invoice as paid, and there's no question of van der Meer knowing about Kromme Palmstraat. Do we need to go to see him at all now?'

'I still want to go, firstly to check that the delivery Gerrit made was the one to van der Meer, but also to ask how he found father and when he placed his order with him.'

Jos and Maaike were certainly right about Johannes Vermeerstraat, it was a different world to the Jordaan. Number 2 was at the city end, just as Jos had said, in fact it backed onto the Museumplein next to the Rijksmuseum. Together with Irene they walked up from the tram stop on Johannes Vermeerplein, marvelling at the houses, until they stood outside the mansion which was the residence of Matthijs van der Meer.

For a moment they just looked at each other, unsure whether to ring the bell or to go through the heavy iron spiked gate to the side door, which looked like the tradesman's or even the staff entrance. Suddenly the decision was made for them as Irene ran up the three steps and started knocking on the wide oak door.

'Irene! Come back here.'

Maaike started to go towards the steps but he was faster, joining the girl on the top just as the door opened. A woman in her thirties smartly dressed in a two-piece black suit and white blouse looked at him, Irene and finally at Maaike, who was still slowly climbing the steps.

He gave her his best smile. 'Goedemiddag, can we speak to Meneer van der Meer?'

'And who might you be?' The woman looked him up and down, noting no doubt his second-hand coat and old shoes. She turned her attention to Maaike, staring at her crutches and single leg 'Have you got an appointment?'

'No, I'm sorry, we haven't.'

'Can I tell him who you are and what it's about, perhaps?'

'Please tell him I am Simon Mendelevski and it's about gold watches.'

The woman started to close the door when a tall, distinguished, bald man with a goatee beard dressed in an expensive three-piece suit and bowtie appeared behind her in the huge hallway.

'Thank you Joke, I'll handle this.'

The woman nodded and turned away, disappearing into a back room.

'I'm Matthijs van der Meer, how can I help?'

'I am Simon Mendelevski, son of a watchmaker, and my friend is Maaike de Vries and this is Irene. I think you had business with my father during the war.'

'You'd better come in, Joke will look after Maaike and Irene while we talk.' He rang a bell on a table in the hall and Joke reappeared. 'Joke, can you look after these two young ladies for me, I'm sure Irene would like some lemonade.'

Joke managed a smile for the first time. 'Of course, please come this way.'

Maaike looked at him anxiously, keen to stay with him. 'Will you be alright?'

It was too late, Irene had already taken Joke's hand and was halfway down the long hallway.

'Come into the study. Can I take your coat? Please sit down.'

He handed over his shabby overcoat and perched nervously on the edge of a studded leather armchair across from an enormous inlaid and highly polished mahogany desk. The room was hung with a huge number of paintings, mainly portraits reminiscent of the Golden Age paintings he had seen in the Rijksmuseum. An ornate pair of silver inkwells sat in a polished wooden tray, a brass reading lamp with a dark green glass shade and an ornate telephone occupied the desk. Everywhere he looked he saw antiques, old Delft pottery, paintings and items of precious metal or cut glass. Two large framed certificates hung on the wall behind the desk.

Van der Meer settled himself in a high-backed leather chair and rang a bell. Joke appeared again, and he ordered coffee. 'Is coffee alright or would you like something stronger?' He indicated a well stocked drinks cabinet.

'No, thank you, coffee is fine.'

Van der Meer looked at him, 'So Meneer Mendelevski, what can I do for you? May I call you Simon?'

'I think you bought three watches from my father. I'm trying to piece together the details of his last weeks of work. He died in Auschwitz.'

'I'm sorry to hear that. What about the rest of your family?'

'I was the only one of my family to survive, Meneer.'

'Please, call me Matthijs. So, your father was Mendelevski the watchmaker?'

'Yes, and I think he did some work for you.'

'That's correct. Your father made me three of the finest watches I have ever owned.'

He opened a drawer in the desk and took out a polished wooden tray with three gold pocket watches laid on a velvet cushion. 'Your father's finest work. Please handle them if you wish.'

Simon picked up one of the watches. It was much heavier than David Meijer's and the gold case totally enclosed the watch. He opened it to see a beautiful enamelled face and delicate hands.

'It's magnificent, isn't it? What a loss that your father can never again create more beautiful watches like that, he was so skilled. Press that catch there and open it up further. Now, remove that dust cover and look at the superb workmanship, the heart of the watch.'

He looked in awe at the wheels and spring, moving gently. He noticed 'A.M. Amsterdam' engraved proudly but discreetly inside. He gently replaced the watch in the tray.

'Thank you for letting me see them, I am so proud that my father could produce something so perfect. We were sent to Westerbork then on to Auschwitz in late 1942. My father only finished your watches just before we were arrested. I have his copy of the invoice he sent to you.'

Van der Meer interrupted him. 'He didn't send the invoice, it was delivered here by a man I think worked for your father. He also brought the watches with him and I paid him in cash. He just turned up here, like you did today. I was here with a client but Joke showed him in, he handed me the watches and the invoice, and I paid him. My client, like you, thought the watches the most beautiful objects. I do hope your father got the money by the way, it was in very large denomination notes.'

'I'm sure he did.' He thought of the large notes in the box. 'Yes, I'm sure he did.'

'To be honest I'd given up on ever seeing the finished articles. I sent my driver to check on your father's progress, but he came back and said your father had gone from his business address. That would have been sometime in 1941. I thought he had already been arrested or that he had registered the business and that all the assets had then been taken and compulsorily paid into the LIRO bank by the Nazis.'

'My father closed the business down in 1941 to avoid that and worked from home until we went into hiding.'

'You were in hiding?'

'Yes, and I think we were betrayed.' He looked at van der Meer, trying to gauge his reaction. 'I believe my father finished making your watches while we were hiding.'

'That's awful, so many of those who hid, both Jews like your family, and good Dutch patriots too, were betrayed.'

'Can I ask how you found my father to give him the work?'

'He was recommended as the best watchmaker in Amsterdam by a friend of mine who was the managing director of the company who supplied your father with parts.'

'Prins Horloges in Arnhem?'

'That's right, how did you know? My friend was killed in the fighting at Arnhem in 1944.'

'We found some of his invoices to my father. When did you order the watches?'

'I know exactly when it was, it was August 1940, three months after the invasion. I went to your father's workshop personally to place the order and talk money.'

'Did you provide the gold cases?'

'No, I left it all to him.'

'Can I ask why you ordered three watches?'

'That's a good question, how can I put it? After the invasion it was clear to me that money was going to be worthless or the guilder was likely to be replaced by the German mark, and I had a lot of very large denomination notes from some, let's call them unrecorded, dealings only I knew about before the war and also some money from commodities that I sold at a good rate in the days after the invasion in May. I saw gold as a good investment; beautiful watches in gold cases were even better.'

He felt himself suddenly become very angry. 'So you ditched your dirty money on my father?'

'Simon, Simon, calm down. Your father was an astute businessman as well as an outstanding watchmaker. He knew exactly what the situation was with the money. We agreed he could double the price. He drove a hard bargain, laundering the money if you want, he was no fool, so I actually paid him double what it said on his invoice. In fact, I was surprised when the man delivered it that your father raised an invoice for the transaction at all, if you follow me. I presume you have a copy?' He grinned. 'I can't show you mine, it has mysteriously disappeared.'

'I have father's copy. He even marked it 'paid'. He was always very correct with his paperwork.'

Van der Meer laughed. 'Even if it showed only half of the amount. It's a shame he's not still with us, I had all sorts of problems when they demonetised the old guilders last month. A few more gold watches would have been useful.'

He forced a smile, remembering his father's often slightly dubious business dealings and his eye for a bargain. Then it suddenly dawned on him that his father's decision to take van der Meer's dirty money had actually backfired, resulting in Simon being forced to accept only a third of the value when Jos had re-laundered it for him.

The coffee arrived and they made small talk. The atmosphere, on his side at least, was strained. He couldn't help feeling that van der Meer had used his father, but he was unsure whether he could have committed an even worse crime.

For his part van der Meer was a perfect host and gentleman, but it was clear that whatever business he was in, while clearly providing untold riches, was likely to be shady at best and questionable if not downright illegal at worst.

Joke came through with Maaike and Irene and they prepared to leave.

'Thank you both for coming. I hope I have filled in some blanks for you. If you ever need my help or advice, personal or professional, please telephone. Joke is my secretary, she will take a message. Take my card.'

"Matthijs van der Meer, Advocaat'. So you're a lawyer?'

Van der Meer smirked. 'Among other things. I have, shall we say, many interests.' He winked at Maaike. 'Goodbye Simon, goodbye my dear, tot ziens.'

Maaike was anxious to know all the details of his conversation with van der Meer. He told her about it as they walked to the tram stop.

'So Gerrit did deliver the invoice and the watches. Someone at that Arnhem company recommended your father, that's how van der Meer found him. He paid in those large notes as part of a special deal your father negotiated so the amount on the invoice was really just half of what was paid.'

'In a nutshell, yes. But it was dirty money from some obviously illegal dealings and my father saw an opportunity to benefit. I already knew he was crafty on occasions but this rather taints my view of him.'

'Simon, don't, please remember that when your father agreed to the deal the country had just been invaded by the Nazis, who were intent on wiping out your entire race. He probably thought that having more money might help, perhaps he hoped he could find somebody and pay them to help you all get away.'

'Maybe, I'm just totally confused and a little shocked. Father was often a bit cunning but the thought of him dealing with someone like van der Meer has upset me. I'm used to dealings within our own community where everyone was looking to outdo everyone else, it was like a game really.'

'We've established, I think, that van der Meer couldn't have known where you were hiding so he's not the one who betrayed you, right?'

'I suppose so, but he was an odious, creepy, patronising man. I wouldn't put anything past him, quite frankly. Like Jos said, he obviously did very well out of the war. I think he was probably a collaborator or that he made money out of dealing with the Germans somehow. It's obvious he wasn't cold or starving last winter.'

'He's not short of money, however he got it. That house was like nowhere I have ever been, the kitchen alone was bigger than my place on Slootstraat. One thing's for sure, Matthijs van der Meer wouldn't have needed the thirty guilders reward he would have got for betraying your family.'

He thought for a moment. 'Maybe not, Maaike, maybe not.'

They got back to Slootstraat just a few minutes before Grietje returned and came to collect Irene. The girl was excited to tell her mother all about 'the big house' she had visited that afternoon.

'In a moment, darling, I just want to ask Simon and Maaike something. What progress today then, you two?'

'We made some, I suppose.' Simon looked at Maaike for her agreement. 'Theo, the man on the ship, said his brother-in-law had delivered the watches to van der Meer and he confirmed it.'

'His was the luxury house Irene liked so much?'

Maaike chipped in, 'Oh Grietje, you should have seen it. It's the sort of place you can only dream about.'

'Not for the likes of us then,' said Grietje and quickly brought her down to earth. 'It sounds like the places I clean over at Vondel Park.'

'And not exactly legally obtained either, I suspect. I didn't take to him at all. Maaike doesn't think he could be the one who betrayed us though.'

'And you, what do you think?'

'In fairness it's difficult to see how it could have been him, he didn't know where we were hiding. Gerrit took the watches to him. But I didn't like him, everything about him was sleazy and I certainly wouldn't trust him.'

'But if he's off the list, where do you go now?'

'We still have to find Berger and somehow find out who is renting the stable at Kromme Palmstraat and if they had it in 1942, but all that's for another day. I have to go to the station this evening to ask about trains to Leeuwarden for Maaike so she can reply to her aunt, and then I need to write to father's insurance company and the Jewish Coordination Committee in Arnhem. I think they have an office here in Amsterdam somewhere, but I need to know the address.'

'But first you need to eat, both of you. Come on, upstairs, we'll eat together again tonight.' She took Irene's hand.

They looked at each other, shrugged and followed her.

TUESDAY 23RD OCTOBER 1945

'I can't write to Aunt Nel until I've asked Jos about time off.'

'Right, well, ask him tonight and agree the date at the same time. I'll go with you to help with changing trains at Amersfoort and you'll need to make sure someone can meet you at Zwolle when you change again. If they can't get there I'll go on to Zwolle with you and put you on the Leeuwarden train.'

'I'm sure one of my cousins will meet me, but it might be best if I give Aunt Nel a couple of dates, then she can write back to say which one is best.'

'All this writing makes it very complicated. Isn't your aunt on the telephone?'

'She certainly won't have one and probably has never used one, she's in rural Friesland not Amsterdam, remember. But I'll ask in the letter if there is a number I can contact her on.'

'How long are you thinking of going for?'

'I thought a week so I'll need five days off, oh, and I'll have to speak to Grietje about Irene. Maybe I'd better just make it a couple of days.'

'Grietje and I will manage somehow I'm sure, I think she's going to Utrecht again soon so maybe you could go while she's away. Ask her this afternoon before you ask Jos and before you write.'

She touched his leg and smiled. 'I was rather hoping we might spend some special time together the next time Grietje goes away and we have the house to ourselves. Won't you come with me to Leeuwarden? It would be nice.'

'I don't think your Aunt Nel would appreciate the 'special time' you have in mind.' He laughed and touched her hair.

'I'll miss you.'

'I'll miss you too. Now I have to get to work, it's half past two already. I'll post my letters on the way and I'll see you at six.'

'Can I go with you to see Nel, please Maaike? I promise I'll be good.'

Maaike laughed. 'Maybe one day, Irene, I think Mama is taking you to see your Oma and Opa again soon.'

'We have to be careful what we say in front of her, she's so bright, she picks up on everything,' said Simon.

Jos was behind the bar when he arrived at work. It was a typical weekday early evening.

'Simon, on time as always. How did things go yesterday afternoon?'

'It was just as you said, his house was huge, he had a female assistant, his study was amazing, but he was a very unpleasant character.'

'Made his money from the war?'

'Officially he's a lawyer, but, yes, he virtually said as much. He paid my father in those large denomination notes we found. It was a scheme to change that money into gold when the Germans invaded. He tempted my father with a double payment deal and my father agreed, probably because he thought having money might help us. At least, that's what I prefer to think.'

'The bastard, I just knew he was going to be a crafty bugger. I thought maybe I was being biased because of his smart address but having three gold watches especially made just smacked of black market dealings.' He smiled. 'After all I should know. Main thing is though, was he the one?'

'No, on reflection I don't think so, he wouldn't have known our address. It was just as Theo said. Gerrit turned up there with the watches and took the payment. He knew father had gone from Peperstraat, he sent his driver there to look for him and his watches but other than that he just sat at home until Gerrit arrived with the watches and my father's invoice, which of course he's destroyed.'

'So now what?'

'I rather hoped you had some news for me, about the car and the man we saw?'

'Tonight, I hope, I have another meeting with my contact. He will hopefully have the information we want.'

'Can I come with you to see him?'

'I'm sorry but that's not possible, he's passing me information from official police records. Apparently, it's all a bit confused at the moment, they're re-organising the police into municipal and Rijkspolitie because of what happened in the war and the records about cars might go to the national force. No one really knows who is in charge of them at the moment. I can't allow anyone to know who he is, and anyway, I need you here to work this evening.'

'What time are you going? Maaike wants to talk to you about some time off and I might need a couple of days too.'

'Bloody hell Simon, I can't manage if both of you are missing. Her upstairs would have to run the bar, who knows how many customers I'd lose. I'll be back by seven at the latest, it won't be a drinking session, just a quick meeting. We'll talk about it when Maaike's here.'

Maaike arrived at six. The usual crowd of early evening drinkers were in. Two of them flirted with her while the others discussed the mounting tension in the East Indies. Simon worked down in the cellar getting ready for the delivery the next day and stocking the bar with splits.

Jos was as good as his word, he was back just before seven and sober.

'Did you find out? Who was he?'

'Just a minute, be patient, I need a beer and a chat with Maaike.'

Maaike explained that she wanted to visit her father's sister and family but the train service meant changing at Amersfoort and Zwolle so arrangements had to be made to help her on the journey.

'How long would you be away?'

'I don't know yet, all contact with my aunt has been by letter so far so arranging it takes time, but a week maybe? It depends on Grietje too because of Irene.'

'And you, Simon?'

'I just need to go with Maaike to Amersfoort or maybe Zwolle. I'm not going to Aunt Nel's, and I'll be straight back.'

'Alright, if you could travel on a Sunday or Monday when we're closed it would help me, I'll leave it to you to tell me the dates. This lot are going to be unbearable while you're away.' Jos indicated the row of regulars at the bar. 'They'll probably stay at home or drink somewhere else until you get back. Only joking, you need to see your family and of course I understand.'

'Thank you. Simon persuaded me I should go, I haven't seen them since we moved away. My father wrote to say mother had been killed but I don't think he told them about me and now he's dead too.'

'Right then, that's decided. Now I need to talk to Simon, privately, away from these ears. He'll tell you later, I'm sure.'

Jos sat down in his corner while Simon perched on a beer crate.

'Well? Do you know who it was that we saw in Kromme Palmstraat?'

'I know who owns the car, it doesn't have to be the same man, but chances are it is. But I'm not sure it's going to take you much further.'

'Jos, please don't keep me in suspense, who is it?'

'The car is owned by Edwin B...'

He interrupted. 'Berger! I knew it! I knew it, it's him, he's the one, I just know it.'

'Hold on, it's not all good news, that's why I said it might not help much, the car is registered to the Lijnbaansgracht address.'

'But it can't be, it's an empty shop.'

'Maybe, but he's never notified the police of a change of address.'

'So we don't know where he lives. That means I still can't speak to him.'

'No, but if you're sure he's the one who betrayed you, do you really want to approach him? What are you going to say?'

'I can ask him about his two dealings with my father for a start.'

'And where is that going to get you? He's hardly likely to admit to selling you out to the Germans under your gentle questioning, is he?'

'It has to have been him. No one else could have known we were up above that stable.'

'But we don't know for sure if he was renting it during the time you were in hiding there.'

He sat in silence, thinking. 'It would be amazing if he wasn't, we know he put his stuff in storage in 1942. Couldn't we ask de Jong who they were renting it to?'

'They're hardly likely to tell us, and anyway it still won't help you find him, he probably hasn't told de Jong where he is living or trading from either. As long as he pays his rent they won't care.'

'Maybe we could keep watch until he visits again. It's all we have, it's the only way we're going to find him. The man in the bar on Lijnbaansgracht said Berger closed the shop there in 1942 and he didn't know if he was opening somewhere else or just putting the stock in storage long term. Is the stuff in the stable all his stock, in which case he isn't trading any more, or has he got a new shop somewhere? If he's not in business anymore I just don't see how we are ever going to trace him.'

'It's just not practical to watch the place twenty-four hours a day, seven days a week. Besides you can hardly challenge him in the street. We need to find his house or shop if there is one.'

'I suppose not, I was just grasping at straws. This is the end of the road then, I think I know who might have betrayed my family, but I can't confront him.'

'Not necessarily.' Jos gave him a conspiratorial look. 'Leave it with me. I know someone who might help.'

'You always know someone.'

Jos closed early so they walked along their favourite canal and sat on 'their' bench.

Maaike was excited about Jos's findings. 'So it looks like it was Berger after all.'

'Out of the people we know had some sort of business or contact with father after we went into hiding it certainly does look that way. It's not certain of course, but if he was the man renting the stable while we were hiding there, it looks very much like it.'

'I knew it. There is something not right about the two invoices between him and your father. How did the two get exchanged and, in particular, how did Berger's invoice get to your father? Like I said before, something just doesn't fit. I'll have to look at the invoice from Berger again, after all, what could he have been selling to your father? He was hardly likely to be buying antiques while he was in hiding and Berger was just as unlikely to be selling watch parts.'

'Perhaps it was for a watch case he supplied.'

'Maybe, but somehow I doubt it, all the other watches were ordered long before delivery. It took your father a long time to build a watch, yes?'

'Yes.'

'And these two invoices are close together date wise, so I doubt Berger supplied the case. In fact, I wonder if the watch ever existed, but don't ask me what the invoice was really for though.'

'What do you mean?'

'What if Berger was blackmailing your father and the invoice from him was really a demand for cash? I won't know what it was supposed to be for until I look at it again, but it might have been issued by Berger to cover where the money was coming from and why.'

'But why bother at all? Why not just demand cash from father?'

'That depends on how many others he was threatening and how much money he was getting. He might have had to devise a way of explaining it all in his records.'

'But father sent him an invoice for a watch.'

'Alright, so what if there was a watch, a very expensive one like those your father made for van der Meer, and Berger demanded it as another sort of blackmail payment? He might have wanted gold rather than just money, remember what van der

Meer said. You know what your father was like when it came to issuing paperwork to keep his records right, so he wrote one out for the watch. It's not marked 'paid', of course.'

'You think father may have got a demand for cash or payment in kind?'

'Or both.'

'It sounds a bit unlikely.'

'Have I been wrong so far? One thing's certain, Berger must have actually seen your father in late 1942, whether there was an exchange of goods or not. Even if it was just money and invoices, they must have met. It does explain everything, and have you got any better ideas?'

'No, I haven't, but Jos says he has. I don't know what he's got in mind this time, but you can bet it's going to be ever so slightly illegal.'

She laughed. 'Luckily I'm going to be away then, although I'd hate to miss any excitement.'

'Don't worry, I don't know what his plan is or when it's going to happen and we still have to sort out when you're going. I'll speak to Grietje tomorrow morning.'

'Can we speak to her together when she brings Irene down? After all I'm the one who will be going away and leaving her with a problem. I'll check that invoice from Berger to your father when we get home to see exactly what it was for.'

'Will it take us any further though? I've got to find him or at least figure out where he is now. But like Jos said, what am I going to say to him? What am I going to do even if I can prove he betrayed us? I'm useless, out of my depth, kidding myself.'

'Do you want to stop then? Have we taken it as far as we can?'

'I really don't know, for my parents and Esther I feel I have to trace whoever did it, but it won't change anything. I've lost my family and turned my back on my religion, my faith and even who I am, sometimes I've even tried to forget I'm a Jew.'

'But for your own peace of mind?'

'I'll never be at peace, it's always going to be there gnawing away at me, but even if I identify the culprit it won't bring them back. It won't blot out Auschwitz and why they died when I didn't.'

'It might help you to start rebuilding your life though, I don't think you can start again until you know for certain or until you can go no further.'

'We'll have to wait and see what Jos can come up with. Of course, it doesn't even have to be Berger, it might be someone we know nothing about at all and that possibility is even worse. This has taken over my life.'

'I hope there's room left for me.'

'I'm sorry, but when Jos said Berger was the owner of the car we'd seen at Kromme Palmstraat I was so excited, I was convinced it was him, then Jos said there was no more information. It was like a kick in the teeth.'

She stroked his arm and kissed him on the cheek. 'You're just tearing yourself apart, we're going around in circles. Let's see what tomorrow brings.'

WEDNESDAY 24TH OCTOBER 1945

Grietje wasn't pleased at first when they told her about Maaike's proposed trip but when they explained that they would try to fit in with her plans and that he was only accompanying Maaike as far as either Amersfoort or Zwolle, she mellowed. She agreed to ask one of her clients for a couple of days off to go with some time she had already arranged with another client who was going to be abroad on business.

He left it to them to finalise as he had to get to work for the brewery delivery and he also wanted to get another look through the gap in the stable doors at Kromme Palmstraat. If he was honest he was somehow hoping that Berger would be there, but of course it was a silly idea. As Jos had remarked, what was he going to say if he saw him? The last thing he wanted would be for Berger to come up behind him as he was peering through the crack in the doors.

He had just enough time to go to the stable before work. He hurried across the busy Westerstraat and Lindengracht then through the narrow residential streets until he came to the broad Palmgracht and the short dog-leg alley that was Kromme Palmstraat.

He was apprehensive approaching 3B, half expecting Berger to suddenly appear, but the doors to the stable were securely locked, the heavy padlock and chain barring entry to all but Berger himself. He looked each way before pressing his eye to the doors. Just sufficient light came in through the gaps for him to see the stall and the furniture and crates stored there. He had imagined he would be able to gauge if it constituted Berger's entire stock or just excess items, but soon gave up on the idea. Nothing appeared to have changed since he last looked, four of the eight stalls were full, but it was impossible to tell what was contained in the various crates.

Suddenly he heard a voice behind him. 'You again. You've missed him, he was here yesterday in his car, he normally comes at weekends or on Tuesdays. He delivered some stuff yesterday, so I don't expect I'll see him for a couple of days. He often collects on a Saturday. Shall I tell him you're looking for him?'

He panicked and said the first thing that came into his head. 'No, no, really, it's alright. I'll go to his shop and see him there. I want to surprise him, but I just keep missing him. Please don't tell him I was asking for him, you'll spoil the surprise, we're old friends, you see.'

'Suit yourself, I was only trying to help. Looking at him, I suppose he's got a really posh shop up in town, Spiegelgracht probably or somewhere like that. Antiques and things?'

'That's right, and thanks for the offer.'

The woman showed no sign of going back into her house so he smiled weakly, moved away and walked out onto Lijnbaansgracht. He ran to work, afraid of being late. Crossing Bloemgracht and Egelantiersgracht he marvelled at the colour of the trees and the carpet of the leaves now covering the ground and the still surface of the water. A heron stood motionless on a houseboat, staring down into a patch of clear water. He decided that, despite its heavy concentration of run down and in places virtually derelict houses, the Jordan was the most diverse and oddly beautiful district ot the city.

As he approached the bar he saw the dray pulling up outside and Jos, complete with his leather cellar apron, in the doorway. 'Come on lad, you're late.'

'Sorry, I was at Kromme Palmstraat'.

'What the hell for? No, tell me later, let's get this man unloaded so he can be on his way.'

The drayman, presumably in the hope of a free beer, was unusually helpful and the three of them made short work of the delivery and loading the empties. Refreshed with a bottle of Brand, the drayman went on his way and Simon and Jos settled down for a well-earned coffee in the cellar.

'Sorry I was a bit late.'

'Don't worry, you're normally so prompt, that's all. Well, go on, what were you doing at Kromme Palmstraat? As if I didn't know.'

'It was a bit stupid really, I suppose. I just thought Berger might be there.'

'You silly young bugger, and exactly what were you going to say if he was there?'

'I don't know, I hadn't thought it through, but I'm so sure he's the one. Anyway, he wasn't there so the problem didn't arise.'

'Don't risk it again.'

'The nosy woman from across the road came out. She misses nothing, in fact if Berger didn't give us away to the Germans she'd be my next suspect. She said Berger often comes on Tuesdays or Saturdays and that he was there yesterday delivering something.'

'That fits, it was Saturday afternoon when we saw him, remember? It's also very useful for what I have in mind.'

'What are you planning? Which of your 'contacts' can help this time?'

'Wait and see, wait and see.' He grinned. 'Trust old Jos.'

'She said she thinks he might have a shop in the city somewhere, a posh shop, she called it.'

'Do you realise how many antique and second-hand shops there are to choose from in Amsterdam? They're all over the place, so that doesn't help us much. Now, can you manage until Maaike arrives? I need to go out and look for someone.'

'Of course.' He looked at Jos who winked at him and finished his coffee.

Things were very quiet most of the afternoon. Jos's wife put her head around the door at about three, more he suspected to see if her husband was back than to check on him or to see if he needed any help.

The regulars started to arrive at about four, taking their places on the stools at the bar.

All the talk was about Quisling, the Norwegian collaborator Prime Minister, whose execution earlier that day had just been announced on Dutch radio. Attention naturally turned to Anton Mussert and when he was going to be executed. One regular pointed out that he had not even been tried yet, but his friends regarded that as a total inconsequence and urged the Dutch government to 'get on with it'.

It began to get busy at about five thirty with men stopping for a beer on the way home from work and he was pleased to see Maaike arrive at six.

'I don't know where Jos is or what he's up to, he left me here at about eleven.'

She laughed, indicating upstairs. 'He'll be in for it with her when he finally gets back, I expect.'

'Did you sort anything out with Grietje?'

'She's going to Utrecht a week on Monday, staying until Friday. You could take me to either Amersfoort or Zwolle on the same day and you'll be back at work on the Tuesday, so Jos will only be missing me for the week.'

'So when will you be back?'

'If it's alright with Jos and Aunt Nel, I thought I could come back on the following Monday as it's your day off so you can meet me.'

'You'll be away for a whole week?' He frowned and looked disappointed.

'I don't have to go, but it was your idea, remember?'

'I know, and I do think it's important that you see your family, it will soon pass I expect.'

'I'll ask Jos if it's alright with him, if he ever gets back. Then I'll write to Aunt Nel and ask her for a telephone number so I can make the final arrangements about who's meeting me and where.'

Jos arrived back after eight, slightly the worse for drink but he had been away for ten hours so neither Simon nor Maaike were surprised. 'Hello you two, looking after my bar, I hope. I'm sorry I've been so long, but the man I was looking for was rather elusive and I had to visit a number of bars before I found him. But good news, he's willing to help us. Come downstairs and I'll tell you about my plan. Can you manage, Maaike?'

'I'm fine, they know that if they want drinks at tables or upstairs they'll have to collect it. Go on, off you go. I hope you're going to let me in on it later, Simon.'

Jos settled himself in his chair and opened two bottles of beer, passing one to Simon. 'Come on, do tell me, what are you planning?'

'I don't really know how to put this. I don't know if you'll like it. It's a little bit illegal. No, it's more than that, it's totally illegal, but it's all I can think of to try to make progress on your problem.'

Simon was doubtful. 'Go on.'

'I think it's clear you're at the end of the road trying to trace Berger, but you're convinced he's the one you're looking for so....'

'Yes, yes, go on, spit it out.'

'There's only one thing left that we can definitely connect to him.'

'The stable.'

'Got it in one. That bloody stable and his stuff that's in it.'

'Continue.'

'For goodness sake Simon, you've got to be the most innocent lad I've ever met.' Jos was totally exasperated. 'We've got to get in there, look at what he's got stored. Maybe there will be something that will give us an address or lead us to him.'

'Get in there? How can we possibly do that?'

'We probably can't, but I know a man who can, and we can go in with him.'

'Break in, you mean?' Simon sounded horrified. 'I really don't think....'

'There won't be any 'breaking' as you put it. My contact is a wizard with locks.'

'What if Berger turns up while we're in there?'

'Thanks to your chat with the neighbour, we know the days he's most likely to appear, so we'll avoid those days and go early in the morning when it's quiet. We can't go after dark as we'd need a torch and the light might be spotted. I think the neighbour is a bigger danger than the man himself. She sounds like she's always at the window and if she sees us she might tell him.'

'How can we do it then?'

'As early as possible, first light, just after dawn, and hope she's still in bed. You don't have to come, you know. My friend and I can go on our own. We're just looking for an address on paperwork and how much stuff is in there.'

'Your friend won't steal anything, will he? Promise me.'

Jos looked at him angrily. 'What do you think he is? He's doing you a favour as he's a good friend of mine. Don't insult him or me!'

'I'm really sorry, this is all a bit strange to me but of course I'm coming with you. When can we do it?'

'My friend is coming here on Saturday, he wants to meet you and talk to you before he agrees. He's naturally a bit suspicious, in case you're the police or something. I've vouched for you, but he wants to see you for himself.'

'Policeman? Do I look like a policeman?'

'No, you're far too intelligent.' Jos laughed and opened another bottle just as his wife appeared at the top of the cellar steps.

'And where the hell have you been all day, Jos van Loon?'

'Sorry my dear, important business.' He started to giggle uncontrollably which only made his wife even angrier.

'Get your arse to work in that bar and you too, Jewboy, the tables are filthy, the ashtrays are full and the crippled girl needs help.'

Jos was still giggling as she stormed out. 'Well that told us, come on, better do as she says. It's alright for you and Maaike, you go home at night, I have to stay here with her.'

Simon told Maaike all about Jos's plan as they walked home.

She stopped and looked hard at him. 'I don't like it. It's breaking the law, you could get caught, and what's it going to achieve?'

'We won't know until we try, there's nothing left. I'm out of ideas, so anything is worth a try. What did Berger's invoice to my father say?'

'Strangely it was for exactly the same amount as the one from your father to him. It just said 'goods' and your father had written 'paid' on it and dated it 3rd October 1942.'

'Goods? That's ridiculous. What would my father want with 'goods' from an antique dealer? We were a family of Jews living in hiding in an unoccupied furnished apartment. I never saw any antique goods being delivered, in fact I never saw anything delivered. All we had was what was already in the place, the few bits of clothing and small stuff my parents brought from Dijkstraat plus the supplies Gerrit brought in to us. I'm even more sure now that Berger is the one and that you were right about the invoices being just to cover money, and possibly a watch, that Berger was blackmailing out of my family under threat of exposing us.'

'If your father had given in and was paying, why would Berger tell the Germans?'

'I don't know, perhaps father said 'no more' and stopped paying.'

'Is it worth breaking into the stable though? You may not find out anything.'

'But we just might and there's nowhere else left to go.'

She reluctantly agreed. 'Be careful that's all, I'm not visiting you in prison.' She smiled and lifted her face to kiss him. 'When will it be?'

'I don't know yet, I think we're arranging it on Saturday.'

'Just make sure it's done before I go to Friesland, I need to know you're safe before I leave.'

They walked slowly back to Slootstraat. In his mind, the immorality of what Jos had suggested they should do was fighting with his determination to find Berger and somehow prove his guilt.

They kissed goodnight on the step outside. She pressed herself against him and his hand moved onto her breasts.

SATURDAY 27TH OCTOBER 1945

Jos hadn't said what time his padlock expert was coming to see him. Friday evening had been very busy, and Jos had kept the bar open until one in the morning. He and Maaike had been very late home but he was up early as usual to go to the market. As Grietje was working and Maaike was looking after Irene, he went shopping for them both. Grietje had now agreed to let him pay for the shopping as part of his financial contribution but Maaike still insisted on being independent and paying her own way. He decided to try to slip in some extra items for her as she was feeding him lunch on most days.

He was frustrated that he'd not been able to make any progress for two days. He and Maaike had spent Thursday morning together. She had written to her aunt, giving her the dates for her visit and asking for the telephone number of a neighbour. Jos had agreed that if it could be arranged, she could use his telephone upstairs in the bar. He had started to sort through his father's correspondence again in the hope of finding any letters or notes that might yield more clues, especially to Berger, but there were so many that by lunchtime he had barely scratched the surface. After lunch he had visited the dentist for what he was told would have to be the first of many visits to sort out his neglected teeth.

He'd received a letter on Friday, his first ever mail other than birthday cards as a boy. It was a reply from his father's insurance company in The Hague. He had sent details and the numbers of all four policies but now they were asking for death certificates for his parents and Esther and they also pointed out that no premiums had been paid since May 1942. He decided to ask Jos or, when they replied, the Jewish Co-ordinating Committee for advice, but it looked like the insurers were not going to pay. He recalled that another survivor he had met at the Red Cross office had told him that the Germans had confiscated money held by insurance companies on policies taken out by Jews as well as Jewish money in the banks.

He was becoming quite proficient at shopping and a number of the regular women at the market were starting to recognise him. He finished the shopping by nine thirty and delivered Maaike's to her. She was playing with Irene, but he could see she was tired after their late shift the previous evening. He dropped off the items for him and Grietje and was at work by ten thirty.

Jos was cleaning up in the bar, having left that task the previous evening. 'Good morning, bright and early. That's good, give me a hand with these empties and finish mopping the floor, why the buggers don't use the ashtrays I don't know and sometimes I think they spill more beer than they pour down their throats. I'll catch up on washing glasses and restocking. How are you?'

'I'm tired, last night was a late one and I had shopping duties this morning. Maaike's shattered and she's got Grietje's daughter to look after as well.'

'Sorry lad, but the business is still getting back on its feet, if they want to drink I'd be a bloody fool not to sell to them, wouldn't I? Anyway, there's overtime in it for both of you.'

'I wanted to talk to you about money, Jos.'

'I hope you don't want a pay rise.'

'No, no, nothing like that. I've still got money downstairs and you pay me a good rate but I want to get my own place and set myself up properly. I thought the life insurance policies we found in the box would bring in some more money but it looks like the insurers are not going to pay out. Look at their letter.'

Jos studied the letter carefully. 'It looks to me like you've had it, Simon. They've got you all ways, how can you possibly get death certificates and you can't get around the fact that the premiums weren't paid. I'll ask someone who knows more than me if you want, but I think that's it. You can write back and point out where they died and when you were all taken but you'll need a lawyer, I reckon. Your friend van der Meer maybe, he sounds like a clever devil,' he joked. 'Seriously, I bet there are going to be hundreds of people, many of them Jews who survived the camps or came out of hiding, in exactly the same situation as you. In fairness to the insurance people, if the Nazis took the money the insurers are powerless too, it's all going to take years to sort out.'

'I suppose the same applies to our house?'

'I'm afraid it might, but you want to be careful there. I'm sure the city council is going to try to screw returning residents for unpaid rents, taxes and city rates. Are you sure your father owned it outright? You should check the paperwork carefully.'

'It's starting to look like those of us who survived are not going to get any sympathy or help to get our property back, or any money that is due to us.'

'I'm afraid you're right, and don't forget all the money and deeds and valuables that were declared and paid into that Nazi run bank. Thank goodness your father didn't follow the instructions and hid that stuff in his box instead.'

'That's the other thing I need to do. Can you speak to someone about selling the gold for me, all the coins and the watch cases? I'll just keep father's tools, stamps and David Meijer's watch.'

'I will if you want, if you trust me, that is. I'll need to find out the current gold price and then calculate the weight. I know someone who knows someone who buys gold. We might have to weigh a coin of each size.'

'Of course I trust you, you've been so good to me, I couldn't have done anything without your help and contacts. You've been like a father, I suppose.'

'Father indeed! You cheeky young bugger! Seriously speaking I'm quite touched, it's a nice thing for you to say. Why are you in a hurry to turn all the gold into money? You've still got a lot of money in notes.'

'I can't carry bags of gold coins around, can I? Opening a bank account is difficult and going on what you said they're not going to make it easy for us Jews to sort that out either. Besides, I have plans, well, dreams really. I'm not sure I want to stay in Amsterdam or even the Netherlands for the rest of my life. I need to broaden my horizons; my life so far has been the Jodenbuurt and Auschwitz.'

'What have you got in mind? Where are you hoping to go?'

'I've no idea yet but not a word to Maaike, please. Promise me.'

'Of course, but don't hurt her or you'll have me to deal with, I feel like her father too, you know.'

He nodded. 'I know and I thank you for it. I'll never let her down Jos, she's part of my plan, if she wants to be. I think I love her.'

'Bloody hell lad, that's a bold statement and very dangerous. I told her upstairs I loved her once, now look at me. Come on, get that door open and let them in. I'll make coffee.'

'Before I do that, when is he coming, the padlock man?'

'I don't know, but it will be when it's quiet, maybe very early this evening. Now get the bloody door open and earn those wages.'

All the talk at the bar was of another Nazi who had cheated the executioner. News had come through that Robert Ley had committed suicide two days earlier, ahead of the big trial in Nuremberg. Simon had never heard of him and didn't know if he had had anything to do with the camps. The attitude of most of the regulars was that he had saved the Allies a bullet or a rope by doing the job himself, but some thought he should have stood trial.

Daft Willem had a rather radical view. 'If they don't get on with it, the rate they're doing themselves in, there'll be nobody left to execute soon. I wrote to the Queen and volunteered to do it, you know.'

Hendrik was much more interested in matters closer to home.

'So long as that bastard Mussert doesn't do away with himself before the firing squad get to him.'

Lunchtime was hectic as usual on a Saturday and many of the female customers who called in for a drink and to rest their arms from carrying shopping recognised him from the market.

'They like you Simon, good-looking young lad behind the bar. Some of these old girls will stay for an extra bessen just to chat with you, isn't that right, Liese?'

Liese, a fat middle-aged woman with a hairy top lip who was smoking a pipe, looked him up and down. 'He's a bit scrawny but I'll have him if Grietje Blok doesn't want him.'

Jos turned to him and winked. 'Maaike might have something to say about that, eh Simon?'

He felt himself blushing and made an excuse to go outside to collect glasses.

Jos's wife came down at about one and the three of them worked hard all afternoon. She sat on Maaike's stool serving beers to those lining the bar, Jos took trays to those upstairs and outside while Simon washed glasses, emptied ashtrays and brought up crates.

By four thirty many of the lunchtime and afternoon customers had left and Jos's wife made a swift escape upstairs, leaving just him and Jos to manage until Maaike arrived at six.

Soon afterwards a small man of about fifty with heavily tattooed hands and neck came in and spoke to Jos. They came over to the bar together and sat on two of the vacant stools.

'Simon, this is a friend of mine, you can just call him Piet.'

To Piet he said, 'This is Simon, he's the one with the problem you might be able to help with.'

Simon held out his hand, but the man ignored him and just nodded in his direction. 'Pour him a beer, please. We can't talk here, too many ears. I'll take Piet downstairs and give him the details and you can join us when Maaike arrives.'

Maaike was early so he was able to join them in the cellar after only a few minutes. They were sitting in Jos's 'hideaway' corner and he noticed Jos had given Piet the chair while he perched on a beer crate.

'I've told Piet the details and the address, 3B, wasn't it? Green double stable doors. I've also told him the man often visits on Saturdays and Tuesdays and that there's a nosey neighbour. He wants to have a look at the place tonight and he suggests we do it as early as possible, at first light on a Sunday preferably as the woman will hopefully still be in bed.'

Piet sat in total silence, letting Jos do all the talking.

'I have explained that you want to go and look at whatever is stored there. He's not happy, but he understands your reasons, so he has agreed you can be there. I'll be the lookout in the street. We leave when he says we leave, we disturb nothing and only look in crates or boxes that are already open. Agreed? If you don't agree we don't go, and Piet here has another beer and leaves.'

'Of course, whatever Piet wants. I'm really very grateful you're doing this for me, thank you.'

Piet spoke at last in a heavy accent he didn't recognise. 'I'm doing it for Jos as he's a friend and he tells me you've had a shit time so if I can help to identity whoever betrayed you, I will.' A smile crossed his normally serious face. 'It will be the first time that I've opened a lock and gone in somewhere without actually taking anything.'

The two men stood up. Simon offered his hand but once again it was ignored. Piet finished his beer and he and Jos went up into the bar and out into the street.

Maaike wanted to know what was going on. Simon told her Piet was the man who was going to open the doors at Kromme Palmstraat.

'He looks really evil, can you trust a man like that?'

'I've got no choice, I have to, and he has to trust me even more I suppose.'

'But who is he? What's his name? Where's he from?'

'I don't know anything about him, I think that's the idea. He's just 'Piet', one of Jos's contacts.'

'His most frightening contact yet. Where does Jos get all these people from? Money changers who also steal jewellery, a man who can open any lock. What next I wonder?'

He thought it best not to tell her that he would be going in with Jos and Piet.

Piet came back at ten thirty. Maaike gave him a fierce look as she poured his beer and he disappeared with Jos into the cellar. They spoke very briefly before he left again, placing his empty glass on the bar and smiling at Maaike as he passed. Jos called Simon down to the cellar a few minutes later.

'It's tomorrow morning, be here at six thirty.'

He was suddenly very frightened. After desperately wanting to get into the stable to look at Berger's store of goods in the vain hope of finding a clue, now it was actually happening he wanted to back out.

'It will be alright, won't it? I've never done anything like this before.'

'There are a lot of things you haven't done, young Simon, but if you can get through what you've experienced in the last three years you can do this. Of course it'll be fine, don't worry, Piet is an expert. How do you think he's still free and not in prison?'

'True, but does it have to be tomorrow?'

'It's October, the mornings are going to get darker, we don't want to be going in there when dawn is at eight or nine, the nosey old girl might be up, so the sooner the better. We'll have to bring torches as it is.'

'I thought you said no lights in case they're seen.'

'Yes, but I forgot that when the doors are closed behind you it's going to be dark in there. I've got two torches I used in the war, they have a metal shield to shade the light downwards. You can use those but don't flash them about, especially upwards.'

'You're going to shut us in?' he asked in a total panic.

'You won't be shut in but I'll have to close the doors, we can't leave them wide open.'

'Maaike mustn't know, Jos.'

'Of course, now get back in that bar. It's Saturday night, we're getting busy.'

He was relieved that he had no time to talk to Maaike during the evening. Once again Jos stayed open after eleven despite the fact that both he and Simon had to be up before dawn the next day.

As they walked home Maaike was clearly even more worried about the plan after seeing Piet.

'Doesn't Jos know anyone who isn't a criminal?'

He laughed out loud.

'What did I say that's so funny?'

'I asked him exactly the same thing earlier. He said it wasn't possible to work on the docks and run a small bar in the Jordaan without meeting a few criminals. Then he said he knew two who weren't, me and you.'

'It'll just be me soon, you'll have joined the criminal classes. So, when are you doing it?'

He felt guilty as he lied to her for the first time, but he didn't want to worry her any more. 'I'm not quite sure, soon I expect.'

'Thank goodness we're not working tomorrow and I don't have Irene. We can both get up late. Will you come down and see me after lunch? Perhaps we can go out somewhere.'

'I'd like that.'

SUNDAY 28TH OCTOBER 1945

He hardly slept at all. He was terrified he would oversleep, so he borrowed the old brass alarm clock Grietje used as a timer in the kitchen when she was making cakes. He worried it would wake her and Irene when it went off, so he slept with it under his pillow in an attempt to lessen the noise. He needn't have bothered; he was awake at two, three and five so eventually he turned off the alarm and got up, dressed as quietly as possible, and went down the bare wooden stairs carrying his shoes, carefully avoiding the two squeaky ones so as not to wake Maaike. He replaced the alarm clock and went out into the street, sitting on the step to put on his shoes.

It was still dark as he made his way slowly through the narrow streets towards the bar. Everywhere was virtually deserted with just the odd tram driver or railway worker carrying his lunch and a can of coffee on his way to work the early shift. There was a hint of rain in the air and he was grateful for the overcoat. Here and there a light came on in a window and he heard a tyre-less bicycle rattling along a street nearby.

He was at the bar before six, so he sat on the bench outside, loathe to wake Jos any earlier than necessary. After about half an hour a light went on upstairs, followed after a few minutes by one in the bar. The door opened and Jos peered out.

'I thought you'd be here, come in, come in, but keep it quiet, I don't want to wake her upstairs. I've made coffee, it's on the bar.'

They sat at a table just inside the door.

'It smells fresh out there, I think it's going to be a nice day.'

'It feels like rain at the moment.'

'Never mind lad, you'll be back home and in bed again by nine.'

'I'm still worried about this, excited but worried.'

'Don't be, I'll be keeping watch at the bend in the road so I can see both the Lijnbaansgracht and Palmgracht ends. If he should turn up, which he won't at this hour, it'll be in his car and I'll hear the car and see the headlights in plenty of time.'

'What will you do though? We'll be inside, there won't be time for us to get out and lock the doors again.'

'I don't know, I'll worry about it if it happens. I'll think of something.' He laughed and said, 'Run in front of him and act drunk, lay down in the road, I don't know, I haven't really thought about it.'

'It's not funny Jos, I'm scared.'

'Stop worrying, you'll be in and out, Piet isn't going to let you look around for long.'

'What about the woman opposite?'

'Unless she's a tram driver I don't see her actually coming out or looking out of the window at this hour either, even if she's up and awake, which I doubt. Piet isn't exactly going to rattle the lock and chain. If the light goes on I'll be straight to the doors to get you out.'

'But what if she does come out or look out?'

'I'll charm her so she'll only have eyes for me.'

'Seriously, what will we do?'

'Run like hell, you'll be in third place behind me and Piet.' He laughed again. 'Just don't let her recognise you. She'll tell Berger, if and when she sees him, that some men were in his lock up, he'll find there's nothing missing, so end of story. All he'll do is add another lock or two. Come on, let's go, we're meeting Piet there, I've got the torches.'

They made their way quickly towards Palmgracht without seeing another soul. It was not yet dawn, but the outline of roofs and gables was becoming visible to the east. As they crossed Palmstraat a figure stepped suddenly and silently out of a doorway and joined them.

'Ready to go?'

'Of course, the lad here is shitting himself though.'

They crossed Palmgracht and turned left towards Kromme Palmstraat.

'You walk through to the other end and check it out, we'll wait here until you call us in. Leave the torches with us,' Piet instructed Jos.

After a few moments Jos gave a low whistle from somewhere near the bend halfway down the street.

'Right, come on and keep quiet.'

He and Piet went straight up to the doors. As they approached, he could see Jos virtually outside the nosey woman's house, looking carefully to his left and right in order to observe both ends of the street.

Piet produced a ring of keys and after trying only two or three opened the padlock before gently pulling the heavy chain through the hasp.

Simon reached to open the doors but Piet grabbed his arm and whispered, 'Steady lad, slowly, slowly, we only need to open one enough to slip through and do it carefully in case it scrapes on the ground or those hinges squeak.'

Dawn was breaking by the time they went inside but, despite trying to adjust his eyes, after pulling the door closed it was too dark and he couldn't see anything. Piet switched on his torch so he did the same.

'Keep it pointing down, don't flash it about. Now what do you want to look at?'

'There's just so much I don't know where to start.'

'Get looking, I'm not staying here all day, in and out, that's me.'

Together they shone their torches over the stalls.

Piet cast what was obviously an experienced eye over the

furniture. 'There's some really nice antique stuff here. Look at that inlaid desk, that bureau, those chairs and that lamp. It's all expensive stuff but not enough to stock a shop. This is just a store I reckon.' He pointed to some open crates and boxes. 'What about those?'

Together they examined a number of wooden crates of all shapes and sizes.

'Look at the labels. You want an address for this man, don't you?'

'They all say Lijnbaansgracht, that's his old shop address. They look like old boxes.'

'Let's look at the labels on those over there, the ones that haven't been opened, they look newer.'

'Lijnbaansgracht again and this place, Kromme Palmstraat.' He shone his torch on a label. 'Bloody hell, look closely, they're in German. Look at that, it's the Nazi eagle. These are from German forces.'

'Stuff he bought after the war, when they surrendered?'

'No, they're addressed to him by name, they're not just boxes of military surplus. Look at the dates. He's been dealing with the Germans, I bet.'

'Can't we open one?'

'Don't be stupid, we can't let him know we've been here. Check out some more of the open ones over there, I'll look here. Get on with it, two minutes and we're going, what are you waiting for?'

'I've just realised, this piece of furniture here, and that one over there, and that piece there.'

'What are you talking about?'

'Some of it is Jewish, I just know it's Jewish stuff, it's just like the things we had at home. I'd know it anywhere, look at some of the symbols carved on that cupboard door. I just know it's from a Jewish home.'

'The rest of the stuff is antique and very Dutch, I've been inside enough rich Dutch houses to recognise quality.'

'Maybe, but all that lot is from Jewish homes.'

'Get looking in those the crates and let's get out of here. What have you got?'

'More Jewish items: tzedakah boxes, menorahs, some silver Kiddush cups, everything. There's a pile of mezuzahs, they were on door frames in Jewish houses, and there's even an aron kodesh, a holy ark, which belongs in the shul. He's been robbing Jews.'

'I've got paintings, small antiques and silverware in this one, I don't think they're particularly Jewish, but come and look.'

Simon shone his torch down into the crate and suddenly he reached down and grabbed a book, frantically opening it. He shook as he looked at the inside of the cover. Trembling, he turned to Piet. 'It's mine, it's one of my medical books, I brought it with me when we were hiding. There's more. That's mine too, and that's mother's.' He started to gather up the things just as Jos whistled.

They froze.

'Come on, out now!' Jos hissed. 'The old woman's bedroom light is on, her old man must have got up for a piss or something. It's almost daylight. Let's get out of here.'

Piet turned to Simon. 'Put them back as you found them and let's go. There's no time.'

'But they belong to me and my family! I have to see if there's a painting of a girl in there.'

'No, come on!' Piet dragged him away and pushed him out into the street and Jos's arms.

'What's going on?'

'I'll tell you later, this silly young sod took a liking to some stuff.' He quietly re-threaded the chain, snapped the lock closed and they hurried away.

Back at the bar Jos poured Piet and himself large Canadian Club whiskies.

'What went on in there?'

'Better ask the lad.'

Simon had tears rolling down his face and felt unable to speak.

'Simon, come on, what happened in there? Did you find out where he lives or where his new shop is? If he's got one, of course. Whatever's the matter with you, boy?'

'He's upset. He found a whole load of Jewish religious stuff and what he says is Jewish furniture. There were some very tasty Dutch antiques, furniture, paintings and silverware in there too, made my fingers twitch, I can tell you. I don't know how I resisted, I must be going soft. There's not enough there for a shop, it's only his storage, I'm sure of that, but we had no luck finding an address or anything.'

Simon spoke at last. 'That's only half the story, I know now it was definitely Berger, some of our things were in there; my books, father's books, mother's things, all the stuff we left behind when we were taken away. As well as betraying us he stole our belongings. I bet the painting of the girl is in there somewhere, but I had no time to look. There were crates and crates of things he's obviously got from Jewish homes, there was even stuff from the shul.'

'Probably bought them from the police or the Nazis or both, they didn't turn in half the stuff they collected from Jewish homes after the occupants were shipped out, my mate in the police told me that.'

'There were crates that hadn't even been opened with German labels on them, he was obviously dealing with them. I think the lad's right, whoever owns that stuff is an evil bastard.'

'But I still don't know where to find him. I was desperately hoping we would find an address or a clue in the stable but nothing. I'm even more certain now that he's the one but I'll never find him. Like you said Jos, we can't stand outside the stable for ever.'

'We will, we will, and when we do I'll have a word with him for you, make no mistake about that.'

'There were so many Jewish things there, not just from my family but things from others who probably suffered the same fate. Perhaps he was betraying lots of Jews and not just us.'

'Not necessarily, like I said, he may have just bought them.'

'Whatever, the point is he profited from Jewish families being arrested and killed and he was working with the Germans. While I'm more sure than ever that it was him, there's still the biggest question of all. How did he find out about us being upstairs? I've got to know, I've got to know if we gave ourselves away or worse, if it was me personally in some way. It's killing me not knowing. If I do find him that's the first thing I want to find out.'

'I'll get it out of him if ever we meet, I promise.'

Piet drained his glass. 'I must be off, call me if you ever need a lock sorted.'

'Can I pay you for your help Piet?'

'Keep your money lad, don't insult me. I did it as a favour to Jos and because you've had it bloody hard. I don't want paying, in fact I rather enjoyed it, made a change from my normal lock opening adventures if you follow me.' He laughed, his stern face showing some emotion for the first time. 'Find out where his shop is and we'll take a look in there too if you want. Tot ziens.'

'Thanks for arranging this for me Jos, I appreciate it.'

'Don't mention it, I'm just sorry we're no further forward. Now get off home before Grietje gets up and starts asking questions. What are you going to tell Maaike?'

'Everything, I suppose, I've got to tell somebody.'

A screech came from upstairs. 'Jos van Loon, what the bloody hell are you up to? Who have you got down there? Get your fat arse up here now!'

Simon made his way slowly back to Slootstraat.

Jos was right, it had turned into a beautiful autumnal Amsterdam morning. The streets were still relatively quiet as it was Sunday, but he passed a number of Jordaan locals on route to the early morning service at the Noorderkerk.

Grietje and Irene were already up when he walked in.

'Where on earth have you been? I've been worried. Irene woke up early and I had to take her downstairs to the toilet and you weren't in your room.' She looked guilty. 'I even asked Maaike, I thought you might have spent the night with her, I'm sorry.'

'Oh Grietje, you didn't. How could you?' He sounded hurt and he was angry, but he was actually more concerned that Maaike would have to be told where he'd been.

WEDNESDAY 31ST OCTOBER 1945

He and Maaike hadn't spoken since Sunday afternoon. He'd gone down to see her straight after speaking to Grietje and tried to tell her about what they'd found in the stable, but it had quickly developed into a huge argument because he had lied to her. He had tried to explain that he had thought it best not to tell her as she had been so worried about it. He was upset as he wanted to share things with her. He desperately needed to talk to someone about it, especially about finding some of his own family's possessions.

They had spent their day off on Monday apart. He went through his father's letters again, separating the business ones from those between his parents, hoping to find something he had missed but without success. All that appeared to exist linking Berger and his father, apart from the possessions in the stable, were the two unexplained invoices. An afternoon walk and visit to the book stands in Oudemanhuispoort had done nothing to ease his pain.

Work on Tuesday evening had been very difficult. Jos had noticed the tension between them but had kept quiet, clearly not wanting to get involved and risk the anger of another woman as well as his wife. He had hoped that they might walk home together after work, but Maaike had left early claiming a headache.

He still felt thoroughly miserable at breakfast, noticed first of all by little Irene rather than Grietje. 'What's the matter, Simon? You look sad.'

'I'm alright, I'm just thinking about things, that's all.'

'Maaike was sad yesterday as well, she didn't want to play with me. I think she cried so I gave her kisses.'

Grietje sounded almost pleased. 'You two still not talking then?'

'I'm afraid not, I should have told her, it's my fault, but I thought it was for the best.'

'She'll come around if she has any sense, you'll just have to wait and serve your sentence.'

'I hope so. I'm off to work, delivery day today. I don't know if Jos will keep me on all day or if I'll get a few hours off this afternoon. I'll try and speak to Maaike then if I can, it's no good at work.'

'Go and see her now.'

'No, she might not be up and dressed and I want to get in early, I have some questions for Jos.'

The mail arrived just as he got to the bottom of the stairs. Maaike must have seen the postman passing the window and her door opened just as he was picking up the mail.

He straightened up to see her standing in her doorway.

'Is there anything for me? I thought Aunt Nel might have replied by now.'

He looked at the envelopes. 'Yes, there's one from Leeuwarden.'

He passed her the letter. She took it without a word and closed the door. The rest of the mail was for Grietje and Aart. He left it on the shelf in the hallway so they would see it when they passed and went out into the street.

He took a slow walk to the bar.

Jos was sitting outside with a coffee, smoking a cigar. 'Nice morning, chilly but at least it's fine and the sun is up there somewhere.'

'Hello Jos, yes, nice day.'

'Alright, so what's the matter? What's going on with you and Maaike? The atmosphere last night was awful, put the customers off their beer. You'll have to keep your lovers' tiffs away from work, I won't have it interfering with my business. Understood?'

'I'm sorry, I'll sort it out.'

'You'd better. What is it all about anyway?'

He explained why they had argued and how they hadn't spoken since Sunday because he had lied.

'Bloody hell, is that all? If that's the worst you're ever going to do, you're in for a rough life. Just look at me. Sort it out now before it gets out of hand, put your foot down and tell her you did it for her. Don't you know anything about women?'

'No, I don't. I don't know much about anything apart from death, hunger and loneliness. When I went to the camp I was a boy, it may have forced me to become a man, but a very bitter one. I know nothing of real life. Life outside the camp only goes up to when I was seventeen or eighteen.'

Jos sat in silence for a moment. 'You're making a great job of rebuilding your life. You might be totally innocent in the ways of the real world, but you've been through more than we'll ever experience. You've got Grietje, me and best of all Maaike, grab it with both hands, lad. Put this Berger stuff behind you. You're tearing yourself apart. Look to the future and make sure it's with Maaike. Right, end of speech, let's get ready for the delivery.'

'Thank you, you're right, of course. What would I do without you? I have some things I want to discuss and ask you about.'

'What? More jobs for old Jos? Only joking, we'll talk after the delivery.'

Jos's wife called him upstairs, so he handled the delivery on his own, assisted by the drayman. He remembered to double check everything before he signed for it and was pleased with himself when he noticed the delivery was one case of Amstel short. It turned out to have been on the cart all the time behind the barrels for another bar. The drayman dragged it out reluctantly and rather shamefaced, handing it to him before he signed the receipt. He offered the usual beer but the driver declined, saying he was busy and behind schedule but he suspected he was too embarrassed to accept.

Jos went into town at lunchtime for one of his mysterious business meetings, which inevitably also led to a drinking session, leaving Simon to run the bar so he didn't get any time off in the afternoon as he had hoped. Business was slack so he coped easily and didn't have to call on Jos's wife for help.

Maaike arrived early, closely followed by Jos. She settled herself on her stool and exchanged greetings with the early evening regulars. Jos, slightly the worse for drink, went straight upstairs to face his wife, casting him a glance and pointing towards Maaike as he left. He had to change a barrel, so he took refuge in the cellar for a few moments before facing her. He began hesitantly. 'Maaike, can we talk?'

'Can I go first? I'm sorry, I've been acting stupidly, like a little girl. I know you didn't tell me because you didn't want to worry me. Can we start again? I've hated us not being friends.'

'I'm the one who needs to apologise, please let's go back to how things were between us. This Berger business is ruining everything. I've made a big decision. I know it was him, but I'll never prove it and if I could what would I do? It's over, no more, finished. I just want to concentrate on rebuilding my life, forgetting as much as I can and starting again.'

He leaned forward and they kissed.

Three of the regulars at the bar applauded and they both blushed.

'Stop it you lot and drink your beer. Simon, I need to know, will you still help me go to Leeuwarden?'

'Of course, I was always going to help you.'

'Aunt Nel says she can't get to use a telephone. I think she's a bit afraid of using one, but she's written to say her sons, my cousins, will be at Zwolle station on Monday at three when the Amersfoort train arrives. Can you go with me to Amersfoort and put me on the Zwolle train?'

'I'll go as far as Zwolle with you if you want, just in case they're not there.'

'They'll be there, I'm sure. If Aunt Nel has said so it'll happen. They've checked what time the train arrives so there's no need to get in touch again. We just need to work out the times from here to Amersfoort to catch the train that gets to Zwolle at three.'

'Thank you, I'm glad we're friends again.'

'So am I, and Jos will be too, he told me off this morning. He said we were spoiling trade. Well, he hinted at it.' He indicated the men at the bar. 'These four seem pleased we made up anyway.'

Jos came down at seven thirty and, unusually, told them to take a break for an hour. Whether he felt guilty about leaving Simon on his own all day or whether he thought he was helping their relationship they didn't ask, but gratefully took him at his word and went out into the dimly lit street. The recent change of clocks had brought the darkness forward.

They sat on their bench by the canal, watching the reflection of the lights on the water.

'I hated it when you weren't talking to me.'

'So did I, I was being very silly. But tell me what happened when you went to the stable?'

He told her all about his Sunday morning adventure and finding some of his and his family's possessions in the crates.

'How awful for you, I'm sorry we didn't talk about it on Sunday, you must have been so upset.'

'There were lots of things from other Jewish homes, much more than there was from ours. Furniture and many religious items too, there were even unopened crates—who knows what's in them. Berger was obviously working with the Germans or at the very least dealing with them. There was nothing to indicate where he is living or trading from so that's it, it's over. No more heartache. Jos is selling the gold for me. I'll keep father's tools and stamps, at least for now. I'll have one more try with the insurance company and the house if I can get professional advice, and then it's all over. Life starts again from then.'

She snuggled up close to him and he put his arm around her.

'Does that new start include me?'

'It certainly does. I have plans, big plans and dreams, and I hope you'll want to join me in them.'

'What plans? What dreams? Do tell me Simon.'

'Not yet Maaike, not yet, it's just a crazy idea at the moment. I'll tell you when.'

She playfully smacked his thigh. 'That's awful! Don't tease me.'

He changed the subject. 'I'll go to Centraal tomorrow and check those train times.'

They went back to work to find the bar absolutely packed, so much so that both Jos and his wife were behind the bar. She looked her usual angry self.

'Ah, there you are. Get yourselves back to work right now, I don't know what the old fool was doing giving you time off halfway through the evening. What we pay you for I really don't know.'

Jos smirked and his wife stormed off upstairs. Simon put on his apron and Maaike hopped to her stool.

'You two lovebirds look happier, all sorted?'

Maaike smiled at Jos. 'Yes, thank you, all sorted. Now where on earth have all these customers come from?'

'It's some wedding anniversary party, they ran out of booze at home I'm pleased to say. Could be a late night, you'll be glad I gave you a break.'

Jos was right. It was after midnight before he finally bolted the door behind the last of the revellers, a couple who had just returned from the East Indies after years of internment as civilians under the Japanese. Totally unconnected with the anniversary group, they had come in for a quiet drink and had been swept along with the celebrations and free drinks from Jos when he had learned what they had been through. 'Poor sods, starved by the Japs for years and now there's a bloody civil war so they can't even live in their home anymore. They'd been out there for twenty years, he was in rubber. Now they've got nothing and if this independence thing goes through I suspect they'll never go back.'

'At least I have father's box.'

'That reminds me. Pour some drinks while we clear up. Maaike, you stay there, we'll do it, and then I need to talk to you about your father's gold.'

He and Jos wiped the tables and counter and emptied the ashtrays while Maaike washed the glasses behind the bar.

'That'll do for tonight, it's late. I'll mop the floor in the morning. Let's sit down, I have some news for you about your gold.'

209

'You saw someone?'

'Yes, not the man who's buying but a contact of his. The man himself, the buyer, sent a message that he wanted to see us at his place tomorrow, but I said I wasn't keen on you and me carrying all that gold across town to an area we don't know.'

'So, what's happening?'

'He's coming here before opening tomorrow. He'll have someone with him but there'll be two of us so it should be alright.'

'Isn't it a bit risky, him knowing the gold is here?'

'I don't think so, my contact vouches for him. He's one hundred percent reputable allegedly, and anyway we won't let him see where we keep it. He'll weigh it and work out a price but the rate per gram changes so we may not be able to finalise it tomorrow. I don't expect he'll have all the money with him just like I didn't want us to take the gold to him. Also, I'll need to verify the current price with an independent source. I know someone who knows the weights and the prices but he doesn't buy, not in this quantity at least.'

'How will we do the deal?'

'I'm not sure, we'll have to see what we think of him and he of us. One of us is going to have to transport money and gold across the city eventually. Let's meet him first and let him examine the goods here under our control.' He laughed. 'I suppose it depends on whose bodyguard is the biggest.'

'Who's my bodyguard?'

'You're looking at him.'

'Do you know who the buyer is?'

'I've never met him, and I don't know his name, but I do know he's one of your lot.'

'A Jew!'

'Yes, another survivor like you.'

'What time is he coming?'

'I didn't think we'd be so late tonight so I said nine, that gives us two hours before we open. We won't be able to dash into negotiations, we'll have to offer drink and talk first. Is that alright with you?'

'I'll be here.'

Simon and Maaike took their normal route back to Slootstraat without stopping at their bench in view of the lateness of the hour.

'You're quiet, aren't you excited about selling the gold? I'm sure it's going to be worth a lot of money.'

'Yes, of course I am, but it's yet another connection to my father that's being severed. In this case I'm cashing in on what he thought would be our family's investment for after the war. He put it away so we could rebuild our lives and not be in poverty.'

'And that's exactly what's happening. Those coins are your inheritance, a legacy he left for you and you're using it just as he would have wanted, to rebuild your life.'

'But it was meant for all of us, father, mother and Esther, not just me.'

THURSDAY 1ST NOVEMBER 1945

Jos took the bags of coins and the watch cases out of the hiding place in the cellar before the buyer arrived and put them behind the bar.

'I don't want them to know that we keep them in the cellar. I think my secret place in the floor is quite safe but there is no point in risking it.'

The door rattled at exactly nine and Jos went to unlock it while Simon stayed sitting at the table facing the door. Two men entered, each vastly different to the other. Jos locked the doors again behind them and drew the heavy leather curtain, which ran on a curved rail, across the doors.

The man he took to be the buyer was at least seventy if not eighty years old. Bent and shuffling he sported a long straggly goatee beard, a black velvet yarmulke on his thinning grey hair and a threadbare and stained black knee-length jacket. He carried a small leather case.

His companion was totally different. He was clearly Dutch, at least two metres tall, unshaven, barrel chested with close cropped blond hair and dressed in a smart blue suit.

Jos offered his hand. 'Goedemorgen gentlemen, I'm Jos van Loon, please sit down. This is Simon, he's the owner of the goods you have come to see. I'll bring coffee and anything else you want to drink.'

The big Dutchman spoke. 'Just coffee for us, please.'

The old man spoke at last. 'Shalom.'

Instinctively he replied, 'A gutn tog, Shalom Aleichem.'

A look of surprise crossed the man's face. 'Aleichem Shalom. You're a Jew?'

'Yes, meneer, I am.'

'I'm Abraham Hirschfeld, but please call me Abe.'

He felt the ice was already broken.

Jos arrived with the coffee and they settled down to talk.

'You survived Simon. Did you hide?'

'We did, but they found us. We were in a camp, I survived but my family were killed. What about you?'

'I hid from 1941. I was in a farmhouse near Nieuwlande in Drenthe. The whole place was full of Jews, all over the village and the surrounding countryside. I was very lucky, my wife Miriam and her brother and I, we all survived. The Canadians came in April and we were back in Amsterdam in early May.'

'We were betrayed. I am the only survivor.'

'I understand you have gold you wish to sell. Can I ask how you still have it? Our people who were sent to the camps lost everything. All the gold the Nazis found was sent to Berlin.'

'My father put it in a box and hid it where we were in hiding. The Germans and the police didn't find it and a Dutchman who was helping us rescued it.'

'And he kept it safe for you?' Hirschfeld sounded incredulous. 'You got it back when you returned?'

He felt the old man was checking him and his story out.

'A relative of his kept it, they had promised my father it would be kept safe for our return. The box was still locked and what I want to sell was hidden in the bottom.'

Jos spoke up. 'I'll get the items, shall I? Then you can see for yourself. Simon, lay that cloth on the table, please.'

He spread a clean drying cloth out on the table between them and Jos placed the wooden box containing the watch cases and the two cloth bags of coins in the centre. 'I'll speak for Simon if I may, Abe, I've been helping him since he found the things his father left behind.' Jos reached for one of the bags. 'What would you like to see first. I presume you want to make a close examination?'

The old Jew grabbed his arm. 'Wait a moment please, let me look at the bags before you open them.'

Simon looked at Jos then at Hirschfeld with a puzzled then worried look on his face. 'Is there a problem? They are just as they came from my father's hiding place.'

Hirschfeld picked up each bag, seemingly oblivious to the weight of the gold each held. He took out a magnifying glass and, holding both bag and glass close to his rheumy right eye, closely examined each one in turn before returning them to the table.

'These were your father's, you say?'

'Yes, meneer.'

'What was his profession?'

'He was a watchmaker, some say the best in Amsterdam.'

'Where was his workshop?'

'Peperstraat.'

'And which shul did he attend?'

'Father was a reader, a baal keriah, at the shul on Nieuwe Uilenburgerstraat, it was the nearest one to our home.'

Hirschfeld smiled, showing a single tooth. Seemingly satisfied he held out an almost skeletal hand. 'Simon, Simon Mendelevski, I am honoured to meet you. Your father was a fine and much respected man, I was proud to know him, and I am proud to know you too. I am sad to hear of his death, so many friends and acquaintances have gone.'

Simon looked confused. 'Thank you, but how do you know who I am?'

'The coin bags and, I assume, their contents. I sold gold coins to your father five years before the war and then again when the Germans came. Look, the bags have my mark, if you look closely you can just see it. Your father had closed the business and sold many of his things. He didn't want to put the proceeds into that Nazi bank. He was already investing in gold coins, but when the war started he wanted to change all his guilders into gold. He thought they would be worthless if the Germans introduced the Reichsmark. It was good business for me, I admit it.' He smiled and rubbed his hands together. 'Especially as I also knew where I could get rid of the guilders again and buy more gold.'

It sounded to Simon just like the dealings with van der Meer all over again, but somehow his father dealing with a fellow Jew made it more palatable. He guessed his father had paid more than the going rate per gram on the gold he bought after the Germans invaded and he suspected, that if he and Jos were not careful, the old man's price for buying it back would also be heavily to his, rather than their, advantage.

Hirschfeld slowly untied one bag and then the other, his eyes lighting up as he gently tipped the contents onto the cloth. 'Ah, yes, I remember most of these coins well, but here, and here, these are ones I did not sell to your father.'

With Jos's help the old man sorted the coins by type and together they began to count.

'Can you both keep a record of this?' Hirschfeld looked at his companion and then at Jos. 'Unless you would prefer to record it, Simon Mendelevski?'

He shook his head. 'I'd like Jos to do it for me.'

The young Dutchman took a notepad and pencils from the leather case, handing a sheet of paper and a pencil to Jos as Hirschfeld began to dictate. 'Seventeen gold twenty gulden pieces Koning Willem and sixty-five gold twenty gulden pieces Koningin Wilhelmina, agreed?'

Jos nodded.

'Twenty-two gold ten gulden pieces Koning Willem and hundred and eight ten gulden pieces Koningin Wilhelmina, correct?'

'Correct. Do you agree, Simon?' Jos looked at him and he nodded.

'And two hundred and seven silver gullders all Wilhelmina.'

Once again, he and Jos indicated their agreement.

'Now these.' Hirschfeld looked closely at the remaining gold coins, a puzzled look on his face. 'Your father didn't get these from me, Simon. I think he must have invested in these long before the war or even before we dealt with each other, ten or more years ago. I haven't seen German coins since I left Konigsberg in 1905 and then I never owned any. The Russian coins are special ones for collectors, 1897 was the only year they were minted. They are very fine. Could it be your father was a coin collector, not just investing in gold? The Dutch coins he bought just as gold, not for the coins themselves, I just happened to have coins instead of gold ingots or jewellery, but these, well, these are different.'

'I don't know, I didn't know anything about any of these at all. He was a stamp collector, I recall him often looking at his stamp collection and working on it, but I never saw him with coins.'

The old man shrugged. 'Well, write this down anyway, please. There are fifty-two gold German twenty mark coins, Wilhelm I and Wilhelm II, and six gold Russian fifteen roubles coins dated 1897, from Nicolas II. Now each of you initial and then exchange your lists, gentlemen. A little security measure, Simon, you have my list and I have yours.'

Jos and the Dutchman swapped their pieces of paper.

'More coffee or maybe a beer?' Jos was clearly in need of refreshment and a short break.

Hirschfeld spoke first. 'Coffee again for me.' He looked at the Dutchman. 'But I think my friend here would like a beer this time.'

Simon asked for coffee, a little concerned that Hirschfeld might not approve of him drinking beer. He had begun to acquire a taste for beer since he had started working for Jos. He remembered his first ever taste during the job interview and how much he had disliked it just a few weeks before.

Jos poured two beers and went upstairs for coffee, indicating to Simon before he left to keep an eye on the coins laid out on the table.

'Well Simon, your father left you a very nice legacy here, you're a rich young man.'

'I think he intended this to be the future for all of us after the war, for the whole family not just me, Meneer Hirschfeld.'

'Please, Simon, call me Abe. I know you are showing me respect, probably because I am old.' He laughed at himself. 'But I prefer if you use my given name, we are friends after all, your father called me a lot worse!' He laughed again.

Jos served the coffee and they sat in silence for a few moments.

Eventually Abe spoke. 'I must get on with testing and weighing. I know exactly what the twenty and ten gulden coins should weigh, and I am happy with them. I know them better than my wife and I can tell just by handling them that they are genuine. Of course I sold almost all of them to your father, but I think I will weigh and test a few anyway. You understand I hope—please don't be offended.'

He produced a small pair of hand-held balance scales from the leather case, placing a small lead weight on one pan and a ten gulden coin on the other. He repeated the process on five of the Willem coins and just two from the Wilhelmina issue. Then he took a small bottle and, after making a small scratch on each of the seven coins, he allowed a drop of fluid to fall on each one.

'Perfect!' He turned to Simon with a beaming smile. 'All weighing in more or less correctly at just under six and three quarter grams each. They are gold and I am happy they will be ninety percent pure, which makes a gold content for each one of just over six grams, six point zero six to be exact for the more recent 1930s Wilhelminas.'

Jos interrupted. 'And there are a hundred and thirty of them.'

'Yes, don't worry, we will do the final calculation at the end, the earlier ones are worn, they were coins of the realm, don't forget, and were used in everyday life so they will be a little lighter. I sold them as gold, not collectable coins in mint condition. Well, the 1933 ones, the last issues, are very fine, but we will need to weigh them all together in bulk.'

He moved on to the twenty gulden coins, repeating the process after changing the lead weight. 'Each of these should weigh double the weight of the tens, just under thirteen and a half grams each.' He weighed four of the Willem coins and three of the Wilhelminas, scratched them and applied a drop of fluid before once again stating he was satisfied. 'Correct, just under thirteen and a half grams, ninety percent pure, gives a gold content of just over twelve grams each, give or take. Some are again very worn.'

Jos spoke again. 'Multiplied by eighty-two.'

'Yes, yes. We'll weigh them all together, the tens and the twenties, they're all ninety percent so we can mix them.' The old man smiled at Jos, perhaps irritated initially by his interruptions but then amused as Jos was clearly trying to work out the totals in his head. 'Please, don't worry, we'll write it down and do all the calculations together, but we will need to do it on another occasion when we have the big scales.'

Jos tried to cover his embarrassment. 'What about the silver guilders Abe? There are...' He looked at his list. 'Two hundred and seven.'

Hirschfeld thought for a moment, fidgeting with his beard. 'They're not really my thing. I deal in gold and there's not a lot of value in silver. The earlier dates up to 1922 are ninety-five percent, they were withdrawn but many people kept them for the silver content. The later ones are only seventy, so we'd have to sort out the two types for a start then weigh them and I haven't got the bigger scales here. Then I'd have to sell them on to someone with the facility to melt them down into ingots. No one collects them as coins, they'll have to go in the pot. The Yanks are minting new ones, not silver of course, but you can spend the later ones if you want, they're still legal tender, only the Germans stopped us using them.'

Simon spoke, 'So you're saying they're just worth their face value, two hundred and seven guilders?'

'The silver value is obviously more than that Simon, but with all the work involved and I'd have to sell them again...' He opened his palms and shrugged his shoulders. 'It's not really worth my time but, for your father's sake, I'll pay twice the face value.'

Jos jumped in. 'You make it sound like you're doing the lad a favour.'

'I am meneei, I am.'

Simon tried to defuse the situation. 'That will be fine, I accept.

It's a good offer Jos, I'm happy with it. The value is really all in the gold ones.'

Jos didn't look convinced. 'Are you absolutely sure?'

'I'll pay you that today.' Abe looked across at the big Dutchman and grinned. 'Joost here can carry them home for me, he's a big strong fellow.'

'What about the German and Russian coins?' Jos was clearly anxious to get the conversation back to the gold. 'Young Simon here needs as much money as he can get. He's starting his life again, but on his own since his family were killed.'

'I know that only too well. I was lucky, my beloved Miriam and I lived through it all so we still have each other, but both my sons are dead. They saw to it that we were safely hidden, away from Amsterdam, but they stayed behind and the Germans took them. Maybe to Auschwitz like you, maybe Sobibor, I don't know where.'

'I'm sorry, I had no idea.' Simon looked shocked and saddened. 'Sometimes I forget that others suffered the same as me, I'm so sorry.'

'It was the fate of thousands I suspect, the final number will not be known for years, maybe never. But you, Simon, are one of the next generation. There are now so few of our young people left, we must care for them and nurture them if our race is to survive. For me it is all over, I have a few more years and maybe a few more deals to be done.' He rubbed his hands and smiled. 'But it is now just an existence for us. Our home thankfully was also saved, first my sons then my neighbours looked after it for us. Most of the contents were taken but the building is still standing and a few valuable trinkets and items with a sentimental value, like your father's, were kept safe for me.'

'There were good people around for us, Abe, like Jos here.'

'So, to the rest of the coins. The German ones have a different gold content for the two emperors, one Wilhelm is more valuable than the other. I need to check that and also check what they should weigh. I haven't bought or sold any of these, but I have friends who have, or at least I had friends, I don't know if they are still alive. The Russian roubles I think your father must have obtained before he came to Amsterdam.'

'It's possible. Could they have been a wedding gift from his family or from my mother's family?'

'I think that's very likely. I told you they are very special, the date is the only year they were made, so a present is the best explanation. Either way, I will buy them if you wish, but perhaps it would be better if you kept them as they are collectable and maybe the German ones too. Gold will rise in price in the future, at the moment it is little more than what your father paid.'

At this Jos gave him a very knowing and noticeable sideways look, which Abe clearly recognised.

'Please check the price per gram yourself meneer. The total value is enormous, so Simon has a lot of money to come but the actual profit on the coins will not be great. I was going to suggest that he sells the Dutch gold, if we can agree a price of course, but that he keeps the other coins for the future when the price goes up. The condition and rarity may mean they will be worth even more to collectors in years to come.'

Simon nodded his agreement and turned to Jos. 'Can we show Abe the watch cases, Jos?'

Jos leaned over and opened the polished wooden box.

The old man's eyes lit up again. 'Ah, I wondered what was in the box.'

He took out the cases and examined them carefully in turn. 'These are nice, very nice. I can't weigh them today as I don't have the scales or the right weights, but I can test the gold for purity. I don't expect it will be over seventy-five percent. Anything purer would be too soft for watch cases, they would be too easily dented or scratched or the hinge would bend, but they are still valuable. Do you want to sell them?'

'Yes, I have a complete watch my father made, I think these were for watches he had hoped to make in the future.'

'In that case, let me see.' He reached into his leather case and brought out a square rough stone and a metal instrument with finger-like points. He spread out the points and gently scraped them down the stone making five noticeable lines. Then he scraped the edge of one of the watch cases down the stone leaving another faint gold line. Taking the small bottle of liquid, he drew a line of fluid across the lines on the stone. One of the five lines and the line made by the watch case reacted to the liquid. 'As I thought and expected, about seventy percent pure gold.'

Jos, as before, was defensive. 'How do we know that? Neither of us understands what you have just done.'

'It's a standard test for the purity of gold. Please have them tested yourself by someone else if you think I am deceiving you. I like a good deal, but I am an honourable man and not a liar. In fact, sell it all somewhere else if you want.'

Simon desperately tried to calm the situation. 'Abe, please, I'm sure Jos didn't mean to insult you, please understand he is only trying to look after my interests and that all this is totally foreign to both of us.'

'Meneer Hirschfeld, I am sorry, I am a simple man who worked on the docks and now runs a bar. All my life I have had to be careful about business and people who are not honest. Honourable men are few and far between in my experience and many of them are no longer with us, after the war. My apologies, I just want to look after this boy, I didn't mean to doubt your honesty.'

It was the longest, most eloquent and swear-word free speech Simon had ever heard from Jos and it seemed to satisfy Hirschfeld, who smiled and extended a bony hand. 'I totally understand, and I expect you will check the current gold price before we can do a deal, in fact I hope you do so that we are all satisfied. Whether you then accept my offer we will have to see. The gold coins alone will be worth many thousands of guilders which somehow I will have to pay you.'

Relieved Simon looked at Jos, who nodded his acceptance. 'I understand. So what do we do now, Abe?'

'I need to weigh all the coins on a heavier scale to get a total weight, so you will have to bring them, and the watch cases, to my home. I can send Joost over to accompany you, and Jos may come along. Before then I will try to work out, if my mathematics allow, approximately how much I will have to pay you. I may need to involve a friend in the transaction in order to raise enough money. In the meantime, you should check today's gold price and also what it was in 1935 and 1941 so you will see it has risen little since your father bought the coins from me.'

Jos spoke up, still a little defensive. 'Until then we keep everything here.'

'Of course, except the silver which I will pay you for now, four hundred guilders, agreed?' The old man opened a fat, worn leather wallet and handed him the money.

Simon quickly agreed and took the notes before Jos could argue.

'Now the gold.' Hirschfeld picked up the German and Russian coins and passed them over to him. 'You keep these for the future, Simon. Now I will put the Dutch ones back in the two bags.'

Jos watched intently, clearly counting, as the gold went back into the cloth bags. Hirschfeld then took a stick of sealing wax from his case and, lighting a match, he melted the wax until it was soft, rolled a piece of the molten wax onto the knots in the drawstrings of the bags and impressed his signet ring onto each one. 'A security measure, I'm sure you understand.' He grinned to Jos. 'And, knowing you, I'm sure you approve. Please take care not to knock off or break the wax seals.'

Jos put the two sealed bags into the wooden box with the watch cases and his copy of the note and brought a large linen bank bag from behind the bar for the silver coins, which he filled and then handed to the younger man. 'You need to take care not to damage the German and Russian coins if you want to sell them to collectors in the future. Don't throw them all in a bag together, will you? Treat them gently.'

'Thank you, I won't.'

'Joost will call here in a few days' time to arrange a date for you to visit me with the gold.'

The four men shook hands and Hirschfeld and his silent companion left.

Jos breathed a huge sigh of relief. 'Thank goodness that's over, the things I do for you, lad.'

'Thank you Jos, but what's the problem? I thought he was a nice old man.'

'Nice man? Bloody hell, you are so innocent, I hope you counted your fingers after you shook his hand. I didn't like it at all, I've dealt with some right villains as you know, and I can hold my own in most dealings, but I just didn't feel confident. I was out of my depth and I admit it.'

'We've started things off at least.'

'Maybe, but we have to get across town to his home area, on a date which he's going to pick, with all that gold, then back with the money. That's if we even do the deal. He clearly hasn't got enough cash, he's going to cut someone else in on it and anyway if the offer isn't right I'm not going to let you just agree to it. He might be one of your own but he's a businessman. Money first and Judaism second.'

'But he knew father, I'm sure he's alright.'

'Your father was his customer first and friend second, believe me. I'm just playing devil's advocate and looking after your interests, call me a soft old bugger but I care about you.'

'I've still got a problem. I'm selling gold and getting thousands of guilders that I can't put in a bank as I still have no account and if I did, how could I open it with so much money? What am I going to do?'

Jos thought for a moment. 'I don't know, I didn't think about that. Like you said, I thought selling it in one go was the right thing, after all you were right, you can't carry two bags of gold around with you for years selling a few bits here and there when you need money, can you?'

'But I can't carry thousands of guilders around either.'

'Leave it with me, I'll have a word, but it may be another case of you having to pay someone for the privilege and I don't want to see your inheritance swallowed up by damn sharks.'

'Thanks, I appreciate it. Cheer up, we did sell the silver.'

'Yes, and I think he got the best of that deal too, four hundred guilders indeed. Now get off home, it's nearly time I open up. I'll put everything back down in the cellar. I'll see you at four and don't be late. You might be a rich man, but I have a living to earn.'

Simon raced home to tell Maaike while Jos sat in the cellar with a large jenever and tried to multiply the number of coins by the weight of gold in grams, but he couldn't remember what the old man had said each coin weighed. It gave him a headache so he soon gave up and, mentally exhausted, reached for another drink before opening up.

MONDAY 5TH NOVEMBER 1945

Everyone in the house, apart from Aart who was on a late shift, was up early. Grietje wanted to go to the Monday market in the Westerstraat to get some last-minute items to take to her mother and father-in-law in Utrecht. She had already shopped at the Noordermarkt as usual on Saturday, buying enough to keep Simon going for a month rather than the few days she was going to be away. He had pointed out that she would be back on Friday, but she had seemed firmly convinced he was going to starve in her absence.

Maaike hadn't needed anything for herself as she was going to be away for a full week, and she didn't think she needed to buy anything to take with her as food and provisions were still more plentiful in Leeuwarden and had been even during the recent winter. She was in the bedroom packing, so he was looking after Irene while Grietje was out.

He'd been to Centraal Station on Saturday and bought the tickets. A return for himself to Amersfoort, return tickets to Leeuwarden for Maaike, and tickets to Utrecht for Grietje and Irene. Jos had arranged for yet another 'contact' of his to pick them up in his car and take them to the station. The railway network was still in some disarray, and to get Maaike to Amersfoort in time to catch the train which would arrive in Zwolle at three, they would have to leave Amsterdam before eleven. Grietje's train left at about the same time.

Jos's friend drew up outside at just after ten fifteen. The car, a large black Citroën, and its driver, dressed in an immaculate suit, attracted considerable attention from the neighbours in both Slootstraat and nearby Madelievenstraat. Just as they were getting into the car, the postman arrived and handed Simon a letter. The envelope showed it was a reply from the Jewish Co-ordination Committee. He put it in his pocket to open later and finished loading the luggage into the car.

They were at the station in just a few minutes, but it had saved them, and particularly Maaike, the long walk along Brouwersgracht. They were early, but they needed time for Maaike to get up the steps to the platform for the Amersfoort train while Grietje and Irene carried on to the Utrecht platform.

Irene turned, waving frantically. 'Goodbye Maaike, I love you, see you soon, lots of kisses, I'll miss you.'

'Goodbye darling, I'll see you soon.'

She blew a kiss. 'Give my love to Aunt Nel, Maaike.'

The war weary and badly maintained old train left on time. Simon and Maaike had a compartment to themselves and they settled down on the dirty, worn seats for what threatened to be a slow, stop-start journey.

'You're quiet, Simon, what's wrong?'

'I'm sorry, it's the train and the station, it reminds me of the train journeys after we were arrested. Bad, bad memories.'

'Of course, I'm sorry, I didn't realise.'

'Don't worry, it's alright.' He tried to joke but failed miserably. 'This carriage might be scruffy, but it's better than how we travelled in 1942.'

She changed the subject. 'What's in the letter?'

'Oh, I forgot all about it.' He tore open the envelope. 'It's as I thought, it's a reply from the Jewish Co-ordination Committee. I wrote to them in Arnhem but this is from Amsterdam.'

He read the letter. 'That explains it, their head office was in Amsterdam all the time. There is an office in Arnhem but they've sent my enquiry back here, that's why it took so long. Why didn't someone at the Red Cross tell me when I first enquired? Some others who had returned were complaining that the Dutch Red Cross weren't exactly doing a great job.'

'What does it say?'

'Just that they have all my details and those of my family, no point in that now, I suppose. It gives their address in Amsterdam if I need anything, and guess where it is?'

'I don't know, just tell me, please, no games.'

'18 Johannes Vermeerstraat, we must have walked right past it when we were going from the tram to van der Meer's house. It says here that as well as it being their head office, it's a registration office and a reception centre for repatriates and they also operate a child welfare office and a clothing warehouse. They've been open since August, that's a week or so before I got back. I wish I'd known all this then or that someone had told me. They might have found me somewhere to stay instead of me having to sleep on the streets.'

'Then you wouldn't have moved in with Grietje and we would never have met.'

He smiled and took her hand. 'That's true, but it would have made things a lot easier. It also says they distribute clothing, blankets, food parcels, and even pots and pans and things from there, and from an office on Museumplein. I wish I'd known that, I was sent to a place on Nieuwendijk and given rags to wear.'

'You don't need any of that stuff now.'

'No, but I still need their help. It's obvious they're the people to ask how I can get a new ID card. There must be lots of us with old cards identifying us as Jews or others who have come back with no card at all. I'm going to ask if they can help with the house and father's insurance too and see if they can assist with a bank account.'

'I certainly hope they can do something, it's a shame you didn't know all this earlier, it would have helped you so much. I think there will be lots of other survivors who are still struggling to cope but don't know where to go.'

They had over an hour to wait at Amersfoort station for the

Zwolle train, so after changing platforms they went for coffee. The station was in a state of disrepair with broken glass panels in the roofs over the platforms.

'I think this place was bombed by both sides in the war. The British attacked the railway lines. It was a really big railway hub and an army town. There was a camp as well, I met a couple of men from around here when they arrived in Auschwitz. They said that when the Germans invaded in May 1940 all the people had to leave the city, but they were soon allowed back and then of course the Jews got arrested.'

The train for Zwolle was already waiting so she boarded it a little early, struggling to get up the steps. He went on with her, carrying her suitcase.

'Now, you're sure your cousins will be at Zwolle? This train gets in at two minutes past three, delays permitting.'

'Stop worrying, they'll be there I'm sure. If they're not, I'll find someone to help me down with my case and I'll wait for them.'

'But what if they don't come at all?'

'Then I'll get someone to help me onto the next train to Leeuwarden.' She laughed at him. 'Don't worry, you're like an old woman.'

'I'm sorry, but I do worry about you.'

'I know and it's nice. Now you'd better get off or you'll find yourself coming to Zwolle with me, the train's about to leave. I'll write as soon as I know what time I'll be back here on Monday so you can meet me.'

'Please do, I want to know you got to Aunt Nel's safely.'

He kissed her and stood on the platform watching her through the grimy carriage window until the train pulled out. He waved until she was out of sight.

Back in Amsterdam he was at a loose end. With both Maaike and Grietje away, and no work to go to, he decided to go to Johannes Vermeerstraat. He realised that the Jewish Co ordination Committee office would almost certainly be closed, but he thought he could at least identify the building and see if the opening times were displayed.

He took a tram from Centraal Station to Johannes Vermeerplein. He felt both confident and quite pleased with himself having safely negotiated a tram journey through the heart of the city without Maaike's help or Jos's directions.

Number 18 was, like all the properties in the street, an imposing three storey building with a small attic window up at roof level forming a fourth level. Built of granite blocks at street level and brick above, a small notice pasted to the wall announced it to be the office of the 'JCC' with opening hours of nine until four on weekdays.

He decided to walk back to Slootstraat via the Rijksmuseum tunnel. It was a beautiful autumn evening and he had nothing to rush back for. Approaching the back of the museum he saw the house of van der Meer ahead. As he got closer, the front door opened and van der Meer appeared with another man. The two walked down the steps, speaking briefly and shaking hands on the pavement before van der Meer went back into the house while Edwin Berger turned, crossed the pavement, got into his car and drove away.

For the second time he watched helplessly as the man he believed had betrayed him and his family to the Nazis disappeared into the distance.

He burst through the doors of Café van Loon, sweating profusely having run all the way from van der Meer's house.

'Jos! Jos! I've just seen him again. Berger, I've seen him, and he was at van der Meer's!'

'Simon, lad, calm down, you'll frighten the customers going on like that.'

'But I've just seen him again. He was there, twenty metres away from me at most, just the same as when we saw him in Kromme Palmstraat that day. It was the same car and everything.'

'Just a minute, we can't talk in front of this lot. I'll get her upstairs to come down for a minute.'

Jos's wife eventually appeared and they went down to the cellar. Jos settled himself in his chair, opened a beer and turned to him. 'Now tell me again, calmly this time.'

'I was passing van der Meer's house and he came out with Berger. They shook hands and Berger drove away.'

'Is that it?'

'Yes, that's it. But Berger knows van der Meer. Surely this changes everything.'

'Maybe, but he's gone again, gone somewhere in this huge city and we haven't got a clue where.'

'But he was there, right in front of me, just like before.'

'What could you do? You could hardly have grabbed hold of the rear bumper.'

'But what could Berger have been doing with van der Meer? I didn't like him when we went to see him, there was just something about him. He was an odious, smarmy man.'

'There could be a dozen reasons at least why they were together, it's probably a complete coincidence.'

'I'm going to find out.'

'And how the hell are you proposing to do that?'

'I'm going to ask him.'

'Are you sure? You'd better be careful. How are you going to introduce Berger's name?'

'I don't know yet, I haven't thought it out.'

'Well you'd better think about it, don't jump in. Take Jos's advice and sleep on it for a day or so.'

'I will, but I've got to do it. I was prepared to give up after we found nothing in the stable. I told Maaike it was all finished but seeing him again today started it all off again. I can't leave it now, I have to go on.'

'I wish you wouldn't, but if you are set on it then be careful, that's all. If van der Meer is a friend of Berger's, be very careful indeed. Do you want me to go with you?'

'No, this is one where even you can't help me. I have to do it myself. I'll keep you in reserve until I meet Berger face to face, if I may.'

'You can rely on that, I'll sort the bastard out for you.'

TUESDAY 6TH NOVEMBER 1945

He had thought about it as Jos had advised. In fact, he had thought about nothing else leading to yet another disturbed night to add to the many since he returned to the city. As well as thinking about how to approach van der Meer, he was wondering and worrying whether Maaike had arrived safely in Leeuwarden.

Unable to sleep he was up very early, taking care not to wake Aart, and made himself breakfast. It felt strange not having Grietje to prepare it for him and Irene there chattering to him while they shared the kitchen table.

As soon as he had eaten he went out into the Jordaan in an effort to sort out his thoughts and to try to come up with some ideas. Early mornings were his favourite time, he loved being out in the narrow streets before the area was fully awake. Bar owners like Jos were sweeping outside their premises, deliveries were being made to shops and restaurants and the smell of bread and cakes hung in the air. Night workers were returning to the residential streets as others made their way to work in the city centre.

He passed local residents; many recognised and greeted him, adding to his newfound feeling of belonging, but he was still bothered and confused by thoughts that perhaps he should make a completely fresh start away from Amsterdam and maybe even the

Netherlands if only Maaike could be persuaded to leave with him. Abraham Hirschfeld's comment about how few of the young generation of Jews were left had merely increased his already growing feeling that perhaps he should once again embrace his religion and return to the shul.

Standing alone in the morning silence on a bridge on Bloemgracht, quietly observing a resident heron, he realised the only way to ease his turmoil and sort out his thoughts was to place and then address each problem in order and he decided that, despite what he had said to Maaike, van der Meer and Berger must be dealt with first.

He turned on his heel and set out for Johannes Vermeerstraat.

Once again van der Meer's secretary Joke answered the door. Van der Meer was in court and was not expected back until midday, but she appeared to have mellowed a little since his first visit and invited him to come back then.

As he had time to kill he walked up to the JCC office. A tiny lady, he guessed in her sixties, matronly and obviously Jewish, greeted him in the front office. He gave her his details and those of his family. She confirmed all were on the search record already together with his address. He told her that sadly the search for his parents and sister was over and she noted the record. He was, however, unable to provide her with a date of their death.

'Is there anything the JCC can do for you?'

'Two months ago I would have said yes, but as you can see I have somewhere to live, although it's temporary. I'm now reasonably clothed and I have work although I'd like to go back to my studies sometime in the future. Perhaps you can help with that. For some reason I didn't know about you when I got back, that was when I badly needed help.'

'You were in Auschwitz I think, yes?'

'Yes, from late 1942. I stayed on after liberation to help where I could. The Russians weren't very helpful, but I wasn't a priority to be shipped out and anyway I was hoping to find my mother and sister. I made my own way back. Lots of others were sent back via Odessa. But what about you? You survived too?'

'I was very lucky. I left the Netherlands before the war. We went to England with my husband's work. I feel awful that I sat there in safety for the whole war, so as soon as I could I volunteered to come back to help and the JCC needed people. There have been quite a few Auschwitz survivors through here, none from Sobibor though. Have you found any friends or relatives, from your shul maybe?'

'Not really, just the woman who told me about mother and Esther. I haven't been back to the shul yet.'

'And your home?'

'My home is still intact, unlike some, but there is a Dutch family in it. Can you help with that?'

'We're trying to help a number of people with that problem, but it's very difficult and the city authorities seem more interested in trying to charge survivors for unpaid rents and taxes than helping them to get their houses back. I think you might need a lawyer if you know anybody, and it could take years.'

I know one, he thought. *But can I trust him?*

She went on. 'It's the same with life insurance too. Did your parents have insurance at all? They're all refusing to pay, no death certificates, unpaid premiums, the Germans took the money as those insured were Jews—they're using excuses. I think it will go on for years.'

'A friend warned me about that. He also said it was going to be difficult for me to open a bank account even though I have ID.'

'That all depends how much you have. Most survivors have absolutely nothing. If you have enough money to open an account, or so much that it's a problem, then you're a very, very lucky boy indeed.'

'Father left some valuables behind but I can't prove it, the banks seem totally fixated with identifying money from the wartime black market.'

'I'm not being very helpful, am I?'

'There is one thing I hope you can advise me on. I have my ID card stamped to show I'm a Jew and I'd like to get a new one which doesn't single me out because of my religion.' He showed her his card and the prominent letter 'J' stamped in black on it.

'I can help with that. I've had lots of survivors through here with no identification at all and many who survived in hiding still have their original cards, which they want to change. I'm told all cards will be valid for two or maybe three more years before they will be replaced, and that's if the government decides to continue with them at all. The issue of ID cards was suggested and turned down before the war and the Germans simply used the prototype design. Issuing new ones to everyone in the country is going to be a huge job, but I think you can get a new one issued now if you apply to the registry at the relevant city hall, Amsterdam presumably in your case. I'm not sure they're compulsory anymore now the Germans have gone. You've changed a lot though, so you'll need a new photograph, that's for sure.'

He smiled. 'You're very diplomatic. I went to Auschwitz a fit teenage boy and came back a haggard old man.'

It was her turn to smile. 'Nonsense, you're a very good-looking young fellow, a pretty girl will soon snap you up, I'm sure.'

With one question answered at least, he thanked her and prepared to leave.

'Please come back if there is anything we can do to help you, I think we will be working for many years yet. Bits and pieces for your home perhaps, or simply advice. Surviving must have been extremely difficult, but I'm afraid that for many returning to normal life is proving harder. Tot ziens.'

Back at van der Meer's Joke again answered the door and showed him into van der Meer's study.

'Simon Mendelevski, how nice to see you again. How can I help you this time? Are you here to see me professionally?'

'No, although I may need your help soon about my family house, my father's insurance and some financial matters.'

'Of course, I told you last time that if there is anything, please ask.'

'I have another question about my father's watch making business, and in particular about another of his customers I am trying to contact. Do you know an Edwin Berger by any chance?'

'The antiques dealer? As it happens I do, he's a client of mine. Why do you ask?'

'I think he also bought a watch from my father and I want to ask him about it.'

'Did he really? I thought he might have, but he never told me.'

He looked puzzled. 'What do you mean?'

'He was here the day when your father's employee delivered my watches, he was the client I said I was with when they arrived. I paid your father's man and then after he had left I showed Berger the watches. Like me, he was extremely impressed with the outstanding quality. I told him I had had them specially made, and he said he too would like to have one, but I told him I thought the maker, your father, had closed his business down. He didn't ask who had made them so I assumed it was probably no more than a passing thought on his part.'

Suddenly a thought flashed into his mind. 'Did he ask the man who brought the watches to you?'

'No, he didn't speak to him at all, he was just sitting in the room while I paid the man and showed him out again.'

'But he saw him?'

'Of course, why do you ask?'

'No reason, I just wondered if that was how he got in touch with my father. Do you know how I can contact Meneer Berger?'

Van der Meer thought for a moment. 'It's difficult, he's a client, or rather he was, so I am bound by confidentiality, but our business was purely a civil matter about shop leases and it's finished as of yesterday. I can tell you I believe he may have premises in the Spiegelstraat area, but I can't give you his home address.'

'I understand that and thank you. You've finished your work with him, you say?'

'Yes, it was a long-running problem about a shop lease going back to 1942. I never thought it would end. I won't be seeing him again, thank goodness I hope when you find him that he is as proud of his watch, if he ever managed to get one, as I am of mine. And don't forget, if you need my help or advice, don't hesitate to contact me.'

'Thank you, I will.'

He got to Café van Loon an hour early anxious to see Jos and to explain that he now thought he knew how Berger had realised his father was a Jew in hiding and where he was.

It was was very quiet, and Jos was behind the bar on his own when he walked in.

'Simon, what are you doing here so soon? I'm glad you're here, but it's only three.'

'I've just seen van der Meer and I'm convinced I know how Berger found out about us, and I also think I might be able to find him. I've just got to tell you.'

'Calm down, you're more and more excited every time I see you, this is twice in two days.' He looked at the three sitting at the bar. 'They're alright for a moment, come on, let's sit up there.'

It all came tumbling out. 'Van der Meer and Berger aren't friends at all. Van der Meer was just acting for him professionally about the Lijnbaansgracht premises and that's all over now. He wouldn't tell me Berger's home address but he said there's a new shop somewhere on Spiegelstraat, so I'll look for him there.'

'You're sure they won't be speaking to each other again? He won't tell Berger you're asking?'

'No, no, but Jos, there's more. I think I know how Berger found us. He was in the room when Gerrit delivered the watches and father's invoice to van der Meer and when van der Meer paid him. Van der Meer showed Berger the watches and Berger admired them and said he wanted one then van der Meer told him the maker, my father, was no longer at his business address.'

'Slow down, how did that lead to Berger knowing where you were all hiding?'

'Jos, don't you see, it's so obvious. Berger must have recognised Gerrit as the man he'd seen going in and out of the Kromme Palmstraat house when he was at his store in the stable. He probably saw Gerrit going in there with food and things when it was supposed to be an empty house and put two and two together. It all fits. He knew from van der Meer that the watches had been made by someone who had closed down his business and

236

disappeared, so he must have guessed the watchmaker was a Jew. It's the answer to the biggest question, how the person who betrayed us knew we were there.'

'I agree it fits, it's one possibility, but you can't be absolutely sure, can you? Berger must have somehow communicated with your father, they exchanged invoices, don't forget.'

'I'm sure that's how it happened, it's the only explanation. I'll find out when I find Berger. I'll ask him.'

'Not without me, you won't. You'll steer clear until we think it through.'

'But Jos, I'm so close now, it's all falling into place.'

'All the more reason to take care, you can't go challenging the man who you think sold you out to the Nazis on your own. What about van der Meer?'

'I have to say I've changed my opinion of him. I still don't like him, but I don't think he was in any way involved. Him and Berger was just business, I'm sure. In fact, I think he can probably be trusted, he's offered to help me if I need anything.'

Jos looked concerned. 'In what way?'

'With father's insurance, the house and stuff, possibly. The woman at the Jewish Co-ordination Council said I should get a lawyer.'

'You didn't mention the gold, I hope.'

'Of course not. I'm going to look for Berger's shop tomorrow after the delivery.'

'But you don't approach him, understand?'

'Of course not,' he lied.

WEDNESDAY 7TH NOVEMBER 1945

He slept well, so well in fact that without Grietje to wake him he was almost late for the brewery delivery. He had wanted to be early, and he had hoped the delivery driver would be too, as he had a dental appointment at twelve and was determined to find Berger's shop and visit the registry at City Hall about a new ID card if Jos was able to spare him between the delivery and starting work again at four.

He arrived at the bar breathless and without having eaten breakfast just as the brewery dray was pulling up.

'Bloody hell, you're cutting it fine again, that's twice recently, what's going on?'

'Sorry, but Grietje's away as you know and I overslept.'

'Let's get on with it, it's a big order today.'

'Do you need me after this? I have the dentist and I want to see about a new ID card.'

'No, I suppose I can manage until four. You said you would need a new photograph, didn't you? A friend of mine, Ruud, has a little studio on Rozengracht. He'll do some photos for you and develop them in a couple of hours.'

He laughed. 'Thanks Jos, once again one of your contacts comes to the rescue, but he won't take long, will he?'

'You've got all day till four, what's the rush? What else have you got to do?'

'Just the dentist, but I can't go for the ID card until I have the photographs.' He felt guilty about not telling Jos the truth as he didn't want him going near Berger on his own, but he knew that if he managed to find the shop he wouldn't be able to resist.

The delivery went smoothly and he was at the photographer's by eleven thirty. Ruud told him he could have the photographs ready by one, which fitted in with his dentist appointment in nearby Lauriergracht.

Complete with a very sore mouth, an appointment for yet more dental treatment and his two head and shoulders sized photographs, he made his way to the City Hall in the Prinsenhof only to find that the entire staff of the 'Persoonsbewijs Sectie' were all still out at lunch. Abandoning all thoughts of a new ID card until another day, he hurried over to Spiegelstraat.

Van der Meer hadn't specified exactly where Berger's new shop was, so he found he had the choice of Nieuwe Spiegelstraat or Spiegelgracht. He decided to work his way down one side and back up the other, looking for Berger's name.

A large number of the shops were stocked with high-quality antiques and many did not even carry the owner's or dealer's name above the door. He had almost given up hope when, halfway back up towards Herengracht, he saw a slightly less expensive looking shop, its frontage narrower than many of the others with an untidy window full of mixed objects rather than the single Golden Age painting or large Delft pot of the more expensive businesses.

The name above the small window announced it to be 'E.B. Antiek', which initially meant nothing to him, his attention being immediately drawn to a painting on a small easel in the centre of the window. In its beautiful gilt frame, he found himself looking at the portrait of the girl, the missing sister painting to the one hidden by his father in the base of the box.

His head was spinning at the sight of the painting, made worse by the realisation that 'E.B.Antiek' was of course Edwin Berger and he had at last found the man he thought had betrayed his family. Forgetting Jos's warning, he entered the shop.

Hearing the bell, a man emerged from the back room. Simon recognised him immediately as Edwin Berger from his earlier sightings of him at Kromme Palmstraat and outside van der Meer's house. Immaculately dressed in a crisp, freshly laundered white shirt and silk tie, waistcoat with a heavy gold watch chain visible between the two pockets and matching, beautifully pressed trousers, Berger looked him up and down, noting no doubt his old overcoat, cheap trousers and scuffed shoes.

'Can I help you with anything?' Berger almost sneered at him then, smiling, he showed his gold teeth and smoothed his moustache.

Simon's mouth was dry and at first he was unable to speak. Despite waiting for weeks for this moment he realised, that as Jos had warned him, he didn't know what to say.

Eventually he managed to ask, 'The painting in the window, the one of the young girl. How much is it? I might be interested.'

Berger gave him another disparaging look. 'It's not cheap, it's a very well executed portrait and the frame is very fine too. I've only had it a month or so, a very expensive looking lady came in and sold it to me from her family's collection.'

'How much is it?'

Berger sneered again. 'I told you it's expensive, a hundred and twenty guilders, but it's a good painting in a very valuable frame. Can I suggest that you may find it a little beyond your means?'

He was tempted to take out his wallet and pay for the painting on the spot if only to wipe the patronising look off Berger's face. He knew he just had to have it, he had to recover it somehow from this evil man, but he quickly realised that once he had bought it he would have no reason to return to Berger's shop.

'May I see it? You bought it recently from a woman, you say?'

Berger reached into the window and handed him the painting. 'Yes, a very well-to-do lady came in. She said times were hard, after all the Nazis have left the country on its knees, so I paid her a hundred guilders. I'm only making twenty on the deal.'

240

He examined the painting closely and was left in no doubt that it was indeed the other one of the pair that had hung on the wall above his father's desk in Peperstraat. A glance at the back confirmed it when he saw his father's initials 'A.M.' in pencil in the corner. Added to the discovery of the books in the crate in the stable, he was sure that the story of a woman selling the painting from her family collection must be a complete lie and that Berger had either obtained the painting from the Germans and police after they looted the Dijkstraat house or, more likely, from Kromme Palmstraat after his betrayal of them and their subsequent arrest.

'I would like to buy it but as you say I can't afford it today. If I give you a deposit, will you keep it for me?'

Berger smiled and replied in a condescending voice, 'If you think you will be able to raise the money I would be absolutely delighted to hold it for you. You are obviously a man with a good eye. Can we say twenty guilders today and the rest in a month? I'm sorry, but if you can't pay the balance by then I reserve the right to sell it elsewhere.'

He gave Berger twenty guilders, taking care not to let him see that he had sufficient funds in his wallet to pay the full price five times over.

Feeling more confident, he quickly thought up a story and, in an effort to draw him out, asked Berger about two battered silver pocket watches in the window.

'You like watches too?'

'Not really,' he lied. 'My uncle collects them, only cheap silver ones of course, not gold or anything.'

'I don't suppose he can afford it but tell him to get himself a gold watch or two, a great investment, the others will never be worth anything. Those two in the window are worth virtually nothing. Do you want them?'

'No, not today, but I'll tell him they're here.'

Berger was patronising again. 'Tell your uncle to save up his cents until he can afford one like this. A Jew made it for me during the war.'

Berger reached into his waistcoat pocket with his thumb and

forefinger, pulling out a gold watch, which Simon immediately recognised as identical to those made by his father for van der Meer. Proudly opening the case, Berger showed him the beautiful face of the watch.

Simon felt the anger rising within him at the sight of an example of his father's wonderful skills in the hands of the evil man, who he was sure had sent its maker, his wife and his daughter to their deaths. He made his excuses, promising to return with the money for the painting, and left the shop before he blurted out his real reason for being there.

His head was spinning, his brain working overtime and he remembered little of the walk back to the Jordaan. He had no idea of the time until he walked through the doors of the Café van Loon, which was extremely busy for mid-afternoon.

'Simon! There you are, half an hour early, thank goodness. Get your apron on and start collecting glasses. It's been as busy as hell all afternoon for some reason. I could have used you here, her upstairs has been no help at all. Come on, don't just stand there. Whatever's the matter with you? Get working!'

'I'm sorry Jos, something's happened with Berger, I need to talk to you. I don't know what to do.'

'I'll tell you what to do, get those bloody glasses collected and washed, bring up two crates of Heineken and then we'll talk.'

Without Maaike at six, and Jos's wife refusing to come down to help, they were busy and unable to talk at any length until ten when Jos, apparently satisfied with the day's takings, decided to close the door. They settled down at an upstairs table, Jos with his usual beer and jenever and Simon with a beer.

'Now then, what the hell has been going on? I thought you were off to the dentist, the photographer's and then the Prinsenhof about your ID.'

'Well, I was, I mean I did. I went to the dentist and got the photographs but they were out to lunch at Prinsenhof, so I went to look for Berger's shop.'

'And you found it?'

'Yes, and I found him as well.'

'You didn't approach him, I hope.'

'I did. I'm sorry. I know I said I wouldn't but I saw…'

Jos interrupted angrily, 'You bloody fool, what did I tell you? Why on earth couldn't you leave it just for today?'

'But I saw father's missing painting in the window. It was there, right in the middle on a little easel, the one of the girl that went with the one of the boy we found in the box. I just had to go in and try to find out about it, I'm sorry, but I just had to.'

'And it was definitely him? The man we saw that day and the one you saw at that lawyer's place?'

'Yes.'

'And it was definitely your father's painting?'

'Yes, he tried to say he bought it from a woman a few weeks ago but father would never have sold it. It was obviously a lie, there was no woman, it was probably with all the other things of ours that I saw in that crate in the stable when we went in with Piet. It even had father's initials on the back. He was trying to charge a hundred and twenty guilders for it.'

'It's strange though, why was that painting separate from the other one? Why didn't he put both paintings in the box and how did Berger get his hands on it?'

'It must have been on the wall at Kromme Palmstraat, up in the attic where father was working. I never saw it though, we weren't allowed up there, but it's the only possible explanation. Maybe he wanted to be able to look at it every day and he just never got around to putting it in the crate with the other one before we were arrested and the Germans got it. Either that or Berger got it from my father another way, by blackmailing him or something. I just know a woman couldn't have walked into his shop with it, how would she have got it? He even said it was part of the woman's family collection.'

'So, what did you do about it?'

'I said I wanted to buy it, but Berger obviously thought I couldn't afford it. He looked at me like I wasn't fit to be in his shop, which isn't one of the better ones by the way, so I asked if I could leave a deposit mainly to give me an excuse to go back. I've got to have it, even if I have to pay his full price. I don't care, I've just got to get it back.'

'You won't be paying for it, trust me, we'll get it back without you giving him a cent. Did you find out anything else?'

'You were absolutely right, I shouldn't have spoken to him on my own. I really didn't know what to say so I didn't challenge him or accuse him or anything, but I did manage to get him to show me the watch father made for him. Seeing him with the watch felt worse than him having the painting. He even said a Jew made it for him in the war.'

'We'll get that back as well, don't worry.'

'It's not just those things though, I want him to admit it was he who betrayed us, and I need him to tell me why. Of course he'll never admit it and we'll never prove it either.'

'He will, he will, I'll see to that.'

'He gave me a month to pay the balance for the painting or he'll put it back on sale.'

'We'll give him a visit before then. Now get off home and take this with you. Give it to Grietje Blok.' Jos handed him a parcel wrapped in brown paper.

'Whatever is it?'

'Two bicycle tyres and two inner tubes for her bicycle, they're still hard to find but these came from...'

'A contact of yours.'

'I thought it would help, she'll be able to cycle to work instead of all that walking. She might even lend the bike to you at weekends.'

'I've never ridden one, we always walked. I don't know if I can do it.'

'Bloody hell, you're supposed to be an Amsterdammer and you can't ride a bike?'

Simon walked slowly back to Slootstraat feeling strangely disillusioned rather than elated about finally meeting Berger face to face and desperately wishing Maaike was with him.

He let himself in and found a letter on the floor in the hall. Maaike had arrived safely and had written to him literally as soon as she had arrived at her aunt's house. She was coming back on Monday as planned and needed him to meet her at Amersfoort station from the Zwolle train which was due to arrive at two thirty.

All thoughts and concerns about how he was going to approach Berger went out of his head and he went to bed a happy man. Maaike was safe and coming back and he resolved to talk to her about his plans for their future.

FRIDAY 9TH NOVEMBER 1945

He had hoped to hear something on Thursday from Abraham Hirschfeld about the gold purchase or perhaps from Jos about how they might approach Berger, but neither was forthcoming.

In the morning he'd visited City Hall at the Prinsenhof and presented himself, his old card and new photographs before the staff in the ID card section could disappear for lunch. They'd taken his details and material but were unable to issue a new ID card until his personal record had been located in the central registry at the Public Records Office on Plantage Kerklaan.

He'd thought about going past Berger's shop again but realised there was no point so he'd walked back to Slootstraat for lunch after which, with time on his hands, he'd gone into work early.

On Friday morning, however, he was particularly busy. Grietje was due back but he didn't know what time, and as he wanted to get some food in for her return he made his way to the shops very early.

When he got back he ate breakfast before enlisting the help of Aart, who was on his day off, to put the new tyres on Grietje's bicycle as a surprise for her return. He'd never changed a tyre or even mended a puncture before, but Aart produced tyre levers and a pump and made short work of it. It transpired that the second tireless bicycle in the hall was Aart's, and as part of the deal he promised to try to get him a set of tyres too so he could cycle to the tram depot again.

Simon had decided some days before that he would visit his old shul and in the hope that his personal record card had been retrieved, he called in at City Hall on the way. A bored front desk clerk told him it would take more time as some of the cards, which he assumed included those under the letter M, were still in a 'state of disarray' following an attempt by the resistance to burn them in 1943. It struck him that to take two years to reorganise, the staff in the Plantage Kerklaan office must be in a greater state of disarray than the cards they managed.

Leaving City Hall, he made his way via Nieuwmarkt to his old shul next to the diamond factory on Nieuwe Uilenburgerstraat. He resisted the temptation to walk through Dijkstraat; part of him had wanted to see his old home again, but realistically he knew there was no point. The shul was set back from the road and as he approached he saw to his surprise that the doors were open. An old man shuffled across the steps sweeping away fallen leaves, presumably in preparation for the prayer service that evening.

The man turned as he approached. 'Goedemorgen, can I help?'

'Shalom aleikhem.'

'Aleikhem shalom, young man. What can I do for you?'

'I just wanted to visit the shul again, my family worshipped here before the war.'

'You're a Jew then, I'm sorry I didn't realise. I should have known when you greeted me. What is your family name?'

'I'm Simon Mendelevski, my father was...'

'Aviel Mendelevski, you're Aviel Mendelevski's son? The last time we met you were just a young boy.'

'Hardly a young boy but yes, I have changed a little. I'm sorry but I don't remember you.'

'The war aged us all but welcome, welcome, and your father and mother?'

'Both dead, and my sister Esther.'

The old man shook his head. 'They're all dead, there's no one left. Our community is finished, all the young ones are gone. There is a service tonight if enough people attend for a minyan. Our shul was desecrated by the Nazis but it survived and thankfully most of our precious things like the torah were safely hidden away. But sadly, most of our congregation is dead. I was lucky, I was in Bergen-Belsen but I lived.'

'We were in Auschwitz, I am the only survivor.'

'Would you like to come inside?'

'I don't know, I have been non-observant now for three years and I am in love with a Gentile woman.'

'Many find themselves in that position, but you are all still Jews, you must return to us, to this shul, you are wanted and needed. Come this evening or tomorrow, make up the minyan.'

Simon looked down at his feet in shame. 'I work this evening and on the Sabbath.'

The old man was silent for a moment. 'We all have to live. Please come inside for a moment, look around and remember. Your father was a reader here.'

'That's right, he was.' He followed the old man through the doors, collecting a yarmulke from a basket in the hallway and covering his head for the first time in three years. All his memories returned as he saw the ark and the reader's podium once occupied by his father. He turned and hurried back into the hallway.

'I'm sorry, it's all too much for me.'

'I understand but please, come back to us, we are all your family and we need you. I fear our shul will close forever.'

He walked slowly back to the Jordaan, making a diversion along Rapenburgerstraat past the Ashkenazi Seminary, where he had studied until late 1941, the Rapenburger Shul next door and the Ashkenazi Girls' Orphanage. All were standing but in a poor state of repair and deserted, their pupils and congregation gone, he assumed, forever. He was lost in deep thought about his own shul, his community, such as it now was, his culture and his religion. He knew that he must return and that he could never, and must never, allow that which had killed his family to ruin his life and separate him from Judaism. Quite how and when he would be ready and able to return he didn't know, and much depended on Maaike being part of it.

He got back to Slootstraat at about one and heard Grietje in the kitchen.

'Simon, is that you?'

'Grietje, welcome home! Where's Irene?'

'Still in Utrecht, she wanted to stay a little longer with her Oma and Opa. I had to come back to work but I'm going there again next Saturday and bringing her home on Sunday.'

'Did you both have a nice time?'

'Irene certainly did, they spoiled her terribly. Thank you for getting the shopping by the way. I hope you had enough to eat while I was away, there was no Maaike here either to feed you. Did she get to her aunt's safely?'

'She did. She's back on Monday as planned. I'll go to the market for the rest of the shopping tomorrow as you're working. Now, didn't you see your surprise?'

'What surprise?'

'You walked past it. Go and look in the hall.'

'Simon! Simon!' She almost screamed. 'How did you get them, how did you do it? Thank you, thank you so much.' She started to kiss him profusely.

'Don't thank me, thank Jos, and old Aart upstairs as well, he fitted them. I had no idea how to do it.'

She clapped her hands with joy like a small girl. 'It's wonderful, I can cycle to work, to the shops to...well, everywhere again in fact, I think I'll cycle this afternoon when I take the washing.'

'Take it easy to start with,' he joked. 'You might be out of practice.'

'Now, tell me what you have been up to while I've been away.'

'Nothing very much. All very boring, ordinary things really. I went to the dentist and the Jewish Co-ordination Committee, and tried to sort out my ID.'

'Nothing very exciting then?'

His face broke into a grin. 'I'm kidding you. Something absolutely amazing has happened, although I don't know what to do next. I saw him again, I saw Berger, he was leaving the house of the lawyer I told you about.'

'Go on then, don't keep me in suspense.'

'I asked the lawyer about him and he told me where his shop was and I found it. It's on Nieuwe Spiegelstraat and I found him there too, and guess what? That painting, the one of the girl in the gilt frame, you know it, the one that goes with the matching one of the boy, remember, you told me that you helped father pack them in Peperstraat. There it was, in his window. Now I absolutely know he is the one, he betrayed us then somehow he got hold of the painting. He tried to tell me he bought the painting from a woman, but I just know he was lying.'

She said nothing and hurriedly looked away, her mind reeling at the mention of the painting.

'What do you think? You don't seem very pleased for me. I've found the man who betrayed us. Jos is thinking of a way to get him to admit it and get the painting back. Berger is trying to sell it for a hundred and twenty guilders.'

She sounded shocked. 'A hundred and twenty?'

'Yes, why do you ask?'

'No reason. It just sounds a lot, that's all.' She changed the subject. 'Now what do you want for lunch? It's getting late and you have to be at work at four, don't you?'

Jos motioned to him to go down to the cellar as soon as he walked in. His wife was behind the bar and, seeing them disappear down the steps, unleashed her usual barrage of anger.

'Don't you two lazy sods hide away down there. The kid is here to work, and you can take over from me, Jos van Loon.'

He called up to his wife. 'I'm just changing the barrel, dearest, and Simon is getting his apron.'

He put his finger to his lips and whispered, 'Hirschfeld's man has been in, that big fellow who was here with him before. He wants to meet us and discuss the deal on Sunday. I suppose tomorrow was out as it's the old man's Sabbath but it suits us best anyway as we're closed on Sunday and it's your day off. The main thing is he wants to meet here so we won't have to take the gold to his place. Is that alright with you? Ten thirty in the morning?'

'That's fine by me.'

'I'll find out the latest price per gram from my friend tomorrow so we're right up to date. The price is quoted in US dollars, so I imagine that's what Hirschfeld will use.'

'You mean he'll pay me in dollars?'

'I really don't know, it's obvious he's had to get at least one other person in to help finance things, that's why it's taken him a week to get back to us, but I don't know if he'll actually pay and take the gold on Sunday. I suspect he may just want to weigh the bulk, do the calculations, and make you an offer.'

'What am I going to do if he pays in cash of any currency?'

'I don't know, but get yourself a bank account when you get your new ID card, open it with a couple of hundred guilders, which should be alright, and we'll go from there.'

'I'll do it on Monday first thing before I go to meet Maaike.'

'Good, the place has been awful since she went away. The regulars are miserable and I'm working too damn hard. I can't wait to have her back.'

SUNDAY 11TH NOVEMBER 1945

He was at the bar by ten fifteen, soaked to the skin in the pouring rain. He knocked and Jos let him in almost immediately.

'Good morning, hell you're wet, come in and get that coat off. I'll make coffee. Keep as quiet as you can, I don't want her upstairs waking up and poking her nose in.'

He heard a car and looked out of the window to see Hirschfeld and his burly friend getting out of a huge maroon Mercedes-Benz saloon with a uniformed driver. The two men hurried across the pavement and approached the door, Hirschfeld with his old leather satchel and his colleague carrying a large wooden box.

He opened the door before they could knock and drew the heavy curtain across the door behind them just as Jos re-appeared with coffee.

Hirschfeld spoke first. 'Shalom aleikhem Simon, goedemorgen Meneer van Loon.'

'Aleikhem shalom Meneer Hirschfeld, goedemorgen Joost.'

Joost remained silent as usual, busying himself opening the wooden box and setting up a large pair of scales while Jos served coffee.

'To business. All I want to do today is get the gross weight of your coins and the watch cases, calculate the weight of gold, and apply the current price, which I am sure Meneer van Loon has already checked for you, to arrive at a total on which I hope we can both agree. You must appreciate Simon that the price of gold can go down as well as up and therefore my offer may not exactly match the final total of our calculation.'

Jos gave him a sideways 'I told you so' glance before opening his mouth to say something which would undoubtedly have offended the old Jew.

Simon spoke first, cleverly keeping the peace between them. 'Of course, we understand, don't we, Jos?'

Jos mumbled his agreement and poured the coffee before retrieving the two bags of gold coins and the watch cases from behind the bar where he had put them prior to Hirschfeld's arrival.

The old man closely examined the wax seals on the tapes securing the two bags before he broke them and opened the bags.

'Have you got your lists?'

Jos produced his and Joost took the other one from Hirschfeld's leather satchel.

'You recall that I told you that both the twenties and the tens were ninety percent gold.'

Jos nodded. 'I checked on that, it's correct.'

'So I can weigh both together. Agreed?'

Hirschfeld poured the contents of the first bag onto one pan of the scale and placed a one kilogram weight, after showing it to him and Jos, on the other pan. He then added more coins from the second bag until the scales balanced.

'We have one kilo gross weight so far. Are we agreed? If so, please note it on your respective lists.'

After emptying the first pan Hirschfeld poured the remaining coins into it, changing to a selection of smaller weights. The scales balanced at a weight of 965 grams.

After showing the weights to him and Jos, Hirschfeld asked, 'Are we agreed on that, gentlemen? 965 grams?'

Both nodded and each made a note.

'So, if my old brain still works and my mathematics are correct, we have 1965 grams gross weight. Yes?'

Jos wrote the figure down.

'Now for the complicated bit, the calculations. The gold content is ninety percent, so ninety percent of 1,965 is...'

Jos started frantically scribbling, shook his head in despair and quickly handed the paper over to Simon. Moments before he could complete his calculations, without even writing anything down, Hirschfeld announced the total.

'I make it 1,768.5 grams. You're going to be a very rich boy, Simon.'

'Absolutely correct,' Jos laughed. 'Just what I was going to say, but you were too quick for me.'

'Now to the difficult part. We have to apply the price per ounce not per gram, as that is how it is quoted on the market. Also, as you will know from your checks, the market price per ounce is quoted in US dollars. Now, Meneer van Loon, let's hope we both have the same rate.'

'I was told the rate was thirty-seven and a quarter dollars an ounce.'

'I have thirty-seven dollars and fifteen cents but we'll use your rate, I hope we're not going to argue over ten US cents an ounce.' The old Jew stroked his beard and smiled at Jos, clearly humouring him.

'But first we have to change grams to ounces, how do we do that?' wondered Simon. 'I don't know the rate. I've never heard of ounces.'

'Fortunately, I do know,' said Abe and took a chart from his bag. 'Thanks to this I can tell you that 1768.5 grams is equal to roughly sixty-two and a half ounces.'

Jos looked uncomfortable. 'Roughly? How do we know that's right?'

'Please check it for yourself, look at the chart if you don't believe me. I'll give you the conversion rate if you want to work it out for yourself.' He handed Jos a pencil.

Simon quickly covered both Jos's embarrassment and Hirschfeld's rising anger. 'That won't be necessary, I accept your figure is correct.'

'Thank you, now for the all important calculation, and this time I want Meneer van Loon and Joost to both work it out.'

Simon interrupted again to spare Jos. 'Why don't you and I do it and we can write our totals on the other's sheet.'

'An excellent idea.'

Jos looked suspicious, but both he and Joost seemed extremely relieved that they had been left out of the final mathematics.

Hirschfeld finished first and waited for him before he spoke. '2,328 dollars, Simon. Do you agree?'

'I do.' He showed Hirschfeld his figures.

'You're a bright lad, your father would be so proud. It's a nice amount of money, equal to over 6,000 guilders, but I'm afraid it's not a huge profit on what your father bought them at before the war. The rate then was about thirty-five dollars an ounce and the price hasn't gone up all that much despite the war. Lots of people were panic buying gold and paying ridiculously high rates when the Nazis first arrived as they feared for the guilder.' He smiled weakly and spread his hands. 'In fact I think your father may have paid me a little more in 1940, but I'm buying at the proper market rate today, less a little of course for my trouble and in case the rate goes down.'

Simon was thinking of van der Meer's hugely inflated deal with his father when Jos said angrily, 'How much less exactly, Meneer Hirschfeld? How much are you taking?'

The old Jew looked hurt. 'I know you are looking after Simon's interests, but you must understand I have to make a little, obviously I cannot sell at the same price as I buy.' His eyes twinkled mischievously. 'Surely you don't do that with beer or, say, Canadian Club whisky?'

The hint passed over Jos's head but Simon picked up on it.

'I think perhaps our guests might like a drink before we seal the deal Jos.'

'I certainly need one.'

Jos brought a tray of drinks, beers for him and Joost, beer and a jenever for himself, and a large Canadian Club for Hirschfeld.

'Now we come to the watch cases. But before we start, are you content with my opinion that they are seventy percent gold?'

Simon nodded in agreement and Hirschfeld placed all three cases on the scale.

'450 grams gross weight, 150 grams each, agreed?'

Once again the old man demonstrated his mathematical prowess, arriving at the total weight of the gold virtually in the blink of an eye.

'At seventy percent, this gives us 315 grams of gold.'

Jos looked concerned again but kept quiet, presumably to avoid being invited to do the calculation himself.

'My chart tells me that is equivalent to just over eleven ounces which at thirty-seven dollars and twenty-five cents an ounce gives us...' He quickly scribbled the figures down. 'Near enough 410 dollars.'

'I bow to your outstanding mathematics.' Simon smiled at the old Jew. 'I'm sure you are absolutely correct.'

'Thank you. What about Meneer van Loon, are you satisfied?'

'If Simon is, then so am I.'

'Now to the difficult bit, the negotiations. We have a total gold value of 2,738 dollars.'

He noticed Jos out of the corner of his eye checking the addition of the two totals on a beer mat. Clearly this calculation was within Jos's mathematical capabilities and he nodded his agreement.

'As you are probably aware I have had to seek a financial partner to join me in this purchase. It is equivalent to almost 7,300 guilders. Before we discuss how much I can offer you, I need to tell you that my partner wants to pay by cheque or, if you prefer, by banker's draft. Do you have a bank account?'

'No way!' Jos finally reverted to type and interrupted before Simon could answer. 'I'm sorry, but there is no way Simon is going to accept a cheque.'

The atmosphere was extremely tense for a few moments but Hirschfeld forced a smile and attempted to defuse the situation and assure Jos.

'Please gentlemen, hear me out. The coins and the watch cases remain here with Simon until the cheque has cleared. In fact if my partner obtains a banker's draft it is absolutely guaranteed to clear very quickly. The man financing this purchase with me is both extremely honest and upright and very well to do. I can't divulge his name but he is quite a prominent figure in his field. Please understand the payment will not be a problem in any way.'

Jos jumped in again. 'In that case, why can't he pay Simon in cash?'

'Meneer van Loon, Jos, if you try to deposit over 7,000 guilders in cash or 2,700 US dollars into your bank account in the current climate, questions will be asked. If my co-investor pays one of his legitimate company cheques into your account, it will almost certainly be seen as the proceeds of a house sale or a genuine business transaction. Cash would cause you a problem, I think.'

'That's true, Jos and I have already discussed that.' He turned to Jos.

'I suppose it would solve a problem but the cheque or draft thing has to clear. We do nothing until the amount is credited to Simon's bank.'

'Agreed, but now we need to discuss the final price. The approximate value in guilders is 7,300. My offer to you is 6,500.'

'What! You must be bloody joking.' Jos almost exploded. 'If that's all you can do the deal's off. You're virtually stealing from the lad.'

'Jos, please, don't be hasty.' Simon desperately tried to keep the peace between the two men.

'Meneer, I have to make a profit and that profit will have to be shared with my partner, a few hundred guilders that's all, not much for my trouble. I'm already being generous to Simon as he is one of us. After all, the price could go down tomorrow.'

'Oh please, you're breaking my heart.' Jos said sarcastically.

'Abe has a point Jos, he is a businessman, not a charity for young Jews.'

Simon laughed but no one else saw the joke.

'I'm sure this 'businessman' could do a little better, Simon.'

Hirschfeld held up his hands. 'Simon, your friend is a much cleverer trader than he wishes to appear. He wants to deal, he is trying for a better offer from me.'

'And you, my friend, have quoted a price that gives you room to move.'

The old man smiled knowingly, stroking his beard and thinking deeply. Feigning hardship and defeat he answered Jos almost in a whisper, 'Meneer, how can I live, how can I feed my wife if I have to deal with you? You are a hard man.' He drained his glass, and looked up at Jos, and smiled. 'The Canadians brought us more than just our freedom, their whisky is excellent.'

Jos fetched the bottle and Hirschfeld refilled his glass.

'I like this boy, he is the future of our race and his father was a fine and honest man, a skilled workman who spent money with me. 6,650, last offer.'

Simon opened his mouth to accept but Jos grabbed his arm. The bar owner turned to Hirschfeld again. '6,800, last offer.'

The old man shook his head but grasped Simon's hand. 'I give up, it is agreed. We have a deal but promise me you will go back to your shul and make an old man happy. Now, give me your bank account details, please.'

'I don't have one yet. I plan to open one on Monday.'

'Oh dear. Very well, it will delay things but perhaps you could tell them you are expecting a large payment from a business transaction, it will help to smooth the way. I will arrange for Joost to deliver a cheque, or preferably a banker's draft, as soon as I obtain it from my partner and then you can pay it into the bank yourself. When it clears, Joost and I will come to collect the goods.'

The younger man packed the scales while Hirschfeld resealed the coin bags as before, but this time placing the watch cases inside with the coins.

Hirschfeld shook hands enthusiastically with Jos. 'You're a hard man but you were a good opponent and thank you for looking after this young man's interests. We must leave soon, our borrowed driver has been waiting outside in the car but perhaps one more small whisky to keep out the damp?'

The two men shared another drink while Joost took the scales out to the car.

'Zen ir bald Simon, tot ziens Jos van Loon. Remember old Abraham Hirschfeld in your prayers, won't you?'

'We will, we will, you can be sure of that,' Jos muttered under his breath.

'Thank you for looking out for me with Abe like that.'

'I just didn't want him to swindle you, he's a crafty old devil. You've agreed to a deal where he pays you 500 guilders less than the full value and it could even be more depending on the rate of exchange of the US dollar.'

'I know all that, but he has got to make something out of it and so does his backer, whoever he is, plus the gold price might go down.'

'I doubt that very much, and he's already made money selling it to your father in the first place. I'm sure the money man can afford to sit on it until it goes up, which it will.'

'I'm not sure now the war is over, after all it didn't go up that much during the war. It was just that people were paying more than the going rate in order to get gold instead of guilders.'

'Tell me about it, I did the same thing with my jewellery purchase. If it's not the rising price, then all I can think of is that the money man must be getting rid of some dodgy cash.'

'I'm sure you're right.'

'And you don't mind? Bloody hell Simon, you're learning at last, lad, I'll make you streetwise yet.'

MONDAY 12TH NOVEMBER 1945

He was up and about early, excited by Maaike coming back and anxious to get to a bank but first he had to go back to City Hall to collect his new ID card as the bank would almost certainly need some form of identification.

Grietje was getting breakfast as usual but without having Irene to worry about. 'What time is Maaike back?'

'I have to meet her at Amersfoort at two thirty.'

'You'll be pleased to see her again, I suppose.'

'Yes, very pleased.'

'Me too, I know Irene is missing her, she told her grandmother all about her, and you too.'

'Only good things I hope.'

'Of course, and speaking of good things I'm cycling to work today. It will be the first time in so long, I can't wait.'

He was at City Hall as soon as it opened and, to both his amazement and relief, his new ID card, no longer bearing anything to identify him as a Jew, had been prepared and was ready and awaiting collection. His personal record card had been retrieved, undamaged by the fire, from Plantage Kerklaan. It bore his old Dijkstraat address, followed by an entry showing his transportation date and the Westerbork destination. He noted his new address in Slootstraat had been added.

On Jos's recommendation he went to the Rabobank on Rokin. He presented himself together with his ID card and an introductory note from Jos to a counter clerk. He was extremely doubtful that Jos's reference, however well it was meant, would carry much weight, but the clerk, who apparently knew him personally, was impressed.

'Ah yes, Meneer van Loon, from the Café van Loon. He has had an account here for many years, a good customer and a very honest and reliable man. If I recall correctly, he spoke to me about you wanting to open an account some weeks ago.'

To his surprise the creation of an account was relatively easy and took only a matter of minutes. He deposited 200 guilders and told the clerk he was expecting a large amount to be deposited or transferred into the account within days. The clerk assured him that, providing the funds were not in cash, were the proceeds of a genuine business transaction, and came from a reputable source, there would be no problem. Clearly, having Jos van Loon as a referee carried an amazing amount of influence.

Feeling guilty that the clerk was under the false impression that the forthcoming large deposit was from a genuine business deal, he quickly collected his new account details and first ever bank book. The clerk even apologised that his cheque book would take a few days to arrive.

Resisting the temptation to divert to Nieuwe Spiegelstraat, he made his way directly to Centraal Station. He wanted to look in the window to check on his father's painting but he decided against it because he knew that, if he saw Berger, he would almost certainly weaken and hand over the balance in order to get the painting back.

He arrived in Amersfoort an hour before Maaike's train was due, so he waited in the station buffet with a coffee and a newspaper. The news was all about the fierce fighting that was taking place in Surabaya as the war in the East Indies intensified. He put the paper aside, unwilling to read any more about yet another war. Instead he pondered over how he was going to tell Maaike his plans for the future and, more importantly, how he was going to persuade her to join him. Now that the gold sale was all but complete, he had a new ID card and bank account and Berger had been found, if not yet actually challenged, his path ahead was clear and he knew exactly what he wanted to do but it had to include Maaike.

The train was a few minutes late and he was waiting anxiously on the platform as it finally pulled in. He saw her at the door and, opening it, she literally fell from the train into his arms and kissed him. The Friesland air had obviously agreed with her and clearly she had been eating well; she had rosy cheeks and her face no longer looked as grey and drawn as it had in Slootstraat. 'Simon, I missed you so much!'

'I missed you as well. Let me get your suitcase, the Amsterdam train leaves in three minutes. We really have to talk, I have so much to tell you. I've found him, I've found Berger, you'll never guess who knows him, and he's got father's other picture. I changed my ID card, opened a bank account and I sold the coins and I've got nearly seven thousand guilders coming for them. Oh, and I went to my old shul and I'm thinking of...'

'Slow down, slow down. I've got something to tell you as well, let's talk on the train.'

They settled into their seats and Maaike looked at him. 'Go on, tell me all. I thought you had given up on Berger.'

'No, you go first, it's a really long story and I'll probably still be talking when we get back to Amsterdam. Besides, I have one big thing to say, or to ask you rather. How was Aunt Nel?'

'She was lovely, they all were. Uncle Johannes was at home. He fishes out of Harlingen and normally only gets home to Leeuwarden every few weeks, so I saw him as well, in fact I think all the Bootsma family came around to see me. They were all a bit shocked about my leg and they fussed over me to start with but when they saw I can manage quite well they relaxed a bit. They didn't suffer too much in the war, thank goodness. Leeuwarden airfield was bombed by the Americans I think, and the Germans commandeered uncle's fishing boat for two years so he couldn't fish. The coastal area was restricted anyway, but food wasn't too short for them last winter. In fact they helped people from Amsterdam who were starving and came to Friesland looking for food.'

'You look really well, it obviously suited you up there. Fresh air and good food, I suppose.'

'It was wonderful. Clean, not like Amsterdam at all, wide open spaces, a much slower pace, everything was lovely. I'd forgotten how nice Leeuwarden was, after all I was very young when we left. My family made me feel very at home.'

'I thought you said there was nothing there for you?'

'I did, but this visit has made me see things differently. It's made me realise I don't want to be in Amsterdam anymore. After all, I only stayed here in the hope my papa would return.'

'You want to leave?' He was initially terrified she wanted to leave him, but then suddenly hopeful that it might be easier to persuade her to go away with him on the adventure he had planned.

'Only if you come with me, I don't want to leave you. If you don't come, then I'm not going.' She looked at him and felt for his hand. 'I love you Simon, and I want to be with you wherever I go.'

'But where to?'

'To Leeuwarden. I told Aunt Nel and Uncle Johannes all about you, all about us, and they want to meet you.'

'You told them I'm a Jew?'

'I told them all about you, absolutely everything, how you survived the camp but lost your family and how much you mean to me. They have a very small house my uncle's mother left to him, they said you could rent it and live there.'

'But what about you?'

'I'd have to live with them of course, we couldn't live together unless we were... Anyway, both the boys have left home and uncle is away a lot so there is plenty of room just for me and Aunt Nel.'

'I don't know. I have to be with you and if you want to go then of

263

course I'll go too, but Leeuwarden for the rest of our lives? I'm not sure.'

'We don't have to decide now. What about that plan for the future you mentioned? I hope that still includes me. We could go to Leeuwarden until you make a final decision, perhaps.'

'I have got this crazy idea, you might not like it but of course it includes you.'

'Go on, tell me, don't keep me in suspense any longer. I don't really care where we go or what we do so long as we are together.'

'Not yet, I still need to sort it all out in my head. First though I must tell you all about what's been happening while you were away.'

He told her how he had seen Berger at van der Meer's and then found him and his shop thanks to information van der Meer had given him and that his father's missing painting was in the shop window.

'He said he'd bought it from a woman recently, but of course that's a lie. He had a watch that was obviously my father's work too.'

'So there was a watch matching the invoice after all?'

'Yes, father issued an invoice and made a watch but I'm sure Berger never paid for it.'

'What are you going to do about it?'

'Jos is going to come up with something, he doesn't want me to accuse him outright.'

He told her about his new ID card and opening a bank account.

'And what about the coins? You said 7,000 guilders, that's a fortune!'

'Abraham Hirschfeld came to the bar again, weighed it all up and gave me a price. He's not financing it all himself though, he's got a backer who's going to pay me with a banker's draft, which puts the money straight into my bank.'

'Now you're a very rich man, with that, the money you already had in Jos's place and the other coins. Plus there's the insurance and the house.'

'I don't know about those things, both are a bit of a problem. I've had an idea that I might ask van der Meer to handle that for me, especially if we're going to be leaving Amsterdam. There's something very special I want to do with some of the money that I might ask him to deal with as well. I can afford to pay him.' He laughed. 'Wouldn't it be ironic if he was working for me?'

'Even more surprises? When are you going to tell me what else you have in mind?'

He kissed her. 'As soon as I have thought it all through you'll be the first to know, I promise. I want you involved in everything, I want our future to be together.'

They took a taxi from the station. The driver looked surprised that the couple hiring him asked to be taken to one of the poorest streets in Amsterdam, but grinned happily as he pocketed a large tip.

'I can't wait to see Grietje and Irene, I hope they're in.'

'Grietje probably will be now she's cycling back from work again.'

'Cycling? How on earth did she get tyres?'

'A friend got them through a contact.'

'Let me guess, Jos.'

They both collapsed with laughter.

'Grietje said something about cooking us both a meal tonight as you have no food in, but Irene is still in Utrecht. Grietje is going back there on Saturday to collect her.'

'And staying the night?'

'I think so, why do you ask?'

She giggled and snuggled up to him as he opened the door. 'I thought we might manage that special time together.'

WEDNESDAY 14TH NOVEMBER 1945

He and Jos finished the delivery, managed to get rid of the drayman without the usual lengthy chat over a beer, and sat down with coffee.

'Great to have Maaike back last night, all the regulars think she's wonderful, you know.'

'So do I, I missed her very much. Nothing's decided yet, but she has been asked by her family to move back to Friesland.'

'I hope she's not going. Well, if she wants to then I suppose she must, but I'll miss her, the business will miss her.'

'So would I, that's why I might go too.'

'Bloody hell, not you too.'

'If she goes I'll go as well. I have to be with her, I love her.'

'Love! You've only got to look at my wife to see where love gets you.'

They sat in silence for a few moments then he spoke. 'I haven't worked it out yet, but I was seriously thinking of leaving Amsterdam anyway and starting again somewhere away from all the bad memories this place holds even before Maaike mentioned Leeuwarden. My plan would take us a lot further than Friesland.'

He outlined his idea for his future and for his newfound wealth to Jos, the first person he had shared his thoughts with.

'That's a lot to take in, it's massive, very ambitious. What does Maaike think?'

'I haven't told her anything yet, you're the only one I've spoken to. Please keep it to yourself until I've thought it through. It will be a while yet, there will be paperwork to sort out before we can go so it's Leeuwarden for now with Maaike's family.'

'Of course lad, I'll miss the both of you but if you do it then it will really be the start of a new life after what the war did to you both. I'll be proud to wave you two off.'

'Whether we go or not, whatever progress I've made is down to you, I can never thank you enough.'

'You're welcome, I care very much for you and Maaike. I'd better get on with sorting Berger out quickly then if you're about to leave me.'

The front door rattled and Jos turned angrily. 'Bloody people, can't they read the opening times?' He shouted, 'We're closed, come back at eleven.'

The door rattled again and whoever it was began knocking too. Jos strode across to the door, drew back the bolts and prepared to give the caller a mouthful of obscenities.

Instead he fell silent as the large figure of Abraham Hirschfeld's assistant stepped into the room holding an envelope.

'Goedemorgen Meneer van Loon, I'm sorry to bother you before you are open, but I have something to deliver from Meneer Hirschfeld, or rather from his partner, in the business Meneer Mendelevski and he discussed. Perhaps he can pay it into his bank as soon as possible? It will clear almost immediately and Meneer Hirschfeld wishes to collect the goods on Saturday.'

'Is he allowed to do that? I thought he wouldn't be able to work on Saturday, it's his Sabbath or something, isn't it?'

Joost laughed. 'Meneer, where there is money involved Abraham Hirschfeld always conveniently bends the rules.'

'Well, check it then, Simon.'

He opened the envelope and took out a banker's draft made out to him for 7,000 guilders drawn on the account of 'Mokum Investments'.

'I think there's a mistake, it's 200 guilders too much.'

Jos gave him a 'keep your mouth shut you silly boy' look before Joost spoke.

'My employer's partner thought the deal was rather hard on you and wanted the amount to be rounded up as a gesture of good faith. Meneer Hirschfeld agreed when it was established that it would not affect his share of the profit.'

All three of them laughed.

Jos visibly relaxed and, inviting Joost to sit down, opened three beers.

'A toast. To young Simon, Abe and his mystery backer.' They raised their glasses in Simon's direction and Jos lit one of his cigars.

'Get yourself off to the bank,' Jos told Simon, 'the sooner that's paid in the sooner Meneer Hirschfeld can collect his goods. I don't need you until four. My new friend Joost and I are going to have a few more beers before I have to open up.'

Simon raced to Slootstraat to see Maaike and show her the draft. They went to the bank together and paid it into his account.

'The money will be credited to your account overnight tonight and you will be able to draw on it by lunchtime tomorrow.' The clerk shook his hand and smiled at Maaike. 'Thank you for your business and please do not hesitate to contact us if you need anything further.'

Out in the street Maaike turned to him. 'Oh Simon, or should I say Meneer Mendelevski, you are obviously a very valuable customer. I felt so proud to be with you. The clerk couldn't do enough for you.' She giggled. 'Fancy me having one of Amsterdam's most important citizens on my arm.'

'Stop it! He probably ingratiates himself with all his customers, I expect it's all part of the bank's service, but it is nice to have some standing again. Even as a boy I was respected because of father, but I was a nobody when I returned. A lot has happened in a few weeks.'

They celebrated his newfound wealth with lunch in a cafe, a treat for both of them.

'I want to show you something or rather somewhere. Can you walk a little further? I think we can get a tram part of the way back.'

'Of course, what is it?'

'First I want to show you our old house but mainly I want to show you our old shul, our church you'd call it. I've been thinking about my religion a lot recently.'

'You want to go back to it, don't you?'

'How did you know? I'm not sure, but what would you say if I did?'

'Simon, it's you I love, I knew you were a Jew and what that involves from the first day we met. You must do what you feel, I'll be there with you and I'll share it with you if that's what it takes.'

He gripped her arm and kissed her on the cheek.

They walked slowly down Dijkstraat, passing the house with its illegal occupants.

'It's a lovely house, I can just imagine your family in there. It's awful that someone has taken it, you simply must get it back.'

'It was lovely, a lovely cosy family home. We were so happy there. I'm not sure I even want to try to get it back, it won't be the same without mother, father and Esther.'

It would be ideal for us, she thought but she said nothing.

They came out onto Kromboomssloot.

'What a beautiful canal! You know I like canals, this is as nice as anything in the Jordaan and I love those old warehouses.'

'I used to play here as a child. We had a small rowing boat, it was perfect.'

Crossing the Oudeschans, they came to Nieuwe Uilenburgerstraat and the shul.

'This is where you and your family worshipped?'

'Yes, my father was a reader here. He read the Torah, the scrolls. He was quite an important man and well respected. I spoke to someone here last Friday and he said the congregation was almost gone, and that they don't always have enough men to hold services so it will probably close.'

'Can't you return, for your father's sake?'

'I want to, but if we leave for Friesland and if my plan for the future happens we won't be in Amsterdam much longer. Perhaps I could go back to a shul wherever we are living.'

'Do you want to do that?'

'Yes, I think I do, for no reason other than to ensure that all those who died did not die in vain, that Judaism lives, and that it will grow in strength again. The woman who told me mother and Esther were dead, the old man who was here the other day and even Abe Hirschfeld all said things that made me think I should return to my faith.'

He fell silent. They walked on to Waterlooplein, took the tram and went straight to work.

Jos greeted them enthusiastically. 'Simon, Maaike! You're early, very early in your case Maaike, what's happening?'

'We paid the money into the bank and, as Irene is still in Utrecht, Maaike decided to come in with me.'

'I'm pleased to see you both, I can have a few minutes' rest downstairs while you work up here. When will the money be in your bank?'

'Tomorrow lunchtime, they said.'

'You'll have to go there again before work and check, I'm not letting those coins go anywhere until I know you've been paid.'

'You should have been there, the bank clerk was bowing and scraping to Simon, I was so proud to be with him.'

'He's not a millionaire but he's a very well-off young man, marry him as soon as you can.' Jos laughed and disappeared down the cellar, his sights no doubt set on a quiet drink.

The evening passed quickly. The bar was busy but they had developed such a good working system between them that however crowded it became, they coped easily.

They walked home in the rain without stopping at their bench. Something was clearly playing on Maaike's mind.

'When are you going to tell me your plan? I'm dying to know.'

'Not just yet. I'll telephone van der Meer to ask him to take on the house and the insurance claim for me, so we can leave as soon as the thing with Berger is sorted out. You do understand that now I've found him I'd like to see it through. I'm waiting for Jos to come up with something. I've found him and I'm sure it was him but if I'm honest I don't think he's ever going to admit it to me, so really that just leaves father's painting, I can't leave without that. I have money in the bank and the cash in Jos's cellar that we can take with us. I'm sure he will look after father's box and the things still in it until we are settled.'

'Leave? Settled? Where do you mean?'

'Leeuwarden of course, for a while anyway. We'll have to tell Jos and Grietje.'

'When are you thinking we might go?'

'You need to write to Aunt Nel first to tell her and ask her if she can arrange that place for me to stay. I'll get money for rent to her somehow.'

'Are you sure? Don't do it just for me.'

'I hope we will be going much further than Leeuwarden together, but Friesland will do for now.'

SATURDAY 17TH NOVEMBER 1945

Grietje was working again, and as she was leaving for Utrecht in the early afternoon she started early so he and Maaike, with no Irene to look after, did all the shopping. They also had an early start as he had no idea what time Hirschfeld was coming for the gold and he suspected he might arrive before Jos opened at eleven.

He'd checked at the bank and the money as promised was in his account. The clerk had also presented him with his cheque book. He had felt very proud, and Maaike had been excited, although he hadn't the first idea if he ever might need to actually sign a cheque. He'd also telephoned van der Meer who had been surprisingly friendly and, despite having an important criminal trial coming up at the end of the month in The Hague, had agreed to see him on Tuesday morning.

Maaike had written to her aunt the previous afternoon and although she wasn't working until six, she wanted to go in to work with him so they could tell Jos together that they had made up their minds to leave. Simon was pleased as it meant he wouldn't have to work the busy Saturday lunchtime and afternoon period with Jos's wife.

They were at the bar by ten. Jos was in his cellar apron changing a barrel and stacking empties. He was delighted to see them both, and early to boot, as they had finished late the previous evening and there were still floors to be swept, ashtrays to empty and glasses to wash.

'Lovely to see you Maaike, but I'm not paying overtime, you know.'

'What time do you think he'll come for the coins and watch cases Jos?'

'I've no idea, I hope it's before we get busy, but the money is already dealt with so really all we have to do is hand over the bags.'

'Jos, can Simon and I talk to you about something?'

'That sounds ominous, whatever is it?'

Maaike looked nervous and turned to Simon for support.

'You remember I mentioned to you that Maaike and I might move to Friesland, well, we've decided to go so I'm sorry but we'll have to leave you.'

Jos sat in silence looking at the floor for a few moments. 'I really don't know how I'll manage without you two, and I'll certainly miss you both. You've been like children to me, I suppose. My wife and I never had children.' He laughed. 'Perhaps we were never speaking to each other for long enough.'

'We'll miss you too, you've been wonderful to us. First you employed me then Simon, we couldn't have managed to live without you.'

'So will Friesland be permanent then?' He gave Simon a sideways glance. 'Or are there other things planned?'

He spoke quickly before Maaike realised he and Jos had already discussed it. 'Possibly Jos, possibly.'

'He's got something in mind, but he won't tell me.'

'When are you planning to leave me?'

'As soon as we hear back from Maaike's aunt about somewhere for me to live.'

'If you got married you could live together.'

Maaike blushed and looked away while Simon gave Jos a hard stare, afraid he would blurt out part of his secret.

'I've got to sort out the Berger thing first though, I must have that painting and I want to instruct van der Meer on some outstanding things and an idea I've got.'

'Leave Berger to me, he's not going to tell you anything. I might be a little more, shall we say, persuasive.'

He was about to argue when the front door rattled.

'That must be Hirschfeld and Joost, let them in, and Maaike, can you get the Canadian Club bottle and two glasses while I make coffee.'

He unbolted the door to find Abe and Joost on the doorstep. Parked on the corner was the same car and driver that had brought them three days before but on this occasion, there was an extra passenger sitting in the back.

'Goedemorgen gentlemen, please sit down.' Jos indicated a table. 'Whisky for you, Meneer Hirschfeld, and what about you, Joost? Coffee or beer?'

Hirschfeld greeted them. 'Shalom Meneer van Loon, shalom Simon, and who pray is the beautiful young lady?'

'Shalom Abe, can I introduce you to Maaike de Vries, she and I are...'

'In love, he means in love, don't you, Simon?'

'Jos, really!' Maaike blushed again. She came out from behind the bar and joined them at the table while Simon and Jos carried the drinks.

Jos poured two generous measures of whisky for himself and the old man and a beer for Joost while Simon and Maaike had coffee.

'Well, my friend's payment is safely in your bank Simon so may I have the goods?'

Jos fetched the two bags from behind the bar. Hirschfeld examined the wax seals and pronounced himself satisfied.

'Gentlemen, the transaction is complete, let us drink to our success and the future for all of us.'

Jos refilled Hirschfeld's glass and poured himself another before Hirschfeld spoke again.

'There is just one more thing. My friend, who has financed most of the purchase, is outside in his car. With your permission I will bring him in. He specifically mentioned that he wanted to speak to you Simon and meet you Meneer van Loon, and of course I would like him to see his goods before we leave here.'

Simon looked at Jos who nodded. 'Yes, of course.'

Joost crossed to the door and opened it, holding back the curtain as Matthijs van der Meer entered the room.

'Goedemorgen Simon, Juffrouw de Vries, and you must be Meneer van Loon.' He held out his hand to Jos. 'I'm Matthijs van der Meer.'

He turned to Simon. 'We meet earlier than expected.'

'You! What are you doing here?' Simon was visibly shocked. 'What have you got to do with this?'

'Abe here didn't tell you? Good. I asked him not to in case you refused to sell to me for some reason.'

'This is your lawyer friend then? I'm not surprised you didn't trust him.'

'Jos, please.' Simon was embarrassed, 'I know Meneer van der Meer better now, of course I trust him.'

'Please let me explain.'

'I think you'd better.'

'Abe and I have known each other for years. I helped him and his wife when they needed somewhere safe to spend the war. He told me about a quantity of gold in the form of coins that was for sale, the price of which was too much for him but which he regarded as a good investment for someone who could hold it until the price rose. He told me the gold was being sold by a young man called Mendelevski who was the son of a Jewish watchmaker, and straight away I knew it was you. I knew I could never have any more of your father's wonderful watches, but I could invest in his gold. I had an amount of money I needed to dispose of, not for the same reason I bought the gold watches in the war, but so that the taxman didn't get hold of it. This time though I couldn't pay twice the going rate like I did for the watches, but I decided to round the figure up to 7,000. I thought old Abe had struck too hard a bargain with you.'

'It's black money then?' Jos glared at van der Meer and Hirschfeld.

'I wouldn't exactly call it that. It's just a few guilders I earned without broadcasting it. Surely you have done the same on occasions in the past. Bar takings are notoriously hard to calculate correctly for tax purposes, I believe.'

Jos looked sheepish then broke out in a grin. 'As you say, as you say. Please will you take a drink with us?'

Simon was still concerned. He thought van der Meer had used him in some way just as he had felt he had used his father years ago.

'I only wish I'd known.'

'And if you had known? Would you have refused my money? It's not stolen, you know.'

'But it is in a way, from the tax people I mean.'

Jos broke in. 'Ignore him, please, our Simon is still learning the way of the world. He's a little too honest and innocent sometimes.'

Simon shrugged his shoulders in acceptance and even managed a smile. 'Then it appears that I have you to thank for both parts of my father's legacy, thank you.'

Hirschfeld poured himself another drink. 'Your father wanted you to benefit from the gold, he hid it knowing that if he did not return then maybe, just maybe, you would come through it all and it would help to start your life again.' He turned and smiled at Maaike. 'Now you can afford to marry, perhaps?'

Van der Meer reached across the table and picked up one of the bags. 'Can I see what you have spent my money on, Abe?'

He broke the seal, untied the tape and poured the contents out on the table. It was the bag with the watch cases, and he picked up one of them.

'If only your father was here to make more watches to fit these cases.'

He nodded sadly and felt Maaike reaching for his hand.

'These two young people are leaving me to go to Friesland.' Jos looked at them kindly.

'That's why I want to see you on Tuesday, I have some things I want you to do for me professionally before I go,' said Simon.

'Until Tuesday morning then.'

Hirschfeld, van der Meer and Jos all shook hands. Joost swept up the coin bags and the three men made their way to the door.

Hirschfeld turned and spoke. 'Tot ziens Maaike, look after this young Jewish lad, make an honest man of him and produce lots of children.'

They sat in silence for a few moments until Simon spoke. 'Well, I didn't expect that!'

Jos nodded, 'I see what you mean, he's somehow too crafty, too smooth. Not the sort of man I normally rub shoulders with.'

'He's a highly rated lawyer, his life is a long way from ours, but love him or hate him he's helped make my Simon a rich man.'

'And he's going to sort out your remaining business so you two can leave.'

'On the subject of remaining business, what about Berger?'

'I told you, I don't want you confronting him. Leave it to me, I'll sort the bastard. Sorry Maaike.'

'But I wanted to challenge him I...'

She interrupted. 'Leave it to Jos, let him do it for you.'

'Just make sure you get father's painting.'

'I will, and a confession too if I can.'

Jos sent them home early as both of them had been in since ten.

They sat and talked long into the night and, the coin sale being concluded, Jos dealing with Berger for him and van der Meer handling the other matters, he nervously told her his plan for their future, fearing she might not agree.

'Of course I'll go with you. I'll go to the end of the earth if you ask me. I love you and want to be with you.'

'I don't know how we'll get there, I still have to sort that out, and I don't know where we'll live but I have plenty of money. It will be totally foreign to both of us and you know I'm going to be an observant Jew again.'

'I don't care so long as we're together.'

It was two in the morning before he took her in his arms, kissed her and carried her into the bedroom. They undressed, each of them shy and embarrassed seeing the other naked for the first time. She looked down at her stump and then up at him, biting her lip, terrified of his reaction. She need not have worried. They lay naked on the bed, each exploring the other's body, before they made love for the first time. Their inexperienced lovemaking was hurried and frantic, lasting only a few moments before they lay back exhausted in each other's arms and fell asleep.

MONDAY 19TH NOVEMBER 1945

After a wonderful start Sunday had turned sour. They had made love again and stayed in bed until lunchtime, then they'd spent the afternoon deciding what they had to take with them and Maaike had cooked a meal for Grietje and Irene when they returned.

After the meal they had told Grietje their plans. She had become very angry and then upset that they were leaving and had said some very unpleasant things but, like on previous occasions, by breakfast time the next morning she acted as if nothing had happened.

'When are you hoping to leave?'

'As soon as Maaike's Aunt Nel replies. We don't have a lot of belongings to pack, just clothes.'

'What about your jobs?'

'Jos is upset of course but he understands and is pleased for us.'

'So am I, it's wonderful to see you starting a new life, and Maaike too. What is she going to do about her rooms?'

'The rent's paid until the end of the month so she's just going to leave I think. She doesn't own any of the furniture or anything. She and her father arrived here with nothing.'

'I wonder if old Aart might want to move down, it would be easier for him, and less noisy for us,' she laughed.

'Maaike and I were concerned about who would look after Irene for you.'

The girl looked up from her porridge. 'I can look after myself, I'm nearly four, you know.'

'She can go to the kindergarten, they'll take her as she's almost four and it's not too expensive.'

'Can I come and see you and Maaike? I'm going to miss you so much. Are you getting married?'

'Eat your breakfast, too many questions for a little girl. I'm sorry, she's a bit nosey.'

'I'm not nosey.'

'It's alright, Grietje, we'll miss her too.'

He took Irene downstairs to Maaike and the three of them spent the whole day together.

Jos walked purposefully down Nieuwe Spiegelstraat and it was a few minutes before five when he entered E.B. Antiek. The bell rang as he closed the door and Berger came through from the back room.

'I'm sorry, I'm closing now.'

'That's alright then, we won't be disturbed.' Jos locked and bolted the door, turned the sign to 'gesloten', pulled down the blind and approached the counter.

Berger managed a worried smile. 'How can I help you? I really don't have long.'

'I hope it won't take long. I'm interested in the painting in the window, the one of the little girl in the gilt frame.'

Berger visibly relaxed and smiled, showing his gold teeth. 'Ah yes, meneer obviously has a good eye. It's a lovely work in an extremely fine frame. There has been a lot of interest. Would you like to see it?'

He reached into the window and, looking Jos up and down to judge his ability to pay, passed the painting out.

'Just 300 guilders, and cheap at that.'

Jos feigned interest in the painting. 'It's nice, that's true, 300 you say? Where did you get it from?'

'A lady brought it in just a few weeks ago, it's from her family's collection I believe.'

'Really? That's strange.' He moved menacingly towards Berger. 'It's part of a pair owned by an old Jewish friend of mine. Perhaps you know him, he made watches.'

'I don't know anything about that, a woman sold it to me a couple of months ago.' Berger looked frightened as Jos moved even closer. 'I don't know any Jewish watchmakers.'

'Like hell you don't.' Jos grasped Berger's collar and with his other hand he tore the gold watch and chain from the terrified man's waistcoat. 'He made this watch for you, didn't he?'

'Alright, yes, yes, a Jew did make me the watch but I didn't get the painting from him, I swear. Please, you're hurting me.'

'How did you know the Jewish watchmaker?'

'I didn't know him at all.'

'So how did you order a watch from him?'

'Through my lawyer, his name is van der Meer, you can check.'

'He introduced you?'

'No, no. I was at van der Meer's house when a man delivered three watches he'd had specially made. They were beautiful and I decided I wanted one.'

'How did you get in touch?'

'I... I don't remember. Please, you're frightening me.'

'So bloody tell me. How did you order the watch?'

'I recognised the man who brought van der Meer's watches. I'd seen him before.'

Jos tightened his grip. 'Where had you seen him and how did you know about the Jew making the watches?'

'I'd seen the man before, going in and out of the door to an apartment above where I store some of my stock. He never saw me, I saw him through the crack between the doors. I'd always thought the place was empty, but when I saw him taking food in and when van der Meer said the watchmaker had closed down at his business address I put two and two together.'

'Meaning what?'

'It was obvious, the man had to be helping and working for a

Jew who was hiding upstairs making watches. I wanted a watch so...'

'So what, you little bastard, what did you do?'

'There was a key, it was on the ring I had with the stable key. I think de Jong who rents me the stable must own the upstairs too, and somehow I'd got a key for both. I tried it in the front door and it worked. The Jew came to the top of the stairs as I went in, he looked frightened so I knew straight away he was hiding.'

'So you threatened him?'

'No, not at all, I just asked if he'd make me a watch.'

Jos pinned him to the wall and his large docker's hand closed around Berger's throat. 'You lying bastard, you threatened him, tell me the truth. What did you do? Did you threaten to tell the Nazis about him?'

'Please, I can't breathe.'

'So tell me, you little shit.'

'He agreed to talk to me down in the stable. He said his family were upstairs. He said he'd make me a watch but he wanted a ridiculous price, the dirty Jew was trying to double or even treble what the watch was going to cost.'

'So you threatened him?'

'I said I wouldn't tell anyone if he made a watch for me for nothing.'

'You blackmailed the poor bastard?'

'He could afford it, the Jews have been getting rich on us Dutchmen for years.'

'And what else did you get from him? The painting, I suppose?'

'No, honestly, I bought it from a woman, I swear to you.'

Jos punched him in the stomach. 'You lying bastard. What else did you take from him?'

Berger doubled up, gasping for breath. 'Alright, alright, please don't hurt me. I admit it, I asked him for money, 2,000 guilders. But not the painting, I swear, a scruffy looking woman came in with it.'

'And he had to pay or you would report him?'

'Yes, he paid, he could afford it. You know what? The dirty Jew asked me to send him an invoice for his records to show where the cash had gone, unbelievable.'

'And the watch, I suppose you got it for nothing?'

'Yes, he was scared, I got it for free, but would you believe it, he actually gave me an invoice. He actually thought I was going to pay him for it.'

Jos tightened his grip on Berger's throat. 'And then you betrayed him.'

'No, no, really, I didn't, please let go.' Berger started to cry. 'Why would I do that?'

'Because he refused to pay you any more money? Tell me, you fucking bastard, or by God I swear I'll kill you.'

'Yes, yes, I did, he got angry. He said I'd had enough out of him. He said he was going to tell those who were hiding him.'

'So you sold them all out to the Nazis you little shit.'

Berger begged then whimpered, terror showing in his eyes as Jos moved closer. 'Please don't hurt me, please, I beg you. What do you want? I have money, anything.'

Jos put both hands around Berger's throat and squeezed, lifting him off the floor. To his surprise Berger didn't put up a fight. His arms hung loosely by his side, his tongue protruded hideously between the gold teeth and, after convulsing for a few moments, he went limp and Jos allowed his body to fall to the floor, out of sight behind the counter.

Back at the Café van Loon Jos poured himself a very large jenever then he placed the watch and chain, Simon's twenty guilder deposit, the thirty guilders betrayal reward money and the painting of the girl alongside its matching brother in Simon's box. He couldn't understand why Berger hadn't fought him or even struggled. It was almost as if he had been resigned to his fate.

'Is that you, Jos?' His wife's voice came from above, 'What the hell are you doing down there and where have you been? Get your arse up here, I've got your meal ready.'

'I had something I had to do for Simon, I'll be up in a minute.' He poured himself another drink and tried to stop himself shaking before he saw his wife.

TUESDAY 20TH NOVEMBER 1945

The fearsome Joke must have heard of his good fortune. He was received as a highly respected client on his arrival at Johannes Vermeerstraat, rather differently to his reception on his first visit. 'Meneer Mendelevski, goedemorgen. How nice to see you again, please come in, he is expecting you.'

Van der Meer was equally welcoming, if perhaps a little patronising. He felt that he might be reminded any minute where the money that he now wanted van der Meer to handle had come from. The lawyer was as polished and if possible even more professional than on their previous meetings. 'What can I do for you? Do I understand that you wish to instruct me?'

'Three things, I hope. I am leaving Amsterdam and I want you to deal with some outstanding matters for me in my absence Firstly, these four insurance policies on my parents, my sister and myself.'

Van der Meer put on his spectacles and quickly scanned the policies and the letters from the insurers. 'I can try for you, but I'm afraid it is not an uncommon problem. There are many Jewish survivors, or relatives of those who did not return, who are in your situation and I fear it could take a long time and may not be worth pursuing in the end. I can't see a way, certainly not in the short term, that any of the companies are going to pay on the life policies of those who died in the camps, without death certificates, especially when the premiums were not paid. It's harsh but there it is, I'm being very honest with you. I can take your money but in fairness it may be better for you to accept defeat and sadly I think the same will apply to your sister's policy.'

'What about the one in my name?'

'As far as yours is concerned it is true that it lapsed when your father stopped paying the premiums, but it should be regarded as a 'paid up' policy to that date, so although it won't pay the full amount that would be due when you turn twenty-five, there should be something to come. I will fight this one for you.'

'I have these papers about our house on Dijkstraat. Dutch people have taken it over, and I don't know if I can get it back.' He passed the documents to van der Meer. 'I don't really understand them.'

'I'm sorry, but it's clear your father did not own the house. It was leased to him on a long-term lease by the City of Amsterdam so you have no real claim on it. In fact you need to be careful. I have it from an inside contact that the city council is about to start charging people for unpaid ground rents and city taxes.'

'Charging taxes and rents that were unpaid because people were in the camps?' He sounded incredulous. Jos had mentioned it to him before, but to hear it confirmed by a lawyer shocked him. 'That's crazy. How can they do that?'

'I know, and I'm sure people will fight for years to get it reversed. It's probably best that they simply don't know where you are now so they can't charge you.'

'But they do know.' He looked frightened. 'They put my new address in Slootstraat on my central record card when I got my new ID at the Prinsenhof.'

'That could be a problem, but as you are leaving Amsterdam can I suggest, and you didn't get this idea from me, you understand, that you keep a low profile and ignore any letters from City Hall and don't leave a forwarding address when you go. Where are you going, by the way? A long way from Amsterdam might be best.'

'Friesland to start with, but after that much further away than you might imagine, and I want you to administer my bank account and do certain things for me in respect of payments here in Amsterdam. Can you still do that if I have 'gone missing', so to speak?'

'Providing the financial arrangements you want me to make in no way involves City Hall, or if they do, are not made in your name.'

Van der Meer smiled and once again Simon saw the face of the unscrupulous rule-bending lawyer he had seen when they first met.

'So tell me what you want me to do.'

He outlined his plan for his and Maaike's final destination and what he wanted van der Meer to do for him after their departure in respect of a property to be arranged through his account at Rabobank.

'You want me to have the power to make those arrangements for you, and to have access to your account to finance it?'

'Yes, and to take your fee from the account as well.'

'That's very trusting of you, are you absolutely sure?'

'Completely, I trust you implicitly. The arrangement I want you to make is very important to me, and I know you won't let me down.'

'Thank you, I will be proud to represent you as your lawyer and there will be no fee. We need to draw up an authority to the bank for me to make payments from your account. I will ensure it has a clause that you must also agree to any withdrawals before I make them, so I will need to know your address, and we need another document to say I am acting for you in respect of the other business.'

'That sounds acceptable, I hope you can complete most of the arrangements while I am still at the Friesland address. I will give it to you when I have it and I will need to give it to the bank as well.'

'Hmm, you may not wish to do that until you get a little further away than Friesland, just in case the Amsterdam City Council somehow gets hold of it. Banks are sometimes not as discreet as they ought to be. As I am your lawyer, it is quite in order for you to use my address here as your official address. Any correspondence will come here and I will of course be bound by client confidentiality regarding your whereabouts now I have officially taken instructions from you.'

'If you think that would be best then yes, I agree, you're the expert after all.'

'Yes, I am rather, aren't I?' He laughed at himself. 'Excellent, I'll have Joke type up the necessary paperwork now while we have coffee. Then I really must get back to my brief, I am defending in a big trial starting in a week's time and I'm not ready. I don't think it will last long, and I will make your matters my first priority after that.' He reached over and rang the bell for Joke.

The necessary paperwork completed and only his Friesland address still outstanding, he made his way back to the Jordaan via Nieuwe Spiegelstraat. To his horror, his father's painting was no longer in the window of Berger's shop. In a panic he went to the door only to find it locked, the blind drawn and the 'closed' sign showing. Distraught, he rushed to work to talk to Jos, who was behind the bar serving two customers as he burst in.

'Jos! It's gone! The painting's gone, Berger must have sold it! I knew we should have gone back sooner.'

'Steady lad, slow down.'

'It's Berger...'

Jos interrupted, his voice strangely anxious. 'What about him?'

'He's sold the painting. I went to his shop but it was closed so I didn't see him, but the painting was gone from the window.'

'Calm down.' He breathed a sigh of relief. 'Get a beer and come downstairs, these two are alright for a minute or two.'

'But the painting, it's gone! We should have done something.'

'Not here, get down the cellar.' Jos almost pushed him down the steps and slumped into his chair.

'Are you alright?' Simon asked Jos. 'You're shaking.'

'Nothing, nothing at all. I must be getting a cold or something.'

'We've lost the painting, we left it too long.'

'We haven't, it's in your box with the other one and the gold watch your father made for Berger is in there too.'

287

'What? How?'

'I went to see Berger yesterday. You were right, he recognised Gerrit that day at van der Meer's. He'd seen him coming and going from the house when he was visiting his store in the stable. He had a key to the house and he simply went in and met your father. He guessed you were Jews who were in hiding, and he demanded money and a watch from your father. When your father stood up to him he told the bloody Nazis about you. It was just as you and Maaike said, the first invoice was fake and was just to cover the money. When your father handed him an invoice for the watch, Berger got angry and decided to turn you in after your father said there would be no more payments.'

'And he confessed all this?'

'Yes, with a little persuasion. I think he was glad to get it off his chest, clear his conscience you might say.'

'And he gave you the painting and the watch?'

'Not exactly, I pointed out to him they belonged to your father, although he still said he bought the painting from a woman right to the end.'

'End? What do you mean, 'end'?'

'To the end of our conversation, of course. He saw the sense in returning the painting and the watch to you, my argument was obviously a good one.'

He opened the box and took out the paintings. Holding them side by side he looked at Jos. 'How can I ever thank you? I already owe you everything but now this. The paintings are reunited. I am forever in your debt.'

'Don't talk rubbish, boy, I'm just glad to have finally sorted out the Berger question for you. He's admitted everything, you know who betrayed you and your family, so it's over I hope. You can now go off with your Maaike without that hanging over you. The watch is there too, have a look.'

'But the gold chain is still attached to it, that wasn't from father, so it's not really mine, is it?'

Jos spoke angrily. 'Please, don't start that holier than thou, honest little boy routine again. You'll want to give the bloody thing back next. Just leave it, will you.'

'I just think I'd like to face him, to look him in the face now I know for sure, tell him who I am and tell him what happened to my family.'

'No! Absolutely not. It's over, leave it! He knows who you are, he knows what happened because of him. I told him all about you and what you've been through,' he lied. 'There's no more to be said to him about it. Keep the bloody chain as some sort of compensation, God knows it's worth nothing compared to what he did to you all. Please, for me, put him behind you now, it's over, my last favour to you. I told you I'd sort it and I have.'

Simon had a strange feeling and he asked, 'You didn't hurt him, did you, Jos?'

'Now would I do that? Let's just say I was at my most persuasive, the odd bloody nose maybe. He deserved a bit of pain after what he did.'

'Thank you, from the bottom of my heart.'

'Just get upstairs to work, it's after four.'

Jos poured himself another drink and clasped his hands together to stop them shaking. His wife always said he was an awful liar, he just hoped and prayed the boy hadn't noticed and that he would never find out what had really happened.

He told Maaike as soon as she arrived at six. She was delighted that at last his search was over and his question answered, realising what a difference it would make to him. She was also rather smug as it appeared that the dealings between his father and Berger had been virtually as she had predicted.

'Thank you Jos, you're a wonderful man.' She kissed him. 'Simon couldn't have done this without you. Perhaps now he can forget.'

Jos was lost in thought, wondering if he could ever do the same. He headed to the cellar.

'Simon, I must tell you some other good news, Aunt Nel's reply has arrived and she says we can go as soon as we want. They're all looking forward to meeting you and uncle's little house is all ready and it will be rent free! It's been standing empty so they're just pleased someone will be living in it.'

'That's marvellous news. We'll tell Jos later, I don't want to leave him in the lurch so we may have to work a few more days. We'll have to tell Grietje too. I think she is quite pleased for us now, but when we say we are actually going and tell her the date I expect she might be upset again.'

'As long as she's not angry, about us I mean.'

'We'll have to tell your aunt and uncle our long-term plans as well and that we will only be with them for a few months or so. I hope they'll understand.'

'I'm sure they will, especially after they've met you and know I'm in safe hands.'

'Maybe so, but what we have planned is a big move and I don't know how it will sound to them.'

She laughed. 'Possibly, I'm afraid my family do tend to think the world ends at the border of Friesland and Groningen.'

'I hope they won't mind if we just stay there temporarily, I don't want them to think we're using them.'

'Don't worry. They just want the best for me and when I say we're starting a new life together they'll be delighted.'

'Assuming they like me.'

'They'll love you, after all I do.'

'We need to finalise what we're going to take. I want to leave father's box with most of the remaining things in it here for Jos to ship to us when we reach our final destination. I want to take the two paintings, father's prayer shawl, and the cash from the box, and I'm going to ask Jos to dispose of father's tools. I'm not going to need those, I don't see myself as a master watchmaker somehow, do you?'

'All I've really got are clothes and the odd small item from Rotterdam, father's picture, letters and a couple of trinkets. I think all my things will go in one suitcase.'

'Clothes-wise I don't have many things to take either. I have less than you, so mine will probably fit in your suitcase too. What I do want to do is buy new clothes for us both, plus some basic household items to fill father's box for when Jos sends it on. He can hardly send an empty box, the only contents being in the false bottom can he?' We'll go shopping tomorrow morning as soon as I've done the brewery delivery.'

'I can't wait, I'm so excited. I've never had money to spend on new clothes and things. Can I choose things for our new home?'

'Of course, that's your department not mine, make a list of what you need to buy and I'll do the same.' He laughed. 'You'll be the one in the kitchen wherever we end up.'

'In your dreams.' She laughed too and swung a crutch at him. 'You can ring van der Meer and give him Aunt Nel's address as your contact point for now.'

'We'd better get to work if we're going to ask Jos how soon we can leave.'

FRIDAY 23RD NOVEMBER 1945

'You'll ship the box to us when we get settled?'

'Of course, just let me have an address when you have one and leave it to me.'

'I've put all our new clothes in there and the kitchen and household stuff, crockery, cutlery and things that we bought. Can you refit the false bottom for me, so it can't be seen? I'm taking the cash and the two paintings to Leeuwarden but I want the coins, stamps, two watches, photos and letters and mother's jewellery all to go in there. I think it would be safer than trying to take them on our journey. Do you think it will be alright or is it too risky?'

'Simon, Simon, trust me. No one will ever know it's there, don't worry.'

'I don't want to keep father's watchmaking tools, I have no need of them. I've got the photos and the jewellery and his prayer shawl, so I have some memories of my parents. Do you think you can dispose of them for me?'

'I'll try.'

He laughed.

'I think I know someone. They are very good quality technical tools and hard to come by, if I can find a buyer they should fetch a good price.'

'I hope so. I want you to give whatever they make to Theo's sister as a thank you for what her husband did for my family. I'd like to give you something too.'

'There's no need for that, I don't want anything from you. You'll need all your money and more when you reach your destination.'

'But you did so much for me and for Maaike, we owe you a lot.'

'You owe me nothing, I just helped where I could and you both worked damn hard for me.'

'Please, I'd like to give you something. Would you take Berger's watch? You know it's solid gold.'

'No, no.' Jos looked horrified. 'I don't want it. I don't want anything in any way connected to that man. Please don't insult me! You keep it, sell it when you need money wherever you end up. You've got that other watch as a memory of your father's work.'

'I'm sorry, I didn't mean to upset you.'

'I know, lad, I know. Now get yourself back to Maaike and finish your packing and don't forget these.' Smiling, Jos handed him the paintings and all the cash. 'Just get your arse back here for your last shift, but make it a six o'clock start, the same as Maaike.'

Back at Slootstraat Maaike was still trying to pack their clothes into a suitcase while keeping Irene entertained at the same time. 'Can you finish this? Irene wants a story and this is the last time I'll be looking after her. I'm going to miss her so much.'

'I'm going to miss you too, Maaike. Mama says it's a long way to Freezingland.'

'Maybe you can come and see us there, darling.'

'Yes, please, Maaike. I love you both so much.'

Simon carefully wrapped the photograph of her father in a pair of his trousers, put the paintings in-between the clothes and closed the suitcase. 'Jos says I don't have to be at work until six, so we can go in together.'

'I'm going to miss him terribly, he's been so good to me ever since my father left.'

'Me too, I just couldn't have sorted everything out without him, and all his contacts of course.'

They both laughed.

Grietje came home before four and, finding them both still at home, announced that she wanted to cook them a farewell meal before they went to work. 'It'll just be pan-fried chicken and potatoes but I've made one of my special apple pies, I hope that's alright.'

'Grietje, that's very kind. Really, you shouldn't have bothered.'

'Nonsense, my two favourite people are leaving tomorrow for a new life together, I have to do something. I love you both, you know that, and I'll miss you both so much. I'm coming to the station with you tomorrow morning as well, I'm not working and I know Irene wants to wave you goodbye, no arguments.'

As they approached the bar just before six they could see a large number of drinkers standing outside despite the bitterly cold November evening. And as they reached the door they could see the place was absolutely full.

'Look at this, what on earth is going on? I bet Jos wishes he hadn't told me to come in late. Where have all these people come from?'

They squeezed in through the partially open door and started to push their way through the crowd to get to the bar.

Jos and his wife, smiling for once, were busy serving drinks.

Jos looked up and saw them. 'Here they are everyone, the happy couple. Our Maaike and Simon.'

A cheer went up and they recognised all their regular customers, Saturday faces and even the occasional drinkers. They were totally surrounded by well wishers, slapping him on the back and trying to kiss Maaike.

Jos moved people away and beckoned them further in. 'Come on you two, there's a table here for you both. Welcome to your farewell party!'

'Jos, this is wonderful, you didn't have to do this, we've come here to work!'

'Not tonight you don't Maaike. We wanted to give you a proper send-off, so shut up and enjoy yourselves. Just about everybody's here.'

Jos's wife appeared with trays of food which, still smiling, she offered around the ravenous crowd. Coming close to their table she stopped and bent to speak to them. 'Thank you Maaike, and you, Simon, for your hard work here. You've been an absolute godsend to Jos, the old bugger couldn't have managed without you two. We've had to build the business up again after the war, in fact you helped to keep it going during the war, Maaike, and I just want to say I appreciate what you've done.' She looked suddenly nervous and uncomfortable. 'I know I haven't always been nice or helpful to either of you, I'm afraid that's just my way, but I do thank you.' Then just as suddenly she regained her confidence and brusqueness. 'After all, someone has to keep control of things with that drunken lazy old devil in charge.' With that, she moved back into the crowd, leaving them both speechless.

'Well, that's a Mevrouw van Loon I've never seen before.'

'Nor me, Maaike, nor me.'

The door opened and Grietje and Irene came in and, struggling through the crowd, joined them at the table while Jos brought over drinks. Irene immediately climbed onto Maaike's knee.

'Grietje! What are you doing here?'

'Jos called round last night to let me know about the party. I just had to come, I can't stay very long but it's quite early so it's alright for Irene to be here for a couple of hours.'

'You kept it very secret earlier while we were eating.'

'I was worried Irene was going to blurt it out, I had to promise her chocolate if she kept quiet.'

'I like chocolate, but Mama said if I eat it all at once I'll be sick so I'm giving you some tomorrow to eat on the train.'

Maaike smiled and gave the girl a hug. 'That's very kind of you, can I give some to Simon?'

'Maybe one piece.'

The evening passed very quickly. Many of the guests drifted away around nine o'clock, leaving the regulars. All of them wanted to say their farewells, especially to Maaike, and to wish them well.

Talk between the hard-drinking regulars inevitably turned to the report of the opening speech by the prosecution in the Nuremberg trial which had started two days before, and to the

Mussert trial due to start the following week. 'Daft' Willem was still offering his services as executioner if required until Hendrik opened the morning newspaper and pointed out the huge number of defendants. At this point he tried to enlist Jos as his assistant.

Jos interrupted, 'Come on you buggers, this is no time to talk about war crimes, it's a farewell party, these two are starting a new life away from all the bad memories and you lot, so get drinking.' He quickly took the paper from Hendrik, folded it and put it under the bar before Simon could see the small item at the bottom of the front page:

Amsterdam Friday 23rd November 1945. Amsterdam Police are appealing for help following the discovery on Wednesday of the body of forty-four-year-old antiques dealer Edwin Berger in his shop on Nieuwe Spiegelstraat. Police believe he was strangled some days before his body was found. The motive for the murder is unknown, theft has been ruled out as the contents of the cash register and the stock do not appear to have been disturbed. Anyone with information is urgently requested to contact the Gemeente Police at the Central Police Station on Elandsgracht.

By ten only the hardened barstool crowd, Maaike, Simon and Jos were left, Jos's wife having run out of pleasantries and disappeared upstairs an hour earlier.

'We must be going soon, our train is at nine thirty tomorrow.'

Jos produced two bottles of champagne, each boldly marked 'Canadian Forces' from under the bar. 'Not yet, not before we toast your departure and wish you luck. Don't worry about getting to the station. I have arranged for my friend to pick you, Maaike and Grietje up at quarter to nine.'

He opened the bottles and poured everyone a glass. 'Gentlemen, raise your glasses. To Maaike and to Simon, you will be sadly missed here in the Café van Loon. Go with all our good wishes for a new life together.'

They said their goodbyes. Jos pumped Simon's hand. 'I don't know how I'll manage without you two.' He laughed. 'Saturday tomorrow, the busiest day of the week, and just me and her upstairs to run the place. I'll have no time for a quiet drink downstairs anymore.'

'Thank you for everything you've done for us. I remember when I came here for a job, you took a chance on me and I'll always remember that. I don't know how we're going to manage without all your contacts to help us.'

'Bugger off lad, I just did what anyone would have done.'

Jos turned to Maaike who was trying to disentangle herself from Willem. 'Come here Maaike, my lovely little lady. I'll miss you so much, you've been like a daughter to me. I love you, you know that.'

His huge arms enveloped her and lifted her off the ground and Simon thought, just for an instant, that he detected a tear on the burly landlord's face.

Maaike was in floods of tears and clung to him. 'I'll never forget you, Jos.'

They walked slowly back to Slootstraat, sitting on their special bench by the canal for a few moments. 'I'll miss this, this is the last time we'll see the Jordaan. It's where we met, where we got our bad news and where we fell in love. So many memories.'

'We'll come back one day, I promise, perhaps we will be able to show our children where we lived but for now the future awaits.'

'We must, and you must tell them about your family, what happened to them, what life was like for you as a Jew in Amsterdam in the war and about your father's box.'

THURSDAY 27TH JUNE 1946

'Do hurry up, Irene. Mama has to get you to school and then I have to get to work. Put on your shoes, please. Quickly now, I don't want to be late again, you'll have to leave the rest of your breakfast. Come on.' She left the breakfast dishes in the sink unwashed and pulled on her coat while making her way to the top of the stairs.

'Coming Mama, I can't fasten my shoes.'

Cursing herself for buying ones with laces, she hurried back into the kitchen, tied the girl's shoes and buttoned her coat.

Aart, now living on the ground floor, was in the hall below, moving her bicycle so he could get his own out to go to work. He called up to her, 'Grietje, there's a letter for you. I'll leave it here on the shelf so you can pick it up on your way out.'

She eventually got Irene downstairs and picked up the letter, putting it in her pocket to open later. With Irene finally installed on the child seat, she cycled down the road to the kindergarten and dropped her off before heading for the first of her three jobs.

Taking a mid-morning break from her cleaning she remembered the letter and, seeing the Leeuwarden postmark, excitely tore it open. She was a little angry not having heard from Simon and Maaike since they left, and was very anxious to hear their news. The contents of the letter both shocked and delighted her while leaving her feeling desperately guilty at the same time. She had to read the letter over at least three times before it all sank in.

Leeuwarden, 25th June 1946

Dearest Grietje, I'm sorry I haven't been in touch for such a long time. This is just a short note to let you know that Maaike and I were married three months ago in a civil ceremony at Leeuwarden Town Hall and that we have secured two places on a ship which will be leaving Marseille for Palestine next week.

I have rediscovered my faith and emigrating to Palestine, we call it Aliyah (or 'going up'), and starting a new life there is something I feel the need to do. Maaike has said she wants to convert to Judaism when we are settled.

We will hopefully be there before our baby is born in August.

Enclosed is the key to Apartment 113B Zaandammerplein. The apartment is yours and Irene's for as long as you need it. Matthijs van der Meer, Advocaat, of 2 Johannes Vermeerstraat will deal with the payments of the rent and you can contact him if you have any problems. He also has access to an emergency fund should you ever need it.

I know your beloved Jaap and the boys will not be there to share your new home with you, but I am sure that he will somehow know that you did eventually get to the Spaarndammerbuurt as he promised.

There is a parcel on its way to you containing the paintings of the boy and the girl in the gilt frames, which I know you admired so much and which I would like you to have. As you know, my father left one, the boy, in his box for me and the other one, the girl, was recovered from the man who must have stolen it when he betrayed us. He insisted it was sold to him by a woman, but surely that can't be true, can it?

Maaike and I have no words to thank you for everything you did for both of us. You picked me up from the street and gave me a home, love, hope and a new life and for that I will be in your debt forever.

I will write again when we are safely in Palestine.

Maaike sends her love and says that if our child is a girl she will have your name. Simon

Her hands were shaking as she took the key out of the envelope and realised that the young Jewish boy, whose family she once cleaned for and then stole from, whom she had taken in when he returned alone from the horrors of Auschwitz with nothing, had changed her life forever.

AFTERWORD

Simon and Maaike Mendelevski and their son finally arrived in Palestine on the 18th of December 1946. Despite holding valid immigration certificates, their original journey was interrupted by a British Royal Naval patrol vessel, which intercepted and boarded the ship on which they were travelling off the Palestinian coast near Haifa on the 20th of July 1946, before escorting it to Cyprus.

Many of those on board were German Jews, a number of whom were returned to displaced persons camps in Germany. Others, including the Mendelevskis, who were Dutch nationals, were held in one of many detention camps near Larnaca in Cyprus. Their son Joshua Kees (Jos) was born in the Jewish wing of the British Military Hospital in Nicosia three weeks after their arrival.

From November 1946 detainees were allowed by the British to leave the camps for Palestine at the rate of 750 a month. As a nursing mother Maaike qualified for release under a special quota and on the 25th of November the Mendelevski family became one of the first to continue their journey to Palestine.

Simon's father's box arrived safely, courtesy of Jos van Loon, at Haifa docks in early February 1947, the British Mandate controlled Palestine Customs Service being blissfully unaware of the German and Russian gold coins, stamp collection, jewellery, watches and photographs in the false bottom.

Simon and Maaike's second child, Esther Grietje, was born in Tel Aviv on the 21st of May 1948, a week after the Declaration of the Establishment of the State of Israel.

On completion of his compulsory service in the armed forces, Simon became a doctor specialising in paediatrics in Tel Aviv. Jos fought with distinction in the army in the Six-Day War in June 1967 and Esther qualified as a nurse at Haifa General Hospital.

Grietje and Irene Blok moved into their new apartment in the Spaarndammerbuurt, the two paintings in their gilt frames taking pride of place in the hallway where they could be seen by everyone.

Jos van Loon and his wife continued to argue and run the Café van Loon until their retirement.

Relatives of Jewish Holocaust survivors continue to fight to this day for payouts due from insurance companies and for the refund of fines and ground rents charged to survivors on their return by the Amsterdam City Council.

Arthur Seyss-Inquart, Reichskommissar for the occupied Netherlands, was convicted at the Nuremberg trials and hanged on the 16th of October 1946.

Anton Adriaan Mussert, the NSB leader, was executed by firing squad on 7th of May 1946 in the dunes at Waalsdorpervlakte, the site of Gerrit's execution, despite two appeals by his defence lawyer Matthijs van der Meer.

Edwin Berger's murder remains an unsolved crime in Dutch police records.

Lightning Source UK Ltd.
Milton Keynes UK
UKHW020048290822
407933UK00007B/667

9 789493 056107